Outstanding praise for M.V. Byrne and
Meet Isabel Puddles!

"I was very happy to meet Isabel Puddles and I'm
sure readers will enjoy making her acquaintance,
too. M.V. Byrne's small-town sleuth with a big heart
sees the *possible* in impossible, whether she's cooking
up a delicious pot roast or solving a devious crime."
—Leslie Meier, author of *Irish Parade Murder*

"A charming debut, a captivating cast, and
many spells of laugh-out-loud humor."
—*Kirkus Reviews*

"When you meet the delightfully witty and no-nonsense
Isabel Puddles, you'll never want her to leave."
—Lee Hollis, author of *Poppy Harmon and the Hung Jury*

"I've met Isabel Puddles and I love her. She's a smart, funny
AARPster who can whip up a mean pot roast while solving
a diabolical murder. I eagerly turned the pages of this
charming, action-packed whodunit. What a fun read!"
—Laura Levine, author of *Murder Gets a Makeover*

Books by M.V. Byrne

MEET ISABEL PUDDLES

ISABEL PUDDLES INVESTIGATES

Published by Kensington Publishing Corp.

ISABEL PUDDLES INVESTIGATES

M.V. BYRNE

KENSINGTON
PUBLISHING CORP.

www.kensingtonbooks.com

KENSINGTON BOOKS are published by

Kensington Publishing Corp.
119 West 40th Street
New York, NY 10018

ISBN-13: 978-1-4967-2834-0 (ebook)
ISBN-13: 978-1-4967-2833-3

First Kensington Trade Paperback Printing: December 2021

10 9 8 7 6 5 4 3 2 1

Printed in the United States of America

To Rick, with love and thanks,
for decades of friendship, inspiration, and endless laughs

Chapter 1

Whenever the wind was blowing from the north, which was always a cold wind even in the summer months, Isabel Puddles could hear the faint, haunting blasts of the SS *Badger*'s horn wafting down from Wellington Harbor, some twenty miles north of her cottage on Gull Lake, the place she had called home most of her life. The sound was as familiar to her as the wind rustling through the poplar trees surrounding her property or the frantic barking of her dogs after successfully treeing another squirrel.

Isabel's father, Buddy Peabody, bought the little white clapboard-and-river-stone cottage when Isabel was just a girl, and her mother, Helen, named the plot of land it sat on Poplar Bluff. Buddy intended the cottage to be an investment— a rental property for summer people—but after the insurance agency he worked for folded, the Peabody family found themselves in reduced circumstances, so their handsome brick Colonial manse in town was sold, and they moved into their quaint little clapboard cottage full-time. One day, after Buddy was back on his feet and heading up his own agency, their old house in town came back on the market, and he jumped at the chance to reclaim it. Buddy surprised his wife and daughter at dinner that night by telling them he had made an offer, to which Helen and Isabel responded, and in no uncertain terms, that he should rescind it immediately. Poplar Bluff was their home now, and they were staying put, they told him. Buddy did as he was told, having grown accustomed to losing two-one majority votes to his wife and daughter.

Many years later, Isabel raised her own family at Poplar Bluff. And when Buddy and Helen decided the Florida retirement community they had retired to was not what they had signed up for, they moved back to Gull Lake and happily settled into the cozy garage apartment Buddy had built himself years before. But after Isabel's husband, Carl, died, and the children had gone off to college, Buddy and Helen moved back into the main house at their daughter's insistence, and Isabel moved into the apartment. As Helen and Buddy entered their elder years, Isabel looked after them in the same home where they had once looked after her. "The circle of life," Buddy often liked to point out. But now her kids, Charlie and Carly, were living on opposite coasts, a decade had passed since Carl had died, and it had been five years since Buddy and Helen passed; Buddy first, and just six months later, Helen. So for the past five years Isabel had been living alone for the first time in her life. Well, alone in that she was the only one living at Poplar Bluff who walked upright. She did have roommates—her Jack Russell terrier, Jack, short for Jackpot, and her cocker spaniel, Corky, a black-and-gray-speckled beauty Isabel had recently adopted. At some point, two cats—one a gray tabby, the other an orange-and-black calico—had moved into the garage, so she now counted them as neighbors. Because she was a devoted admirer of Jane Austen, she named them Mr. Darcy and Miss Bennet.

Isabel's son, who now went by Charles, although she still called him Charlie, was a successful architect living in San Francisco. Years before he had changed his last name to his mother's maiden name of Peabody. "Do you know what it's like to spend your entire childhood being called Mud Puddles in school?" Charlie said to his mother in defense of his decision to establish a more professional persona. But she understood. It took a few years for her to get used to her new last name too, but after a while she decided she liked the uniqueness of it. Isabel Puddles . . . It had kind of a lilting ring to it. But Charlie had evidently decided at some point he was not a fan of lilting rings, and that was fine by Isabel. He also decided at some point after changing his name, to change his religion too, converting from Congregationalism to Buddhism. That one threw her for a loop at first. All Isabel knew about Buddhism was that the Dalai Lama seemed to be the man in charge, and she thought he looked like a very kind person, so she figured it must be a friendly sort of religion. But did this mean Charlie was going to shave his head, dress in robes, and wear sandals year-round? That might be hard for her to get used to. After Charlie assured her he was not becoming a Buddhist monk, only a Buddhist, and made sure she understood the difference, she embraced his decision wholeheartedly. And after doing some reading on the subject, she concluded it was a religion that made a lot of sense. She could see the appeal for Charlie, who had always been a deep thinker. Charlie even suggested to his mother that she consider becoming a Buddhist, but since Isabel considered herself an agnostic, she was going to stick with Congregationalism, which wasn't quite as strict as other denominations were about uncertainty when it came to one's faith. When Isabel finally shared her pendulum-like philosophy concerning the existence of God and heaven with her minister, the Reverend Curtis, he assured her that pondering His existence was perfectly understandable and nothing to be ashamed of. He even admitted he had pangs of disbelief himself from time to time. Isabel told him she did her very best to live by the Golden Rule, and if that wasn't enough to get her into heaven, assuming there was a heaven, she would just have to hope St. Peter would give her the benefit of the doubt. Reverend Curtis, knowing the character of one of his favorite parishioners, assured her that she would likely make the cut.

During a recent visit home for Christmas, after Mr. Darcy and Miss Bennet had moved into the garage, Charlie decided that his grandparents, Helen and Buddy, had *trans-mutated* and come back as cats, taking up residence in the garage in order to keep an eye on things. Isabel assumed this was something Buddhist's believed in, although she found it to be a bit of a stretch. Charlie arrived at this conclusion after being startled more than once by Mr. Darcy and Miss Bennet sitting on the windowsill outside, casually but very intently observing what was happening inside. "They look like they're plotting . . . like they want back in . . . it's a little spooky." Charlie's canine brother and sister, Jackpot and Corky, were not big fans of the practice either, but their barking did nothing to scare the cats away. They just looked down at them in disdain as they swished their tails. Carly, a banker, who now lived in Boston, was of a different mindset altogether regarding the cats. All she wanted to know was how much her mother was spending on cat food per month, and how that would amortize after five, and then ten years, allowing for inflation.

"I can assure you," Isabel said to her son over blueberry pancakes one morning, "that if your grandparents were going to reincarnate or trans-*whatever*, it wouldn't be as feral cats living in the garage." Then, in an effort to calm her daughter's fear that feeding two cats would eventually lead her to financial ruin, "And just in case they *are* your grandparents, I think eight ninety-nine a month in cat food is the least we can do . . . They *are* the original owners, after all." And that ended that conversation.

★　★　★

The SS *Badger* was a massive, four-hundred-foot car ferry, and the only remaining coal-fired steamer left on the Great Lakes. It had been running between Wisconsin and Michigan, from May to October, for well over fifty years. When she was a girl, Isabel Peabody was fascinated by the enormous ship, and longed to sail across the Big Lake on her one day. Every summer she asked her parents if they could make the four-hour journey to Wisconsin. Her mother, always the voice of reason in the Peabody household, didn't want to discourage her daughter's adventurous spirit but also wanted to manage any expectations that it would ever happen, knowing her husband's aversion to the state of Wisconsin. "Honey, if you can think of a good reason to go to Wisconsin, we can talk about it . . . but I really can't think of one. They have trees and they have lakes . . . and we have that right outside our picture window."

Buddy Peabody was quick to invoke the tragic fate of the *Titanic* whenever his daughter brought up sailing on the *Badger*. "Why would you want to risk your life to visit a state that counts cheese making as its crowning achievement? In Michigan we make automobiles. In Wisconsin they make sharp cheddar. Enough said." The world was a very black-and-white place for Buddy Peabody.

For years her father's contempt for the state of Wisconsin had been a mystery to Isabel, but one day her mother offered up a simple explanation: "Your father is as kindhearted and fair minded as a man can be. But everybody needs to hate something . . . For me it's mice. For you it's lima beans. For your dad it's Wisconsin . . . We just have to let him have that."

When Isabel got into high school and began dating Carl Puddles, a transfer student from Wisconsin, her father was surprisingly calm . . . at first. But the day her new boyfriend came to pick her up wearing a University of Wisconsin sweatshirt, Buddy stopped him cold at the front door and made him wait outside, in December, in falling snow. Fifteen minutes later, Mr. Peabody finally announced to his daughter that her date—still standing on the front stoop shivering—was there to pick her up. The stunt resulted in a good scolding from both his wife and his daughter, and from that day forward, Isabel's dates with Carl began with a friendly honk from the driveway.

Eventually Isabel learned that her father's disdain for Wisconsin, and virtually anybody who hailed from America's Dairyland, could be traced back to a Milwaukee boy who spent a summer living in his family's very grand lakefront estate and working as a lifeguard alongside Buddy at a nearby Lake Michigan beach. But when he wasn't lifeguarding, the handsome young rich kid devoted his free time to trying to woo a beautiful local girl named Helen MacGregor away from her boyfriend—Buddy Peabody. The unwelcome interloper, who was an heir to a famous beer fortune, was about to begin his freshman year at the University of Wisconsin. He was so smitten with Helen that he implored her to dump Buddy and go steady with him. He even dangled the possibility of a marriage proposal after he graduated. But in the end, Helen stayed true to the boy she had been going steady with since seventh grade, resisting the temptation of one day marrying into great wealth and privilege, and a lifetime supply of beer. Instead, she promised to marry Buddy, who was destined for a career in the insurance business, and provided her with a lifetime supply of laughs. Although they were far from rich, financially speaking, they were rich in every other way that mattered. Buddy had been a good provider, a devoted husband, a wonderful father, and a pillar of the community, and Helen MacGregor Peabody had never for a moment regretted her decision. And she wasn't much of a beer drinker anyway. But ever since that brazen romantic coup attempt—which ended with the handsome rich kid from Milwaukee going home on

Labor Day with a black eye, courtesy of Buddy Peabody—he had remained contemptuous of the boy's home state *and* his alma mater. He also prohibited the brand of beer that bore his family's name from ever coming into the house.

After Isabel married Carl, which was a marriage Buddy blessed only after his future son-in-law laid his hand on the family Bible and swore he would never move back to Wisconsin with his daughter, she finally made the journey she had always dreamed about, setting sail on the SS *Badger* one summer with their first child, Carly, to visit Carl's grandparents in Green Bay. Thirty minutes into the four-hour voyage, Isabel and the baby both got terribly seasick, and suffered for the remainder of the journey. After their visit in Wisconsin, Isabel and the baby flew home, and Carl and their Ford Country Squire took the *Badger* home alone.

When Buddy and Helen picked their daughter and granddaughter up at the airport, Isabel began to gush to her mother about her trip, although she had the good sense to wait until her father had gone to get the car. Isabel loved Wisconsin. She loved Wisconsinites, the cheese was wonderful, and she couldn't wait to go back the next summer and see more of it, just not by way of the *Badger*. She then slipped her mother a wedge of white cheddar. Helen smiled, dropped the cheese into her purse, and patted her daughter's hand. "Well, I'm happy to hear that, honey. I'm sure it's a lovely place. But don't tell your father, it'll kill him." To this day, whenever Isabel heard the *Badger*'s familiar horn blast, it brought back fond memories of that first trip to Wisconsin, although these waves of nostalgia were often accompanied by waves of nausea.

The sound of the *Badger*'s horn could also stir up sadness for her, especially in stormy weather. On those days, the horn sounded almost mournful, reminding Isabel of the many thousands of souls who had perished on Lake Michigan over the years. But she loved Lake Michigan. It felt like it was almost a part of her. Through the woods, the Big Lake was only a quarter mile or so from Poplar Bluff, and she made the hike with Jack and Corky as often as she could. And every time the trail ended and the lake revealed itself, she was still awestruck by its beauty. Looking out across that seemingly endless expanse of water was as second-nature to her as looking up at the sky. "Salt free and shark free for ten thousand years," the locals liked to say. But just as the skies in this part of Michigan could go from a brilliant blue one minute to dark and ominous the next, so could Lake Michigan. Those who loved the beauty and majesty of the lake as she did also had a healthy respect for the unexpected and deadly dangers it could present.

For her Michigan history class in high school, Isabel wrote an essay inspired by Gordon Lightfoot's ballad "The Wreck of the Edmund Fitzgerald," about the doomed freighter that went down on Lake Superior in 1975, taking with it its twenty-nine-person crew. The song still brought tears to her eyes whenever she heard it. She nearly came unglued at the Kroger recently while standing in the checkout line with a carton of orange juice and a loaf of whole-wheat bread when the song came on.

In her essay, which won first place in an essay-writing contest held by the *Gull Harbor Gazette*, Isabel also wrote about a sad event recounted by her grandparents, who told her in somber recollections about what came to be known as the Armistice Day Storm, which hit the Midwest on November 11, 1940. The unexpected and brutal early-season blizzard tore across the upper Midwest, wreaking havoc with every vessel sailing on any of the Great Lakes, but Lake Michigan was hit hardest. Captains and their crews had virtually no warning, so they were caught completely unprepared. Three large freighters sank just off the coast of Gull Harbor.

After the storm cleared, anybody with a boat went out in search of survivors, but found only a handful of bodies. At dusk, hundreds of locals went down to the shore holding lanterns and candles. Led by the choirmaster from the Methodist church in the nearby town of Hartley, they sang hymns so that anybody who might be out there struggling to stay alive would know there were people on shore pulling and praying for them. But in the end, there were no survivors. Tragically, sixty-four men met their deaths on those three ships.

In the spring, when the lake began to thaw, bodies that had been frozen in ice all winter began to wash up on shore. Isabel's grandmother, Hazel Peabody, was out beachcombing one morning when she found the body of a young sailor lying face up on the beach. Grandmother Peabody never got over it, and she never swam in the Big Lake again.

Chapter 2

It was the Friday morning before Memorial Day weekend, and Isabel was on her way to the Land's End to meet Frances, her very best friend, for breakfast. Gull Harbor was already beginning to buzz with the usual influx of summer visitors, and it wouldn't stop buzzing until Labor Day. Some were tourists who had come to town for the holiday weekend, some were only passing through on their way to other points north, but many were Gull Harbor's usual summer residents who traditionally arrived on Memorial Day weekend to open their summer homes and cottages, either on the Big Lake or on Gull Lake. Other summer people sailed into the harbor and moored their enormous yachts at the exclusive Gull Harbor Yacht Club, where many would spend their summers onboard.

This morning, Gull Harbor merchants and their summer employees, mostly high school and college kids, were busy sweeping, washing windows, and pulling racks of merchandise out onto the sidewalks, preparing for the larger onslaught of summer tourists who would be streaming in over the next three months, ready to shop. The regular summer residents—most of them from the wealthier suburbs of Chicago, Milwaukee, and Detroit—were not really the souvenir-buying types, but by Isabel's observation, there seemed to be a whole species of tourist who were unable to check the place they were visiting off their list until they had purchased a T-shirt or a coffee mug to remind themselves of where they had been.

Isabel Puddles was not a fan of the crass commercialism on display in her hometown during the summer months, but this aversion was not an opinion she shared with others around town. People had to make a living, and she didn't want to insult anybody's livelihood. And she had done well by the summer tourists, too, for the past few years, so she didn't want to be a hypocrite either. Still, despite the many changes Isabel had witnessed over the years, and not all of them for the better, Gull Harbor was still as charming a shoreline village as you could find anywhere on any of the Great Lakes, and she was proud to call it home. Living anywhere else had never even occurred to her.

When Isabel Peabody was a girl, downtown Gull Harbor, all three blocks of it, was as quaint and wholesome as a Norman Rockwell painting. The Ben Franklin Five & Dime store was Isabel's favorite, and always her first stop on Saturday morning after she received her two-dollar-per-week allowance. They had a luncheonette counter with a soda fountain, where she and her mother would have lunch together nearly every Saturday afternoon—Isabel spinning in her stool and drinking a vanilla Coke, while Helen talked to whoever was working behind the counter and drank her chocolate Coke—soda concoctions younger generations couldn't quite understand. Mother and daughter would usually split a grilled cheese sandwich on rye bread with mustard and dill pickle chips, still one of Isabel's go-to comfort foods, and an order of onion rings.

Lining either side of Gull Harbor's Main Street, which

was still paved with brick, was the Harbor Bakery, a movie theater called the Royale, Wurzburg's gift shop, Longwood's department store, a corner market called the Pixie Plaza, the post office, Birke's Boot Shop, Herb's Tackle and Bait, and her cousin Flora's florist shop, called Flora's Florist Shoppe, which had caused Isabel years of confusion over the proper spelling of *shop*. Surrounding the village proper were gracious old clapboard homes and cottages with manicured lawns and big clumps of hydrangea, all sitting proudly along streets canopied by giant sugar maple trees. Most of the homes in town, many of them owned by summer people now, had been meticulously preserved, but a few of the older families who struggled in the off-season to keep the lights on had let their places fall into various states of disrepair. Locals understood that the choice between putting groceries on the table, or putting a fresh coat of paint on your hundred-year-old house, wasn't a difficult one to make.

One home did stand out as an eyesore by anybody's definition, however. It was a three-story Victorian—a style very common in Gull Harbor—that looked as though it had not been given a fresh coat of paint since Queen Victoria was still on the throne. The house sat on two lots and was set much farther from the curb than the other homes on the street. It also had a good-sized barn covered in ivy, where the owners stored God knows what. The home was owned and occupied by two brothers named Emmett and Elliot Twistleman, identical twins, who were now well into their seventies, and whose family had owned the property since it was built back in the 1870s. According to local historians, Colonel Twistleman, the twins' great-grandfather, was a Civil War hero who retired to Gull Harbor after the war and built himself what was, at the time, considered quite a grand estate.

Everybody in town knew *of* the twins, because they were out and about all the time, but nobody really *knew* them. They were, to be kind, kind of the town oddballs. Both had wispy red hair and long beards that looked as if they were trimmed maybe once a year, and they wore matching overalls. They were also notorious hoarders, who drove around town in a beat-up old red pickup truck collecting whatever caught their eye, which was just about anything. If you had an old dresser you wanted to get rid of, all you had to do was take it out to the curb, and the next time you looked out your window, the Twistleman twins would have scooped it up. Every Memorial Day weekend, the twins' yard sale opened, and didn't close until Labor Day. At night or when it rained, they simply covered their merchandise with tarps. Every summer the neighbors, especially the summer neighbors, complained to the town council, asking them to shut down the twins' yard sale, and every summer the council reminded them that nowhere in the town charter did it say that homeowners couldn't hold yard sales, nor were there any restrictions on how long they could last.

Isabel stopped in at least once every summer out of pure fascination. You never knew what the twins might have dug up over the winter months for one thing, but the twins themselves had always intrigued her too. She always enjoyed her conversations with them, as awkward as they often were, because neither of them would make eye contact. They both looked up and around like they were following birds around the yard. But she always found something to buy, sometimes only because she felt it would be rude not to. "I don't know why you insist on stopping by and talking to those nutjobs," Frances scolded her one morning at breakfast. "They scare the *bejibbers* out of me! I'm afraid you're going to wind up in their crawl space one of these days! 'Where's Isabel?' 'Last time I saw her she was buying a cup and saucer off the Twistleman twins!' " Isabel rolled her eyes and sipped her coffee, as she always did when Frances turned on the drama.

When Isabel was growing up in Gull Harbor, it took her less than five minutes to walk from one end of town to the other, and she wouldn't pass a single person whose name she didn't know, and who she would most likely stop and chat with. Except for the Amish, who would come into town on the weekends in their buggies. A faint smile and a polite nod were usually the best you could ever get out of them. There were still some Amish families scattered around the county, but she rarely saw them in town anymore. Thankfully they did still have the Amish Dairy, which Isabel and many others considered the mecca for dairy products in this part of Michigan. Their ice cream was highly coveted, and you needed to be there early if you wanted black cherry or butter pecan. Isabel recognized a lot of the summer people too, and they might smile and nod politely, but they were not the stop and chat types, unless it was with each other. For them, the locals seemed to serve only as window dressing who added to the country charm of the place.

Anchoring the north end of town were the offices of the *Gull Harbor Gazette*, and on the other end was Shumway Park, with a vast lawn that meandered down a gentle incline and hugged the shore of the harbor. The town's gazebo was the focal point of Shumway Park, and where concerts were held every weekend in the summer. During the holidays, the gazebo was home to the town's Christmas tree, with a Nativity scene off to the side intended to, as her father used to say, "Keep the Baptists happy." Thankfully those traditions hadn't changed. There was still music every weekend during the summer, and the lighting of the town Christmas tree was still a beloved Gull Harbor tradition. And the same Nativity scene, now slightly worse for wear, was still set up beside the gazebo on the same day the tree went up.

A few years back, some local hooligans kidnapped the baby Jesus one night and returned him the next morning wearing a toddler's University of Michigan sweatshirt. "That's the sort of thing you'd expect from a Michigan fan," she remembered a loyal Michigan State supporter remarking at breakfast after hearing about the prank. The following year, this time on Christmas Eve, baby Jesus was kidnapped once again, and returned on Christmas morning in a hooded Michigan State sweatshirt. Local clergy of all denominations failed to see the humor, and it became a hot topic for a sermon or two, but most of the townsfolk just thought it was funny. "All you have to do is look around you," Frances joked, "to see that God has a great sense of humor!"

The largest structure in town was the Gull Harbor Yacht Club, an expansive, beautifully maintained property that sat along the harbor on the opposite side of Shumway Park, surrounded and secluded by tall, thick hedges on three sides. On the fourth side were slips for about two dozen yachts. The clubhouse was a grand old Edwardian structure, painted white, with yellow-and-white-striped awnings and an enormous wraparound porch lined with white wicker furniture, where members could sit and look out over the grounds and the harbor. Yachtless members, usually those more elderly, stayed in the suites on the second floor of the clubhouse, while members with children and grandchildren stayed in small bungalows that peppered the property. The club had an Olympic-sized swimming pool, a couple of clay tennis courts, and a croquet court. GHYC members represented old money, steeped in old-money tradition. These were people of privilege who had been "summering" in Gull Harbor going back three and four generations. Aspiring members, no matter how rich, who were without a family history at the club, were rarely allowed to join. For most locals, members of GHYC seemed as mysterious and remote as the Amish, but with suntans and much more colorful clothes.

Although the population of summer people stayed fairly

fixed, for the past few years Isabel had been noticing more and more folks coming from farther away. She was now seeing license plates from back east: Pennsylvania, New York, New Jersey. And there was a recent smattering of European tourists—French, German, and English, mostly—who had apparently discovered the place after a popular European travel magazine published a glowing article about Gull Harbor and some of the other picturesque hamlets along the Big Lake. Going to Europe was high on Isabel's bucket list, but until she could get there, if she ever did, she kind of enjoyed Europe coming to her. Frances, who had also lived in Gull Harbor all her life, and had been friends with Isabel since kindergarten, was not as enamored of the European influx. But then she didn't like tourists no matter where they came from. Last summer at the Land's End diner, where Isabel and Frances had breakfast nearly every morning, two large tables were occupied by stylishly dressed German tourists enjoying their breakfast, all excitedly chatting with each other in German, naturally, just laughing and having a grand time. Frances was clearly annoyed. "I feel like an extra on *Hogan's Heroes*," she remarked. "Where's Sergeant Schultz?" Isabel and Kayla both shushed her simultaneously, and thankfully her xenophobic remarks were not overheard.

After finally finding a place to park, Isabel walked two blocks to the Land's End to meet Frances for their standing eight a.m. breakfast date. Frances was at their usual table hidden behind a newspaper when Isabel walked in and sat down. Their waitress, and now dear friend, Kayla, met her at the table with a steaming pitcher of hot coffee.

"Morning, Iz. Did you hear?" Kayla asked, flipping Isabel's cup over on its saucer and pouring her coffee.

"Hear what? I haven't read the paper yet." Isabel reached for the little metal pitcher and poured milk into her coffee, stirring as Frances folded the newspaper in half and handed it across the table.

"Kid went missing coming across on the *Badger* yesterday. His girlfriend was there to meet him, but he never got off the boat."

Isabel took the newspaper and gave it a shake before opening it. "Maybe he never got *on* the boat," she suggested as she began reading the front-page article.

Kayla was still hovering nearby. "No, he was definitely on the boat. He took a selfie after he got on board and sent it to the girlfriend."

Isabel looked over the top of the paper and scrunched her nose. "A selfie? What's that?"

Frances laughed. "Kayla, have you forgotten who you're talking to? This woman is still waiting for the Bee Gees to come out with a new album." Then turning to Isabel, "a *selfie* is what the kids call it when you take a picture of yourself with your phone and then send it around for the whole world to see."

Isabel shook her head. "Who takes pictures of themselves? Sounds like the height of vanity to me."

Frances continued, "I don't spend a lot of time trying to figure out what young people are up to these days or why . . . I mean, who can keep up? But my grandkids do educate me on the lingo . . . and I let 'em think I give two shakes."

"So what do you think, Iz? Foul play?" Kayla asked, her voice dripping with intrigue.

Isabel folded up the paper and set it aside, then put her napkin in her lap. "Probably more like foul weather. That was quite a storm that moved across the Big Lake yesterday. He wouldn't be the first to have been swept off the deck of that boat."

Kayla was refilling coffees again. "The Coast Guard is still out there looking for him. Maybe he's a strong swimmer."

Isabel was not so optimistic. "Even if he had the stamina of an Olympic swimmer, I'll bet the water temperature isn't much over fifty degrees now. It wouldn't take long for hypothermia to set in. Who was he? Do we know?"

Kayla shook her head. "Haven't released his name yet. Safe to say he's not a local boy or we would have heard."

"What if he jumped?" Frances offered. "Wouldn't be *my* first choice if I was going to do myself in, but then to each their own."

Kayla added her two cents to the abrupt change in topic. "I think I'd just take a handful of sleeping pills if it ever came to that. No point in being melodramatic."

Frances had always loved anything morbid or ghoulish, so she was thrilled *that* door had just been opened. "Did you ever hear about that Hollywood actress . . . I forget her name, it was back in the forties, I think. Anyway, her career wasn't going so hot, and I think she'd just been jilted by her boyfriend, so she must have decided she'd had enough, and planned this very elaborate final farewell scene. She dressed all in white, made sure her hair and makeup was perfect, and then lit candles all over the bedroom of her Beverly Hills mansion. Then she washed down a handful of sleeping pills with a glass of champagne, and laid down on her bed with her arms folded across her chest . . . then she waited." Frances closed her eyes and struck the pose she had just described before continuing. "Unfortunately, after a little while, the enchiladas she'd had for lunch started to come back up on her, thanks to all those pills and the champagne, so she had to get up out of bed and dash to the bathroom to be sick. But the pills had already started to do the trick." Frances took a dramatic pause with a deliberately slow sip of coffee.

Kayla was enraptured with the story. "Well? What *happened*, Frances?"

Frances took another sip before she brought the curtain down. "Her maid found her the next morning, dead, with her head in the toilet."

Kayla's mouth was hanging open. "That is *not* true. You made that up, Frances!"

"I most certainly did not. I saw it on a TV show. But it just goes to show you that it doesn't matter what grand plans you make in this life, there's always a very good chance you're going to end up with your head in the toilet." Frances suddenly realized Isabel was staring at her. "What?"

"Is that really a story that needs to be shared at the breakfast table, Frances? Or *anywhere*, for that matter?"

"I thought it was interesting," Frances replied, defending her story. "Anyway, Kayla . . . if you ever do decide to throw in the towel with pills, make sure you steer clear of the Taco Bell!" Frances and Kayla both laughed. Isabel shook her head and drank her coffee, trying to forget Frances's dreary story, and the poor young man who had disappeared off the *Badger*.

After they finished their breakfast, it was time to get on with the day ahead. "So what are your plans for the day?" Isabel asked Frances as she got ready to pay her check.

"Hank and I are off to pick up his mother. It's her eighty-fourth birthday today, so we're taking her to lunch at the Sizzler in Wellington. The woman loves a salad bar! His sisters and their kids will be joining us too. They make my teeth itch, but you do what you have to do."

"That sounds nice," Isabel said as she scooted her check to the end of the table and slapped a ten-dollar bill on top.

"Does it?" Frances replied, as she did the same with a twenty. "You've never seen that old woman go after a bowl of tapioca pudding. She sounds like a nursing calf. Myrtle Spitler has put me off pudding for life, I can tell you . . . And what are your plans for the day, Mrs. Puddles?"

"I'm going home, taking the dogs for a walk, putting on some soup, and then I have to finish writing my last paper of the semester."

"What kind?" Frances asked.

"Advanced blood spatter analysis."

Frances stared at her for a beat. "I meant what kind of *soup?*"

"Oh!" Isabel laughed. "Split pea. Hannah Wilcox brought one of her smoked ham hocks by the hardware yesterday."

"What time would you like me? I'm free for dinner. Hank's bowling tonight."

"Come on by any time after six. And by the way, you have more of my Tupperware than I do, so if you'd please bring some back?"

"I guess if I'm going to bring home any soup, I'll need to. You're always thinking of me, Izzy. I love that about you." Frances smiled and finished her last sip of coffee, just as Kayla came back with a final splash.

"So have you decided if you're going to the commencement exercises, Izzy?" Kayla asked as she poured.

Isabel had been debating whether or not she would take part in her college commencement ceremony when the time came, and Kayla brought the subject up at least twice a week. She was still on the fence, and it was a long way off, but she was leaning against it, afraid people might make fun of a woman her age wearing a cap and gown. But Kayla was emphatic. "You need to get up there and get your diploma! You ought to be proud of yourself, Isabel, just like we're all proud of you."

Kayla had been one of Isabel's most ardent supporters after she announced she was going back to college to get the degree that had eluded her for so many years. When she and her husband, Carl, went off to Michigan State University together, her plan was to get her teaching degree and teach literature, inspired by her very favorite high school teacher, Gladys DeLong. But Fate stepped in and derailed that plan about halfway through their sophomore year, and gave her a daughter instead. Carly, and then two years later, Charlie, were the two shining stars in her life, so she had no regrets, but she always secretly wished she had found a way to get her degree. Carl eventually got his civil engineering degree thanks to night school courses at the same college Isabel was now attending, but she remained mostly a stay-at-home mom, except for her part-time work at her cousin Freddie's hardware store in Hartley during school hours, along with some part-time hairdressing at a shop owned by an old friend from beauty school called The Mane Event. But Fate had recently stepped back in, and had steered her back not only to college but in a dramatically different direction. Next year, assuming she passed all her remaining classes, Isabel would be matriculating with a degree in criminal justice, a field in which she had recently acquired some unplanned, but fairly significant firsthand experience.

"I have plenty of time to think about graduation, so I don't know . . . I might do it," she assured Kayla. "But," she added, "I don't want to be the only graduate in my class who needs help getting up onto the stage."

"You're already the only one in your class with corns and an AARP card," Frances cracked. She was proud of Isabel too, but she could never resist the occasional jab about her age, even though they were only two months apart.

"I do *not* have corns, Frances! Honestly. The things you come up with," she replied indignantly.

Frances was still laughing when Gil Cook, the local funeral director and Isabel's dear friend since high school, walked into the diner. Frances stopped laughing. "Uh-oh . . . here comes the grim reaper! Who are you here to collect, Gil?" Frances looked around the diner. "It looks to me like everybody's still sitting upright. Sorry to disappoint!" She laughed, then looked over at Floyd Pickering, an asparagus farmer just shy of a hundred, who was sitting at the counter eating his usual stack of pancakes. "Floyd, you better check your pulse!"

Floyd was as deaf as a post, so he couldn't hear her, and Gil just ignored her as he always did, having grown accustomed to Frances's snarky remarks about his profession. They had known each other since high school too, but they were never really friends. For Gil, like for many others, Frances was an acquired taste he never really acquired. "Morning, Iz . . . Kayla." Then, yelling over at Floyd, "Good morning, Floyd!" He deliberately skipped Frances.

Isabel could tell right away that Gil was in a bad mood, something that rarely happened. She always told him he was the most cheerful mortician in America. "What's wrong, Gil? You look upset."

"That's because I *am* upset," Gil said as he sat down with a heavy sigh. He grabbed a piece of toast off Isabel's plate and took a bite. "One of those plaid-shorts-wearing idiots just backed into my poor little Bug with an SUV the size of a bulldozer. Smashed in the driver's-side door so bad I couldn't even open it. I had to put the roof down and crawl out. Then he had the gall to claim it was *my* fault because *he* couldn't see me. I said, 'My God, man, it's a bright red Volkswagen! You can see it from space!' What a . . . ." Gil took another bite of Isabel's toast. "I'd like just *one* summer without summer *people*." Gil flipped his cup so Kayla could pour his coffee. "And they don't even have the courtesy to die here so I could at least take in a little extra income . . . like you do with your pickles, Iz."

"Very inconsiderate of them . . . Would it kill 'em to die here?" Isabel offered, trying to cajole Gil out of his funk. "And maybe you've forgotten, Gil, but I'm out of the pickle business, at least for the time being."

Like Gil and most other year-round residents, Isabel had mixed feelings about the summer people who invaded their otherwise sleepy community, but Gil was right. She had benefitted financially over the past few years from the summer influx, selling her pickled asparagus, beets, and bread-and-butter pickles at a handful of local farm stands. Puddles Pickles had been a big hit with the summer people, and a nice source of extra income. She had also been baking cherry, blueberry, and strawberry-rhubarb pies for local restaurants that catered to summer people. Pies baked by the Peabody Pie Company—named after her Grandmother Peabody, whose recipes she used—were almost as popular as her pickles.

And not only was Isabel keeping the summer people fed, she was also keeping them warm. After she placed an ad in the *Gull Harbor Gazette* one summer promoting her hand-knitted scarves, special orders came pouring in, most of them pre-ordered as Christmas gifts. For an up charge she would gift-wrap them and then ship them off to the buyers' chosen friends or family. Scarves by Isabel had become somewhat lucrative, too, but very time consuming. And for the past couple of years this operation would have been more aptly called Scarves by Bertha and Lila Purdy, the two spinster sisters from nearby Shelbyville to whom she had been farming out most of the knitting. But this summer, Isabel's cottage businesses, or, as Charlie called them, her "side hustles," were a thing of the past. There was no longer any time for pickling, or baking, or knitting. And, sadly, the Purdy sisters' arthritis had prevented them from carrying on with the knitting any longer.

Isabel loved to knit, and she had been doing it for as long as she could remember, but the only time she got her yarn and needles out nowadays was at home, usually in the evenings, and strictly as a form of meditation. The end products were new scarves for her kids, new jackets for her dogs, and last week, a new tea cozy for Frances, who had somehow managed to light the last one she knitted for her on fire and nearly burned her house down. But Isabel Puddles was still a member in good standing with her knitting circle, the Knit Wits. However, due to her busy schedule, she had been forced to relinquish the presidency. There just wasn't time enough to be an effective chief executive. Evelyn Utley had been campaigning pretty hard for the job anyway, so she figured it was time to pass the baton, or the needles, as it were. Frances always made fun of Isabel for taking her role as president of the Knit Wits so seriously, but the position required more time and attention than Frances or anybody understood. The club's local charity work—mostly food and yarn drives—required loads of prep work, and so did knitting the ornaments for the town Christmas tree, which had a new theme every year. It was Isabel's idea to sell the previous year's Christmas ornaments at their annual holiday bake sale and bazaar, which was also quite an undertaking. And for years the Knit Wits had been turning out several dozen pairs of slippers every few months for the all too often forgotten residents of the county old folks' home, known coldly as "the facility." That project was a labor of love, but it did eat up a lot of time. At their monthly meeting, just before Isabel stepped down, Dottie Dorfman offered a plan to streamline the slipper project. Given that the facility, not surprisingly, lost residents on a fairly regular basis, Dottie thought maybe they could start recycling slippers. Isabel was mortified by the mere suggestion and let Dottie know it. "Who in the world wants to wear a pair of slippers somebody died in?" Wanting to dispense with the idea as quickly as possible, Isabel immediately put it to a vote, and the measure was defeated twelve to one, with Dottie voting yes, and her sister-in-law, Enid, abstaining.

It wasn't General Motors, but the Knit Wits' presidency did require a firm hand, solid organizational skills, and a fair amount of problem-solving ability. Evelyn Utley was Frances's cousin, and she warned Isabel that Evelyn might not be up to the task. "Well, she must know how to knit, because she's no wit, that I can tell you!" Frances chuckled after hearing of her cousin's elevation to such high office. "My father's side of the family didn't turn out a whole lot of mental heavyweights, but Evie, bless her heart, was still on coloring books in the eleventh grade!"

In keeping with presidential precedence, Isabel didn't think it was fitting to comment on her successor's performance, but, given how things were beginning to unfurl under Evelyn's administration, it looked like Frances may have been right.

While Gil was trying to calm his nerves with a warm cinnamon bun, Isabel's other favorite cousin, Ginny, and her new husband, Grady, formerly the Kentwater County sheriff, walked in. "What happened to your car, Gil?" Grady yelled across the diner as he entered the restaurant. Gil shook his head in disgust, licking his fingers and answering with his mouth half-full.

"I wish you were still sheriff, Grady. I'd ask you to go arrest the fool who backed into me!" Grady smiled as he pulled out a chair for his wife. Today was the day Ginny and Grady, who had married the previous summer, were leaving on a belated honeymoon, and intending to be away all summer. After twenty years as sheriff, Grady had finally decided to retire. Ginny, who had worked for the sheriff's department for twenty-*five* years, was happy to follow suit. They had just purchased a new motor home and were now "off to destinations unknown," as Grady liked to put it. But Isabel knew her cousin. Spontaneity wasn't her thing. Ginny was a planner. Isabel was certain Ginny had a travel itinerary all planned out, she just hadn't shared it with her husband yet.

"So this is it, huh?" Isabel asked with a melancholy smile. "You kids are hitting the road?" Isabel and Ginny grew up more like sisters than cousins, and they had never in their lives gone more than three weeks, tops, without seeing each other, so to have her gone for three *months* was hard to imagine. But she was happy to see Ginny so happy, and she adored Grady, so she would just have to accept her new normal for the summer.

Ginny was quick with her answer. "Yep! First thing in the morning, we are *outta* here! I'll miss all of you terribly, but I cannot *wait* to get away from all these tourists! I'm ready to be one *myself* for a change!"

"You're preachin' to the choir, Gin," Gil said as he popped the rest of his cinnamon bun into his mouth and licked his fingers again. Frances looked over at him with her eyebrows slightly furled.

"You really ought to meet my mother-in-law, Gil. I've watched gulls at the beach pick apart a washed-up perch more delicately than you did that cinnamon bun." Everybody laughed except Gil. Frances then turned to Grady. "You two must have *some* idea where you're headed, don't you, Grady?"

"I want to head west to Yellowstone, but Ginny wants to head south to Orlando so the grandkids can meet us and we can all go to Disney World *again*. I think we're going to have to play a game of rock, paper, scissors to finally settle it."

Ginny turned to Isabel and Frances, saying in a whisper, "We're going to Orlando."

After Ginny and Isabel shared a hug and a slightly tearful goodbye, the Land's End kaffeeklatsch broke up. Isabel stood up and put her sweater on as Kayla returned with their change. "Kayla, I'll bring you some split-pea soup tomorrow. You can have it for your lunch."

"You know how I love your soups, Isabel," Kayla yelled back as she went into the kitchen to pick up another order of pancakes for Floyd.

Frances stood up next. "What goes with split pea? Red, white, or the pink stuff? I'll pick up a box."

"Surprise me. I still have a loaf of your rye bread in my freezer so I'll make us some grilled cheese too." So with dinner plans now confirmed, Isabel left the Land's End and headed home to Poplar Bluff. With traffic getting heavier, she was going to have to think seriously about riding her bike into town. But then she had thought seriously about that last summer, and the summer before.

Chapter 3

Isabel had the day off from the hardware, so after taking Jackpot and Corky for a brisk walk through the woods and over to the Big Lake, she returned home with two happy dogs and a pocket full of morel mushrooms, one of the many perks of living in the north woods of Michigan. She had been picking morels for more years than she could count, and always in the same spots where they appeared every year in the early spring. Hunting morels in these closely guarded secret spots had always been a spring ritual for Isabel and her dad. Her mother would then cook them up in a variety of ways: omelets, quiches, and Isabel's favorite—a creamy morel mushroom lasagne, which was also Charlie's favorite. She always made sure to freeze enough to prepare that dish for him when he came home, and then send him back to California with the rest in a ziplock bag, which he smuggled onto the plane like contraband. When Charlie told his mother that morels went for over fifty dollars a pound at the Sausalito Farmers' Market where he shopped, she was bowled over. Yes, they were indeed delicious, but they were not fifty-dollars-a-pound delicious, but then she couldn't think of anything that was.

The subject of morels always reminded Isabel of the story

of poor old Art Huffine, a member of the Kentwater County board of supervisors, whose wife, Maybelle, prepared some delicious morels her husband had found while hiking in the woods. Maybelle sautéed them in butter and brandy just the way Art liked them, and served them over a strip sirloin she had lovingly grilled for him. It was the last steak Art ever ate. It seems Maybelle tossed in another variety of mushroom she found in the backyard growing under her birdbath, one commonly known as the death angel, which later became Maybelle's nickname around the county. By breakfast the next day, Art was in a coma, and by lunch he was dead. Everybody was pretty sure she did it on purpose, but during her trial, Maybelle took the stand, turned on the waterworks, and managed to convince at least one member of the jury it was all just a terrible accident. It turned out that one juror was a local businessman who, five years earlier, had lost his bid to build a large storage facility when his plan came before the board. Supervisor Huffine had cast the deciding vote *against*. Apparently in the mind of this particular juror, Art's no vote was so egregious that death by mushroom poisoning seemed a perfectly appropriate punishment. Jury pools in a county the size of Kentwater didn't have too many degrees of separation, so it wasn't the first time a score had been settled from the jury box, and it wouldn't be the last.

Isabel put the mushrooms in the fridge, took out the plump ham hock, courtesy of Hannah Wilcox, and started putting together her split-pea soup, using Gran MacGregor's recipe, which she knew by heart. But now she gave it a little kick she had learned from Charlie, who had become quite an accomplished gourmet cook; a couple of dollops of Dijon mustard and a handful of fresh dill elevated it to something Julia Child would have been proud to serve. As the kitchen filled with the aroma of simmering soup, Isabel sat down at the kitchen table and flipped open her laptop and got to work on her paper. This was not her favorite class by any means, and she would be glad to have it behind her.

By the time she wrapped up, dusk was falling over the lake and a north wind had come up, so she went into the living room and built what would likely be her last fire in the fireplace until the fall. She then sat down in her favorite overstuffed chair next to the fire with the new mystery she had just checked out from the library and a cup of chamomile tea, then immediately bookended by Jack and Corky, who snuggled in and went to sleep. Isabel read for an hour or so as the fire crackled, then drifted off to sleep herself until she was awakened by the sound of the *Badger*'s horn as it left Wellington Harbor for its evening crossing to Wisconsin. She was instantly reminded of the sad story of the young man who had disappeared from the ship the day before.

Isabel was in the kitchen stirring her soup when the phone rang. It was her new friend, famed Michigan defense attorney, Beverly Atwater, whom she had met during the Jonasson murder investigation—a case in which Beverly and Isabel found themselves at one point, quite literally up to their necks. But as a result of that hair-raising chain of events, the two women had forged an unlikely friendship. Beverly was born and raised in Birmingham, a wealthy suburb of Detroit, and Detroiters were a very different breed from the folks along the western shore of Lake Michigan. But Beverly had become enamored of Gull Harbor, and now owned a beautiful summer home overlooking the Big Lake, where Beverly seemed to shed her big-city-attorney persona and mellow out a bit.

It was Beverly who encouraged Isabel to get her private investigator's license. Having proved her uncanny sleuthing abilities in the Jonasson murder case, Isabel Puddles was now famous in her own right for cracking a case the county sheriff's department and the Michigan State Police could not.

Beverly said she wanted to be able to hire her in the future if the right case presented itself, but told her she would have to be licensed by the state in order for her to do that. So while Isabel was studying for her college degree, and still working at Freddie's hardware, she managed to complete an online correspondence course, so she was now a licensed private investigator in the state of Michigan. Freddie Peabody, who had always supported his favorite cousin in any and all of her many ventures, renovated an old office above the store for her, and on the frosted-glass office door, had stenciled ISABEL PUDDLES—PRIVATE INVESTIGATOR. She was now officially in business. So when she wasn't in class, or studying, or working at the hardware, Isabel Puddles, P.I., was investigating.

But so far, her docket had not only been pretty light, it had also been pretty dull, consisting of tracking down a couple of long-lost relatives, one deadbeat ex-husband owing back child support, and finding Lois Randall's yellow lab, Murray, who had somehow ended up in Kalamazoo. Isabel had turned down more than one case involving suspicious husbands or wives looking for proof that their spouses were cheating. Although turning away clients wasn't a great way to get her business off the ground, Isabel wanted nothing to do with anything as tawdry as that. So despite the quasi-celebrity status she had gained as a savvy small-town sleuth, her notoriety had not brought any terribly interesting cases her way. But that was fine by her, at least for now. She'd had more than enough excitement freelancing on the Jonasson case to last her a while.

That said, she wouldn't be opposed to a financially rewarding assignment from Beverly, whose firm apparently paid private investigators an obscene amount of money. Given the additional expense of school, two new crowns, having to replace her water heater that winter, and the looming reality that she was in need of a new roof, Isabel found herself even more worried about money than usual, so she hoped maybe this was the reason Beverly was calling. It wasn't.

"Hi, Bev . . . how's everything?" Beverly Atwater was a talker, so an opener like this was risky. Fifteen minutes later, Beverly finally took a breath, providing Isabel with an opening. "So are you coming up for the holiday?" Isabel's eyebrows furled. "What holiday? It's Memorial Day weekend, Bev," Isabel reminded her as she walked over and closed her laptop. "I understand you're very busy, but . . ."

Ten more minutes passed, with Beverly explaining why she couldn't come up for the holiday weekend. Something to do with a trial she was preparing for. Isabel stirred slowly and listened semi-attentively until it was her turn again. "All right, Bev. I'll see you here for my Fourth of July barbecue, then? Perfect . . . Yes, my kids are coming . . . Who else? Well, let's see, Frances and Hank will be here, Freddie and Carol, of course, Meg, Larry and the rest of the Jonasson clan I'm not sure about . . . No, Ginny and Grady will still be on the road. Shall I send you the guest list? Bev, everybody you have ever met in this county, and a couple dozen more you haven't, will be here."

Beverly was on to the next subject as Isabel tasted her soup. "Yes, I'll swing by this week and check on the landscapers . . . Yes, I'll call Toby and make sure the doghouse and the enclosure will be finished by the Fourth . . . No, nobody wants to see Diego eaten by a wolverine." Diego was an adorable Chihuahua puppy Isabel was going to foster, but when Bev saw him, it was all over. She took him home that day, and with the exception of the courtroom, the two had been inseparable ever since. And Toby was the handsome young local contractor, and local heartthrob, Beverly always seemed to find projects for. After Bev acquired the property, Isabel had agreed to play the role of de facto caretaker of Beverly's impressive new log home. There wasn't much to it, really, and it was less than a mile away from Poplar Bluff, so she would have been happy to do it purely out of friendship, but Beverly insisted on paying her. Isabel was not in a position to say no to any additional income right now, so she relented. And Beverly could well afford it.

"Speaking of wildlife," Isabel said excitedly, "there was a bald eagle perched on my dock yesterday. Absolutely thrilling! No, I'm not kidding. We've always had bald eagles around here, not many, but they do seem to like Gull Lake . . . I wouldn't add that to your list of concerns, Bev. I doubt bald eagles like Chihuahuas. Too spicy . . . Listen, I have to run, Bev. Frances is coming for dinner and I have to season my soup. Yes, I'll call you next week." Isabel hung up before Beverly could ramp up again. Whew! It's no wonder she was such a successful defense attorney, Isabel thought, she must just talk until the jurors in the case see a not guilty verdict as their only means of escape.

The dogs started barking, signaling Frances's arrival. "Yoo-hoo! The lady with the wine is here!" Frances sang from the foyer.

"The lady with the soup is in the kitchen!" Isabel sang back.

After dinner, Isabel and Frances retired to the living room and plunked down next to the fire, each with a glass of what remained of their wine. "So what's Hank up to tonight?" Isabel asked. "Oh, that's right. It's his bowling night."

"Yes, and old Hank is back to his old tricks. When I told him I was coming over to have dinner with you tonight, he had the *audacity* to ask me to make *him* some dinner before I left, and leave it in the microwave for him. I mean, the man didn't even want to go to the trouble of lifting a plate out of the refrigerator and putting it into the microwave!"

Isabel smiled. "And did you?"

Frances scoffed. "Isabel, have you met me? I most certainly did *not*. What I left in the microwave for him was a menu from Rizzo's Pizza and Sub Shop and a ten-dollar bill."

Isabel laughed. She had been through the last standoff between Frances and Hank, which resulted in Frances moving in with her for several weeks, and Hank eventually caving in to her list of demands—an actual list she made him sign—in order to get his wife to come back home. It seemed to do the trick for a while, but it looked like there might have been some backsliding, and a refresher course was clearly in the works.

Frances got up and put another log on the fire. "You know, this winter he started to talk about early retirement. I told him he better think twice about it. If I had to have that man under my feet all day every day I may end up needing the services of your friend Beverly." She sat back down. "I'll tell you what, Isabel, you don't know how lucky you were to have been widowed while still in your prime."

"What a thing to say, Frances! Carl Puddles may not have been Husband of the Year, and yes, our marriage was less than ideal, but the poor man died *too* young."

"Would you ever have left him, or do you think you would have just stayed the course?" Frances asked.

"I don't know, Frances. After the kids left, Carl and I just sort of fell into a routine, you know? I still loved and cared about the man, most days, and I know he loved me too, in his own way, but we became more like roommates. He did his thing and I did mine. There wasn't any romance, but there wasn't animosity either. We had breakfast together every morning and dinner together most nights. I did the cooking, and I taught Carl to do the laundry. That man got to where he could fluff and fold like nobody's business. Boy, I do miss that!" Isabel laughed. "But we had a system: I cooked, took care of the yard, and tended the garden, and he did things like putting in the dock, fixing the roof, and taking care of the cars. We put on more of a show when the kids were home, but they've both told me since their father died that they could see how distant we had become from each other."

"After giving you those kids, dying is the nicest thing Carl ever did for you."

Isabel was genuinely shocked at such a statement. "I'm going to blame that remark on your third glass of wine, Frances."

"It's the truth, and you know it," Frances said with a shrug.

"I would much rather Carl was alive, Frances. I might not want to live with him again, but I certainly never wished him dead."

"I still think he did you a favor," Frances muttered as she headed back into the kitchen to pour her fourth glass of wine. When she came back into the living room a minute later, she was looking somewhat contrite. "I'm sorry. You're right, Isabel. That was an unkind thing to say. It's not like I'm married to Mr. Wonderful . . . Sometimes I just blurt things out without thinking."

Isabel responded with a deadpan stare. Frances Spitler was to "blurting things out without thinking" what the Wright brothers were to flight. Frances collapsed on the sofa again and grabbed the remote. "It's almost nine o'clock. Let's flip on the Wellington news and see if there's any word about that kid who went overboard on the *Badger*."

It was their lead story, but still not much to report. There was a quick interview with the local Coast Guard commander, who didn't exude any confidence that they were going to find him alive, and then a brief interview with the new Kentwater County sheriff, Will Chase, who was Grady's former senior deputy. The sheriff was asked if he would release the name of the missing man, but he said he was not at liberty to say.

Sheriff Chase hadn't been in the role very long, but so far his reviews had been mixed. Isabel, being fair-minded, was still reserving judgment regarding his law-enforcement abilities, but he definitely did not cut the same impressive figure of a man as his predecessor. Will Chase was rail thin, somewhere in his mid-forties, and wore a mustache, which only made his weak chin look slightly weaker. He always seemed a little nervous and shy, too, so he didn't come across as terribly self-confident. But Isabel liked him very much, personally, and she trusted him. She was sure he would grow into the job. Frances, however, had landed squarely on, "The man is completely inept! He makes Barney Fife look like Eliot Ness."

Isabel's mind drifted off after the news story ended. She couldn't imagine how distraught this young man's family must be, not knowing what happened to him, how it happened, or if he was dead or alive. But sadly, by all accounts, it looked like the Big Lake had swallowed up yet another poor soul.

Chapter 4

It was the afternoon of Memorial Day, and the time had come for Isabel's tri-annual visit to the Gull Harbor cemetery to check in on the family. Her other two visits were on her mother's birthday in August, and her father's in October. As she pulled in to the driveway and under the ivy covered iron trellis, she spotted a couple of old-timers from a nearby VFW post who were just wrapping up their own traditional Memorial Day visit, sticking little American flags into the gravesites of all the veterans. Each time the two old soldiers, both in full uniform, stuck a flag into the ground, they stood back, stiffened up, and saluted before checking their list and moving on to the next grave. Isabel had witnessed the same scene before on these Memorial Day visits, and had always found the occasion very touching and somber. She knew either the soldiers themselves or the families of virtually all of them, but as the nearest VFW post was in Wellington, she didn't know these particular old soldiers. She did notice that each year there were fewer of them. This time she noticed the frail-looking old vet with the trumpet who used to play taps at each gravesite after the flag was placed was noticeably absent this year.

Isabel's parents, her husband, and her grandparents and

great-grandparents on both the Peabody and the MacGregor sides, were all buried at the Gull Harbor cemetery, although the family plots were on opposite sides of the grounds. The MacGregor plot sat under an enormous weeping willow next to a meandering stream that ran to the Big Lake, while the Peabody plot sat on a small knoll shaded by two giant sugar maple trees with a beautiful view of the Big Lake. Buddy used to lament that it was too choice a piece of property to be wasted on the dead. Helen on the other hand liked the idea. "We're going to be there for a while, Buddy," she would say, "we may as well have a nice view."

Cousins from both sides were scattered all over the place, many of whom Isabel had never known, or had only dim memories of. She once commented to Frances that "a trip to the Gull Harbor cemetery is like a family reunion without the lawn darts and potato salad."

Being a devoted daughter, granddaughter, and great-granddaughter, Isabel always saw to it that the urns in both family plots were well tended. She cleaned off the headstones and pulled up any weeds that had come up in the spring. Next, she opened the side door of her van and pulled out several pots of red and white geraniums, a bag of potting soil, a spade, and her gardening gloves. These cemetery visits gave Isabel a familiar sense of calm, providing a time for quiet reflection. It also gave her a chance to get Buddy and Helen up to speed on whatever was happening in her life and in the lives of their grandchildren. Conversations with her husband were not as involved, but Carl had never been a big talker, nor was he terribly interested in what she had to say when he was above the grass, either, so why waste the breath?

Before leaving, she always walked behind Buddy and Helen's headstone to say hello to Vern and Maggie Buchanan, her parents' very best friends, and who had always been Aunt Maggie and Uncle Vern to her. Vern had two dachshunds named Rum and Coke, who had been taught to do various tricks. One was to sit up, which was not exactly advanced for most dogs, but no easy task for a dachshund. And because they were so well trained—"they're German," Vern would say, "they do as they're told"—the two sweet little pups would sit up, then stay that way, until Vern gave the command to get down. The poor things would bend back and forth and side to side as if they were blowing in the wind, their eyes pleading for relief, while Isabel pleaded with Vern to give them the command to get down. Then she would try, but they wouldn't listen to her, only to Vern. Remembering it now made her smile, but as a girl it made her crazy.

As a surprise to Buddy and Helen one year, Vern bought the two cemetery plots right behind them, so that one day they would be head to head. "So we'll always have four for bridge," Vern told them. Buddy thought it was a grand idea, Helen and Maggie thought it was morbid.

"I hope we'll have better things to do in the afterlife than sit around and play cards. We do that in this life every Thursday night," Helen said dismissively.

After Isabel wrapped things up at the cemetery, it was off to Brent Buchanan's annual Memorial Day barbecue. Isabel always reported to Brent that she had said hello to his parents, and would remind him to get some flowers planted in their urns so that people wouldn't talk. No sooner had she walked onto Brent's back patio overlooking Gull Lake, than Frances made a beeline for her. She wanted to be the first to share the news that had the whole party buzzing. The young man who had disappeared off the SS *Badger* four days before, and whose body had still not been recovered, was Randolph "Trey" Bachmeier III, the nephew of Abigail Bachmeier, Kentwater County's most elusive and reclusive resident, other than Madge Clinton, who was a hoarder and would probably like to get out more if only she could find the door.

Isabel knew about Trey Bachmeier, and had seen him around town in the summers for years. He was hard to miss, tooling around Gull Harbor in a different classic convertible sports car every year, and usually with a pretty girl beside him. Rich, handsome, and tanned, Trey Bachmeier also had the reputation of being an entitled and arrogant playboy. At least that's what Isabel had heard. She had never met him and never really paid attention to him. To her, he was just another summer person who would appear at the start of summer and then disappear at the end. Only this year, it looked like he had done things in reverse.

Chapter 5

Memorial Day weekend was technically the beginning of Gull Harbor's summer season, but things didn't usually begin to ramp up until just before the Fourth of July holiday. But traffic this year was heavy for mid-June, and parking in town was getting even more challenging, which meant Isabel had to park a couple of blocks away from Land's End. As she approached the diner she was shocked to see people outside waiting for a table. That was a first. Isabel politely excused herself as she walked past the line and went inside to find Frances already sitting down and reading the paper. "How did you manage to get a table?" Isabel asked her as she sat down.

"Kayla snuck me in through the kitchen. What do you suppose this is all about, Iz? They just keep coming." Isabel shrugged her shoulders and waved at Kayla, who was looking frazzled, but still wearing a smile as she came over with a pot of coffee.

"Have you ever seen anything like this? Why are they here so early? And why so many of them?" Kayla flipped Isabel's cup over and poured her coffee. "Hey, do you girls know anybody who needs a job? I need to hire a part-time waitress for the morning rush or I'm going to just set this tray down one of these days and run straight into the harbor screaming."

"I saw the sign in the window." Isabel looked over at Frances. "What do you say, Frances? Ready to rejoin the workforce?"

"About as ready as you are to rejoin the varsity cheerleading squad," Frances retorted.

Isabel laughed. Just then a tall, thin, pretty young woman, thirtyish, came in and walked over to Kayla wearing a smile. After a brief chat, Kayla reached behind the counter, where she grabbed a job application, and handed it to her. They chatted for another minute, the girl said thank you, and then turned to leave.

"I wonder if she's going to be the new waitress," Isabel said to Frances as she took a sip of her coffee.

Frances looked up at the girl just as she reached the front door. "That skinny thing? She looks like a pixie stick with a skirt on. Look! She can barely pull the door open. How is she going to carry six plates of waffles?"

Isabel could see Frances was in a mood this morning. She was sure it was something Hank-related, but she didn't feel like playing marriage counselor, so she let it go. Kayla walked back over with more coffee. "That was Jasmine. She goes by *Jazz*. She seems nice. Said she worked at an IHOP for a while, so she knows the breakfast business. I hope she works out, because I just can't keep up this pace all summer long, and I don't exactly have applicants breaking down the door."

Frances and Isabel shared the newspaper and drank their coffee in silence until Frances finally put down her section of the paper and looked over at Isabel. "Can you believe they still haven't found that Bachmeier boy's body? I'm beginning to wonder if he staged the whole thing."

Kayla came back with their breakfasts. "Thank you, dear," Isabel said to her as she reached for the salt. "I don't see what his motive would be to stage his own death," Isabel said. "I'm sure his body is still floating around out there somewhere, poor kid."

"The Big Lake gives up its dead when it's good and ready," Kayla interjected before moving on to her next table.

"Oh, well. I've got my own problems," Frances declared. "But I'm not swimming in the Big Lake again till they find him. Can you imagine backstroking into a bloated corpse?"

Isabel wasn't interested in entertaining such a grim possibility. "Can we change the subject, please? Something a little more cheerful, maybe?"

Frances went quiet. Apparently cheerful was not on her schedule today. Although she would rather avoid it, Isabel knew she was going to have to ask her what she was in such a bad mood about. "So do you want to tell me what's going on with you and Hank?"

"I wish I knew!" Frances was clearly relieved to be able to talk about it now. "He's just not himself lately. The man wakes up in a good mood, and he comes home in a good mood. Something isn't right. . . You know what I think?" Frances leaned over to Isabel. "I think he has a girlfriend."

"Hank? *Your* Hank? Don't be ridiculous, Frances!"

"I'm not being *ridiculous*, Isabel. Anything is possible once a man gets north of fifty. That's the sweet spot for a midlife crisis!"

Isabel had known Hank Spitler for more than thirty years. He was not a man who was going to cheat on his wife, if for no other reason than he would be afraid for his life if that wife ever found out. But she could see why Frances might be a little suspicious if Hank seemed to be unusually happy, given that he had been in the same mood for as long as Isabel had known him, which was consistently unenthused about most everything. Isabel remembered him being in a particularly good mood when the Detroit Tigers won the World

Series in 1984, but that lasted only about a week. She also remembered a change in Hank's mood when he was promoted to foreman at the canning factory, where Frances met him while she was working as a secretary. They met on her first day of work, and Frances told Isabel that night he was the handsomest man she had ever laid eyes on outside of a movie theater, and that she intended to marry him. Isabel agreed that Hank was quite handsome, but she thought Frances was crazy at the time for planning her wedding when they hadn't even been on a date.

Much to her surprise, less than a year later, they were engaged, and a year after that, they were married. There had been a few bumps along the way, as with any marriage, but Hank was a good father and a good husband, although according to his wife, he was not as romantic as he used to be. "Hank's idea of romance is patting me on the bottom when he's trying to move me away from the fridge to get a beer," Frances once lamented to Isabel. "And what passes for exciting with *my* husband is a new flavor of Pringles."

Of course Isabel knew Frances was what Charlie called a "drama queen," so she took everything she had to say about her husband with a full shaker of salt. But whatever the inner workings of the relationship might be, Frances and Hank had built a good life together. They had three terrific kids who, unlike their parents, had all gone to college, which was a point of pride for them both. Their kids, two girls and a boy, had grown up to be happy and successful in life; however, they were all now living out of state, which Isabel assumed was the only way they knew how to manage a mother they loved and adored, but one who was not a big believer in boundaries. Everything and anything was Frances's business. That went for her husband, her kids, her neighbors, and her friends, most of all Isabel.

"Isabel, I want you to investigate Hank."

"Frances, are you out of your mind? I most certainly will *not* investigate your husband."

"Why not? I'll pay you."

"I would never take your money, but that's beside the point."

"Then what *is* the point?"

"The point is that this—whatever *this* is—is between you and Hank, and I am not getting in the middle of it. And there is nothing you can say or do to make me change my mind, so you may as well drop it here and now. But I will say this: I think you better have a lot more to go on than your husband simply having a little extra spring in his step before you accuse him of cheating. I would think by now he at least deserves the benefit of the doubt, don't you?"

Frances stared at Isabel for a moment as she let her friend's words sink in. "Well, something isn't right, and I intend to get to the bottom of it, one way or the other."

Isabel found the "one way or the other" sentiment a bit worrisome. Then she panicked for a split-second, thinking what if Hank *was* cheating? She shivered at the thought of what Frances might do to him. Short of murder, or so she hoped, Isabel knew Frances would find a way to make the man pay, and pay dearly.

"Let's change the subject, Izzy. So I was thinking this morning about your London pen pal. Have you heard from him lately?"

Isabel smiled and pulled a letter out of her purse. "As a matter of fact, I just received a letter from Teddy yesterday."

Frances grabbed for it, but Isabel quickly pulled it away and shoved it back into her purse. "Come on, Iz. Let me read it! After all, I'm the one who introduced you two."

"I'm aware of that, but that doesn't mean you get to read

our private correspondence. Would I ever ask to read private correspondence between you and Hank?"

"You're welcome to it! Hank's last correspondence to me was a note he left on the fridge reminding me we were running low on Ding Dongs."

Isabel laughed. "And this is the man you suspect of having an affair? I don't think men who eat Ding Dongs have affairs. Well, the big news is that Teddy's coming to spend two weeks with his daughter and her family at their cottage this summer. I'm hoping maybe he'll be here for my barbecue on the Fourth. I'd love for him to meet the kids."

"Not sure an Englishman would be very excited about celebrating that particular day, are you? That is, after all, the day we officially told the Brits to stick it."

"I hadn't really thought about that, Frances, but Teddy's not the type to hold a grudge."

Theodore Mansfield was a very distinguished British gentleman, a few years older than Isabel, who she had met the previous summer at breakfast, and Frances was indeed the one who had introduced them. It turned out that Teddy, as he liked to be called, was also quite a well-known mystery writer who wrote under the nom de plume Archie Cavendish. Isabel knew his Hampstead Street mystery series well and had been following his brilliantly befuddled Detective Waverly for many years. She tried to play it cool at the time, but she could hardly believe she was meeting such a famous writer. And in Gull Harbor of all places. Crazier still, in Isabel's mind, was that *he* had actually wanted to meet *her*, because, as it turned out, Teddy had read about Isabel's cracking the Earl Jonasson case while he was in Chicago visiting his daughter and grandchildren.

As luck would have it, Teddy's daughter and son-in-law had recently bought a cottage in Gull Harbor, so he came over to see the new place. But, he later admitted, what he was really hoping for was an opportunity to meet "Gull Harbor's celebrated sleuth," as he put it. He was as impressed with her detective skills as she was with his literary accomplishments. Teddy, who was a widower, had come to Land's End by himself for breakfast one morning where he met Frances. Ten minutes later, after Isabel arrived to join her, he found himself being introduced to the newly legendary Isabel Puddles. Teddy invited her to dinner, Isabel accepted, and the two got along swimmingly, bonding over roast duck at the Old Cottage Inn. They followed up with a walk along Isabel's favorite stretch of Lake Michigan beach the next day, but that was it. Teddy had to return to Chicago to catch his flight home to London. Isabel learned that whenever he traveled, his trips were limited to two weeks because he had to leave his two corgis, Fred and Ginger, with his sister, and that was apparently all the dog sitting she could handle. Teddy and Isabel decided they would stay in touch, but do so the old-fashioned way, by writing letters, on paper, using actual pens. Their budding friendship had not taken any unexpected turns in the direction of romance, but Isabel was enjoying whatever connection they seemed to be cultivating, and it seemed Teddy was feeling the same way.

They had been exchanging letters a couple of times a month ever since, mostly sharing current events in their lives, their children's lives, or in Teddy's case, his grandchildren's lives as well. They were both devoted to their dogs, so there was a lot of dog talk, and they both loved to garden, so there was that to talk about too. Teddy had recently started writing a new mystery series, but he didn't like to talk about his work. They did, however, talk about school, and Teddy was fascinated by some of the crime-fighting techniques and investigative technologies Isabel was learning about, and was very impressed and supportive of her making such a bold move by going back to college "later in life," as he diplomatically put it. They both loved to read, mysteries mostly, so whatever was on their nightstand at the time was another topic of conversation. And, of course, if there was a good real-life murder mystery in the news on either side of the pond, that was always a hot topic. Isabel loved writing letters to Teddy, and she loved getting them from him. They had talked about taking their correspondence into the modern era via e-mail, but decided it was more fun and interesting to keep things old school. They both agreed that, sadly, the art of writing letters—putting pen to paper—was likely to die with their generation, so they were going to ride it out while postage stamps were still available for purchase.

Naturally, Teddy was a constant topic for Frances, who seemed determined to get them to the altar, despite Isabel's constant refrain that it wasn't going to happen. "What in the world makes you think two people our age, who live on opposite sides of a very large ocean, are ever going to get to know each other well enough to fall in love and get married?"

Frances didn't see any of this as a barrier. "You should be on him like white on rice! He's obviously very smitten with you. He's handsome, charming, sophisticated, and I would assume rich. Do you think you're ever going to find a marriage candidate with those attributes within a thousand-mile radius of this place? You need to seal the deal the next time he's here and move him over here!"

"You're being ridiculous. And who ever said I was looking for a *marriage candidate* anyway, Frances?"

"Isabel Puddles, you've been a widow for over a decade, and to my knowledge you've been on one date, and that was with Teddy. Do you want to be alone forever? You're in the autumn of your life. You have to think about your future."

Isabel had finally had enough of this conversation. "I happen to like living alone, Frances. And I'm grateful every single day for the life I have. I've been blessed with two beautiful children, a beautiful home, two beautiful dogs, a loving family, and wonderful friends, when they aren't browbeating me and trying to coerce me into chasing after a man who lives five thousand miles away in another country. And I am *not* in the autumn of my life either, thank you very much. If we have to keep things seasonal, I would say I am in mid-summer and maybe thinking about plans for Labor Day weekend."

Frances laughed. "Honey, I hate to break it to you, but the leaves are turning! You either need to get yourself a husband or you need to get yourself a rake!"

And with that, Isabel stood up. "I'm going to get on with my day now, but thanks for the pep talk!"

"Don't go off in a huff," Frances scolded.

"I am not in a huff, but I am going off, so goodbye. I have to get back to my lonely, husbandless, autumnal existence."

Isabel left with a wave to Kayla and out the door she went . . . in a huff. What she stopped herself from doing was pointing out to Frances that she had not exactly been making marriage anything to aspire to of late, but she knew that would just be hurtful and she would later regret it. What Isabel knew about her best friend was that even though she would, from time to time, say things that were hurtful, it didn't happen often, and they were never intended to *be* hurtful. Frances was one of the most loyal, kindhearted, albeit kooky people Isabel had ever known, and she loved her dearly. But, boy, could she work her nerves sometimes.

When she got home, Isabel and the dogs went out onto the dock and sat while she read Teddy's letter again and thought about what she would write back. Then she had to ask herself: What if she *was* starting to feel something more than friendship with Teddy? And what if Teddy was feeling that same thing with her? Would it be a smart idea to go any further with it, given the obvious impediments standing in the way? It was all way too much to think about at the moment, so she folded the letter back up and went inside to get ready for work.

Autumn of her life, indeed. That little gem was going to be looping in her head now for the rest of the day.

Chapter 6

Isabel hadn't been scheduled to work, but she was going in to relieve Freddie, who had forgotten about a local golf tournament he was slated to play in. And since the Fourth of July was just around the corner, she figured she might as well decorate the front window.

She and Freddie had done the summer window just before Memorial Day, which entailed replacing snow shovels, snow blowers, and sleds with barbecue grills, rafts, and beach umbrellas. There was not a lot of creativity involved anymore. For many years Isabel had painstakingly designed the front window display, trying to do something clever and eye-catching for every season. Christmas was her favorite. But she didn't have the time or the energy to bother with that any longer. And from what she could tell, her flair for window decorating never did anything to boost sales anyway. Hardware store customers were not big on window shopping. They knew what they wanted or needed before they came in, so a window display, no matter how beautifully executed, was not going to tempt them in a wildly different direction.

But Isabel was as patriotic as the next gal, and Freddie had served proudly in the armed forces, so they both thought

Independence Day deserved some special attention. But even then there wasn't much to it. Some red, white, and blue crepe paper; a handful of American flags; a life-size cardboard cutout of Uncle Sam; and it was pretty much done. For the past few years that task had been assigned to their stock boy, Frank, who had worked at the store for more years than Isabel could remember. Frank was a bit of an oddball, who was north of forty and still lived with his mother. Ambitious was not a word that came to mind when describing him. In fact he seemed to have mastered the art of laziness. Frank was also a narcoleptic, or claimed to be, and was known for lying down and napping anywhere in the store he liked the minute he felt his eyelids get heavy.

Frank was currently laid up for a couple of months after an unusual accident on the job. He had been stocking grass seed on an upper storage shelf outside in the lawn and garden department when nap time called again, so he curled up on a stack of bark chips about twelve feet off the ground. After Freddie and Isabel heard a cacophony of clanging sounds, followed by a cry for help, they ran back to find Frank, now wide awake, tangled up in a display of wind chimes . . . and with a broken leg. Mrs. Abernathy, the store's resident mouser, was so unnerved by the racket that she didn't appear again until two days after the incident.

But Frank's misfortune turned out to be their good fortune, because they now had a new stock boy named Andy, a college student home for summer break. Andy was a breath of fresh air. He was responsible, eager to help, and always wearing a smile; a stark contrast to Frank, whose overall demeanor had years before earned him the nickname "Eeyore" for his uncanny ability to find the negative in virtually everything. Not to be unkind, but for Isabel, in the weeks following Frank's accident, a chronically groggy man who could suck the joy out of a Peanuts Christmas special had not exactly been missed. If there was one personality trait Isabel couldn't tolerate, it was laziness, and "Fall Asleep Frank," as she called him, was the poster child for it. Why Freddie kept him around was a mystery to her, although knowing her cousin as she did, she knew he probably just felt sorry for him. But personnel matters were none of her business, so she stayed out of it, and showed as much patience and tolerance as she could muster when it came to Frank.

It was closing in on eleven a.m. when Isabel parked down the block from the hardware. As she approached, she was pleasantly surprised to see that the front window was already beautifully decorated for the Fourth of July. She stopped to admire it for a moment before going inside, where she found Freddie standing behind the counter. "Did you do that window, Freddie? It's beautiful!"

"Good morning, Isabel my dear! No, I did not. *That* is the handiwork of our new stock boy, Andy. Terrific, isn't it?"

Isabel was duly impressed. "It certainly is. That kid's a keeper! Although I'm guessing he has greater ambitions in life than a career stocking shelves and decorating windows for us."

"Yes, I expect he'll be moving on to bigger and better in the fall."

At that very moment Andy appeared at the front counter wearing his usual smile. "Good morning, Mrs. Puddles."

"Good morning, Andy . . . and please call me Isabel."

A look approximating horror crossed Andy's face. "Oh, no, I couldn't, Mrs. Puddles. If my parents ever heard me address a woman of your age by her first name, they would not be pleased."

A woman of my age? Maybe this kid isn't such a keeper, after all, Isabel said to herself as she slipped her red hardware store apron on over her head, careful not to mess up her hair. Her age had now been referenced twice in the same morning, and she was just about over it. "Well, suit yourself," she replied, looking over at Freddie, who was already reading his cousin's mind.

Isabel was not usually sensitive about her age. In fact she was usually pretty philosophical about the subject. And, being a woman who had never been terribly vain about her appearance even in her younger days, she paid little attention to the outward indications of age. Her hair had gone a beautiful shade of silver years ago, and in those rare times when she did look a little more closely in the mirror to examine the lines in her face, she just shrugged and shook it off. But like anybody else of a certain age, man or woman, when it started to sink in that the end was closer than the beginning, it did create some twinges of anxiety from time to time, especially when she was constantly reminded of it.

Isabel intended to use her parents as models for how to grow old gracefully when she reached her golden years, and she hoped when it was her time, she would go just as peacefully. Her father, Buddy, died well into his eighties, on a beautiful spring day, after spending the morning in the yard planting his wife's flower beds with her favorite annuals, a springtime ritual for half a century. He then enjoyed lunch on the deck overlooking the lake he loved. As a reward for his gardening, Helen, his beloved wife of sixty three years, had prepared his favorite lunch: a BLT accompanied by her famous homemade potato salad, and for dessert, a slice of her equally famous lemon meringue pie. After lunch, Buddy kissed his wife and then went inside and sat down in his favorite wingback chair to read the newspaper. Pretty soon he drifted off to sleep . . . and just never woke up. Six months later, with a salmon loaf in the oven, sitting in the same wingback chair with her needlepoint in her lap and a magnificent display of fall colors blazing outside the picture window, Helen drifted off to sleep . . . never to wake up. If ever there were two people who deserved to go so peacefully, they were Buddy and Helen Peabody. But hopefully, their daughter Isabel's departure from this earth was a long way off, so she wasn't going to let age references made by her best friend or the new stock boy, who was younger than many of the shoes Isabel was still wearing, upset her.

"Oh, Mrs. Puddles," Andy said as he passed the counter with an armload of boxes, "I'm sorry but I almost forgot to tell you . . . an older gentleman stopped by this morning looking for you. He wouldn't leave his name. He just said he would come back later."

"Hmm . . . well, I can't imagine who would be so secretive, but I suppose we'll just have to wait to unravel that mystery." Then, because she was feeling a little bad about being short with him earlier, "By the way, you did a beautiful job on the front window, Andy."

Andy smiled shyly. "Thank you, Mrs. Puddles. I hoped you and Mr. Peabody would like it. Well, I better get these light switches stocked."

Freddie came out of the office and watched Andy disappear down the electrical aisle. He was wearing an expression of admiration and just a touch of sadness. "How are we ever going to get used to Frank again after Andy leaves us?" he lamented.

Isabel smiled. "You mean now that we've seen Paris?"

"Paris, London, and Rome! That boy gets more done in a day than Frank does in a month, and without taking a nap every ten minutes. I'll tell you, that kid is going places!"

"Yes, he is . . . and that place is back to college in eight or ten weeks, so we may as well start getting mentally prepared for the return of Frank van Winkle."

Freddie raised his eyebrows, shrugged, and then sighed. "Well, we all have our crosses to bear, Izzy. Frank apparently is mine, along with my slice, which reminds me, I need to get to the club. We tee off in thirty minutes!" Freddie whipped off his apron and headed for the back door. "Thanks again for filling in! I'll be back in time to close up!"

"Good luck, Freddie!"

No sooner had she heard the back door close than the front door opened, and in walked somebody she was so startled to see she could barely say hello. It was Abigail Bachmeier's chauffeur, Mr. Bajrami, who was almost as mysterious and elusive as his employer. Isabel had never officially met Mr. Bajrami, but she knew who he was, and had seen him around for many years. Their only interaction took place at a local farm stand when they both reached for the same quart basket of plums. He smiled warmly and insisted Isabel take it. That encounter had left her with quite a good impression of the man.

When Mr. Bajrami wasn't driving Miss Bachmeier around town in her black, late-model Lincoln Continental limousine—a vehicle that looked as out of place in Gull Harbor as the Easter Bunny would in a Christmas parade—he could be seen around town driving an immaculately kept, light blue, 1950s-era, wood-paneled station wagon, while he did the shopping and ran various errands for his mistress, so it seemed he wore many hats. Mr. Bajrami was a distinguished-looking gentleman who carried himself with a certain Old World elegance. He was probably somewhere in his late sixties, with an olive complexion and beautiful salt-and-pepper hair as thick as his accent, one which nobody, including Isabel, could quite pin down. For most of the year he was seen in beautifully tailored suits and white shirts, paired with expensive-looking ties. But in the summers, when the dress code at the Bachmeier estate was evidently more relaxed, Mr. Bajrami wore khakis, boat shoes, and assorted colors of sport shirts Isabel had always referred to as "alligator" shirts, although she knew those who could afford them had a fancier name for them. He looked more like a man who would *employ* a chauffeur as opposed to being one. Mr. Bajrami was described by others who had come in contact with him as neither friendly nor unfriendly, and he carried himself in a way that Isabel had once characterized as "pleasantly aloof." Other locals found Mr. Bajrami's slightly imperious demeanor offputting, including Frances, who referred to him, inexplicably, as the "King of Siam."

Mr. Bajrami smiled and dipped his head as he approached the counter. Isabel could only hope words would come out of her mouth when she opened it. Thankfully he spoke first.

"Good day, madam . . . I wonder if you might be of some assistance. I'm trying to locate a Mrs. Isabel Puddles. This is the address I was given, and I understand her offices are above this store, but the door to the upstairs is locked, and has been all morning. Do you know when, or possibly *where*, I might find her?"

Isabel's first instinct was to ask him *why* he was looking for Isabel Puddles before she identified herself, but that seemed like a question only someone concerned with being served a subpoena would ask, so she spilled the beans. "*I'm* Isabel Puddles," she said, as she nervously reached her hand out in introduction. As they shook, she couldn't help noticing he had the softest hand she had ever felt on a man. He also had the most intense brown eyes she had ever looked into.

Mr. Bajrami was confused, and said so. "I'm confused . . . You work in a *hardware* store? I was under the impression you were a private investigator."

Isabel laughed. "I am, but a girl can't live off what a private investigator makes around here. Kentwater County is not exactly a hotbed of nefarious activity, although last year we did set the bar pretty high. Anyway, this was my uncle Handy's store, and now it belongs to my cousin Freddie. I've worked here on and off since I was in high school. It's kind of a family tradition."

It took Mr. Bajrami a moment to process this information before continuing. "I see . . . Well, my name is Bajrami, Ramush Bajrami, and I am in the employ of Miss Abigail Bachmeier. Do you know of her?"

Isabel smiled knowingly. "Yes, of course I do. *Everybody* knows Abigail Bachmeier, although nobody I know has ever met her. And I've seen *you* around for many years as well, Mr. Bajrami, but I have never had the pleasure of meeting you, either."

"The pleasure is all mine, Mrs. Puddles. I'm here at the request of Miss Bachmeier, who would like to inquire about possibly hiring you to do some very discreet investigative work. Miss Bachmeier has recently become familiar with your inspective prowess, and what is, by all accounts, a sterling reputation. I read about your work on the Jonasson murder case. Most impressive. In fact I was the one who suggested to Miss Bachmeier that you might be just the right fit for this assignment."

Isabel was shocked to hear that Abigail Bachmeier knew who she was, and even more shocked by the prospect of working for her. "Thank you for those very kind words, Mr. Bajrami."

"Miss Bachmeier would like to meet with you in person to discuss the job, and a possible arrangement."

"I'm very flattered . . . And I would be very happy to meet with her. When would you like to arrange a meeting?"

Mr. Bajrami looked at her as though the answer was obvious. "Immediately. So if you would be so kind as to follow me back to the estate, Miss Bachmeier is expecting you."

Isabel smiled warmly. "As much as I would love to, Mr. Bajrami, I'm afraid I'm here today until five thirty, when we close up."

Mr. Bajrami looked genuinely surprised. "Mrs. Puddles, we're talking about *Abigail Bachmeier*, and she very much wants to see you *today*. In fact, she has invited you to a late lunch, which I might add is a very rare occurrence."

Isabel began to straighten up the counter, something she always did when she was nervous. And between Mr. Bajrami standing before her and the prospect of meeting Abigail Bachmeier, she was plenty nervous. "That's very nice of her, and I hope you will thank her anyway and send my regrets. And as I said, I would be very happy to meet with her tomorrow, but my cousin Freddie is playing in a golf tournament today, and I'm afraid I'm in charge of the store until he returns."

Mr. Bajrami was clearly annoyed but doing his best to hide it. He stared at her for a moment as if that might change her mind. When he could see she was unmoved, he continued. "Well, then, I suppose tomorrow will have to do. You do know where the Bachmeier estate is located, I presume?"

Isabel nodded. "Yes, I do."

"Shall we say eleven forty-five for luncheon at twelve fifteen?"

Isabel nodded in agreement, "Eleven forty-five it is for a luncheon at twelve fifteen."

"Do you have any dietary restrictions I should inform Chef of, Mrs. Puddles?"

Isabel laughed. "Not as many as I should. No, I'm very easy to please. Shall I bring anything?"

Mr. Bajrami looked at her, slightly bemused. "That won't be necessary. I'll leave your name with Bernard at the front gate. We will look forward to seeing you tomorrow then, Mrs. Puddles." And with that, he dipped his head again, a gesture she now assumed was how servants of the very rich said hello and goodbye.

Andy, who had been out sweeping, came inside a moment later. "So he found you. He looked rich. Must be a summer person." Andy put the broom back in the office and bounced back out. "Is there anything I can do for you, Mrs. Puddles?"

That was a question she had never once heard come out
of the mouth of the man Andy was filling in for. "No, thank
you, Andy. I guess you can just carry on with Mr. Peabody's
to-do list."

"That's all done. Maybe I'll go out to lawn and garden
and do some watering and make some room for tomorrow's
flower delivery."

"I think that sounds like a fine idea."

Andy turned and bounced down the aisle, whistling all
the way, while Isabel's thoughts went to the encounter she
had just had with Mr. Bajrami. She could not believe an opportunity like this had just fallen into her lap, assuming her
lunch with Miss Bachmeier went well and she would be hired
to do whatever job it was she had in mind. But then suddenly
the job she had in mind became obvious. It must be related to
the disappearance of her nephew. Now she was feeling somewhat deflated, because as long as there was an active investigation underway by the authorities, Isabel was not going to get
involved. Still, even knowing she might have to turn down
the job, the opportunity to meet Abigail Bachmeier in person,
and to actually see inside the mysterious Bachmeier estate,
was terribly exciting.

As her mind began to race, imagining what she might
encounter tomorrow, she snapped back to attention when the
front door bell jingled, and in walked Frances. "Hello, Iz. I
brought you a chocolate-chip cookie from Hobson's, fresh
out of the oven. I got the feeling you were a little annoyed
with me at breakfast this morning." She handed her a small
white bag across the counter. "So I thought this might make
up for it."

"I *was* annoyed, but I know you didn't mean any harm.
And, yes, this makes up for it. Thank you." She reached into
the bag and broke off a piece of cookie and popped it into her
mouth. "You want a piece?" Isabel offered.

"No, thanks . . . I just had two. Bobby Hobson said to say hello, by the way. You know the man is still sweet on you, Isabel. You could do worse. At least he lives in the same zip code."

"If you don't stop, Frances, you're going to have to go back and get me another cookie. Please stop trying to marry me off!"

"Fine, whatever. So listen to this: Bobby was putting together a big order when I got there, but he wouldn't tell me who it was for. Chocolate croissants, almond croissants, bear claws, a couple dozen cookies, and a cherry cheesecake. And that's only what I saw. There was more stuff already boxed up! And do you want to guess who came in to pick up the order? Never mind, you'll never guess . . . It was the King of Siam *himself*. And of course he was just as snooty as always. After he left, well, then the cat was out of the bag since I knew who he worked for, so Bobby told me Abigail Bachmeier is one of his very best customers. He said he puts an order like that together once, sometimes twice a week! Can you imagine? Apparently *milady* enjoys her pastries!"

Isabel took another piece of her cookie. "So do you want to guess who was in here not fifteen minutes ago? You'll never guess, either, so I'll just tell you . . . Mr. Bajrami. The King of Siam. He came in to arrange a meeting for me tomorrow with, are you ready? Miss Abigail Bachmeier."

It took a lot to stun Frances Spitler silent, but that little bombshell did the trick . . . at least for ten seconds. "Get outta here! You've got to be kidding me!"

Isabel replied as though it were as casual as a dentist's appointment. "Nope. Not kidding . . . I've been invited to the Bachmeier estate tomorrow at eleven forty-five, for lunch at twelve fifteen. Excuse me, *luncheon*."

"Sounds like the old gal runs a tight ship. What does she want? Oh! Well, she must want you to find out what happened to her nephew. What else could it be?" Frances didn't wait for an answer, and her excitement was building. "You have to take me with you, Isabel! Tell her I'm your assistant."

"I have no idea what she wants to talk to me about, Frances, but you're probably right. However, I have no intention of getting involved in an active case involving her nephew. And I also have no intention of taking you with me. I would be a nervous wreck fearing what might come out of your mouth."

A frown fell across Frances's face. "You're no fun. Well, I hope the balmy old broad doesn't lock you up in the dungeon of that spooky mansion of hers. Rumor has it a couple Jehovah's Witnesses paid her a visit a few years back and have never been seen or heard from again." Isabel refused to react to such an absurd comment, so Frances continued. "It has to be about her nephew. It's been what? Almost a month since the kid went into the drink?"

"The Michigan State Police, the Wisconsin State Police, the Coast Guard, and the Kentwater County Sheriff's Department are all investigating, Frances. I'm sure they'll figure out what happened sooner than later. They certainly don't need *me* butting my head in, whether Abigail Bachmeier wants me to get involved or not."

"Well, if old lady Bachmeier is waiting for our new sheriff to crack the case, she's in big trouble . . . I'd have a better chance of finding Jimmy Hoffa." Frances always loved a good Jimmy Hoffa reference, and of course she had a few crackpot theories regarding what really happened to the old Teamster, one that even involved a sex change operation.

"I guess all will be revealed tomorrow, won't it." Isabel grabbed a cloth and began to wipe down the cash register.

"I'm going to be waiting for you when you get home. I want the whole scoop, in person."

"I'll be happy to share anything that isn't confidential, Frances," Isabel replied calmly as she next wiped off a display case filled with jackknives.

"You know whatever you tell me is safe with me, Isabel," Frances stated boldly.

Isabel stopped wiping, looked at Frances, and laughed out loud. "And you actually said that with a straight face. Frances, Paul Revere was less effective warning that the British were coming than you are at spreading gossip."

Frances turned on her heels. "Okay, we're even, because now *you* are annoying *me*."

Isabel chuckled and shook her head as Frances turned on her heels and swung open the front door. Now it was her turn to leave in a huff.

Isabel closed the store up with Andy at five thirty after getting a call from Freddie's wife, Carol, telling her that after a disastrous round of golf, Freddie had been overserved on the nineteenth hole, so she had to drive to the country club to pick him up and take him straight home to bed.

It was a breezy, beautiful evening, so when Isabel got home from work, and after having her usual bonding time with Jackpot and Corky, she went out onto the dock and sat while the dogs raced up and down, tracking schools of minnows, which, next to treeing squirrels, was their favorite pastime. The lake was starting to quiet down as the summer people were wrapping up their activities for the day and going back to their cottages to grill or get ready to go out for dinner. This was Isabel's favorite time of day, and had been ever since she was a girl. In the summers, as dusk approached, she and her dad would often spray themselves with mosquito repellent and paddle the canoe around the lake, or take the rowboat out and fish for perch or bluegill or, if they were lucky, a walleyed pike. Pike was still her favorite fish, but for what they were charging for it these days, if she couldn't catch one on her own, pike was off the menu.

As she stared out at the lake, her mind began to drift to what she might expect to encounter tomorrow at her lunch meeting with Abigail Bachmeier. Given the many stories she had heard over the years about the reclusive heiress, she felt a little bit like Dorothy being invited in to meet the wizard. It was exciting but also daunting. If half the stories were true, Isabel was in for an interesting lunch.

Stories about Abigail Bachmeier had been circulating for as long as Isabel could remember, stretching back to her parents' day. But other than catching passing glimpses of her from time to time sitting in the back of her limousine, staring blankly out the window while being driven through town by Mr. Bajrami, Isabel had seen her up close only once in her life.

It was about ten years before, on a snowy afternoon just a few days before Christmas, and Isabel was going into Phyllis's Phudge Shop to buy a gift for a friend who was in the hospital. As she opened the front door to go in, Miss Bachmeier was just leaving. Behind her was Mr. Bajrami, holding several shopping bags full of gift-wrapped boxes of fudge. Isabel held the door for the striking-looking old woman who was wrapped in a fur coat and wearing a matching fur hat. Only her rosy-cheeked face was visible above the drawn collar of the coat, and a few tufts of gray hair stuck out from under her hat. Miss Bachmeier smiled and softly thanked the pleasantly dumbfounded Isabel for holding the door. Once outside, Mr. Bajrami helped her down the steps, across the snow-covered sidewalk, and into the back of her limousine. Miss Bachmeier looked to be somewhere in her early seventies then, and based on what she could see of her, seemed quite hearty and healthy, but Isabel couldn't help wondering what her condition might be a decade later.

Just as she stood up to go inside for dinner, her choice of Lean Cuisine still pending, Frances came screaming down the road leading to Poplar Bluff and pulled into the driveway as she always did, like it was a pit stop at the Daytona 500. "Oh, Lord," Isabel mumbled to herself before calling the dogs to follow her in. Isabel loved Frances like a sister, but sometimes she could wear a person out. And because she was as predictable as the seasons, Isabel knew why she was there: she wanted to talk more about Isabel's lunch with Abigail Bachmeier tomorrow, and she was sure to have plenty of advice to impart.

The dogs ran up to greet her as Frances waved with one hand and carried a Tupperware container in the other. It looked as if there might even be some kind of bribery attempt afoot.

"Izzy, have you had dinner yet?"

"No, I have not . . . I was about to choose between meat loaf with mashed potatoes or glazed turkey with stuffing . . . such a dilemma."

"You can forget about that! I made a batch of my deliciously cheesy chicken-and-broccoli casserole to take to Hank's nephew's birthday party tomorrow. Or is it his niece's? I don't know. These people are always having birthdays. It's a potluck, but no point taking the whole batch. Those Spitlers will mow through it like Grant took Richmond. And I guarantee you not one of them will say a word about how delicious it is! Believe me, it will stand out among whatever kitchen disasters Hank's sisters show up with. I still haven't gotten over his sister Jan's take on Chinese lasagne."

Isabel laughed and thanked her. "You want to come in and keep me company while I eat?"

"Of course. Oh, and I have some big news. I'll tell you inside."

After she put the casserole in the microwave, Isabel was ready to hear Frances's big news. "So, tell me."

"Tell you what?" Isabel shot her a look. "Oh! My news! Well, no big digs, but thought you should know. Remember that hippie-looking string bean of a girl who came in to apply for the waitress job at Land's End? Well, Kayla hired her. I stopped in for a quick cup of coffee this afternoon and she waited on me." Frances took a thoughtful pause. "I don't like her."

"And why is that?" Isabel asked casually. Such blanket judgments and knee-jerk assessments were not unusual for Frances, but they were always worth asking about.

"Don't know. I just don't like her. But I'll come up with a reason."

"You work on that, but I think I'll reserve judgment." The microwave timer went off and Isabel took her dinner out, grabbed a fork, and sat down at the kitchen counter next to Frances. "This smells so good, Frances. So *that* was your big news?" She was relieved that Frances's news didn't have anything to do with her ridiculous idea that her husband was having an affair. At least she was pretty sure it was ridiculous.

After Frances went home, Isabel went to bed early to read for a while and then get a good night's sleep before her big lunch meeting with Abigail Bachmeier the next day.

Little did she know it was a meeting that would lead to another memorable investigation, one that promised to have even more twists and turns than the Jonasson case, the case that had paved the way for her unlikely new career as a private investigator.

Chapter 7

Abigail Bachmeier was very well known around Gull Harbor for someone who nobody knew. For decades she had been an enigma, and her life, shrouded in mystery. Rumors and gossip, often tempered with wild conjecture, were all the locals, including Isabel, really had to go on. What people *did* know was that she was a fabulously rich heiress from Milwaukee, Wisconsin, whose father, Randolph Bachmeier, founded the Bachmeier Brewing Company, one of the largest breweries in the country. But despite being born into great wealth, Abigail's life story was, by all accounts, as tragic as it was lavish.

Much of what Isabel had heard over the years came either from stories her mother and grandmothers had told her about Miss Bachmeier and her family or from gossip she picked up over the years, along with several decades of press coverage of the Bachmeier family. It all helped paint a rather sad portrait of Miss Bachmeier's life. But when it came to what was actually true about the inner-workings of the family, or Abigail's personal life, nobody really knew what was or *wasn't* true.

Gull Harbor had once been strictly a summer retreat for the Bachmeier family, albeit a very grand one. They opened the estate, known as Bachmeier Hall, for Memorial Day weekend and shuttered it up on Labor Day. But for the past fifty years or so, Randolph Bachmeier's only daughter had lived in the enormous estate, purported to have forty rooms or more, along with a complement of servants and a revolving pack of Pomeranians. The family's imposing English Tudor estate, built in the early 1930s by the family patriarch, sat on a headland overlooking Lake Michigan, and was considered among the most important homes in all of Michigan, rivaled only by estates peppered around the state built by world-famous architects for world-famous Michigan families like the Fords, the Dodges, and the Chryslers. According to local vendors, and service people who had reason to be there, the once-magnificent structure was described as looking run down now and a little spooky. But whatever the condition of the mansion today, it didn't really matter, because the many acres of lakefront property it sat on was some of the most, if not *the* most, valuable real estate in the entire state.

Abigail Bachmeier's life seemed so extravagant that it didn't seem possible to somebody like Isabel Puddles, whose idea of extravagance was two scoops of ice cream instead of one, or buying steak that wasn't on sale. Miss Bachmeier resided at Bachmeier Hall for most of the year, but apparently spent a few months every winter at her Palm Beach estate, which was said to be just as grand, and where she was said to be just as reclusive. She also had a home in the south of France. But, according to rumor, that estate, which overlooked the Mediterranean Sea, with Monaco in the distance, had been shuttered and abandoned for many decades. Still more rumors swirled around some tragic and mysterious event that was alleged to have happened there decades earlier, and Abigail had never returned.

At one time it was believed she employed a dozen servants. And with the exception of the groundskeepers who minded the estates year round, they all traveled with her be-

tween Michigan and Florida every year. Isabel remembered
her father's reaction to hearing about Miss Bachmeier's min-
ions: "It's like a traveling circus! How in the world does it
take a dozen people to take care of *one* person?" Buddy asked
his wife and daughter rhetorically at dinner one night.

Helen, the perpetual voice of reason and fairness in the
Peabody home, was quick to defend a woman she had never
met, but who she had always felt a little bit sorry for. "Honey,
it's not just *one* person who needs taking care of. Can you
imagine the work that goes into keeping a forty-room mansion clean? Then there's the pool, upkeep of the grounds, and
I'm told—"

"Would it kill her to pick up a feather duster or some
pruning shears?" Buddy snorted. "What does that lady have
to do all day other than sit around and be filthy rich?"

Helen saw a teachable moment—for her daughter, at least.
"It really isn't fair to judge a person so harshly just for being rich. It's not her fault she was born into money. I think
how those with great wealth spend their money is what shows
their true character, and I understand Miss Bachmeier is quite
philanthropic. She runs a large charitable foundation and does
a lot of good work with her money. And hasn't this poor
woman seen her share of unhappiness in life? I think our family is wealthy enough in the ways that matter most in life to
find some compassion for her."

Isabel remembers that her father didn't exactly go along
with his wife's display of largesse that evening. But she had
not yet learned about the deep-seated animosity Buddy had
for the Bachmeier family, namely Abigail's brother, Skip, the
boy who had audaciously tried to steal his future wife that
summer so many years before.

Miss Bachmeier's dedicated entourage, many of whom
had been with the family for decades, had been dwindling
over the years, though, because as they retired, or died, she

apparently never replaced them. According to Dale Everhart, a local plumber who had recently done some work at Bachmeier Hall, there was now just Mr. Bajrami, two maids, an elderly butler, and a French chef. A guard at the front gate, who also served as the groundskeeper, was the extent of her security apparatus.

With the assortment of rumors and legends about Abigail Bachmeier, her family, and what really went on at Bachmeier Hall circulating for so many years, it was impossible to separate fact from fiction, but the story behind how she ended up a recluse living alone in her family's mansion was one Isabel's Grandmother Peabody told her, and it went like this. . .

When Abigail was seventeen, she fell madly in love with a handsome young man named Patrick Pendleton, who came from another wealthy Milwaukee society family, and who had escorted Abigail to her debutante ball. They officially began dating in college, with Abigail at Radcliffe and Patrick at Harvard. After college, Abigail went to study fine arts at the Sorbonne in Paris, while Patrick went on to Harvard Medical School. When Abigail returned from Paris and Patrick graduated from medical school, they were formally engaged, and a wedding date was set. The lush affair was to be held at Bachmeier Hall on the Saturday of Memorial Day weekend. The event was billed by *Town & Country* magazine as the biggest society wedding of the summer, and Abigail Bachmeier was the bride all society women aspired to be: smart, pretty, accomplished, refined, and with a bubbly personality. And, it goes without saying, very rich. When the big weekend arrived, yachts from Chicago and Milwaukee filled the harbor, and when snug little Gull Harbor reached capacity, the massive boats moored out on the lake, and their passengers came ashore on skiffs. Private planes arrived by the dozens at Kentwater County's tiny airport, and press from all over the country descended on Gull Harbor, clamoring around town, looking for faces or names they recognized.

The Wrigley's and the McCormick's had yachted over from Chicago. The Kellogg's from Battle Creek, and the Upjohn's from Kalamazoo were also in attendance. Recently elected Michigan congressman Gerald Ford and wife, Betty, were there, along with Edsel and Eleanor Ford, Walter and Marguerite Chrysler, and several members of the Dodge family, who had summered in Gull Harbor and had been childhood friends of Abigail and her brother, Skip. High society from New York included Governor Nelson and Mrs. Rockefeller, Brooke Astor, Gloria Vanderbilt, and Babe Paley. Betty Hutton and Doris Duke took a private train car all the way from Los Angeles to attend their friend's wedding. It was even rumored that Edward, Duke of Windsor, and Wallis Simpson were among the invited guests and had yachted over from Chicago with the Wrigley's, although they were never seen on shore. Hollywood society was there too. Bette Davis and Joan Crawford attended and were seated at the same table, because Randolph Bachmeier had a sly sense of humor. Jimmy Stewart, Bob Hope, Bing Crosby and their wives all flew to the wedding together on a chartered plane.

But, sadly, the high-society event of the summer turned into the lowest point in poor Abigail Bachmeier's otherwise ideal life. Just ten days before the wedding, Abigail's fiancé, Patrick, went to New York City to sign the lease on a Park Avenue apartment where they would live while he did his residency. On a whim, he stopped at Tiffany's to buy his bride-to-be a gift, and there, behind the counter, he met and instantly fell head over heels in love with a beautiful young dancer, a former Miss Georgia, who had just moved to New York, hoping to join the Radio City Rockettes.

On the day before he was to marry Abigail, the newly

love-struck Patrick flew back to New York and proposed to Miss Georgia. She accepted, and they immediately eloped and retreated to his family's home in Bermuda to avoid the fallout. Poor Abigail was notified on the eve of her wedding day, via telegram, that the wedding was off. The bride who wasn't meant to be was left inconsolable. Adding to her torment on the Saturday the wedding was supposed to have happened was her father's insistence that the reception be held anyway. It was not a decision made out of callousness or pride but merely a misguided act of love.

Randolph Bachmeier adored his only daughter, and she worshipped him. They had become extremely devoted to each other after her mother died when Abigail was just fourteen years old and away at a Swiss boarding school.

There was no explanation given for the absence of a bride and groom at the lavish reception, other than Mr. Bachmeier putting on a brave face and telling guests something urgent had come up and the wedding itself would have to be postponed. But there was no reason the party couldn't and shouldn't go on. It *was* a holiday weekend, after all, he told his somewhat puzzled and not entirely convinced guests. In reality, Mr. Bachmeier was nearly as crestfallen as his daughter was when Patrick deserted her, but he felt carrying on with the party was the best way to stave off the humiliation and social ruin that were sure to be visited upon his daughter after word got out that she had been left at the altar. He later realized not canceling the reception had been a terrible mistake and only made matters worse, and begged his daughter's forgiveness.

So that evening at Bachmeier Hall, after a magnificent sunset over Lake Michigan, the posh, celebrity-studded reception went off as planned, while the jilted bride sobbed uncontrollably in her bedroom, surrounded by her bridesmaids, who tried to comfort her, but were no doubt hoping she would pull it together so they could get downstairs to the party. A distraught Abigail was then forced to listen to the grand soiree below, complete with a full orchestra. The reception intended to celebrate the happiest day of her life instead became the most soul crushing. Adding insult to an already grievous injury was listening to Bing Crosby singing his hit song "True Love" followed by "I Love Paris," which was where the newlyweds were to have spent their honeymoon, in the apartment her father had bought them as a wedding gift.

The mysterious excuse regarding why the wedding had been "postponed" held water just long enough to get through the weekend, after which the real story came out on the society pages of every newspaper in the country, which of course only added to Abigail's emotional unraveling. It was rumored that after her fiancé's heartless abdication, Abigail began to lose touch with reality, which in polite society was a nice way of saying she went crazy. It was rumored that she refused to leave her bedroom for months, waking up every morning in a semi-catatonic state and putting her wedding dress on. From the beach in front of the estate, all summer long, it was said she could be seen from a distance sitting on her balcony at all hours of the day, staring out at the Big Lake, still wearing her wedding dress. There were also rumors of a suicide attempt, with Abigail being pulled out of the lake, still in the dress, and given CPR on the beach by a family servant.

Eventually Abigail's father had her admitted to a sanatorium in the Wisconsin Dells, where she remained for some time. Still more rumors suggested she had been given shock therapy there. After her release, Abigail refused to return to Milwaukee and face more humiliation, so she took up residence at Bachmeier Hall to convalesce. There she was attended by a nurse and a Chicago psychiatrist whom Mr. Bachmeier had moved in to monitor her progress.

And then the story took another tragic turn. Almost a year to the day after Patrick Pendleton abandoned Abigail at the altar, while vacationing with his bride in the south of France, he was driving to a polo match when, as the story went, the brakes on his Alfa Romeo appeared to have failed on a treacherous road just outside Monaco, and he went careening over a cliff. Patrick, who was alone at the time, did not survive.

"Well, he never was a very good driver," Abigail was alleged to have said to the maid who delivered the news. Abigail's once-effervescent personality had by now become jaded and flat. The charm and the bubbles were gone. Over the course of a year that should have been among the happiest of her life, a beautiful young woman went from being a social butterfly to a reclusive moth.

It took another year of psychiatric care and convalescence at Bachmeier Hall before her doctors deemed her ready to rejoin the world. But by all accounts Abigail Bachmeier never really did rejoin the world. Instead, she created a world of her own at Bachmeier Hall, where her life revolved around her Pomeranians, her painting, a greenhouse full of orchids, and an antique doll collection she had inherited from her mother.

Many years before, a friend of Isabel's parents, a local electrician, was hired to do some rewiring at Bachmeier Hall. He spent several weeks quietly observing Miss Bachmeier as he worked, and had gleaned a lot of intelligence regarding how the mysterious old heiress lived her life day to day. He told Buddy and Helen that she walked around the estate wearing flowing gowns, almost as if she were in a trance, followed by her pack of Pomeranians dressed in seasonal wear. He also swore he saw her talking to her collection of dolls, at least one hundred of them, and heard her refer to the room where they were kept as "the children's nursery."

And every day, as sunset approached and he was wrapping up for the day, Miss Bachmeier went onto the great lawn overlooking the lake, and in her flowing gown did what he said looked like the Dance of the Seven Veils, to classical music that began wafting through the house and grounds, surrounded by her dogs.

But the spookiest rumor Isabel had ever heard about Abigail Bachmeier was that for many years she had a ritual on the Saturday of every Memorial Day weekend, the day that was to have been her wedding day so many years before, when she put on her now-tattered and moth-eaten wedding dress and went out onto the same great lawn where the ceremony was to have been held, and strolled through an imaginary crowd, talking and laughing with her imaginary guests. It was after that rumor began to float that Isabel's dear friend and former lit teacher, Gladys DeLong, began referring to Abigail Bachmeier as "Gull Harbor's own Miss Havisham." But for folks in town who were not fans of Charles Dickens, which accounted for most of them, she was just that "crazy old rich lady on the lake."

Chapter 8

After Isabel woke up and had her coffee, she took the dogs for a quick walk, then came home and spent the next half hour trying to figure out what she was going to wear to her meeting with Abigail Bachmeier. Because she didn't want to look like she was trying too hard, or not trying hard enough, and because it was already promising to be a hot and humid summer day, Isabel put on a green-and-white madras skirt and a simple white sleeveless blouse. It was smart and practical, classic, yet stylish . . . a look well suited to Isabel Puddles' personality.

Isabel certainly didn't look like most people's notion of what a private investigator *should* look like. So when Beverly planted the idea of pursuing the P.I. path, Isabel dismissed the suggestion for that very reason. But Beverly convinced her that her "look" was an enormous asset. "Nobody is going to think a middle-aged former asparagus queen who looks like she's on her way to a church potluck, is going to be hot on their trail," she insisted. Isabel thought it over and decided she couldn't really argue that point. It made good sense. She thought about the perpetually befuddled and disheveled-looking Lieutenant Columbo in his wrinkled raincoat, who was never seen as a serious threat to the evildoers he was investigating until he slapped the cuffs on them. But what she *did* argue with, emphatically, was Beverly's suggestion that after she got her P.I. license, she should get a permit to carry a handgun.

"That is *not* happening, Bev, so you needn't ever bring it up again," Isabel responded emphatically, hoping that would shut down the conversation for good. But it didn't. Not with an all-star litigator like Beverly Atwater.

"It's important you be able to protect yourself, Isabel . . . I'm sure I don't need to point out how useful having a handgun in your purse would have been when we found ourselves in a certain predicament last year, do I?"

"You can point out whatever you like, Beverly, and I do appreciate your concern for my safety, but I am not going to have a gun in my purse, in my house, in my hand, or anywhere in my life, period. Guns of any kind scare me." Then out of curiosity, she asked, "Do *you* carry a handgun, Bev?"

"God no! That would be far too dangerous for me. Do you know how many times I wished I *did* have a handgun with me in court?"

Isabel laughed, "Well, there you go, Bev. So case closed on the handgun idea. Maybe I'll take up karate instead."

Isabel didn't realize she was getting nervous about her lunch meeting with Abigail Bachmeier until she approached the guard's gate at the entrance to the estate and realized her palms were sweaty. She slowed down as a friendly-looking older gentleman in a security guard's uniform poked his head out of the guard shack and tipped his hat. Isabel put her window down and smiled. "Hello. You must be Bernard. I'm Isabel Puddles. I'm here to see Miss Bachmeier."

Bernard smiled back and nodded. "Yes, Mrs. Puddles. Miss Bachmeier is expecting you. You'll find her in the main house. Please drive ahead."

Isabel drove slowly up the winding drive for at least a hundred yards until she turned the final corner, and there it was, like something out of an old movie, Bachmeier Hall. It was an enormous ivy-covered, brick-and-wood framed English Tudor, with steep, slate-covered rooftops and large paned windows of cut glass peering across a smooth sea of perfectly groomed lawn. A beautifully manicured boxwood hedge surrounded the lawn, along with clumps of hydrangea in shades of blues and purples. A lilac tree in full bloom acted as an umbrella covering the grand front entrance. Rumors that the place had become rundown and neglected were obviously inaccurate.

The massive structure looked more like an Ivy League university dormitory than it did a private residence, and as Isabel got closer, it loomed even larger. She had seen photographs of Bachmeier Hall in various magazines over the years, and she had seen it from the lake on many a boat trip, but those views were mostly obstructed. Apparently, after the romantic trauma she had endured, Miss Bachmeier decided for whatever reason that she no longer wanted to look at Lake Michigan, so she allowed the trees and shrubs to grow as high and as full as nature allowed, blocking out most of the first floor of the estate from the water, and vice versa. Isabel had never been on a boat trip off Gull Harbor when somebody didn't mention what a travesty it was to have that spectacular view and choose to obstruct it. And most often it was Isabel who had said it. The view of *her* lake, Gull Lake, was one of the things she loved most about her home on Poplar Bluff, and she felt sorry for somebody so detached from the world, even just the raw beauty of it, that they couldn't appreciate the peace and tranquillity such a sweeping vista might offer.

As Isabel crept along the driveway, she looked to her right, where she could see where things did start to look a bit untended. There was an empty pool filled with leaves, and a pool house almost completely covered in wisteria. Across from the pool was an old tennis court with weeds growing up through its many cracks, and its torn and weathered net sagging across the center. It was clear there were not a lot of recreational activities going on at Bachmeier Hall anymore.

Isabel parked her van in the brick driveway that encircled a polished marble statue, at least eight feet tall, of what Isabel surmised was a Greek goddess, draped in a toga and wearing wings, along with a somewhat smug expression as she looked down upon arriving visitors.

As she stepped into the portico and approached the imposing, intricately carved mahogany front door, Isabel felt the nervousness really set in. She quickly wiped her palms on her skirt, then took a deep breath and rang the doorbell. It sounded as if a chamber quartet had just been cued in the foyer, but obviously a simple ding-dong wouldn't do for a home like this. Mr. Bajrami opened the door with a smile. "Mrs. Puddles . . . Please come in."

Mrs. Puddles smiled, wiped her feet, and entered the grand foyer. "Thank you, Mr. Bajrami."

"Please call me Ramush."

"Only if you'll call me Isabel."

Ramush nodded the same singular nod she had noticed at the store. "Welcome to Bachmeier Hall, Isabel."

"Thank you, Ramush." She couldn't believe she was actually standing in Bachmeier Hall. For a local girl from Gull Harbor, it was a little like walking on the moon. Not many had done it. Although she tried to play it cool, she couldn't stop herself from rubbernecking around the magnificent, museumlike interior. "It's quite an impressive piece of architecture," she said as casually as she could.

"Yes, it is indeed. I can give you some of the history another time, and perhaps a tour if you would be interested, but Miss Bachmeier is waiting for you now on the east terrace, so if you'll follow me, please?"

Ramush led the way to the east terrace through what she assumed to be the living room, although it didn't look like there was a lot of feet-on-the-coffee-table living going on in there. It seemed to be more of a showroom for beautiful furniture, artwork, and an assortment of magnificent antiques. Isabel continued looking this way and that as they reached the other side of the room and walked into the most formal dining room she had ever seen, with a long, carved wooden dining table that matched the wood paneled walls. Highly polished antique sideboards of what looked like cherry-wood were positioned around the room, displaying elegant silver tea and dessert services on one, silver candelabras on the next, and crystal goblets on another. At the far end was an enormous breakfront that took up most of the wall, filled with exquisite porcelain. She didn't have time to count, but there must have been seating for thirty people at the table, in chairs trimmed in gold, and upholstered in fabric you would expect to see at Versailles, not in Gull Harbor, Michigan. And to top it all off, hanging over the center of the table was a gigantic crystal chandelier, which, on closer examination, was in need of a good dusting. As they got closer, she even noticed some cobwebs. Next they turned down a long hallway lined with paintings, mostly landscapes, displayed in enormous gilt frames. She paused briefly to study the first few, but after almost bumping into a massive, and probably priceless, Chinese urn, she decided it was better to keep her eyes on the back of Mr. Bajrami's head as he led the way.

When they reached the end of the hallway, they entered a comparatively cozy room lined with bookcases built in from floor to ceiling, which Isabel presumed to be the library. And then the moment of truth, the big reveal, was upon them: In a grand gesture, using both hands, Ramush slowly opened the French doors leading to the east terrace and announced his mistress's lunch guest.

"Miss Bachmeier? May I present Mrs. Isabel Puddles."

With another of his nods, Ramush stepped aside and invited her onto the terrace with a composed smile. Isabel smiled back, thanked him, and stepped gingerly onto the marble terrace. There, sitting under an expansive trellis covered in morning glory, sat Abigail Bachmeier. She looked over at Isabel with an expression that exuded not so much warmth as circumspection. She carefully watched Isabel make her way over to a table set impeccably with white linen, blue-and-white china, sterling silver place settings, and crystal stemware. Isabel had never seen a table set so beautifully in real life. "I'm delighted you could make it, Mrs. Puddles."

If this was her being delighted to see somebody, Isabel wondered what her being unhappy to see somebody would look like. "Well, I'm delighted to have been invited, Miss Bachmeier. And please call me Isabel."

"Very well, Isabel . . . Won't you please sit down?"

Isabel took in as much of her hostess as she could before sitting down across from her, where she would be unable to stare and still maintain her manners. Abigail Bachmeier was a petite woman, with a handsome, suntanned face and stylishly bobbed white hair. She wore a summer dress in a floral pattern of bold pinks and oranges, a yellow cardigan sweater draped over her shoulders, and a simple but exquisite gold-and-emerald necklace around her neck that probably cost more than Poplar Bluff. In short, Miss Bachmeier looked very unlike what Isabel had anticipated, which was a fragile-looking old dowager dressed all in black, and looking more like a rich Italian widow. Instead she looked like a guest at a Kennedy compound lawn party, circa 1959. Isabel sat down, and before she even moved her chair with a single scoot, an elderly gentleman wearing a white jacket and a black bow tie helped her with her chair, then stood quietly beside her.

"What can I have Sinclair bring you to drink, Isabel? I'm having iced tea with a splash of fresh lemonade. Ramush insists on calling it an Arnold Palmer, but since I have absolutely no idea who Arnold Palmer is, or what his association with iced tea *or* lemonade might be, nor do I care, I prefer to call it iced tea with a splash of fresh lemonade. That way we all know exactly what we're getting ourselves into."

That was quite a journey to describe a cold drink, Isabel thought. And wasn't it odd that someone who so perfectly exemplified the country club set had never heard of one of America's most famous golfers? Isabel had never so much as swung a golf club and even she knew who Arnold Palmer was. But then, come to think of it, she had no idea why he had become synonymous with iced tea and lemonade, either. Was it a conversation worth having as an ice breaker? Probably not. She looked up at the man in the white jacket and smiled. "I'll have the same, thank you."

Sinclair disappeared as quickly as he had appeared, and Miss Bachmeier wasted no time getting down to business. "Now, before Sinclair brings us our lunch, allow me to get straight to the point regarding why I've asked you here, then we can enjoy our lunch and get better acquainted. I'm in need of somebody to do some private investigating for me, and *you* are a private investigator with quite a fine reputation in this little corner of the world, I'm told. I didn't follow this local murder case you were involved in solving last year, but Ramush did, and he seemed quite impressed, which was why he suggested you for this job. However, in addition to competence, what I need is an investigator who is, above all else, *discreet*. And because you're a woman, I think that comes much easier for you than it does for a man. Men, I find, are much better at being *sneaky* than they are at being discreet, wouldn't you agree?"

"Well, I'm not sure that's always—"

"Of course I'll still need you to sign a non-disclosure agreement before I can go into any detail regarding the investigation I'm considering hiring you to embark upon. One can never be too careful, can one? Would that be all right with you, Isabel? Signing an agreement that is?" She posed the questions as though she assumed the answer would be yes, but then Isabel got the distinct impression that Abigail Bachmeier was far more accustomed to hearing yes than she ever was to hearing no.

"If what we're talking about is an agreement stating I will not disclose the details of your case with anybody, which is not something I would ever do, regardless of an agreement, signed or not, then I don't see why that would be a problem."

"Marvelous! I'll have it ready for you to sign when you come back tomorrow."

Sinclair returned with their iced teas. Isabel thanked him and took a sip, then smiled at her hostess. "Of course I wouldn't be prepared to sign anything without my attorney going over it first. One can never be too careful, can one?" Isabel said with a smile. Isabel's "attorney" was her cousin Marvin, who was a retired tax attorney living in Florida, but he remained her go-to on those rare occasions when she had to deal with anything of a legal nature. She wasn't trying to be difficult, but she did feel it was important to let Miss Bachmeier know that she, too, would be entering into any agreement between them with caution. "And I'm afraid I'm unavailable tomorrow as I'll be working, but I *am* free the day *after* tomorrow, so perhaps Mr. Bajrami could drop this agreement by the store tomorrow and I could bring it back then to discuss the case. Then we can make a decision about whether or not I'm the right person for the job." Isabel was as polite as she always tried to be with anybody, but she needed to let Abigail Bachmeier know that Isabel Puddles was not going to be railroaded into anything, by anybody.

Miss Bachmeier seemed slightly stumped as she processed the notion that somebody inhabiting her orbit might not be willing to march to her orders in lockstep. But there was also a glimmer in her eyes that implied she respected this local woman's gumption, so she quickly made the correction and continued. "That will be fine. Now, did Ramush tell me you worked in some sort of a retail establishment?" She then turned to her butler. "Sinclair, you may bring our soup course now." He bowed silently and disappeared again. She turned back to Isabel. "I asked Edmond, my chef, to prepare us some vichyssoise for our first course, which is always lovely on a summer day . . . and I thought a lobster salad would be a nice main course. Oh, and for dessert, he makes a delicious poached Anjou pear, served with his homemade kiwi sherbet."

Isabel couldn't help seeing the humor in the fact that she had gone from eating a lunch of lukewarm, leftover chicken and broccoli casserole yesterday, standing behind the counter at the hardware store, to having vichyssoise and lobster salad on the east terrace with Abigail Bachmeier today. "That sounds fabulous," she replied, not letting on that although she had heard mention of vichyssoise—probably while watching Julia Child at some point—she couldn't remember exactly what it was. She continued by answering her hostess's question regarding her employment. "Yes, I do work part-time in my cousin's hardware store in Hartley. It belonged to my uncle before him. It's sort of a family—"

"And what exactly would one find in a hardware store? I've heard of them, but I've never ventured into one," Miss Bachmeier asked in earnest.

"You can find everything from lightbulbs to power tools. Garden rakes, garden sheds, birdseed, we also carry—"

"I see, well, that's all very convenient, isn't it? Isabel, may I ask you a rather pointed question?" She didn't wait for an answer. "What were you expecting when you came here today to meet me? Or rather, *whom* were you expecting?"

Isabel was taken aback by a question she did not anticipate, and one that required a thoughtful response. "If I'm being honest, I had no earthly idea what to expect, Miss Bachmeier. I was born and raised right here in Gull Harbor, so I've heard about you and your family all my life. In fact, it would have been your brother who tried to woo my mother away from her boyfriend, my father, one summer when the two were lifeguards together. My mother obviously turned him down, but my father never forgave him, or your family, or anything having to do with the state of Wisconsin. I'm afraid Bachmeier beer was never even allowed in our house."

Miss Bachmeier threw her head back and laughed heartily. "Such refreshing honesty! I'm so used to people I encounter slathering me with whatever they think will ingratiate themselves to me. It's *so* tedious. So your father was the one who gave Skip the black eye that summer?"

"I believe he was, that is, unless your brother received more than one black eye."

"I only remember the one he received from a local boy here, but I'm sure there were others. Your mother was a smart woman, Isabel. She dodged a bullet with my brother, I can tell you. And what have you heard about *me* exactly? Just out of curiosity."

"Let's just say you're an *enigmatic* figure in my *little corner of the world*, as you put it."

"But surely you must have had some notion of whom you thought you would be meeting today. I have a good idea of what people in this community say about me. Ramush serves as my eyes and ears out among the locals, and I insist he tell me anything he hears. I don't think he does, bless him, but really, did you expect a barking-mad Miss Havisham roaming the grounds of her estate in a tattered wedding gown, talking to imaginary guests at her imaginary lawn parties?"

Isabel laughed nervously, given that she was pretty much right on the money. And her conjuring up the nickname Gladys DeLong had for her was almost spooky. What Isabel definitely did *not* expect was a perfectly lucid, elegant old woman who seemed about as far from crazy as *she* was. "Well, as I said, I really wasn't sure what to expect, Miss Bachmeier, but I would be lying if I said I wasn't very curious about meeting you, and discovering for myself what you *would* be like, but I did—"

"Hear that I was mad as a March hare? You can tell me the truth, Isabel. You mustn't worry about hurting my feelings. I have very few of those left to hurt," Abigail said with a wink and a smile.

Isabel smiled back before proceeding. "I have never heard anything untoward. In fact, I remember my mother speaking very highly of you and your philanthropic endeavors."

"Well, that's very nice to hear. But my favorite story *is* the one about me wearing my wedding gown and talking to imaginary guests at an imaginary lawn party," she said, laughing. "I have to admit, I actually had Ramush plant that story years ago. Isn't it marvelous?"

Sinclair returned with the soup, and just in time. Isabel hoped maybe their conversation might now take a different path as she unfolded the stiff linen napkin in front of her and carefully laid it in her lap. "Bon appétit," Miss Bachmeier said as she dipped her spoon into the soup. "I'm sorry. I shouldn't have put you on the spot like that, Isabel. Now I'm going to let you in on a little secret: I've never discouraged people from thinking I'm a bit off my rocker, and you want to know why?

I'll tell you why. Because it keeps them from prying into my business, and encourages them to keep their distance. I find people tend to leave crazy people alone. I've even put on a few performances over the years to help achieve that end, and for my own entertainment too I must admit. I remember once hiring an electrician from town to come and do some work here at the hall, doing *what*, I have no idea, Ramush handles all such matters. He's really more my majordomo than he is merely my chauffeur."

Isabel had no idea what a majordomo was, so she made a mental note to Google it when she got home. Miss Bachmeier continued. "Anyway, the man was here for several weeks as I recall, and whenever he saw me going about my usual business, I got the feeling he was studying me, as one might observe ants in an ant farm, so I decided to give him a little something interesting to report back to the locals. One has to make one's own fun up here on this lonely bluff sometimes, Isabel. I recall dressing in my most flowing chiffon gowns in the evenings and going out onto the lawn at sunset, when you could still see the lake. Then, holding scarves in each hand, I began interpreting the sunset through modern dance, which I had studied in Paris." Miss Bachmeier chuckled at her conjured memory. "I thought about doing it in the nude, but I didn't want the local population talking *that* much."

Isabel laughed. "Well, I will say there was talk of some eccentricities, Miss Bachmeier. In fact, that electrician you're referring to was a friend of my father's. So, yes, I had heard that you danced the Dance of the Seven Veils at sunset. He also said you had conversations with your dolls."

With that, Miss Bachmeier let out her heartiest laugh yet. "Well, *that* I do! They're such good listeners. My *Pomies* only really listen when there are doggie treats involved. I have five of them, Pomeranians. I'll introduce you another time. Today is bath day, which they absolutely loathe, so they're in hiding now. The groomer comes at three p.m. sharp once a week, and it's as if they have it marked on their calendars. She and her assistant will spend their first hour here just trying to capture them. It can be quite entertaining."

Isabel nodded knowingly. "I have a Jack Russell and a cocker spaniel who I'm convinced can tell time, so that doesn't surprise me at all. Dogs have capabilities I don't think we will ever fully comprehend."

"I'm happy to know you're a dog person, Isabel. I don't trust people who don't like dogs. Being afraid of them is one thing, but if you do not like dogs for no other reason other than you simply do not like dogs, well, then I don't like you. Cats I can do without. Now, Isabel, I'm sure you are under the impression that the investigation I'm interested in hiring you for has to do with my nephew Trey's disappearance. Randolph Heinrich Bachmeier the Third is his full name, but we call him Trey . . . or we did."

"Of course it did cross my—"

"This *does* remain quite a mystery, doesn't it? But I think one can safely assume the poor boy has gone the way of Davy Jones by now, don't you?" Miss Bachmeier looked over at her butler, now standing in statuesque stillness ten feet away, as though she had just remembered something immensely important. "Sinclair! Bring us some of those delicious rosemary dinner rolls Chef made last night." Then, dabbing the corners of her mouth with her napkin, she looked back at Isabel. "I hope you don't find me callous or indifferent, Isabel, but these things happen, don't they? Life happens, death happens, and yet the planet keeps spinning, so we move on. Just wait until you try these rolls."

Both *callous* and *indifferent* did come to mind as Isabel absorbed what she was hearing in well-disguised amazement. *Coldhearted* and a few other unflattering adjectives also raised their hands. She remembered once hearing the expression:

The rich are different. But *this* different? She took another spoonful of soup and thought about what to say next. "Well, Miss
Bachmeier, I did make that assumption—about your nephew,
that is. I couldn't imagine why else you would be interested
in meeting with me," Isabel said, dipping her spoon into her
soup again. "I gather you and your nephew were not terribly
close, or you would not—"

"*Be* so callous and indifferent? Isabel, let me be blunt if I
may. My nephew Trey was a selfish, entitled little twit, who
was the spitting image, both in looks *and* in character, of his
selfish, entitled little twit of a father, my brother, Randolph
Bachmeier Junior. Skip, whom your mother had the good
sense to reject. It says a lot about her character, too, doesn't
it? There weren't many women who *did* reject him. Skip,
like so many men, liked to be the one to do the rejecting.
He was somewhat handsome I suppose and could be charming when he needed to be, and of course he was rich, so for
many women that passed for sex appeal. I admire your mother
greatly. Is she still living? I'd like to meet her."

"No, I'm afraid she's passed away. I miss her every day, my
father too."

"That we share in common. I miss my mother and father
every single day, and they have been gone quite some time
now. I'm afraid that never goes away. But we were blessed to
have them, weren't we. So many people are cursed with awful parents. I've strayed off the path, haven't I. Back to Skip
and Trey. As you have likely surmised by now, I did not hold
either of them in very high esteem. None, in fact. Neither of
them deserved to carry my father's name, as neither possessed
any, not one, of his many fine qualities. My father, Randolph
Johannes Bachmeier, was a man of unparalleled integrity,
loyalty, and honesty with an absolutely sterling character. He
provided these two ingrates, not only with a name they could
be proud of, and exploit when it served them, but virtually

everything they ever had in life. And how did they honor his memory? By flying in the face of everything the Bachmeier name once stood for. You may or may not recall that my brother also had an unfortunate run-in with Lake Michigan many years ago. Or perhaps a *nosedive* would be more accurate."

Isabel's memory was suddenly jogged a bit. She did vaguely recall Abigail's brother being killed in a plane crash somewhere over the Big Lake some time ago. Miss Bachmeier had a sip of iced tea and continued. "There was talk that it may have been mechanical failure, or even suicide, but, knowing my brother, who wasn't good at much other than drinking and gambling and womanizing, which he certainly had a flair for, I'm sure it was a simple case of pilot error. Whatever the cause, it was for that very reason that my nephew refused to fly across the lake, despite having a private plane at his disposal." Miss Bachmeier clapped her hands together. "Oh, wonderful!"

Sinclair had arrived with the rolls, offering one first to Isabel, and then to Miss Bachmeier, who continued talking as she carefully tore her roll in half and began to butter it. "Irony aside, it just goes to show you that one cannot trick the Fates. When they are ready for you, they come for you, no matter where you are, and usually when you are least expecting them." She took a bite of her roll, savoring it before she continued. "Didn't I tell you these were marvelous?"

She wasn't going to get any argument from Isabel there. The rolls were a nice distraction from the very strange and somewhat troubling conversation she was now involved in. "Yes, outstanding. And the soup is delicious too." The soup was indeed delicious, but Isabel was admittedly startled after taking her first taste, forgetting vichyssoise was a cold soup. "Now, if I may, Miss Bachmeier, ask *you* a pointed question?"

"Please go right ahead. Ask away."

"You seem fairly certain your nephew is deceased. Now, I know this is not why you're interested in hiring me, but I have to ask . . . Given that no body has been recovered, do you think there is any possibility that he's still alive? Is it plausible he deliberately disappeared? Or was perhaps even kidnapped?"

"Both those possibilities have crossed my mind. But the boy simply isn't clever enough to plan anything as elaborate as his own disappearance. And because his trust fund, what remains of it, is closely monitored and controlled by my late brother's estate, there hasn't been any movement of funds reported since he went missing. And none of his credit cards have been used. For me that's more telling than a body. The boy couldn't fend for himself fifteen minutes without access to money. As far as a possible kidnapping? I suppose that's a possibility, but it would not have been a terribly well-thought-out plan. Expecting me to pay a ransom for my nephew would be something akin to kidnapping the fox and then asking the chickens to pay for his safe return."

Isabel was feeling more than a little uncomfortable with how cavalier Miss Bachmeier was being about her nephew's likely drowning. She suddenly felt sorry for Trey Bachmeier III. His reputation around town was very much in keeping with how his aunt Abigail had described him, but being a jerk should not be an offense punishable by death. Surely he should be mourned by *somebody*.

The only person Isabel knew who had ever had any direct contact with Trey *or* Abigail Bachmeier was Kayla from the Land's End. She had been working part-time at the Gull Harbor Yacht Club for the past ten summers and had waited on Miss Bachmeier a few times over the years when she came in for lunch, but those occasions were rare. Sometimes she came in alone, other times with old-moneyed club members, and once in a great while with Trey, although she hadn't seen them together for quite some time, she said. According to Kayla, Miss Bachmeier was always pleasant, but rarely spoke to the wait-staff. But then there was really no need to, because whether she was alone or with company, the staff had very clear instructions regarding how to attend to Abigail Bachmeier. First, they were to wait until she laid her napkin in her lap, and then they were to bring her a bottle of mineral water, along with a tall glass with one ice cube. Step two was to bring her a Kir Royale, her fancy cocktail of choice. If, when she finished her cocktail, she pushed her empty champagne flute away from her, it meant she wanted another. If she left it in front of her, it meant she was ready for lunch. Then it was time to bring her the tarragon chicken salad plate, along with six Melba toasts removed from their wrappers, placed neatly on a bread plate, and accompanied by three pats of cold butter—not two, and not four—three. Assuming you followed the script and got all that right, Abigail Bachmeier was a pleasure to wait on, compared with some of the other club members Kayla had to deal with.

Trey Bachmeier was another story. Unlike his aunt, who was polite, reserved, and a very good tipper, Trey was rude, obnoxious, and rarely tipped at all. Not surprisingly, he wasn't very popular with staff at the club. But he wasn't any more popular with his fellow club members, either, according to Kayla, as he was known to throw rowdy, booze-soaked parties during his college years on board the family's vintage mahogany yacht, despite club rules strictly prohibiting rowdy, booze-soaked parties.

Kayla also mentioned to Isabel, not long after Trey Bachmeier's disappearance, that his relationship with his aunt was not a warm and fuzzy one. Their latest falling-out was apparently the result of Trey's skipping out on a two-thousand-dollar bar tab at the club last summer. When it was discreetly brought to Miss Bachmeier's attention, she paid it and then had his membership suspended.

But whatever the nature of his character, or lack thereof, Trey Bachmeier had been a presence who was hard to ignore in Gull Harbor during the summer months. Even with a summer population composed of some very stylish people, the "Bachmeier boy," as he was known by some around Gull Harbor—or the "Bachmeier brat" by others—stood out among the well-heeled summer set. With his good looks and the vintage convertibles he drove around town, he projected the image of a young Cary Grant vacationing in Saint-Tropez, minus the charm and the wit. But, sadly, today Trey Bachmeier was a missing person, presumed dead, and, it would appear, with nobody losing much sleep over him. His aunt Abigail would certainly not fall under the umbrella of *bereaved*, but as she had just made clear to Isabel over vichyssoise and lobster salad on the east terrace, Trey's disappearance was nothing she needed to be concerned with, anyway. But Isabel couldn't help it. In her mind, any caring person would be.

As Sinclair cleared their soup bowls, Ramush appeared on the terrace and stood at attention before Miss Bachmeier for a moment before speaking. "Excuse me, ma'am, I'm going into town now to run some errands. Is there anything you'd like me to pick up for you?"

Miss Bachmeier wasted no time answering. "I'm running *dangerously* low on red licorice, Ramush."

"I replenished your supply yesterday, and had Wilhelmina put a fresh package in the bottom drawer of your nightstand."

Based on her reaction, you would have thought Ramush had replenished her heart pills. "Oh thank goodness! What would I ever do without you, Ramush?"

Ramush smiled, bowed to both of them, and removed

himself from the terrace. Isabel couldn't help but wonder how, with her closest blood relative either floating in or lying at the bottom of Lake Michigan, red licorice would be top of mind, but she could see at this point that any armchair analysis of Abigail Bachmeier was fruitless. She did, however, see this as an opportune moment to try to satisfy her curiosity about Ramush. "Mr. Bajrami is such an elegant, well-mannered gentleman, and with such an interesting accent. I can't quite make it out though."

"Ramush is Albanian. He was orphaned very young. Both his parents were members of some kind of Albanian resistance, although I don't recall who or what they were resisting. Communists I suppose would be a safe bet. But whatever it was, it cost them their lives, and it cost Ramush his parents. How this all came to fruition I have no idea, but my mother and father sponsored him. My maternal great-grandfather you see was an exiled member of the Albanian royal family, so my mother had a soft spot for them. So, at her urging, my father arranged for little Ramush to be brought over here when he was three or four years old, and then arranged for him to be adopted by an Albanian couple who worked in the brewery. I was away at boarding school at the time, so I didn't meet him until he turned eighteen and came to work for the family, and eventually became my father's chauffeur. The two of them developed a very close bond over the years. In fact, they were closer than my father *ever* was with my brother, which became a bone of contention with Skip, as you might expect. When Father passed away, Ramush was devastated. Of course I wasn't going to just turn him loose, so he came over here to work for me, and he has been with me ever since."

After they finished their dessert course, which was quite tasty, despite Isabel being neither a fan of kiwi, or even pears for that matter, Sinclair brought them each an espresso, and the conversation turned back to more mundane things, like the weather and the pollen count. When she finished her espresso, Isabel felt it was time to thank her hostess and say goodbye, so she stood up from the table and reached out to shake Abigail's hand. "I'm afraid it's time for me to get home, Miss Bachmeier. It's been a great pleasure to finally meet you." *Great pleasure* may have been a stretch, but it was certainly an interesting, and educational, encounter. Abigail smiled and took her hand.

"Please call me Abigail. Miss Bachmeier is a bit formal if we're going to be working together. I have a good feeling about you, Isabel, so once we get that paperwork out of the way, and you and Ramush have discussed the financial arrangements, we can meet again. Now, if you'll excuse me, I play bridge with my dolls at one thirty sharp. They get very cross with me if I'm late." Abigail laughed as she stood up and winked at her. "Sinclair will show you to the door. It's been delightful meeting you."

"Thank you, Abigail. And thank you for that superb lunch."

"You're most welcome. Goodbye, Isabel." And with that, the mysterious mistress of Bachmeier Hall turned and walked away, and at a very good clip for a woman her age, whatever age that was, then disappeared through another set of French doors at the other end of the terrace.

Chapter 9

On her drive home from Bachmeier Hall, Isabel relived her somewhat incredible lunch conversation with Abigail Bachmeier. Nothing about her, or their conversation, was anything close to what she had expected. Although she was still shocked by her complete lack of concern over the likely death of her nephew, Isabel still believed Abigail Bachmeier was a good soul, just a badly wounded one. She still couldn't imagine what it was she wanted to hire her to investigate, but to say Isabel's curiosity had been piqued was a colossal understatement.

As anticipated, Frances was champing at the bit to hear all about Isabel's lunch at Bachmeier Hall, and had already left three messages. But Isabel needed a little time to decompress before being subjected to Frances's interrogation, so she decided to stop by the hardware to say hello to Freddie and Andy and pick up her paycheck. But then something unexpected happened. As she passed the Michigander Inn, a motel just off the highway, she saw a familiar face coming out of the lobby holding the door for a very *unfamiliar* face. She nearly drove her van off the road when she realized it was Hank

Spitler, laughing and carrying on with an attractive, well-dressed younger woman as they walked into the parking lot. Isabel cranked the wheel and pulled into Mac's Muffler Shop next door to the motel and turned around, waving a finger at Mac as she headed back to the motel to see if she could get a better look at this woman whose company Hank seemed awfully happy to be in. But by the time she got back, he was waving goodbye to her as she backed out, then tooted her horn and headed for the main road.

Isabel stopped and sank down in her seat a little, peering over the steering wheel. She didn't want Hank to see her, but she did want to get a better look at this woman as she drove past her. The woman was now wearing sunglasses, so it was difficult to make out her face, but she looked to be forty-ish, quite attractive, with well-coiffed blonde hair. Before Isabel even realized what she was doing, she was following her. Isabel's mind was racing as she tried to think about reasons Frances's husband would have for escorting an attractive younger woman out of a motel. Hank wasn't the sharpest knife in the drawer, but he couldn't be dumb enough to carry on an affair in a community as tightly knit as theirs, could he?

She stopped following whoever this woman was after she turned onto the freeway on-ramp and headed south. For a moment Isabel forgot where she was going, as her mind immediately turned to how she was going to deal with Frances now. She was not going to say anything about what she had just seen without knowing exactly what was going on. There could very well be a reasonable explanation . . . or at least she hoped so. Maybe she could arrange to run into Hank and casually mention to him that she had seen him at the Michigander and then see what he came up with in the way of a reasonable explanation. She almost felt like crying when she thought about how poor Frances would react if she learned that Hank really was involved in an affair. It would crush her. And at that very moment her phone rang. It was Frances. Time to play dumb . . .

Luckily Isabel didn't have to do any talking, which was not unusual when Frances called, but what she had to say was disconcerting. Hank had just called and told her he wanted to take her to dinner and talk to her about something. Isabel could tell that Frances was troubled by her husband taking her out unprompted, but she was doing her best to hide it. What was most telling about *how* troubled Frances really was, given her current suspicions, was that she didn't ask Isabel anything about her meeting with Abigail Bachmeier.

After they hung up, Isabel was suddenly riddled with guilt for not sharing what she had just witnessed five minutes before. This was why she had turned down potential clients who wanted her to investigate spouses suspected of cheating. It made her highly uncomfortable to be caught in the middle of matters so personal. And when it involved someone as close to her as Frances was, it made it a thousand times worse.

Isabel walked into the hardware to find Freddie standing behind the counter wearing his usual grin. Seeing his favorite cousin was always a bright spot in his day. "Hello there, Cagney! Or are you more Lacey? Honestly, I never could keep those two straight."

"Cagney was the blonde, Freddie," Isabel answered as she hoisted both her purse and her tote bag onto the counter. "So how's business been today?"

"Meh . . . I think our June is going to be about the same as it was last year. How about *your* business? I want to hear all about your meeting with Baby Jane Bachmeier!"

Isabel almost felt bad that she was going to have to break it to Freddie and the others that Abigail Bachmeier was not the crazy old bat they had heard about all these years, holed up in a spooky mansion wearing her wedding dress, dancing on the lawn and having tea parties with her dolls. She might be a little eccentric, and she was certainly not somebody you would want writing condolence cards, but she was a gracious hostess, elegant in both appearance and demeanor, sharp as a tack, and seemed relatively normal . . . or as normal as anybody that rich could be.

"What did she want to talk to you about? Her nephew, I suppose?" Freddie asked as he reached under the counter and pulled out Isabel's paycheck.

"She wanted the two of us to get acquainted first, so I don't really know what any of this is about yet. What she did make clear, though, is that it *isn't* about her nephew."

Freddie seemed puzzled. "Hmm . . . That's odd. Well, I ran into Sheriff Chase this morning at Hobson's. It doesn't sound like they're any closer to knowing what happened . . . and still no body. It's shaping up to be quite a mystery. They may need your help, Iz!"

"I wouldn't get involved even if that *was* what she wanted to hire me for. But whatever it is I will not be at liberty to discuss, because she asked me to sign a non-disclosure agreement before she tells me anything."

"Probably a smart idea on her part. Who knows what kind of skeletons might be clacking around in the Bachmeier family's closet! You know there were whispers after her brother was killed in that plane crash that it was not an accident."

"She did mention that she had considered suicide as a possibility. But she felt about her brother about the same way my dogs feel about squirrels, so it didn't seem to matter to her one way or the other what actually happened to him."

Freddie slowly shook his head. "I wasn't talking about *suicide*. I'm talking about *murder*."

Isabel had never heard any rumors about a murder, but then she had initially forgotten there was even a plane crash.

Freddie's words sunk in like red wine on a white plush rug as her investigative wheels began to turn, despite her best effort to hit the brakes. She had to quickly remind herself this was not her business, and as far as she knew, had nothing to do with why Miss Bachmeier wanted to hire her. But unfortunately the bell could not be unrung now.

"Murdered? Murdered by *whom*, Freddie?"

Freddie shrugged his shoulders. "I'm not the sleuth in the family, Iz. That's your department. But I've watched enough episodes of *Law and Order* to know that when it comes to premeditated murder, whoever commits the crime is usually the one who has the most to gain from the victim not being alive anymore. I guess that's murder 101 though, right?"

Isabel was thinking out loud now. "But if Skip Bachmeier's death *had* been suspicious, surely there would have been a thorough investigation at the time, given the family that was involved."

"What did I tell you about calling me Shirley?" Freddie said with a laugh. He had been quoting *Airplane* since 1980. It was his *Citizen Kane*. But then Freddie got serious. "Or maybe it was the family involved that *prevented* a more thorough investigation."

Another good point, Isabel thought. But whatever the case, it happened twenty-five years ago, give or take, so the case was as cold as the vichyssoise she'd had for lunch. It did still beg the question, though: What if, for the sake of argument, it *was* murder? Is it possible Skip Bachmeier's son had met the same fate? And if so, could the two murders be somehow related? Freddie knew what Isabel was thinking, so he went in with a final flourish. "Now Skip Bachmeier's son is missing and presumed dead, and under, well, if not suspicious circumstances, certainly mysterious ones. And who would have the most to gain if two of three heirs to a huge fortune turned up dead?" Freddie let the question float in the air.

Isabel pondered it for a moment. It wasn't exactly algebra. It seemed pretty obvious who would have the most to gain in such a scenario, but it was not a path Isabel wanted to travel down. She was not prepared to believe she had just had lunch with a murderess. "Let's not even go there, Freddie." But even as the words left her lips, Isabel knew one thing for sure: like it or not, *going there* for Isabel Puddles was inevitable.

Chapter 10

Isabel woke up feeling unsettled, and for a variety of reasons. She knew she would soon be learning what Frances and Hank had discussed over dinner last night, although she was still hoping against hope it was not what she feared. If Hank really was having an affair with that woman she had seen him leaving the motel with, Frances was in for some rough water ahead, and Isabel knew she would be right there in the raft with her.

Yesterday's meeting with Abigail Bachmeier, and what Freddie later planted in her head about her brother's death, and possibly her nephew's, too, was also weighing heavily on her mind. What if Skip Bachmeier, whose body was never recovered, really had been murdered? And could it have been a decades-old precursor to what happened to his son, Trey, barely a month ago? Of course it could be mere coincidence that both a father and son, heirs to a vast fortune, died in Lake Michigan. It *was* a big lake, after all. But what was most troubling now was this nagging question she couldn't shake . . . Could Abigail Bachmeier have played a role in their disappearances? She had no way of knowing what, if any, evidence of a murder existed in either case, but it didn't take much of a stretch to find a motive, given that she was now the sole surviving heir to the Bachmeier fortune. But each time that suspicion reared its head, Isabel scolded herself. She had no business speculating about whether Miss Bachmeier was involved in a plot so dark and sinister. Yes, her cold, casual attitude about her dead brother, and her more than likely dead nephew, was a bit unnerving, but a lack of compassion didn't make her a murderer.

Isabel was relieved when the phone rang and stopped her head from spinning. When she looked at the number and saw it was Frances, the knot in her stomach got even tighter.

"Good morning, Frances . . . What am I doing? Well, I was going to take the dogs for a walk and then come and meet you for breakfast . . . Okay, I'll see you then." That may have just been the shortest conversation she had ever had with Frances Spitler, Isabel thought as she hung up, and it happened so fast she couldn't really get a read on her mood.

When Isabel arrived at Land's End, Frances wasn't there, which was unusual. She was always there first. It was eight a.m. and the place was already filling up, but their usual table was waiting. Kayla was taking an order so she waved at her and then pointed at the new girl. Isabel had forgotten all about her. The new girl looked over at Kayla, nodded, and then walked over to Isabel's table with a shy smile. She flipped her coffee cup over and poured. "Hi, I'm the new girl, Jazz. Kayla told me this table was reserved for her favorite regulars, but I don't know if you're Isabel or Frances."

"I'm Isabel. Nice to meet you Jazz . . . and here comes Frances now." Frances walked into the room as if she were about to make an arrest. *Oh dear,* Isabel said to herself, *she's in a mood.* She brushed past Jazz and sat down. "Frances, this is Jazz."

"Yes, we've met. Good morning."

"Good morning, ma'am . . . Can I pour you some coffee?"

Frances flipped her coffee cup over without looking at the new girl. "Yes you *may*, thank you. And I take skim milk, not cream. Good morning, Iz."

This was not shaping up to be a very pleasant breakfast. Isabel was familiar with these moods, and although they didn't come often, she knew that when they did, it was best just to put her head down, stay quiet, and wait for things to blow over. Kind of like how her father had told her that, if she was ever attacked by a bear, playing dead was the best hope for survival. Isabel reached down and took the newspaper out of her purse and handed a section across the table to Frances, who shook her head and waved it away. Jazz returned to the table and gingerly set the skim milk down on the table as though she instinctively knew how best to handle Frances's mood too. The neophyte waitress looked at Isabel and took a deep breath. "May I take your order, ladies?"

Frances looked up at her as if she had just spoken to them in Pig Latin. "We've been ordering the same thing here since Moses was a boy. Just tell whoever is in the kitchen today it's for us and they'll know. And if it's Chef, tell him he over-cooked my eggs yesterday."

Isabel smiled apologetically at the new girl, who grimaced slightly and backed away from the table. Jazz got to the kitchen window just as Kayla did, and they began to chat. Kayla looked over at Frances and shook her head, then walked over to the table. "Good morning, Izzy, and a good morning to you, Mrs. Spitler. Is this mood you're in going to pass once you get some coffee in you, or are you going to be brightening up our entire breakfast hour with such a cheery disposition?"

"I have no idea what you're talking about, Kayla," Frances said as she poured the milk into her coffee and stirred.

"Well, you've already put the fear of Jesus into my new girl. Frances, so help me, if you make her quit, I'm going to hand you an apron and an order pad and you're going to take her place."

Isabel chuckled. "Can we please give the poor girl a chance, Frances? She seems very nice to me."

"She is . . . *And* she's a good waitress," Kayla added as she stared Frances down. "So please be nice, Frances, or at least don't bite her head off. How about pleasant? I'll bring you a warm cinnamon bun on the house if you'll just agree to be pleasant."

"You can keep your bun, but I'll try to be a little friendlier. Have her pull up a chair and I'll braid her hair." Kayla topped off Isabel's coffee, but conspicuously skipped Frances before leaving the table, annoyed.

Isabel had reached her limit. "Okay, Frances . . . spill it. I don't want to spend the next hour trying to decipher what this is all about." Unfortunately she was pretty sure she already knew what this was all about, but it was time to rip the Band-Aid off.

Frances took a long sip of coffee, then looked up at Isabel and stared at her for a few seconds before speaking. "My husband dropped quite a bombshell on me last night at dinner."

Isabel wished she was anywhere in the world other than where she was at this very moment. She took a deep breath. "Okay . . . And what was that?"

Frances took another long, dramatic sip of coffee. "Hank's been given a promotion."

Did she just hear Frances correctly? *This* was Hank's bombshell? Isabel's eyes widened as she looked across the table. "And *that's* what has you in such a foul mood?"

"The company that bought out Glickman's Canning and Cold Storage last year held a lunch meeting at the Michigander yesterday with Gerry Glickman and all the shift foremen, along with the bigwigs from the other company. The human resources woman met with Hank afterward and offered him the position of vice-president of quality control. Hank! Can you believe that?"

So that was who Hank was walking out of the motel lobby with in such a good mood! Isabel was awash with a sense of relief. She had never been so happy to have been wrong in her life. But at the same time she felt a little foolish *and* a little guilty for thinking Hank was a cheater. "Well, that's terrific, Frances! Why do you find that so hard to believe? Hank has worked at that plant for twenty-five years. And he's been a foreman for at least fifteen years, right? He's more than earned it."

"I don't know why you're smiling, because that's not the whole story." Frances took another slow, dramatic sip of coffee. "They want him to work out of their corporate office in Grand Haven."

"Grand Haven? That's quite a commute. It's got to be over an hour each way . . . and a lot longer with summer traffic."

"And *that's* why I'm in such a foul mood! He doesn't want to commute. He wants us to move to Grand Haven! And his next surprise was that he found us *a beautiful condo on the water* that he wants to make an offer on." Isabel was at a complete loss for words, so Frances continued. "I guess it's been in the works for a few weeks. He had heard the promotion might be coming, but it wasn't official until yesterday. So that's why he's been in such a good mood lately. I'd rather it *had* been a girlfriend! Let *her* move to Grand Haven with him!"

Isabel was slowly processing what was happening. A moment earlier she wanted to laugh with relief, and now she felt like crying at the thought of her closest friend in the world moving away. But she also wanted to try to stay positive, at least for now. "Grand Haven's a nice town, Frances." The two friends shared a moment of silence looking at each other across the table. "When does Hank have to decide?"

"Oh, he's decided! He's already accepted! And without so much as a word to me. Can you imagine? So typical of him."

"So now what?" Isabel didn't even notice Jazz was back to refill their coffees.

Frances was building up even more steam. "He seemed to think that because they offered him such a nice big salary, I'd be all for it. He even ordered champagne for us to celebrate. I said, 'What are we celebrating? Our divorce? Because wild horses could not drag me away from Gull Harbor! And for what? So you can wear a suit and tie to work and feel important?' It never occurred to the man to run it by his wife. I don't know why I didn't divorce him twenty years ago! In fact, I don't know why I even married him in the first place!"

"I do. Because you were head over heels in love with him! Wild horses couldn't have dragged you away from the *altar!*" Frances ignored her remark, so she kept talking. "How did Hank react? He can't have been surprised that he met with some resistance."

Frances shook her head in disgust. "He's already called the kids to try to get them on his side and convince me to do it. He thinks I'll come around. It's like the man has never *met* me. I've told him it is *not* happening, but he's determined he can get me to change my mind."

"I can't even imagine you not living down the road from me anymore. I mean, even the thought of it breaks my heart. But you have to admit, this is a great opportunity for Hank . . . *and* for you. Hank's got some good earning years left, so this could make your retirement years a whole lot easier."

Frances stared into her coffee for a moment, then looked up at Isabel with tears in her eyes.

"I can't imagine not living down the road from you, either, Iz. And I can't imagine leaving the place I've called home my whole life. All my people, from my mom and dad to my great-great-grandparents, are all buried together just a mile from here. What am I going to do, dig em all up and move em down to Grand Haven with me?"

Isabel couldn't help chuckling. "Don't be morbid, Frances."

Just then Jazz arrived with their breakfasts. Isabel could tell from the look in her eyes that she wanted to get the orders right, so she helped her out. "Scrambled for Frances, over-easy for me . . . and a little more coffee, please. You're doing a great job, by the way." Jazz smiled gratefully and went back for more coffee.

"Isabel, I don't give two hoots about him making more money. We're doing just fine. He's tighter than bark on a tree, so it's not like he's going to be showering me with jewels or furs, which I don't give two *more* hoots about. But between what he's socked away and my secret nest egg, which he knows nothing about, we're just fine. So if I have to crack open my nest egg to divorce him, I'll do it. Because I am *not* moving to Grand Haven. Period!"

Isabel did not envy the fight Hank was up against, but she knew if Frances stuck to her guns—and she had never known her not to—it was a fight he was going to lose. So for the time being, she was feeling relieved that the move to Grand Haven was not inevitable, while at the same time, she was already apprehensive about what a divorce would look like. They ate their breakfast in relative quiet, with Frances barking out anti-Hank sentiments every few bites, until she finally decided it was time to move on to another topic. "I can't believe it, Izzy." Frances took a breath and pushed her plate away. "I haven't even asked you about your meeting with Abigail Bachmeier. So is she nutty as a fruitcake? Any sign of those Jehovah's Witnesses?"

Jazz had just come to clear Frances's plate and overheard her question to Isabel. "Are you talking about Abigail Bachmeier, of Bachmeier Beer? You know her?"

Frances was annoyed. "Eavesdropping on customers is frowned upon here at Land's End."

"What are you talking about, Frances? That's how we get most of our local news. Quit scaring this poor girl to death." Isabel looked up at Jazz. "Yes, we just met. I may be doing some work for her."

"I wasn't trying to be nosy, it's just that I'm from Milwaukee originally, and I've known about that family my whole life. More money than God! I understand Abigail Bachmeier's quite the character too. Terrible thing about her nephew . . . And still no body."

Kayla came to the table just in time, sparing Isabel from answering any more questions about her potential new client. "Jazz, would you go take an order from table six, please? They have the look. Thanks."

"She's a nosy one," Frances said to Kayla as she cleared their plates. "What do we know about her?"

"Who's being nosy now? Frances, why do you have it in for this girl? I called the couple of references she gave me and they checked out. And like I said, she can wait tables so I know all I need to know. Want me to swab her for a DNA sample?"

Frances shrugged her shoulders, put ten dollars on the table, and got up to leave. "I guess you know best, Kayla, but I'd keep my eye on the cash drawer if I were you. Izzy, I'll see you later. I've had about all the interaction with humans I can handle for the day. I'd rather go home and spend the day with my cat." Frances made her way to the front door, then, yelling back across the room, "And I don't *have* a cat!"

Kayla looked at Isabel and shook her head. "That one can be a real pain in the caboose sometimes, can't she?"

Isabel reached into her bag for her wallet. "She's a pistol, all right! Okay, I'm off to the hardware. We have a big shipment of light sockets coming in today, so I don't want to miss that excitement."

Isabel walked into the hardware to find Ramush standing at the counter, talking to Freddie. He smiled at Isabel and held up a manila envelope before setting it down on the counter.

"Good morning, Isabel. I brought the agreement you and Miss Bachmeier discussed yesterday. If you'd like to sign it, I'm happy to wait."

Isabel said her good mornings and reached behind the door to grab her red work apron.

"Thank you, Ramush. I'll look it over and bring it with me to lunch tomorrow. Eleven forty-five again, I presume?"

Ramush nodded. "Yes, that will be fine. We'll see you tomorrow, Isabel. Oh, and I've included a document regarding what Miss Bachmeier would like to offer you in the way of payment for your services. We came up with an offer I think you'll find suitable."

"Thank you, Ramush. I'm sure it will be fine."

Ramush headed for the door. "Good day, Mr. Peabody . . . Isabel." The minute the door closed behind him, Freddie grabbed the envelope off the counter and handed it to his cousin. "Open it! Let's see what kind of money old Miss Moneybags is offering."

"I can't imagine it's going to be enough for me to quit my day job, so I wouldn't worry." Isabel opened the envelope and pulled out the agreement along with the document attached to it. As she read the document, her eyes began to widen. She quickly slipped it back into the envelope before Freddie could peek.

"Well? Are you not going to tell me?"

Isabel smiled slyly. "You might want to start taking applications, Freddie."

"That much, eh?"

"It's generous . . . Let's leave it at that. It will cover the new roof I've been putting off for five years now, and with a little left to spare. And you know I'm only kidding. I'd never leave you, Freddie. Not even if I hit the Powerball."

"If you hit the Powerball, Iz, I'd be begging you to buy this store and *I'd* leave!"

Isabel laughed as she slipped the envelope into her bag and tucked it back under the counter. For some reason the amount made her slightly uncomfortable. It was an offer almost impossible to turn down. Could it be this was the strategy, if Miss Bachmeier thought whatever it was she wanted her to investigate might involve something unsavory? If so, she didn't know Isabel Puddles. Yes, it was a lot of money, and yes, she could use it, but she would make her decision based on what the job would require her to do, not what it paid.

It was late in the afternoon and business was slow. Isabel had just sent Andy down to Hobson's to get iced coffees and two chocolate-chip cookies, which had become an afternoon ritual. She then went around the store organizing and straightening shelves, which was what she always did on slow days. She was organizing fly swatters by color when she heard the front door jingle, her cue to head back to the counter. When she turned the corner, standing there wearing a big grin was Beverly Atwater. "Isabel! There you are!"

"Bev! Hello! What are you doing here?" Isabel walked over to give her a hug. "I'm happy to see you of course, but I didn't think you were coming until Fourth of July weekend."

"Well, that was the plan, but I had a case wrap up sooner

than I thought, and it's hotter than Hades in Detroit, so I thought, what am I doing *here* when I can be in Gull Harbor? I almost forgot I had a home here now!"

The two chatted for a few minutes until Isabel suddenly realized Beverly didn't have her beloved Chihuahua with her. "Where's Diego?"

"He's asleep in his carrier. I left the car running with the AC, so he's fine. But I need to run anyway. Would you like to come by the house for dinner tonight? I'll cook for us."

Beverly Atwater *cooking*? This was not registering.

"Don't make that face, Isabel! I can cook! Well, I can *kind* of cook. Enough to make a salad, throw some potatoes in the oven, and grill us a couple of steaks anyway. See you at seven? We'll have dinner on the deck and watch the sunset."

"That sounds very nice. May I bring the dogs?"

"Of course! Diego will be happy to see them again. I think he's getting bored with me. Okay, I'll see you later then, Iz."

Beverly was out the door before Isabel remembered the documents Ramush had dropped by. No need to bother Cousin Marvin in Florida when she was having dinner with one of the top attorneys in the state. She'd bring them with her to dinner.

No sooner had Beverly left the store when another familiar face walked in the door, although it took Isabel a second or two to place the Land's End's newest employee. "Well, hello there, Jazz."

Jazz looked surprised until the coin finally dropped. "You're one of the breakfast ladies! The nice one . . . Isabel, right?"

Isabel smiled. "Don't let Frances get to you. She can be a little prickly at times but she'll come around. Yes, I'm Isabel. Now, what can I help you with?"

"I just moved into a new apartment, so I need a few things. I'll just look around, if that's okay?"

"Look around all you like. Let me know if I can help you find anything."

Isabel heard Andy come in the back door. He came around the corner and nearly bumped into Jazz. "Oh . . . Hello, Jazz . . . What are you doing here?" Andy was slightly confused.

"Hi, Andy." Jazz was confused as well. "I just needed a few things for the apartment. You work here?" she asked.

"I do," Andy replied as he set the iced coffees and the bag with the cookies down on the counter. "But I thought I mentioned that to you."

"Maybe you did. But I guess I don't remember that," Jazz answered vaguely.

Now Isabel was a little confused. "And how do *you* two know each other?"

"Jazz is renting out my parents' basement apartment," Andy replied.

"Isn't that a coincidence?" Isabel said as she unwrapped a straw and poked it into the lid of her iced coffee.

"Andy's parents are such nice people," Jazz said as she patted Andy on the shoulder.

"I'm not at all surprised," Isabel said, smiling at Andy. "They raised a very nice young man. I hope I'll have the chance to meet them sometime."

Andy was blushing. "Thank you, Mrs. Puddles. Mom and Dad said they're going to come in sometime soon to see where I work, and to meet you and Mr. Peabody."

"That would be lovely. I'm surprised they've never been in the store before, though. Is your family new around here, Andy?"

"We moved over here from Milwaukee about three years ago. My dad's a doctor and he was offered the chief of staff position at Kentwater Memorial. My mom's a nurse there too."

Isabel was duly impressed. "And do they like it here?"

"Dad does, but he's from Michigan originally. Mom misses Milwaukee. Her side of the family's all over there, but they come over here a lot in the summer, especially now that we have a boat."

Isabel looked over at Jazz, who was perusing the seed display. "Didn't you say you were from Milwaukee too, Jazz? Is there anybody left in that town? You all seem to be over here these days."

Jazz laughed. "Thanks to the *Badger*, Gull Harbor's just a boat ride away! Yes, I was born and raised in Milwaukee. That's how Andy's mom and I bonded. We went to the same high school, although she was a few years ahead of me."

"What exactly do you need for the apartment, Jazz? I thought we had it pretty well stocked up," Andy asked.

"Nothing major . . . just a few odds and ends." Jazz looked at her watch. "But I didn't realize how late it was getting! I'm meeting a friend, so I have to run. I'll come back when I have more time to shop. Bye, Isabel. See you at breakfast. And I'll see you around, Andy."

Jazz flew out the door before either of them could say a thing. Isabel noticed an odd expression on Andy's face. "What is it, Andy?"

Andy was quick to answer. "Nothing, Mrs. Puddles . . . it's just that I'm beginning to think my mom's right," he replied as he watched Jazz walk past the front window. "She is kind of an odd bird."

Isabel laughed. "Well, birds come in all varieties, odd and otherwise, Andy my dear. She does seem a little lost to me, but I think she's a good egg."

Andy just shrugged as Isabel reached into the bag and dug out their afternoon cookies. They both took a bite and smiled. "That Mr. Hobson sure knows his cookies," Andy said as he took another bite.

"He does indeed," Isabel said, taking another bite, then putting the rest of her cookie back in the bag. "Now I need to get back to my fly swatters." Isabel started to put the bag away, then reached back in. "Maybe one more bite," she said with a wink.

Chapter 11

Beverly Atwater's spectacular log home overlooking Lake Michigan had been acquired recently in lieu of payment from a client she had successfully defended in a murder trial, one who may or may not have been guilty. Isabel was still reserving judgment on that. Beverly had become enamored of Gull Harbor while working on the Jonasson murder case. It was how she and Isabel had become friends, under less-than-ideal circumstances. She had been looking for a new vacation home ever since she let her ex-husband have theirs as part of their divorce settlement, and decided Gull Harbor was an ideal place for one. It also didn't hurt that the home was worth far more than her attorney fees would have been, but she very astutely cut the deal in advance. If she could get her client an acquittal, they agreed, her client would hand over the deed.

The enormous log-and-stone structure, which sat on a bluff under an umbrella of hundred-year-old sugar maples, had more square footage than a single woman and a Chihuahua could ever possibly need, but Beverly had a brother and sister who had wholeheartedly embraced procreation, so she intended the place be used as a family vacation getaway for her many nieces and nephews and their families, who were all scattered around the Midwest. That worked in theory, but when they all converged for Memorial Day weekend, Beverly was so overwhelmed by the ensuing chaos that she snuck over with Diego and took refuge with Isabel. "It's like a prison riot over there," she said, pulling a bottle of wine out of her overnight bag and uncorking it.

Beverly was in the front yard gardening when Isabel pulled up. *Gardening? Cooking? What's next?* Isabel thought. *Would she be asking to join the Knit Wits?* She had no idea Beverly Atwater had a domestic bone in her body. It was almost jarring to see this sophisticated, citified lawyer, who typically wore only designer outfits, now wearing blue jeans, an oversized sweatshirt, gardening gloves, and wielding a pair of pruning shears.

Beverly smiled and waved as Isabel walked up the drive. She was only too happy to put down her pruning shears and pick up a glass of wine instead, so they took the bottle of chilled Michigan Riesling Isabel had brought and some cheese and crackers out onto the deck and sat down to take in the incredible sweeping view of the Big Lake. It was already seven o'clock, but the sun didn't set until around nine o'clock this time of year, so the water was still sparkling blue, although shadows were beginning to cast themselves among the trees, signaling that sunset was approaching. The massive clouds billowing along the horizon promised another magnificent sunset. Lake Michigan sunsets were one of Isabel's favorite things about living near the lake.

Photographers called this the "magic hour," but so did mosquitoes, so Beverly and Isabel sprayed themselves with plenty of bug repellent, and Beverly lit a citronella candle before they got too comfortable. After a toast, Isabel shared a little bit about her meeting with Abigail Bachmeier, and asked Beverly if she would take a look at the non-disclosure agreement Ramush had given her. After reading through it, Beverly handed it back and gave her the okay to sign it. "It's pretty standard," she assured her. Beverly then began to dig deeper into her meeting with the mysterious old beer heiress. Isabel pulled a pen out of her purse and signed, but she was hesitant to get too far into the weeds regarding what Abigail had already discussed with her. So to distract her, she began describing the estate itself. Then she talked about Ramush and Sinclair, the east terrace, what Abigail was wearing, and even the lunch menu. She also mentioned how surprised she was to find such a lucid and elegant hostess—a woman of refinement who looked more like a throwback to Camelot than she did to the Norma Desmond–like character she had been expecting. Although Beverly seemed to be sufficiently intrigued with Isabel's descriptive storytelling, she was clearly looking for something juicier.

"You know, Isabel, that agreement you just signed is not yet valid, because it is not yet in Abigail Bachmeier's possession. And it doesn't cover what the two of you talked about at lunch today anyway, so. . ."

Isabel mulled this over as she picked a fruit fly out of her wineglass and gave it a flick, then took a sip. In Michigan at this time of year, if you weren't willing to keep drinking after a fruit fly or two had landed in your beverage of choice, you would be perpetually thirsty. "So *what*, Bev?" Isabel said casually.

"*So* tell me what you two talked about at lunch!" Beverly replied with some urgency.

"There's really not much to tell, Bev."

"Of course there is! Here, have some more wine." Beverly's agenda was pretty transparent.

"No, I'm fine. What exactly do you want to know?"

"Did she talk about her missing nephew at all? She must have!" Beverly asked.

Isabel shook her head. "Not that much. She talked more about her brother than she did him."

"And?"

"*And* let's just say there didn't seem to be much love lost between the two, and when I say 'not much' I mean virtually *none at all*. But by the sound of it, he was not an easy person to love. Did you know he died in a plane crash?"

"Yes . . . And I remember when it happened."

"You do? Because I barely remember it and I was right here."

Beverly continued. "I was new at my firm, and one of the senior partners had gone to Harvard with Skip Bachmeier. He didn't think much of him, either, as I recall. But I do remember him speculating that the timing of his death was a little suspicious."

"How so?" Isabel asked, unaware she was being lured in.

"Apparently Skip had been trying to wrest control of the Bachmeier Foundation from his sister by having her declared mentally incompetent. Rumor had it he had paid off some corrupt judge in Florida—take your pick—to have her Baker Acted."

"Baker Acted?" Isabel dipped back into her wineglass to retrieve another fruit fly. "What's that?"

"In Florida there is a provision in the law called the Baker Act, which allows for a person exhibiting signs of mental illness to be taken into custody and then held for observation, *involuntarily*, for seventy-two hours. So one winter, when Abigail was at her Palm Beach estate, the men in the white coats showed up and carted her off to the booby hatch. I'm sorry, that wasn't exactly politically correct. I mean taken to a mental health facility. All her brother had to do next was prove she was a danger to herself or others and she could be committed for up to six months, which would put him in charge and give him all the time he would need to loot their family foundation, which Abigail ran, and considered to be her life's work. Even then it had about a half-billion-dollar endowment, so you can imagine where it's at today."

"No wonder she hated him. That is absolutely diabolical! So what happened?"

"Well, apparently ol' Skip had not paid off all the right people, because he was unable to prove she was nuts, sorry, mentally incapacitated, so when the seventy-two hours were up, she was released. By then, she may very well have become a danger to others, or at least to *one* other."

No wonder Beverly was such a successful litigator. Isabel wasn't even aware she had been sucked in. "Do you mean what I think you mean, Bev?"

"What I mean is that after his sinister plan failed, he'd stirred up quite a hornets' nest with his sister and her camp. Next thing you know, Skip ends up at the bottom of Lake Michigan. I don't believe they ever found *his* body, either."

Isabel looked genuinely shocked. "And you're saying there was speculation at the time that Abigail had something to do with that? Sounds like more of a coincidence to me."

"Sure, that's possible . . . but it certainly was a *happy* coincidence for Abigail. And you know Isabel in my experience, when it comes to murder, there is *coincidence*, and then there is *circumstantial evidence*, and sometimes it's very difficult to separate the two."

"But how could Miss Bachmeier have been involved with causing his plane to crash?"

"There was never any investigation, so we'll never know. As I recall, it was determined the crash was either mechanical failure or pilot error or both. So, case closed."

"I just don't see how she could have arranged for a plane crash even if she wanted to."

"Maybe she hired a hit. Somebody who knew a little something about airplane mechanics, for instance?" Isabel just shook her head. She wasn't buying it. Beverly continued. "I happen to know of a case in Ohio where a wife gave her husband—a private pilot allegedly on his way to Myrtle Beach for a golf outing—a can of grape soda, just before he took off, that had enough sleeping pills crushed up in it to coldcock a bull moose. You see what his wife knew, that he didn't *know* she knew, was that he wasn't really headed to Myrtle Beach. He was flying from Cleveland to Columbus to pick up his twentysomething girlfriend and take her to Miami for the weekend. About thirty minutes after he took off, air traffic control in Cincinnati tried to make contact with him but got no response. The man was sound asleep at the controls and had passed right over Columbus. But he had turned his autopilot on at some point before he drifted off, so he ended up crashing into a swamp in north Georgia after the plane finally ran out of fuel. Gators took care of most of his remains by the time they found him, so there was not much of him left to do any reliable toxicology as far as the jury was concerned."

Isabel was sufficiently horrified by Beverly's story. "So she got away with it?"

"She did," Beverly said with a wink, "with the help of a very good defense attorney."

Isabel was so caught up in the story now developing in her head of what may have happened to Skip Bachmeier that the obvious identity of the grape soda murderer's defense attorney didn't even sink in. "Oh, please, Bev. You really think Abigail Bachmeier might have drugged her brother? Or paid somebody to sabotage his plane? That all seems a bit far-fetched."

"Far-fetched is George Clooney coming to spend Fourth

of July weekend with me. A sister offing the brother who tried to have her declared insane and put away so he could pillage the half-billion-dollar family foundation seems like a pretty *off-the-rack* motive to me." Beverly then laid her last card on the table. "And now her nephew has gone missing, making Abigail Bachmeier the only surviving heir to one of the largest fortunes in the Midwest." She let that sink in, then looked at Isabel and raised her eyebrows for punctuation.

While Beverly grilled the steaks, Isabel set the table, all the while thinking over everything Beverly had just said, which was exactly what Freddie had implied. Was she about to go to work for a woman who could *possibly*—no matter how remote that possibility—be responsible for the murders of two of her own family members? After her last, and first, experience in the murder-solving business, Isabel would never again be surprised by the lengths to which some people would go to get rich. So it only followed that people who were *already* rich were just as capable of going to the same lengths to *stay* rich. But was it fair to even entertain such suspicions when there was absolutely no evidence pointing to anything so dark and devious, beyond decades-old rumor and conjecture?

Isabel made it a point to steer the conversation in a completely different direction once they sat down to eat, so she kept Beverly entertained with some fresh Gull Harbor gossip. After a surprisingly delicious dinner, and two perfectly grilled steaks (Beverly had obviously been concealing her culinary skills), they sat down and watched the sunset with Jackpot and Corky splayed out at Isabel's feet and Diego curled up in the fold of Beverly's arm. Theirs was certainly an unlikely friendship—a high powered, big city attorney and a hardware store clerk and small-town sleuth—but after what they had been through together during the Jonasson case, they now shared an unbreakable bond. And, more and more, Isabel was discovering how much they *did* have in common, not the least of which was both of their being single women *of a certain age.* Beverly suddenly turned to her with a question that came straight out of the blue. "Isabel . . . do you think you'll ever marry again?"

"What in the world brought that up, Bev?"

"I don't know . . . I was just wondering. Have you been in touch with the mystery writer from London lately?"

"Teddy? Yes we've stayed in touch. We write back and forth."

"You write letters? Actual letters?"

"Yes, actual letters . . . pen, paper, envelopes, stamps—the whole shebang."

"That's so cute. Very quaint . . . and *very* Isabel Puddles. I think the only time I put pen to paper anymore is when I'm signing my name."

"Well, there you go. Letter writing is becoming a lost art, so Teddy and I decided to curate it as best we can. And his letters are wonderfully entertaining, as you might imagine they would be." Beverly's smile seemed to be prompting Isabel to say more. "But if what you're suggesting is that we are on our way to the altar? No, that is *not* in the cards. We're pen pals. There's nothing romantic happening between us."

Beverly wasn't entirely convinced Isabel didn't have feelings for Teddy that went beyond those she would have for a pen pal. "And you've never thought about remarrying?"

"Why?" Isabel replied with a chuckle. "It wasn't all that terrific the first time around, if I'm being honest. But as a result, I have two beautiful kids who I cherish, so I'd do it all over again. Although I might abbreviate the timeline a bit if I were given a do-over."

"Don't you ever get lonely?" Beverly asked in earnest.

"Once in a great while. Maybe on a snowy night in the dead of winter it will cross my mind that it might be nice to have somebody to sit next to the fire with and watch the snow falling across the lake. But then I think how lucky I am to have my family and friends, and to have these two down here at my feet to keep me company. I have my cozy cottage, my knitting, my books. So, no, I don't pine away for a man in my life. And what about you, Beverly? Do you think *you'll* ever marry again?"

"I really don't see it. 'Been there, done that,' as they say. And I didn't *done that* very well. I've never had any regrets about divorcing my ex-husband though. I was over the moon at one time for Clay Atwater. He had everything I was look-ing for in a husband. Except, as it turned out, he also had a very fragile ego, along with an initially well-disguised belief that men were superior to women, especially when it came to the law. So after *I* made partner and he *didn't*, the charming man I had fallen in love with became surly and mean . . . and eventually a hopeless drunk. Last I heard he had a time share at Betty Ford."

It was the first time Isabel had ever heard Beverly talk about her ex-husband, and she could see it still pained her somewhat. "I've been alone now for over a decade, and, like I said, no regrets. But I do sometimes think it might be nice to have a man in my life again. But having a man in my *house*? That's something else altogether."

Isabel laughed. "Maybe we'll both grow old together here in the north woods, Bev. *The Golden Girls* meets *On Golden Pond*." They laughed and clinked their coffee cups together, then sat back and watched the sun disappear over the horizon. Once the reds and oranges had turned to black and gray, Isa-bel got up to leave and head back to Poplar Bluff. "Thank you for a wonderful dinner, Bev."

"You're most welcome, Iz," Beverly said as she got up too and tucked one arm under Isabel's, while holding Diego in the other. "Let me walk you to your car."

"You are still planning to be here for the Fourth, yes? I can't imagine you'd want to miss my barbecue. It's one of the social events of the season, and the crème de la crème of Kentwater County society will be there. All the bratwurst you can eat and all the beer from a keg you can drink. It's a very fancy affair."

"I wouldn't miss it," Beverly assured her. As they hugged each other goodnight, they heard what sounded like a loud clap of thunder, followed by a second one.

"Looks like we've got a little weather coming in off the lake," Isabel said as she opened the side door of the van to let the dogs in.

"Weather report said clear skies for the next two days," Beverly said.

"Weather reports around here amount to nothing more than best guesses. It can all change in an instant, as I'm sure you've learned by now."

"Just as in life," Beverly offered as she kissed the top of Diego's head.

"I guess we learned that little life lesson together, didn't we, Bev?"

Beverly's eyes widened as she nodded her head in agreement, then turned and made her way back up the gravel driveway. "Goodnight, Iz. Drive safely," she yelled back. "And watch out for deer!"

On her drive home, Isabel was feeling a bit discombobulated. She couldn't shake this newly planted suspicion, no matter how remote in her view, that Abigail Bachmeier might have been part of a well-orchestrated murder conspiracy. Maybe even two! And the more she tried not to think about it, of course the more she did. By the time she got home she began to ask herself if it was smart to even get involved with Miss Bachmeier at all, no matter what it was she needed investigating. But then again, never knowing what that investigation might be would drive her nuts, so she had to at least follow through with tomorrow's lunch meeting, if only to satisfy her curiosity. It didn't *always* kill the cat, she told herself.

Chapter 12

"Lunch will be on the *west* terrace today, Mrs. Puddles," Sinclair announced after answering the door and graciously inviting her in. Isabel thanked him and proceeded to follow the fragile-looking old butler, who had to be well into his eighties, in the opposite direction she had gone two days before with Ramush. Going in this direction, she was even more impressed with the grandeur of the interior. And because Sinclair wasn't exactly fast on his feet, she had more time to look around. There were more impressive pieces of art hanging on the walls, and more museum-quality antiques and furniture. Sinclair stopped at the threshold of the French doors, which were already opened onto the terrace, and with a slow but elegant hand gesture invited her to step outside. Isabel smiled, thanked him again, and went onto the terrace.

The west terrace looked very much like the east terrace; the only discernible difference was that it was completely shaded by a green-and-white striped canopy. To the west, there would have been what Isabel could only imagine to be a spectacular panoramic view of Lake Michigan, were it not for the barricade of overgrown trees and shrubs stubbornly standing in the way. She could see Miss Bachmeier sitting across the terrace and reading a newspaper at a table set just as beautifully as the other one had been for their first lunch. She wondered if this kind of formality was only for company or if it was everyday living for someone so rich. Abigail looked up from her paper and smiled, folding it and setting it to the side. Isabel smiled back and waved at her hostess, who was wearing a summer dress very much like the one she had been wearing last time, in both style and pattern, but this version was in beautiful ocean-glass greens and blues, and around her neck was the same emerald-and-gold necklace. Abigail Bachmeier was a study in old-school elegance. Isabel, on the other hand, because she hadn't time to do any laundry, was wearing the same skirt she had worn to their last lunch meeting, and was more a study in old-school wash and wear. But at least she was wearing a different blouse, this one a light blue, so she hoped her hostess wouldn't notice.

"Good morning, Abigail," Isabel said in a chipper tone as she approached the table.

"Good morning, Isabel. Do come and sit down."

Isabel did as she was told, sitting across from Abigail, who again wasted no time in getting down to business. "Ramush tells me you've signed the agreement, and have agreed on the offer of remuneration for your services. Are you happy with the arrangement?"

"Yes, Ramush and I spoke briefly on the phone this morning. I have the agreement here in my purse. It's a very generous offer, but I'm still not sure if I'm the right—"

"Splendid! So now we can finally get on with my telling you what this is all about. As I said to you the other day, investigating what happened to my nephew Trey needn't concern you. We will leave that to the proper authorities to sort out. I'm sure they're doing the best they can. I suppose he'll either turn up or he won't."

Isabel was already feeling a little icky again. How could anybody be so callous about the likely death of a member of her own family, even if she wasn't fond of him? She couldn't help but wonder, from a criminal psychology standpoint, which was a subject she had recently studied, if her dismissiveness of Trey's fate might suggest she already knew what happened to him. But before she could put the murder-conspiracy wheels back in motion, Abigail finally began to lay out the details of what it was she wanted Isabel to investigate.

"Trey does, however, play a role here, because you see, Isabel, since his disappearance, it has been brought to my attention that I in fact have—are you ready for it?—*another* nephew. A spare, if you like." That little nugget certainly got Isabel's attention. She straightened up in her chair as Abigail sunk her hook. "It turns out Trey has an older brother, well, a half brother, who, to my knowledge, *he* never knew existed, either. I thought I was his only living immediate blood relative since his mother's passing several years ago, and I assume he believed the same of me." Isabel hoped she wasn't about to learn that Trey's mother had also disappeared into Lake Michigan, but she was in listening mode now so she didn't ask about her cause of death. Abigail continued.

"I know you think I'm not as concerned as an aunt should be regarding a nephew's disappearance, but let me, if I may, give you an idea of the kind of young man Trey Bachmeier was, or the man he had become. Trey's mother, Marjorie, who was a lovely woman, was a Milwaukee girl. She was a Pipp, of Pipp's Pretzels, so what she saw in Skip was always a riddle to me because she had her own money. Anyway, Marjorie had been quite ill for some time, but her death, although not unexpected, did come suddenly. Trey was in the Caribbean with some college friends on their spring vacation when he was notified that his mother had passed away. But because he had only just arrived, he asked his step-father if he would postpone the funeral for two weeks until he came back, so as not to interrupt his vacation. The boy was perfectly content to let his poor dead mother lie in a refrigerator for two weeks while he frolicked in the Caribbean. I told Marjorie's husband to disregard his stepson's outrageously selfish request and to schedule the funeral. I then sent Ramush down to the Virgin Islands in a private jet to bring him back, bodily, if necessary. And it very nearly came to that. The glum look he wore on his face at his mother's funeral had nothing to do with losing her, but had everything to do with his disappointment at having been taken off the beach. This is just one example of many I could point to that would showcase the boy's glaring lack of character and a narcissistic personality. So please don't judge me too harshly for not playing the role of the grieving relative. Hypocrisy is one thing I cannot abide, not in others, and certainly not in myself."

Fair enough, Isabel said to herself. She reached into her tote and took out a notepad and pen. "Do you mind if I take some notes?"

"Not at all. Now I'm going to share with you whatever details I am able to, and then Ramush will fill you in on more of the specifics, since it was he who tossed this little grenade into my lap a few days after Trey went missing. Now, let's see . . . Where to begin? I believe I made clear to you that Trey's father was not a person whom I looked upon with undiluted love and respect. And, I might add, the feeling was quite mutual. But now, two plus decades since his death, I'm learning he was even more despicable than I realized. And that was a very high bar to get over. By the way, today is Chef's day off, so I had him make a batch of his marvelous German potato salad and some deviled eggs last night. And Ramush is going to grill some kielbasa for us shortly. You can take the girl out of Milwaukee, but you cannot take away her love for German food and Polish sausage!"

Sinclair arrived with iced teas, which seemed to put Abigail back on course. "Before my father passed away, he took Ramush into his confidence—they were very close, as I told you—and Father swore him to secrecy regarding this particular family secret. However, he did give Ramush permission to use his discretion and share this information with me if and when he ever felt it was necessary. Ramush is loyal to the core, so despite being in my employ all these years, he stayed true to that promise he made to my father, and did not see any reason to encumber me with this until it very recently *did* become necessary. And, well, here we are." Isabel's curiosity was officially piqued. She knew there was no turning back now. She was all in. "So it seems my brother had an affair many years ago with a beautiful young girl who worked on the bottling line at the Bachmeier Brewery. Her name was Colleen, the daughter of Irish immigrant parents, who also worked at the brewery. She was just nineteen years old and putting herself through nursing school. Skip would have been about thirty or so at the time, so it was an inappropriate arrangement on many levels. Colleen was not the first pretty young girl Skip had plucked from the bottling line and promised the moon, but she was, so far as we know, anyway, the first girl he ever burdened with a pregnancy. Colleen told her parents, who were very strict Catholics, of course, and who were understandably most unhappy. *Her* father then went to *my* father and told him about the unfortunate predicament his daughter was now in, thanks to his son. Father was, as you might imagine, furious with Skip, and he assured Colleen's father there would be a marriage. But that was not to be, because Skip, who was an insufferable snob, thought she was beneath his station in life, so he flatly refused to marry the poor girl.

He instead offered what he thought was a simple and obvious remedy to the problem, but Colleen and her parents wouldn't hear of it, and neither would my father."

Isabel shook her head. "What a mess to be in at nineteen . . . Poor girl."

"A sweet young girl, too, according to Ramush. He evidently got to know her quite well over the course of this whole unfortunate situation. But she was obviously quite naive, as demonstrated by her succumbing to my brother's counterfeit charms in the first place. She told Ramush she actually thought they were in love and that he wanted to marry her. But to Skip, she was just another conquest. Naturally, unencumbered as he was by common decency, he had no problem whatsoever abdicating his responsibility as the baby's father. But if *he* wasn't going to do the right thing, my father certainly was . . . and did. He also made sure Skip would pay the price for being such an irresponsible louse."

Isabel was scribbling notes as fast as she could, enthralled with a story that was getting juicier with every sentence. She jotted down questions she would ask later of Ramush, but she didn't want to interrupt Miss Bachmeier's telling of the story. "Please continue. . ."

"So to that end, my father took half of my brother's shares in Bachmeier Beer, stocks which comprised a sizable portion of his trust fund, which my father still controlled. He then put that stock into a trust for Colleen and his future grandchild to ensure that any and all of their needs would be taken care of in perpetuity. All that he asked of her was to consider leaving Milwaukee in order to spare herself, her family, and our family the scandal that was sure to accompany her pregnancy. I don't have to remind you, Isabel, that there was a time when such a thing as having a child out of wedlock was rather frowned upon. Today it's evidently something to be celebrated, but I digress. To make such a move out of

Milwaukee and away from her family a desirable option, my father arranged for her to attend the University of Wisconsin in Madison, tuition free, and he even bought her a little bungalow close to campus. He then arranged for Colleen's younger sister to attend college there as well so she could help care for the baby. Ramush said that Colleen, being a proud young woman, resisted the offer at first, but at her parents' urging, and my father's—and after finally accepting the fact that the morally impaired father of her soon-to-be born baby was out of the picture for good—she realized it was best for everybody involved to accept my father's very generous offer. Is this beginning to sound like a soap opera to you, Isabel?"

"I don't mean to make light, but this is better than any soap opera I've ever seen." Isabel laid down her pen for a moment and took a sip of iced tea.

"Well, it gets soapier," Miss Bachmeier said, chuckling, as she stirred her own tea and took a sip.

"Your father sounds like a very kind man," Isabel added.

"Randolph Bachmeier was a remarkable man, indeed, and, yes, very kind. You know he immigrated to this country from Germany, by himself, when he was barely seventeen years old. He spoke not one word of English. No, I'll take that back, he knew two words: *hello* and *goodbye*. He always laughed when he recounted how for quite some time he had them mixed up, which he said made for some perplexing introductions and farewells." Abigail smiled at the memory before continuing. "He had fourteen dollars in his pocket when he arrived in Milwaukee to join an uncle, who he learned upon his arrival had sadly passed away. So he was all alone in a foreign land until he met my mother, Brigitte, also from Germany, who had come over with my grandparents when she was seventeen. She met my father at eighteen, and because it was love at first sight for them both, they married only months later. They moved into a tiny little cold-water flat above a beer garden on Brewer's Hill where my father worked as a beer tender and my mother worked as a waitress. Father ended up buying the tavern a few years later after the owner died, and then began brewing beer in the basement, using his grandfather's recipe for ale, and my maternal grandfather's recipe for Bavarian lager. And the rest is, well, beer history. But my parents, God rest their souls, never forgot their humble beginnings. They tried to instill in us the same values that had served them so well in life. I don't know that I turned out to be a complete success story on that front, but I *do* know that at least as far as my father was concerned, my brother, Skip, was an abject failure across the board. Father was very proud of his achievements in business, deservedly so, but I think his greatest disappointment in life was the man his son had become . . . or *didn't* become, as it were. He deemed himself a failure as a father because of it, but he wasn't at all of course. It was Skip who was a failure as a son. And I don't know about you, Isabel, but I think there are people in this world who are simply born bad, and all the devoted parenting in the world isn't going to change that." Abigail reflected for a moment before continuing. "Now, where was I? I'm afraid I've lost track."

Isabel hadn't—she was rapt. "Your father took half your brother's shares of stock in Bachmeier Beer and put them in a trust for his grandchild and Colleen and paid for her to go away to college."

"Oh, yes. So when my brother discovered that his ownership shares in Bachmeier Beer had been cut in half, he was fit to be tied. He hired a lawyer and threatened to sue my father, which was of course ridiculous, because they were my father's stocks to give him in the first place, so they were his to take away. Needless to say, this created a fracture in their relationship—which was not a good one to start with—and a fracture that never healed. In fact, it only deepened in the years to come."

Isabel looked up from her note taking. "So Colleen moved to Madison, I gather?"

"She did, but her whereabouts were known only to my father, Ramush, and to her family, of course."

"And the baby?" Isabel asked.

"A boy she named Jacob. It was my grandfather's name."

Isabel kept scribbling. "And did your father stay in touch with Colleen and the baby?"

"Oh, yes. This was long after my mother died, I was in college back east, and then I went off to study abroad, so I know my poor father had been very lonely in those years. My brother was still around, like a chronic cough that wouldn't go away, but given the sort of relationship they had, he offered no comfort or companionship. So Ramush would drive Father to Madison whenever he could find the time. He was quite the doting grandfather, I'm told, which doesn't surprise me."

Isabel was touched to see Abigail's eyes begin to well with tears. This was not a woman capable of murder, she reassured herself. Abigail composed herself and went on. "I think there must have been a part of him that thought this was an opportunity for redemption of some kind. Having had such bad luck with his son, maybe he hoped he would be luckier with his grandson. Now, as you might imagine, the dramatic scope of this revelation came as quite a shock to me, but it has also provided me comfort in knowing that before he died, my father *wasn't* lonely, after all. He had this little boy, Jacob, in his life . . . his only grandson. Ramush said it was the happiest he had seen him since before my mother died. Looking back, I remember him seeming especially happy whenever I came home to visit during that time. Of course I just assumed he was happy to see me. But knowing he was so happy is exactly why I never believed he—" Abigail stopped short.

"Never believed what?" Isabel asked curiously.

Ignoring Isabel's follow-up, Abigail forced a smile and carried on. "I've certainly been prattling on, haven't I? Are you hungry, Isabel? I'm famished! Sinclair, please go and get lunch organized for us, will you please?" Sinclair, who was standing his usual ten paces away from the table, nodded and left the terrace.

It was clear to Isabel that even to this day Abigail still very much missed her father, something she understood completely. "I can see you and your father were very close."

"Oh, yes!" Abigail suddenly cheered up. "The sun rose and set on my father, as far as I was concerned. Of course I adored my mother, too, and I know she loved me, but she was not as affectionate as my father, and rather more reserved with her emotions. I was away at a Swiss boarding school, which I absolutely hated. After Mother died, my father paroled me from that gulag in the Alps and I came home to Milwaukee. My brother was away at some military academy, one of several he attended and was then expelled from, so it was just Father and me for those years until I left to go to college. We both missed my mother terribly, but they were still wonderful years, just us two."

"When did your father pass away?" Isabel asked delicately.

Abigail looked across the terrace at nothing in particular, as if deliberating over what she was or wasn't going to say next. She looked back at Isabel with a melancholy smile. "My father died on the eve of my thirtieth birthday which is just two weeks before Christmas. I had been in a very dark place in the years leading up to his death. I won't bore you with those details, and I'm not anxious to relive all of that anyway, but I was finally beginning to reemerge into the world. 'Bloody, but unbowed' as the poem goes. And my father was my greatest cheerleader. I would never have gotten through that time of my life without him. I was living here full-time, and had been ever since, well, ever since I was twenty-four." Isabel was sure what she meant was "ever since" she had been left at the altar, but that was a topic she wouldn't dream of broaching. "Father flew over nearly every weekend to see me. We spent my twenty-ninth birthday and his last Christmas right here together, along with my father's sister, Tante, sorry, *Aunt* Dagmar, who came over from Munich. Poor Aunt Dagmar died in an avalanche later that same year while skiing in Austria."

Isabel slowly shook her head. "Your family certainly has had its share of tragedy."

"My mother died quite young too. Cancer took her, but it took her quickly, which was a blessing."

"And what about your father? How did he pass?" Isabel asked once again, but delicately.

There followed an uncomfortably long pause. Abigail looked across the table at her and proceeded to avoid the question by exposing a vulnerability Isabel had not expected. "I don't believe I've ever experienced true happiness since my father died. Although I'm not sure I would recognize it again after all these years. Are *you* happy, Isabel?"

Isabel was surprised by such a direct and personal question. She mulled it over for a moment before answering. "I've always felt as though happiness was not a place you lived, but more a place you visited. If you're lucky, you visit regularly, kind of like your favorite restaurant. Or maybe it's more accurate to say happiness visits you?" She could see Abigail was waiting for more. "So for instance, it makes me very happy knowing my kids will be coming home soon to celebrate the Fourth of July, as they do most every year. So while I'll be very happy to have them here, I also know I'm going to be very sad when they leave. But I think knowing that happy times are very often followed by not so happy times, even sad times, somehow makes you treasure happiness even more when you do have it. Does that make sense?"

Abigail smiled reflectively and slowly nodded. "Perhaps I should have done a better job of managing my expectations of life in my early years. I thought I had found that sort of happiness once, the kind you read about that promises to last a lifetime. But it escaped me, or rather, abandoned me." Abigail stopped herself from descending into the rabbit hole she had just peered into. "But I've had a good life, and I've had a privileged life, depending on how you measure those things. What I am very thankful for is that once I mourned losing the sort of love and happiness I assumed I was destined for in life—marriage, motherhood—I instead, in time, found contentment, which is not a bad consolation prize, I suppose. Still, one always has to wonder what might have been. *That*, I'm afraid, is unavoidable. It's a melancholy that blows in from time to time like a north wind off the lake. It chills you to the bone for a little while, but then it goes away . . . eventually." Almost on cue, music began to waft out onto the terrace. The voice sounded familiar, but Isabel couldn't quite place it. Then she realized whoever it was, was singing in French.

"Who is this?" Isabel asked.

"Edith Piaf . . . I never tire of her voice. And it's a good thing because my chef, Edmond, is obsessed with her, so we hear her daily. Edith and I were friends for a time when I was studying in Paris. She was a lovely, but a tormented soul I'm afraid. Paris was quite a place in those days. I haven't been back in years, so I haven't a clue what it's like today. Probably just as well." Abigail seemed to be whisked back to a time when she truly *had* experienced happiness. But then just as quickly she rejoined the present. A wave of sympathy crashed over Isabel as she looked at the old woman sitting across from her. The last time they met, she had been more than a little taken aback by her callousness regarding her nephew's disappearance, coupled with her hostility toward her dead brother, but today she suspected the emotional detachment she showed was understandable, maybe even necessary. In fact, her detachment from life in general was much easier for Isabel to understand. If finding Abigail's long-lost nephew could bring her some modicum of the happiness that had eluded her for so long, and give her some peace of mind as the end of her life grew near, Isabel was willing to do whatever she could to help. But to do that, she needed more information. "How long has it been since Ramush has seen Colleen or Jacob?"

"It's been quite some time now. My father asked Ramush to look after the boy and his mother for him after he was gone. That came sooner than any of us suspected, but Ramush did as was asked of him, and kept a close eye on them. Colleen gave up her earlier plan of becoming a nurse, and now that she had the means, she went to medical school and became a doctor. Ramush went to her graduation. But not long after that, he received a letter from her saying that she would be going off to do her residency, with Jacob naturally, but she wouldn't say where. She also said she was engaged to be married and would be in touch again after they were settled, but he never heard from her again. And that's the part that unnerves me. How would he have ever known if something happened to them? How do we know they're even still alive?"

"Well, let's stay positive. I'm sure they're both alive and well! It's just a matter of tracking them down now. Jacob would be somewhere in his mid-thirties now, correct?" Isabel asked as she continued scribbling in her notebook.

"Yes, that would be about right. He's a grown man. Ramush has tried his best to track down both mother and son ever since Trey went missing, but to no avail. So *this* is why we have come to you, Isabel. Jacob—assuming he *is* still alive, and assuming Trey is *not*—will now, eventually, become the family torchbearer. He will be next in line to *potentially* control, or be in a position to *gain* control, of everything after I'm gone."

Isabel looked up at Miss Bachmeier as she laid down her pen and closed her notebook. "That is quite a story, Abigail. So somewhere out there is a young man who has no idea that he is in line to one day inherit a multimillion-dollar fortune."

"It's not quite that simple. You see there is nothing left of his father's estate for Jacob to inherit, nor was there for Trey. What he will inherit from *me*, if anything, will be determined once I have met him and I can test his ability to handle the amount of money we're talking about, and measure the sort of man he is. But he is a Bachmeier, and I know my father would want him to be taken care of in some fashion, and he will be . . . in some fashion."

That was odd terminology, Isabel thought . . . *some fashion*. But what intrigued her was how Abigail's brother, one of two heirs to a vast fortune, could die without leaving anything for his son, at least the one he knew about. "So are you saying your brother was broke when he died?"

"Oh, yes! Flat broke! When he died he was millions of dollars in debt, which of course the estate was stuck paying off. Skip spent years selling off his shares of Bachmeier stock and the rest of his portfolio like heads of cattle in order to maintain a lifestyle he could no longer afford, but felt fully entitled to. Father had been kind enough to leave him our home in Milwaukee and a few other real estate holdings, but he sold them all and then squandered that as well. I know this will come across as mean-spirited, Isabel, but the day my brother came to me asking—and when I say asking, I mean *begging*—for money, well, it was a happy moment in my life. He fully expected I would bail him out. And I refused to give him so much as a dime."

Isabel knew she was straying off course, but given what

had been planted in her head by Freddie, and again last night by Beverly, curiosity got the better of her once again. She had to ask just to see what kind of reaction she would get. "Do you think there is any possibility that your brother's plane crash could have been—"

"Suicide? As I believe we've already discussed, I've always thought there was that chance, but only a very slim one. I say that because it would have shown some modicum of decency, which was not exactly Skip Bachmeier's calling card. A plane crash would be virtually impossible to prove to be suicide, which would mean his son would at least be able to lay claim to a sizable life insurance policy, given that there was really nothing left for him to inherit as far as assets. But, you see, my brother was incapable of that kind of selflessness, which is why I'm certain it was an accident. Trey did collect the life insurance. He was a minor at the time, so the money went into a trust, which he was able to gain access to when he turned twenty-one. When that day arrived, and staying true to the theory that the apple doesn't fall far from the tree, especially the rotten ones, he then spent the next several years squandering it in much the same way his father did."

Isabel paused for a moment. "I was actually going to ask you if you thought your brother's plane crash could have been murder."

"That's a novel idea, Isabel," Abigail answered with an odd chuckle. "There was no shortage of people who would like to have seen him dead, but do you not think there would have been more conventional ways to see to that other than arranging a plane crash? That seems awfully elaborate, not to mention a waste of a perfectly good airplane."

Isabel was getting used to Abigail's inability to show any sort of emotion regarding her brother's life *or* death. But she was still stuck by the dichotomy, because she didn't seem to be a heartless person at all. Her love for her father and devotion to his memory were obvious and touching. But Isabel had observed over the years that often people who loved deeply were also capable of hating even more deeply. She opted not to follow up with this line of questioning, or even know how to, so she again reminded herself that whatever may have happened to Skip Bachmeier all those years ago was not her business.

Isabel couldn't help thinking that the Bachmeier family saga had to be the most vivid illustration she had ever seen that money could not buy happiness. In fact, in their case, it only seemed to compound *unhappiness* and tragedy. She had to wonder if Jacob might be better off *not* being found. Maybe he was perfectly happy with his life just as it was. Becoming embroiled with his aunt and all the machinations involving the Bachmeier fortune, could very well end up being a curse. She wanted to know more about Abigail's motives. Maybe she didn't want to be a party to this, after all. "I'm a little confused about the urgency in finding Jacob now. After all these years, why not just let things remain status quo?"

"I want to meet my nephew Isabel! My father's grandson. We share a bloodline and a family heritage. This isn't just about money and inheritance. Skip never understood that, and neither did Trey. I know you probably see me as rather heartless when I speak of my brother and my nephew with such aloofness, but you see they neither wanted nor needed my love. I was nothing more than an impediment to them in getting what they really craved, which was more money. My hope is that this young man, Jacob, will be somebody I can trust to carry on my family's name and legacy as it should, with care and dignity. He may very well be controlling a tremendous amount of money one day, I hope not in the very *near* future, but one day, and I need to know who he is, what he's made of, and then plan accordingly. I had lost any hope that Trey was worthy of that responsibility years ago. My most fervent hope is that Jacob *will* be."

"And what role does the Bachmeier Foundation play in this equation, if I might ask? I know this is something you care very much about."

"Indeed I do! The foundation is *everything* to me. In the end, that will be my family's true legacy. After I refused to bail my brother out, he tried everything he could think of, including going to some rather extreme measures—evil measures, in fact—to try to get me out of the way and gain control of the foundation so he could use it as his own personal piggy bank. And, according to my sources, Trey was exploring ways *he* might do the same, after he learned his own financial future was not looking as bright as he assumed it would be. As I said, he was a very entitled young man, and he believed I was obligated to ensure he had all the money he ever needed or wanted. In our last conversation, which was a rather strained lunch we had last summer at the yacht club, I used his father as a cautionary tale and let him know in no uncertain terms that he needn't ever come to me with his hand out. I told him that once his money ran out, he was on his own, and that he would not be inheriting a *penny* from me. This was not news that Trey received very well at all. I also made quite clear that I was taking every measure available to prevent him from ever gaining access to the Bachmeier Foundation, as his father had once attempted to do. But apparently he saw that as a challenge, and I soon learned that he had already hired an army of vultures with law degrees to explore his options."

"And that was the last time you saw your nephew?" Isabel asked. Abigail nodded. "I understand fully the position you took, but it's still quite sad. You were the only family either of you had left, at least as far as you knew at the time."

"Money can do terrible things to a person, Isabel. Terrible things. But it can also do great good if used wisely and compassionately. Otherwise, what's the point of having it? Yes, the Bachmeier Foundation means everything to me. I want my mother and father's life, and selfishly my *own* life, to have meant something to this world, and to future generations. My last, *best* hope is that Jacob has inherited more of *my* father's character than he has *his* father's, and that he will be prepared, with my guidance of course, to serve as a worthy custodian of the Bachmeier name, the foundation, and our family legacy. It can't *all* just be about beer, can it?" Abigail smiled and took a sip of tea. "I've never liked beer to be honest. Hate the taste of it in fact. Beer has been good to us, but beer is not a legacy. So there you have it. Goodness, I feel as if I have just talked your ear off, Isabel. Shall we have lunch? I can smell those sausages on the grill, can't you?"

On her drive home from Bachmeier Hall, Isabel had a lot more to digest than grilled kielbasa and German potato salad. She had entered a world of wealth that was completely foreign to her. And being a woman who carried a separate wallet in her purse exclusively for coupons, it was a world that was impossible for her to truly wrap her head around.

As she approached Poplar Bluff, she could see a car parked in the driveway that she didn't recognize, and upon closer examination she saw a man sitting in the driver's seat. Isabel pulled alongside and peered in to see a middle-aged man who appeared to be jotting something down on a notepad. He looked up when he saw Isabel's van, then smiled and waved. He seemed harmless enough, but she wasn't used to seeing strange men parked in her driveway. The man put his passenger-side window down and leaned across the seat as she got out of her van. "Hello, are you Mrs. Puddles?"

Isabel grabbed her tote and threw her purse over her shoulder, then slammed the door closed. "I am. Now, may I ask who *you* are?"

The man got out of his car and quickly came around to shake her hand. "I'm Mark Miller. It's nice to meet you. I'm a real estate broker from Chicago. I was just writing you a note, but here you are. I understand you are the owner of this beautiful property, as well as the lots on either side?"

Isabel was instantly annoyed. It wasn't the first time she had found real estate people snooping around Poplar Bluff. "Yes, I am the owner, as my parents were before me, and, no, I have no interest in selling. Now, if you'll excuse me." Isabel smiled politely at him, hoping this was where the conversation was going to end. No such luck. She walked over to the front gate where Jackpot and Corky were excitedly waiting for her and stepped inside, closing the gate behind her. As she leaned down to say hello she noticed the man was walking toward the gate. He had obviously rehearsed a pitch and he intended to give it.

"If I might have just two minutes, Mrs. Puddles. Please. You see, I have a client, a couple from Chicago, who have admired this property for a few years now. They own a big place over on Lake Michigan, but they have also been renting a place here on Gull Lake for the past few summers so their children and grandchildren can enjoy the sort of lake activities that are not really suited to the Big Lake . . . you know, Jet Skiing, waterskiing, kayaking, those sorts of things."

Isabel stood back up and smiled, then stared at him for a moment. "You're only wasting your time. And I don't mean to be rude, but you're wasting mine too. I have a million things to do."

Mr. Miller was not going away quietly. "Funny you should mention that number, Mrs. Puddles, because that is exactly what my client is prepared to offer you for your three properties. One million dollars. It's an offer well over market value."

"Well, you can tell your client thank you anyway, but I have absolutely zero interest in selling. There are lots of nice properties for sale on Gull Lake I'm sure they would be very happy with."

Like most real estate agents, Mr. Miller did not shy away from the hard sell. "My clients have given me some wiggle room to increase the offer if it will seal the deal. Once these clients of mine set their sights on something they like, I'm afraid it's very difficult for them to let it go. And money really is no object."

"Well, how nice for them. Listen, Mr. Miller, is it?" The man nodded. Isabel's patience was running thin, but she was going to make one last attempt to nicely get him to go away before simply closing the door in his face. "You can do all the wiggling you like, but there is no deal to be sealed here, so I suggest you encourage your clients to set their sights elsewhere. So, if you'll excuse me." Isabel turned and headed up the path to the front door, talking to the dogs.

"A million two!" the agent yelled after her.

Isabel stopped and turned back to the man. Now she was annoyed. "Giving up the home where I was raised, and where I raised my own children, in exchange for money, no matter what the amount, is nothing, as I think I may have just mentioned, that I would ever consider. In fact, I find the whole notion rather offensive. So you see, Mr. Miller, money is no object for me, either. Have a nice afternoon, and best of luck to you."

The dejected broker watched as Isabel's front door closed behind her. He reluctantly surrendered and got into his car to leave, but not before putting his business card under one of the windshield wipers on Isabel's van.

Once inside, the dollar amount the broker had yelled out began to sink in a little. Obviously it was a lot of money, but as she had told him, there was something she found offensive about the offer. Something about the arrogance of people like his clients who were rich enough to make such an offer, assuming it would be too much money for someone like her to pass up, bothered her. Many people would probably jump at the opportunity to cash in like that, but Isabel wasn't one of them. She had never aspired to be rich—which was a good thing, because she had never been anywhere close to it—but the thought of trading in her beloved home in order to attain that status was completely alien to her. Abigail was right. Money could do terrible things to people. And after learning about what money had done to the Bachmeier family, Isabel certainly had a whole new appreciation for being, if not poor, a woman of modest means, and one who had no interest in ever giving up her weekly coupon clipping.

Chapter 13

When Isabel walked into the Land's End, Frances was already at their table reading the paper and drinking her coffee. Frances looked up at her, and instead of a simple *good morning*, handed the newspaper across the table to her. The headline of the *Gull Harbor Gazette* read: "Newlywed Sunset Cruise Turns Tragic."

Isabel shook her head and handed it back. "Do you think I could have a cup of coffee before you bombard me with the latest tragedy?"

Frances ignored her friend's very reasonable request and began reading the article to her out loud: "I'll cut to the chase. 'The Indiana couple's twenty-two-foot sailboat was spotted by nearby boaters heading back toward the harbor just after sunset. The boat was next spotted by the same group of boaters capsized at approximately nine fifteen p.m. Coast Guard were notified and were on the scene approximately fifteen minutes later. After righting the boat, the two bodies were discovered inside the cabin. The Indianapolis couple's names have not been released, pending notification of next of kin.'"

Isabel shook her head solemnly. "That's just awful. Those poor kids . . . just starting out their lives together. So sad. But thanks Frances. What a nice story to start the day with."

Kayla arrived with coffee. She could see Isabel was up-set, and she knew why. "Isn't that just about the saddest story you've ever heard? Dying on their *honeymoon*." Isabel contin-ued shaking her head, thoughtfully stirring her coffee before taking her first sip. She then noticed Frances staring across the table at her with a funny look.

"What is it, Frances? Is there another happy tale you'd like to share?"

"What is it? I'll tell you! Those kids must have drowned sometime between nine and nine thirty p.m., which was right around the time I heard the Indian drum—twice!"

"Oh, good Lord. Here we go. I just don't understand why you are so obsessed with something as nonsensical as this old folktale."

"You can 'oh, good Lord' and 'here we go' all you like, but I was sitting out on my porch and I heard it plain as day, two beats in a row, just after sunset."

"Frances, that's just. . ." Isabel's voice began to trail off, and suddenly she looked almost stricken, alarming both Kayla and Frances, who asked in concert, "What's wrong?"

Isabel shook herself back to reality and took another sip of coffee. "Nothing . . . I just remembered something I forgot to do." What she was not prepared to share at the moment was that she had just remembered saying goodnight to Beverly in her driveway the previous night, sometime between nine and nine thirty p.m., and hearing two loud, ominous claps of what they both assumed was thunder, despite clear skies. But that was crazy, she told herself. She was not going to let Fran-ces plant such a ridiculous idea in her head.

"Good morning, Mrs. Puddles!" Andy sang out as Isabel walked into the store.

"Good morning, Andy." She looked around the store and peeked into the office. "Where's Freddie?"

"He's back in lawn and garden. We just got a new shipment of bird feeders. He asked me to watch the counter until you got in. Guess I can go back and help him out now."

Andy disappeared down the broom and mop aisle just as Ramush entered carrying a manila envelope. "Good morning, Isabel."

"Good morning, Ramush. Give me just a moment. I think my cousin forgot I had a meeting scheduled with you." Isabel picked up the phone and hit a button. "Freddie, please pick up line two. Freddie, line two." The phone buzzed five seconds later. "Good morning, my dear . . . Remember I'm starting at noon today? I have a meeting upstairs . . . That's okay . . . All right, I'll see you back here at noon." Isabel hung up and smiled at Ramush. "Shall we go upstairs?"

Once upstairs, Ramush sat down across from Isabel and smiled. "She wasn't at all what you expected, was she, Isabel."

Isabel didn't mince words. "No. If I'm being honest, Ramush, what I expected was what all of us locals believed about her—a spooky old rich woman, rumored to be as crazy as a bedbug, living in a rundown old mansion and talking to her dolls."

Ramush laughed heartily. "I will concede that Bachmeier Hall could use some freshening up, but I would hardly call it rundown. And she's really quite sane, as you witnessed yourself. Of course there was that unfortunate incident with those Jehovah's Witnesses, but we all have our bad days, don't we?" Ramush burst into laughter again. "Not sure where that particular rumor got started, but we've sure had some laughs over it."

Isabel smiled. "I will say that I was happily surprised, and relieved to see she was quite normal, relatively speaking. I do have to admit I'm still a little bewildered by her lack of concern over her nephew's disappearance, not to mention the hostility she still has for her dead brother."

"Her brother was a contemptible human being. I share her hostility toward him to this day. And his son was a chip off the old block. I haven't lost a lot of sleep over his misfortune, either, to be honest. I know that may sound very harsh to you, but that's how I feel."

Well, that didn't leave a lot of room for interpretation. Showing compassion was not a sentiment Ramush shared with Abigail either. But Isabel needed to focus on the task at hand, which was to locate Jacob. Psychoanalyzing Abigail and Ramush or passing judgment on them for their lack of concern for human life was not part of her new job description. She took out her notebook and began to pepper Ramush with some of the questions she had jotted down at her lunch with Abigail. He also then provided her with what little documentation he had brought along. This included a copy of Jacob's birth certificate, which he had acquired from Colleen years before, and their last known address in Madison. Isabel asked about Colleen's family, but there wasn't much to go on there. Colleen's parents were both deceased, and her only sibling, a younger sister, Sharon, had moved back to Ireland and married, but he didn't know her married name.

"She moved *back* to Ireland?" Isabel asked.

"Yes, both Colleen and her sister were born in Ireland," he explained.

"Do you think it's possible Colleen and Jacob may have moved back to Ireland, too? Had she ever mentioned that to you as a possibility? Because that would complicate matters just a smidge."

"I don't think it likely. Colleen was only three or four years old when they came to the United States, so she was a pretty all-American girl."

"But still an avenue to explore, I suppose. Let me ask you this, Ramush. To your knowledge, do you think Colleen ever

told Jacob who his father was? I see Skip isn't listed as the father on Jacob's birth certificate."

"No he was not. And you'll see that Colleen gave Jacob
her family surname of Gallagher. She and Mr. Bachmeier
agreed it was probably best he didn't know who his father
was, at least not until he was much older. But it's entirely possible he may still have no idea. He was very young when Mr.
Bachmeier died, but I would think he would still have *some*
memory of him."

"And I understand Colleen was engaged to be married. So
if her husband adopted Jacob and took his last name, which is
quite possible since he *was* so young, we may not be looking
for a Jacob Gallagher."

"I believe that may in fact be the case, because I certainly
have had no luck finding a Jacob Gallagher or a Dr. Colleen
Gallagher, either, so she is likely no longer using her maiden
name. But of course I'm not the super-sleuth you are, Isabel."

Isabel waved the compliment away. "But what if Jacob *was*
made aware of his father's identity and the circumstances surrounding his birth and simply didn't want to be found? If he
really wanted to disappear, as first-generation Irish he would
be eligible for dual citizenship, if I'm not mistaken. So he may
have moved to Ireland himself, even if his mother didn't."

"These are all avenues to explore, but we must find him
regardless of his name, or where he lives. If he's herding sheep
in the Irish countryside, we still need to find him. There is a
vast family fortune at stake here, and as you now know, the
future of the Bachmeier Foundation to consider. You have
to understand that the foundation is Miss Bachmeier's life's
work. Her brother tried to take it from her once, and her
nephew was attempting to do what his father had failed to
do. If Jacob is not a man of integrity, she must plan her will,
and decide what will happen to the foundation, accordingly.
If we are unable to find him, and he were to suddenly turn up

and lay claim to the estate as the sole surviving heir one day, and with intentions driven purely by greed, he could potentially destroy and dismantle everything, just as his father and half-brother had attempted. Miss Bachmeier has earned the right to leave this world, when her time comes, unencumbered with that concern. And I will do whatever is within my power to ensure that does not happen."

"You're very devoted to her, aren't you, Ramush?"

"Yes, I am very devoted to Miss Bachmeier, and to her father's memory and his legacy. And Jacob is very much a part of Mr. Bachmeier's legacy."

Isabel was touched by his loyalty but she had another lingering question that remained unanswered. "Ramush, do you mind if I ask how Mr. Bachmeier died? It doesn't seem to be a subject Miss Bachmeier is willing to broach."

Ramush stared at her for a moment, as if deciding if or how he should respond to her question. "I'm trying to think of the best way to answer that, Isabel."

His hesitancy in addressing such a simple question, along with Abigail's dodging of the same question, made her think the truth behind how Mr. Bachmeier died may very well be up for debate. Isabel turned to her computer and put her newly acquired Internet research skills to work. She had grown to love the Google and did not at all miss the tedious chore of having to look things up in her outdated Encyclopedia Britannica or make a trip to the library. In an instant she had her answer. "Mr. Bachmeier committed *suicide*?"

Ramush was stumped for a moment, until he realized what had just happened. "Oh! Googled again! I'm still a bit frightened by it, aren't you?"

"Used to be," Isabel replied as she read on, then looked back at Ramush with a pained expression. "A self-inflicted gunshot wound? Poor Abigail . . . That's horrible. I hope she wasn't the one who discovered him."

"No . . . that was me," Ramush said quietly as he stared out the window, wincing slightly as though seeing the grisly scene in his head all over again. "Yes, it was indeed horrible. And it's something I've tried to erase from my memory for decades, unsuccessfully. But you know what was even more horrible?" He didn't wait for an answer. "Knowing to my very core that there was absolutely no possibility that Mr. Bachmeier actually *did* commit suicide." An odd expression then crossed his face, as if he were trying to telegraph what he was reluctant to say out loud.

Isabel got the message. "So you think somebody murdered him?"

Ramush nodded. "I don't *think* it . . . I know it."

"Tell me why," Isabel asked.

"First of all, Mr. Bachmeier hated guns, and I know for a fact that he didn't and wouldn't *own* a gun. Secondly, not since before Mrs. Bachmeier became ill had I seen him as happy as he had been in the weeks leading up to his death. Colleen had agreed to bring Jacob to the Bachmeier estate in Whitefish Bay for Christmas that year. Mr. Bachmeier had finally kicked his deadbeat son out of the house, so there was no longer any concern she or Jacob would cross paths with him. Once that was settled, he had an enormous Christmas tree set up in the great room, and he and I and the maids all drank eggnog one night and decorated it. He had just bought the boy a Shetland pony, too, and had a little stable with a riding ring built on the grounds. Christmas was less than two weeks away and he was so excited to spend the holiday with his grandson, *and* with Colleen, whom he had grown very fond of. Her family was coming for Christmas dinner, and Mr. Bachmeier had his chef plan a veritable feast, complete with a roast goose. Now, does that sound like a man who was planning to kill himself?"

"No, it certainly doesn't. That's just a heartbreaking story. It sounds like he was a wonderful man."

"He was the kindest man I ever knew." Ramush looked out the window again. Isabel felt sure he was fighting back tears. "He never let his wealth corrupt his character. That's quite rare, I've come to understand."

"I would agree that it seems to be the exception to the rule, yes. But who do you suspect wanted to see Mr. Bachmeier dead?"

Ramush sent another unspoken message across the desk, one Isabel quickly received.

"Skip?"

Ramush nodded slowly before speaking. "I am convinced that he either did it himself or hired somebody to do it and then make it *look* like a suicide. Mr. Bachmeier had no enemies. He was beloved by *everybody*, with one exception. His son."

"Was there an investigation into his death?" Isabel asked.

"No. Or if there was, I was unaware of it. I shared my suspicions with detectives of the Milwaukee Police Department, but the coroner had determined it was suicide, so there was really nothing they could do. I was never convinced there hadn't been some bribery involved. Back in those days the Milwaukee Police Department did not have a particularly sterling reputation."

"And did you share your suspicions with Miss Bachmeier?"

"She was even more certain than I was, but again, there was no way to prove it. And she didn't want to invite the publicity that would come along with an investigation naming her brother as a murder suspect. I did not agree, but it was not my place to take things any further."

"And you think Skip was capable of murdering his own father?"

"Skip Bachmeier was, in my opinion, the very definition of a man with narcissistic personality disorder. I think he was capable of *anything*. And he was the only one who had motive."

"And what exactly was that? The stocks he gave to Colleen and Jacob?"

"That, and the fact that Mr. Bachmeier had lost any hope his son would ever become a man he could trust or respect, so he had decided to change his will, leaving his controlling interest in the company to Miss Bachmeier, making her the majority shareholder of the Bachmeier Brewery Company. I'm convinced Skip caught wind of his father's intentions and decided that murdering him would solve the problem. What he didn't realize was that whatever information he received was too late in coming, because Mr. Bachmeier had already made those alterations to his will. It was already a done deal."

"This certainly sheds a new light on why Abigail speaks about her brother the way she does."

"She knew in her heart that when Skip feared their father was not going to leave him what he felt was rightfully his, he murdered him. But, as far as I'm concerned, in the end Skip Bachmeier *did* get what was rightfully his," Ramush said with some authority.

That's an odd way of putting it, Isabel thought. The loyalty Ramush showed for Abigail and her father was certainly an admirable quality, but just how far might that loyalty extend? Far enough for him to somehow arrange for Skip Bachmeier's plane to crash into Lake Michigan more than two decades ago? And, given the suspicious nature of Trey Bachmeier's disappearance, might he have arranged for him to be sent to the same watery grave? This theory left open another possibility, actually two. If this were the case, was Abigail never the wiser for it, or, might she have been complicit?

Ramush stood up to leave. "Isabel, I am going to leave you to your work. Please let me know if there is anything else I can do. I can't tell you what finding Jacob would mean to Miss Bachmeier, and to me."

Isabel smiled and stood up to shake his hand. "I promise I will do my very best to find him."

"That's all we can ask of you. Thank you. Oh, I nearly forgot." He reached back into the envelope and pulled out an old photograph. "Here . . . I took this at Jacob's fourth birthday party." He handed it across the desk to Isabel. It was a photo of a smiling Colleen, Jacob, and Mr. Bachmeier, all sitting around a table with an enormous birthday cake.

"Jacob's adorable. And Colleen really was a beauty, wasn't she? They all look so happy."

"It was a very happy day. I took another of just Mr. Bachmeier and Jacob, which I framed and gave to Miss Bachmeier. It now sits on her bedside table."

Isabel handed the photo back.

"No, I had that copy made for you," Ramush said. "I thought it might be helpful."

"Yes, it may well be. Thank you."

Ramush nodded his signature nod and left Isabel sitting at her desk, trying to process everything she had just learned. Now she was left with a whole slew of new questions, but none of them having anything to do with the job she had been tasked with. Or maybe, everything was related.

Could Mr. Bachmeier's death have in fact been a suicide, despite what his daughter and Ramush believed? And were Skip's plane crash and Trey's disappearance, and likely death, both simply unfortunate, albeit coincidental accidents? Or was it possible three generations of Bachmeier men had *all* been murdered? And an even more disturbing question had to be considered. Could the person responsible for arranging two of those murders be the man who had just left her office? After

all, if there were a first prize for motive, both Abigail Bachmeier and Ramush would have to share the blue ribbon. And
finally, an even more troubling question came to mind . . .
What if Jacob was in danger of meeting the same fate as his
father and half-brother if, in Miss Bachmeier's opinion, he
were deemed unworthy of carrying on the Bachmeier family
legacy and inheriting the fortune that came with it? Would
her most ardent and loyal protector ensure that he was taken
out of the running? Perhaps in finding Jacob she would be
inadvertently sealing his fate. Then again, maybe Isabel had
to ask herself if she had read one too many murder mysteries,
and watched one too many episodes of *McMillan & Wife*, or
Murder, She Wrote over the years, and was now merely letting
her imagination get the better of her. But, in order to be sure
she was not unknowingly being dragged into a murder conspiracy, even though it was a plot even Agatha Christie herself
might call a bit of a stretch, there were still some more threads
that needed pulling for her to be comfortable proceeding. Although it still seemed highly unlikely, such a worst-case scenario was something she had to at least consider. If she didn't,
and she was unknowingly leading a lamb to slaughter, she
could never live with herself.

Isabel still had an hour before she had to be downstairs to
relieve Freddie, so she got right to work. An hour of researching flew by, but she couldn't find a Dr. Colleen Gallagher or
a Jacob Gallagher anywhere in Milwaukee, the suburbs, or
anywhere in Wisconsin. She would expand her search nationwide as soon as she had the chance, and if necessary, start
searching in Ireland. But just before going downstairs, she sent
an e-mail to the University of Wisconsin–Madison Alumni
Association. In the spirit of the means at least sometimes jus-
tifying the ends, she resorted to telling a white lie, inquiring
as to how she might locate her old college roommate, Colleen

Gallagher, whom she had unfortunately lost touch with over the years.

When she walked into the store, Freddie was already taking off his red vest and getting ready to leave. "Hello there, Cousin. Well, I'm off! I told Andy he could take an hour for lunch today. His mother's coming by and taking him over to the Copper Kettle."

"Oh that's nice. All right, Freddie, have a good golf game, or a match, or whatever it is you call it."

"I call it an exercise in patience and futility, with just a touch of masochism. I keep going out there, summer after summer, smacking a little white ball around with a stick, and I *still* can't shoot below a hundred. And we are not talking Pebble Beach here, this is the Kentwater Country Club, which is only slightly more challenging than miniature golf. It might be time for me to finally just admit the truth."

"Which is?"

"Which *is* that I am one lousy golfer!" Freddie laughed his trademark laugh. "But I guess it keeps me out of trouble. I'll see you in a few hours, Iz!"

No sooner had Freddie gone out the back door than a pretty woman with a tan, somewhere in her forties, dressed in a smart and casual summer outfit, walked through the front door. Isabel immediately knew who it was. "You *must* be Andy's mother!" The woman looked a little shocked. Isabel continued, "It would be impossible not to see the resemblance."

The woman smiled and put her hand out. "Judy Wainwright. And, yes, I'm Andy's mother. And *you* must be Isabel."

"Isabel Puddles. Very nice to meet you, Judy," she said as they shook hands. "We just love your son around here. Best stock boy we've ever had! And he's becoming a very good salesclerk to boot."

"That's very nice to hear. Yes, we like him too." Andy suddenly appeared around the corner. She smiled at him and ruffled his hair. "My husband and I are thinking about keeping him."

"Well, we are, too!" Isabel said as she patted Andy on the shoulder and winked at him.

"Hi, Mom," Andy said, slightly embarrassed.

"Hi, honey. You hungry?"

Andy nodded, then turned to Isabel. "Are you sure it's okay for me to take a full hour, Mrs. Puddles? I hate to leave you here alone."

"You go enjoy your lunch. I think I can manage."

"Okay, thanks. But if you get a mad rush, just call me on my cell and I can be back in five minutes," Andy said in earnest as he took off his work vest and stashed it under the counter. At that very moment an elderly farmer in dirt-covered overalls came in the front door.

"And *this* is what constitutes a mad rush here at Freddie's Hardware. Hello there, Bill!"

Andy and Judy laughed and waved on their way out the door. Farmer Bill grunted something that sounded vaguely like a hello and walked up to the counter. Isabel looked him over. "I hope you're here to buy some new overalls. You look like you just crawled in here on your belly. Does your wife know you're coming into town looking like that?"

"No! And what she don't know won't hurt her. Now, I need some batteries, Isabel," Farmer Bill announced as he pulled a battery out of his pocket and set it down on the counter, then looked up at her. "Whatever size this one here is . . . D, I believe."

He stood staring at her for a few seconds. Isabel stared back. "Well, you know where to find them, Bill. Good Lord," Isabel scolded, but in a friendly way. Farmer Bill, one of the biggest cherry farmers in the county, turned and shuffled down the battery aisle. Isabel busied herself at the counter until Farmer Bill returned with two packs of D batteries. "You know, Isabel, if I drive up to Wellington I can get these a whole lot cheaper at the—"

Isabel put her hand up. "Don't you do it! You know how we feel about mentioning that name around here, Bill." She put her reading glasses on and began ringing him up while starting to make some small talk. "So I see cherries have gone up this year. Three ninety-nine a pound?" she said, followed by a whistle for emphasis. "You know, I'll bet if I drive over to Mason County, I can find them for closer to two ninety-nine, maybe even less."

"Yeah, but they ain't near as flavorful as Kentwater County cherries," Farmer Bill replied with indignation. "*And* you have to drive clear to Mason County to get 'em! Waste of time and gas."

Isabel pulled her glasses down onto the bridge of her nose and looked across the counter at her customer. "You see where I'm going with this, don't you, Bill?"

Farmer Bill shook his head and reached for his wallet. "You made your point, Isabel. What do I owe you?"

Isabel happily finished ringing him up, counted back his change, and put his batteries into a little brown paper bag. She slid his purchase across the counter with a smile, then reached under the counter and got one of the lollipops she kept to give out to the kids, then handed it to him across the counter. "You don't get lollipops up at the *you know where*, now do you?"

Farmer Bill finally managed a smile. He took the lollipop, unwrapped it, and put it in his mouth before opening the front door. "Thanks, Isabel. See you next time."

"Bye now, Bill. And thanks for shopping with us!"

Isabel smiled and went back to straightening up the counter, but in no time she was thinking about her meeting with

Ramush. She was anxious to check her e-mails to see if the
Wisconsin Alumni Association had gotten back to her, even
though she knew it was a long shot. She took out a pen and
pad of paper and started making a list of possible ways to track
down either Jacob or his mother. Then she had an idea, but it
would have to wait until Andy and his mother got back from
lunch.

"How was lunch?" Isabel asked when Andy and his mom
walked back through the front door.

"Delicious!" Judy answered as she kissed her son on the
cheek and embarrassing him once again. She turned around
and opened the front door to leave. "I'll see you tonight,
honey. Bye, Isabel. Lovely to meet you."

But Isabel had something on her mind. "Excuse me, Judy?
Before you leave, I wonder if I might ask you a quick question."

Judy turned around. "Sure."

"Andy told me your husband's a physician, and that you're
a nurse. Don't worry, I'm not asking for free medical advice!
Anyway, I know you're from Milwaukee, so I was just wondering if you might possibly have ever heard of a Dr. Colleen Gallagher. She went to University of Wisconsin Medical
School, and I believe she may be in practice in the Milwaukee
area. Or at least was at one time."

Andy's mom's gears were turning. "Colleen Gallagher . . .
hmmm . . . Let me think."

Isabel continued, "She had a son named Jacob. Real pretty
girl. Red hair."

Andy's mom thought it over a little more, then slowly
shook her head. "I'm sorry, Isabel, that name just doesn't ring
a bell. Who is she, if you don't mind my asking?"

"She's just an old friend I'm trying to track down." White
lie number two for the day, but there was no turning back

now. "You know how you lose track of people sometimes? Harder to do *these* days, though, isn't it? Seems like the whole world's connected today, whether we like it or not."

"Isn't that the truth?" Judy agreed and opened the door again. "Well, I'm sorry I couldn't be of more help. But I'll ask my husband when I see him tonight. He may know her, or at least know *of* her."

"That's very nice of you, Judy. Thank you."

"You're quite welcome," she replied before heading out the door.

Andy had his red vest back on and was ready to get back to work. Isabel smiled at him. "Your mother is a lovely woman, Andy. But I would expect no less."

"Thank you, Mrs. Puddles. Mom's a good egg, like you say. She can be a little nosy, though."

"Well, young man, being nosy is very near the top of a mother's job description. It comes just after worrying and right before nagging."

Andy laughed. "She's not a nagger. That's my dad's department. Okay, I'm going back to lawn and garden and do some watering."

Moments after Andy disappeared down the aisle, the front door opened again and Judy reappeared. "You know, Isabel, it just occurred to me that I do vaguely remember a Colleen *Doyle*. She was an ear, nose, and throat specialist. I knew her from St. Mary's, but that's been quite a few years. She was very well regarded. Pretty redhead, and I think I do remember her having a son."

"You know, that could very well be her! Doyle may be her married name. Ear, nose, and throat specialist, you said?" Isabel asked while scribbling her notes.

"Yes, but I'll talk to my husband tonight and see if he knows anything more. If he does, I'll send Andy back tomorrow with the info."

"That would be wonderful. Thanks so much, Judy!"

"You're most welcome," Judy replied, and disappeared out the front door again.

Isabel looked down at her notes. "Hmmm . . . Dr. Colleen Doyle . . . ear, nose, and throat specialist," she said to herself. "Well, I guess it's worth a try."

Chapter 14

Thanks to the promising lead she got from Andy's mother, Isabel was able to track down a Dr. Colleen Doyle, who was indeed listed as one of Milwaukee's premier ear, nose, and throat doctors. Isabel found Dr. Doyle's contact information online and placed a call. When she asked if she could speak to the doctor, she was told by the friendly receptionist that Dr. Doyle could not take any calls at the moment, but she would be happy to take a message. Isabel gave the woman her name and phone number, and was about to hang up when the receptionist asked, "May I tell her what this is regarding?"

Isabel was stumped for a moment. She wasn't sure she even had the right person, but didn't want to scare her off if she did. "Oh . . . it's a personal matter, but rather important, so I sure would appreciate it if she could call me back at her earliest convenience."

"I'll be sure and give her the message," the receptionist replied. "Have a nice day."

Not even an hour passed before Isabel's cell phone rang. It was none other than Dr. Colleen Doyle. "Hello, Ms. Puddles? This is Dr. Colleen Doyle. My receptionist gave me a message that you had a personal matter to discuss with me? What can I do for you?"

Isabel wasn't sure how best to reveal exactly what this personal matter was, but before she could overthink it, she just went ahead and blurted it out. "It's about your son, Jacob."

Dead silence followed, which to Isabel meant this poor woman either had no clue what she was talking about or she knew *exactly* what she was talking about and wasn't sure how to react. It turned out to be the latter. "What about my son? Is he all right?"

Isabel was ecstatic to discover this was indeed the Colleen she was looking for, but now she was scrambling for words. "So far as I know, yes, he's fine, Dr. Doyle . . . but that's why I'm contacting you. I was hoping you might help me get in touch with him."

"And why would you need to get in touch with my son?"

"I don't mean to worry you, Dr. Doyle. Jacob's not in any kind of trouble." Isabel really was flying by the seat of her work khakis at this point, but she figured that just coming out with it might be the best approach. She'd told enough white lies for one day. "I'm a private investigator, and I've been hired to find a young man named Jacob Gallagher. I believe Gallagher is your maiden name, is it not . . . ?" Another awkward silence followed. "My client would very much like to meet with your son, and you, too, if you could just—"

"And who exactly *is* your client? And what do they want with my son? Or me?" Dr. Doyle asked in a less than friendly tone.

"I'm afraid I'm not at liberty to provide you with those details just yet. Would it be possible for me to talk to you or your son about this in person?" Isabel hadn't thought through the fact that this would require a trip to Milwaukee.

"My son and I have not been in touch for quite a while, and I'm not entirely sure *where* he is. But even if I did know, I wouldn't be inclined to tell you. Assuming your client is who I think it likely is, please send my condolences to Miss Bachmeier regarding her nephew, and let her know that neither my son nor I wish to become involved in any matter involving the Bachmeier family. Now if you'll excuse me I have patients to see. But before I say goodbye, I'm going to ask you, respectfully, as Jacob's mother, that you not involve my son in any of whatever Bachmeier family drama may be unfolding in the wake of Trey Bachmeier's disappearance. Jacob has no idea he has any connection to that family. And if you know their history, I think you can understand why I have chosen not to tell him."

Isabel needed to somehow convince her that it was in her son's best interest for him to finally know the truth, but how? "I can certainly understand why you would be concerned, but—"

"I don't mean to be rude, but I really must go. And please don't contact me again. I have no intention of changing my position. Goodbye."

Dr. Doyle hung up, leaving Isabel slightly dumbfounded. She couldn't believe she had been so lucky in finding Jacob's mother so quickly, and how unlucky she had been in convincing her to unveil his whereabouts. She was still holding her cell phone when Freddie walked through the front door. "Hello, Cousin! Have sales been through the roof? Can I retire yet?"

"I wouldn't say through the roof, no, but things will pick up as we get closer to the Fourth, Freddie, they always do."

"You're right. I need to stop worrying. I'm sure that a nationwide hardware conglomerate building a store thirty miles from here, with prices ten to twenty percent lower than ours, won't eventually squeeze me out of business."

Isabel was too busy thinking about the conversation she had just had to go down this well-traveled road with her cousin. "Hey, Freddie . . . do you think you could spare me for a couple days? I think I need to make a quick trip to Milwaukee."

"Milwaukee, huh? I assume this has something to do with the case you're working on for Abigail Bachmeier?"

"Yes, but you know I can't talk about any of the details beyond that."

"Did I ask? If you were able to secure free kegs of Bachmeier beer for the Fourth of July, I might show a little more interest, but otherwise it's none of my business. How do you plan to get there?"

"I'll take the *Badger*."

Freddie thought that one over for a moment. "As I recall, the only other time you were on the *Badger* you had to deal with some pretty awful seasickness. Why not fly? You'll be there in thirty minutes, tops."

"Yes, but I'd have to take one of those puddle jumpers. You know how I feel about flying, anyway, Freddie. You couldn't get me on one of those little planes for all the tea in China. If I skip breakfast and take some Dramamine, I should be fine crossing as long as the lake's not too rough."

"I hope you don't plan on going alone. That would worry me."

"I'm not crossing the Atlantic, Freddie. I'll be fine going alone."

Freddie slipped his red vest on. "I guess I could spare you for a couple days. Andy and I can handle the throngs. When were you planning on going?"

"I was thinking I'd go tomorrow morning and get it out of the way."

"All right, but please be careful, Izzy. We almost lost you once, and none of us wants to go through that again."

Isabel smiled. "I don't either, Freddie. Believe me."

★ ★ ★

After getting home from work, Isabel went out to sit on the dock to enjoy the quiet of the magic hour. She gazed out at the lake and sipped a cup of chamomile tea while Jackpot and Corky ran back and forth, stalking minnows, as usual. She was thinking about her trip across the Big Lake tomorrow and what she might expect when she went in to try to talk with Dr. Doyle in person. But the quiet was suddenly shattered when she heard a familiar sound. There was no need to turn around and look to know it was Frances racing down the road leading to Poplar Bluff as if she were trying to outrun the law. Two loud honks announced her arrival as she skidded to a stop in the driveway. The magic hour had just ceased to be so magical. A minute later she felt Frances's feet hit the dock. "Well, you're not going to believe this!" she yelled.

If that was her opener, Isabel knew she was in for another Frances Spitler supercharged monologue. "Hello, Frances . . . Beautiful evening, isn't it?"

"Sure, whatever." Frances was now standing in front of her with her hands on her hips. "Hank put an offer in on that condo in Grand Haven I told you about without even telling me! Now he wants to put our house on the market! He's already talked to an agent, his brother-in-law, you know the one with the lazy eye? Do you want to know what I told him? I'll tell you what I told him. I said, 'Well, I hope you'll be very happy living there by yourself, Hank, because our home for the past twenty-five years is in my name, too, it's paid for, *and*, I have no intention of selling it!' And you want to know what else I told him? I'll tell you what else I told him. I said, 'Hank, I want a divorce!'"

Isabel was genuinely shocked. She never believed things would ever go this far. "A divorce, Frances? Really? And how did Hank respond to that?"

"He didn't. He just walked out the door, got in his car, and drove off. Probably sitting at the Moose Lodge right now, telling the bartender what an ogre he's married to! But I don't care. I'm done! Now I need to find myself a good lawyer."

"I think you need to slow your roll, as my kids say. There must be some middle ground here, Frances. You shouldn't have to turn the dial all the way up to divorce so fast. Have you talked to your kids about this?"

"I'm not divorcing my kids! I'm divorcing their father! And I don't really care whether they approve or not."

"So you're going to throw in the towel after thirty years of marriage because your husband got a big promotion and bought you a condo on the water? I would hardly call those irreconcilable differences."

"Oh, so you're on Hank's side now?"

"I'm on the side of being reasonable, Frances, and I think you should think about joining me there. You have no idea what kind of Pandora's box you might be opening when you start talking divorce. I still remember going through Ginny's divorce from Ralph. Granted, there was never a husband who needed divorcing more than that deadbeat, but it was still a long and painful slog. And have you thought about what it would be like to be a divorced woman alone at your age?"

"At *my* age? News flash! My age is two months younger than you, Isabel Puddles, and you seem to get along just fine alone. But you don't think *I* can manage?"

"It's not about managing. I just don't think you'd like living in that big house all alone, Frances. You and I are very different animals. I happen to *like* living alone."

Frances paused on this point. "Most of the time I feel like I'm living alone anyway, even *with* him in the house. Can you imagine how alone I would feel living in a new town where I don't know a soul? What am I going to do, just sit and look out at the water and twiddle my thumbs? Here I at least have you to keep me sane."

Isabel laughed. "Well, I'm not sure I'm fulfilling my duties very well if keeping you sane is my role in this friendship."

"Very funny."

"I thought things had gotten better after you left him last year. Didn't Hank sign your list of demands before you agreed to go back?"

"Wasn't worth the paper it was written on. Things improved for a little while, but it didn't last. And I knew it wouldn't." Frances was beginning to calm down a bit, and finally sat down on the bench next to Isabel. "I think it would be good for *him* to live alone, *really* live alone. He's starting his new job pretty soon now, so he was planning for us to be all moved into this condo by the time that happens. Well, it's not *going* to happen!"

Isabel was feeling bad for Frances now. This situation was getting pretty dire. "Frances, I understand completely. I really do. Of course I don't want you to move, and I'm not suggesting you *do* move if you are this opposed to it. Hank had no business making an offer on a new home without consulting with you first, or even accepting that promotion without telling you, knowing it would mean moving. But I don't think *your* next move has to be a divorce. Why don't you go down and see the place? You might love it! Tell him you'll come down on weekends for a while. No need for you to be there during the week anyway, especially if he's working long hours in a new job. Seeing each other only on weekends might spark a little romance again."

"Oh, please . . . I couldn't spark any romance in Hank with a blowtorch. But your idea isn't half bad, if he'll agree to it. Wait! What am I saying? Either he agrees to it or I'll divorce him so fast, it'll make his head swim."

Isabel patted Frances on the leg. "I think you should cool off a little and present this idea to him calmly tomorrow. It's a very reasonable compromise, and if he won't agree to it, I'll support you one hundred percent in whatever you decide to do."

"Sell the house and move in with you permanently?"

"Except that."

They both laughed. "You want to order a pizza?" Isabel asked. "I'm starving."

"Me too. You have any wine in the house?"

"Whatever's left in that box you brought over last week."

"That ought to do the trick." Frances put her arm through Isabel's as they walked down the dock. "I don't know what I would ever do without you, Izzy."

"I don't either, Frances . . . I really don't."

Chapter 15

Isabel opted not to tell Frances she was going to Milwaukee in the morning. She didn't want to hear a whole litany of reasons why she *shouldn't* go, plus she would probably insist on coming with her. One of Frances's daughters lived in a Milwaukee suburb, so she would want to turn it into a whole thing, and all Isabel wanted to do was get there, hopefully accomplish her goal, and then get back as soon as possible. She'd call Frances once she was on board the *Badger* so there wouldn't be time for her to make it to the dock in time.

All she had to do now was make sure the dogs were taken care of. The neighbors down the road had a teenage son named Justin who loved Jackpot and Corky, so whenever she was going to be away for any length of time, which very rarely happened, she paid him to come down and dog-sit. Luckily, the dogs were very fond of him, too, so when he arrived bright and early the next morning with treats and a tennis ball, they barely noticed Isabel slipping out of the house with her overnight bag.

Although the *Badger* was a car ferry, Isabel thought it would be less complicated to travel as a passenger and then rent a car across the lake in Manitowoc. From there it was just over an hour's drive south to Milwaukee. After boarding the massive ferry, she found a seat next to a window. She thought she remembered hearing somebody say that being able to see the water, instead of just feeling the motion of it, would help prevent, or at least lessen, seasickness. Or was it the other way around? She would soon find out. After taking the Dramamine, all she could do was hope for the best.

Once they had cleared the harbor and were out in open water, Isabel was still feeling fine, so she got up and walked around the ship a little. It wasn't as busy with tourists as she thought it would be, given that it was the height of the season, but then this was the 7:30 crossing, the first one of the day, and getting up that early wasn't something most people wanted to do while on vacation.

Isabel saw a friendly face behind the snack bar, so she stopped to buy a cup of coffee. She and the snack bar lady, a heavyset woman with curly black hair who looked as if she had been doing this awhile, engaged in some friendly chitchat until curiosity got the better of her and Isabel changed the conversation to a more serious topic. "Terrible thing about that Bachmeier boy falling overboard, isn't it?" she said. "Hard to believe they still haven't found his body."

The woman looked a little surprised they had just made such a sharp turn, but she went along. "Yes, I suppose it's a shame. I'm sorry to see anybody fall into the drink like that. Not exactly great for business, either. But I waited on the kid that day. He was standing right where you're standing now. He was a real . . ." She leaned across the counter and lowered her voice. "We aren't allowed to cuss on the job, so I'll just say he was a real jerk. I deal with my share of 'em, I can tell you. I had one snobby woman yell at me last week because I didn't have regular cream for her coffee. I just have these little containers of Coffee-mate like the one you just used, and didn't seem to mind. But she got herself all wound up

about it. You would have thought I'd just served her soup
with a fork! I kept my mouth shut for as long as I could until
finally I'd had enough. I said, 'Listen, lady, you're on board
a rusty old car ferry, not the Norwegian Cruise Line!' *And* I
told her, 'You're coming from *America's Dairy Land*! Maybe
next time you ought to bring along your own flippin' cream
for your coffee!' Well, that shut her up. It got me a little
talking-to from my supervisor after she complained, but it
was worth it."

Isabel laughed. She liked this woman. "So you were saying the Bachmeier boy was kind of a jerk . . . How so?"

"He was mad I didn't have ice for the soda he just bought,
then mad that I didn't have the potato chips he wanted, and
madder still that I only had regular yellow mustard for his
turkey sandwich, and not Grey Poupon! I mean, are these the
kinds of things rich people have to worry about? Having the
right mustard, and the right cream?"

Isabel was still chuckling when she asked a question that
had been on her mind ever since she heard about the incident. "I see cameras all around this ship. I'm surprised one of
them didn't catch him going over. *Now* we may never know
what happened. Did he fall? Jump? Or could he have been
pushed?"

"I was about ready to push him overboard myself if he
gave me any more lip. As far as the cameras go, well, they're
always on the fritz. I know the first thing the police and the
Coast Guard asked about were the cameras. So they have all
those recordings. But I understand the cameras on the upper
stern deck were not working that day for whatever reason,
so if that's where he went over, you're right. We'll probably
never know."

"And nobody saw him fall?"

"Apparently not. Or heard him scream. I'd certainly let
out a holler if I was falling a few stories down into that lake!"

"So what do *you* think happened to him?" Isabel asked after taking a sip of very bad coffee.

"I have no idea. In fact I'd forgotten all about it until you brought it up. Why are you so interested, anyway?"

"Just curious is all. Must be hard on the family not knowing how he ended up going overboard, on top of not finding his body."

"We got some weather about halfway across that day, that much I remember. Lots of wind and rain came up all of a sudden. So I suppose he could have fallen overboard if he got too close to the railing and wasn't being careful. Or maybe he *did* get pushed. I think we can rule out suicide, though. Nobody who gets that upset about what mustard he's going to put on his turkey sandwich is going to off himself a half hour later. Unless he took it a lot harder than I thought."

Isabel glanced down at the woman's nametag, then reached her hand across the counter. "It's nice to meet you, Sandy, I'm Isabel."

"Pleasure to meet *you*, Isabel." Sandy's attention was suddenly drawn to a gentleman standing farther down the counter trying to summon her by impatiently tapping a coin on the glass top. Sandy leaned over the counter again. "This one looks like a real piece'a work. Excuse me. It's been nice chatting with you. Maybe I'll see you on your way back across." Sandy turned to the man and started walking his way. "Hold your horses. And stop with that tapping! You crack the glass on this countertop and you're gonna be walkin' the plank, mister!"

Isabel went away chuckling to herself. Sandy was a real character. And Isabel liked characters. She continued walking around the ship while she drank her coffee. It really was terrible but she needed the caffeine. The sun was out and there wasn't a cloud in the sky. The lake looked beautiful too. She rarely saw it this calm, so she had definitely picked a good day to travel. She also realized that more than an hour into the voyage, she hadn't felt so much as a flutter of seasickness.

After going back to her seat she thought about what Sandy had said about her experience with Trey Bachmeier, then quickly redirected her focus onto the job she was hired to do, which was *not* to find out what happened to *him*. She was sure the authorities were more than able to get to the bottom of that. Instead, she began putting together a strategy for the best way to approach Colleen Doyle. She hadn't gotten very far with that, however, before she drifted off to sleep.

Driving through the downtown of a city the size of Milwaukee was a bit of a challenge for a small-town girl like Isabel. Rush hour in Gull Harbor was four cars stopped at a four-way stop at the same time. But she was holding her own, despite her unease driving a rental car just slightly larger than a roller skate. She was able to find Dr. Doyle's office much easier than she had anticipated, so after finding a parking spot in the lot of the sleek, contemporary-looking medical center, Isabel sat in contemplation for a few moments, thinking about how best to handle things from here. *Don't overthink it*, she began coaching herself. *Just walk in, introduce yourself, and then do your best to convince her that finding Jacob is a good thing.*

When she entered Dr. Doyle's office, Isabel was greeted by a chipper young receptionist who she assumed was the same woman she had spoken to on the phone. "Good afternoon, ma'am," she said through the reception window. "Are you a new patient?"

Isabel smiled. "No, not exactly."

"Okay . . . Well, do you have an appointment?" she asked politely.

"No . . . I'm afraid I don't." Isabel winced apologetically, "but I just need five minutes with the doctor."

"I'm sorry, ma'am, but we don't take walk-ins. The doctor has a very full schedule today."

Isabel looked around the office. It was empty. "I'll tell you what I'm going to do if it's all right with you. I'm going to sit down right over here, and if you could just let Dr. Doyle know I'm here, please? Like I said, I only need five minutes."

The receptionist's smile was fading. "Ma'am, if this is an emergency, there's an urgent-care next door. Or St. Mary's is only four blocks away."

"This isn't an emergency. My ears, nose, and throat are all doing fine. But it *is* very important that I speak with her." Isabel sat down on the sofa and picked up an old issue of *Cosmopolitan* and began to leaf through it.

The receptionist's smile was now fully erased and replaced with a look of frustration. "What's your name, ma'am? I'll let Dr. Doyle know you'd like to speak with her."

"That's very kind of you. Isabel Puddles."

The woman looked confused for a moment. "Wait . . . didn't we talk on the phone yesterday?"

"Yes, I believe we did."

The receptionist shook her head slightly as she stood up. "Excuse me." She disappeared for about a minute, then returned to her desk with a look of resolve. "I'm very sorry, Mrs. Puddles, but Dr. Doyle cannot see you today. And I'm afraid I'll have to ask you to leave the office."

Isabel thought things over for a moment, then forced a smile and stood up. "Well, that's a shame. I came all the way from Michigan this morning to meet her in person and to share some very important information with her . . . Information I think she and her son, Jacob, would find very useful. But I'm not the sort of person who hangs around where I'm not wanted, so I guess I'll be off."

She reached into her purse and pulled out the stack of business cards Freddie had printed up for her, which were bound up with a rubber band. She pulled out one of the embossed cards and gave it a quick glance. This would mark the first time she used one. The card was nothing fancy, and contained pretty straightforward information: ISABEL PUDDLES, PRIVATE INVESTIGATOR followed by her cell phone number and e-mail address. She wasn't crazy about the addition of the Sherlock Holmes hat and the magnifying glass, which she thought looked a little cartoonish, but she appreciated the thought. She set the card down on the receptionist's desk. "If you wouldn't mind passing this on to the doctor, I would appreciate it. Maybe she'll change her mind. Thank you, my dear. I'm sorry to have disrupted your day."

Isabel took the elevator back downstairs and sat in the lobby to think about her next move. She was determined not to leave Milwaukee without meeting Colleen Doyle, but she didn't want to get slapped with a restraining order or arrested for stalking, either. She had been sitting there for a little while, directly across from the elevator, when she heard a ding, then looked up and watched the doors open. A distinguished-looking man with silver hair, wearing a white lab coat and a stethoscope around his neck, stepped out and held the door for an attractive middle-aged woman with beautifully coiffed strawberry-blond hair, wearing a stylish navy-blue pantsuit. As she stepped into the lobby, the man, who Isabel assumed was a doctor, said to his elevator mate, "Join me for a coffee?"

"Thanks, Jack." she said, "but I'll have to take a rain check. It's my son's birthday today, so I'm going to drop by with a gift and visit with him a little."

"All right," the man replied as he turned in the opposite direction and headed down the hall. "I'll see you tomorrow, Colleen."

Isabel perked up like a meerkat. This *had* to be Dr. Doyle, who apparently didn't have such a full schedule, after all. She couldn't believe her luck! And she felt luckier still that she was on her way to see Jacob! She couldn't be 100 percent certain, but 90 percent was good enough. Now she had to make a split-second decision. Should she introduce herself and risk being shut down in person or should she do what any good private eye would do, and tail her? Isabel chose the latter.

She waited until the woman named Colleen, and hopefully Colleen *Doyle*, made her way through the revolving doors, then quick-stepped it right behind her. She pushed the door with a little too much elbow grease and nearly went around a second time before exiting somewhat indelicately into the front entrance of the building. Colleen Doyle or not, Isabel was now officially following this lady regardless. She then got into a white luxury sedan parked in a space designated DOCTORS ONLY. Isabel was now at 95 percent certainty that this was her girl. The tiny economy car Isabel had rented was a little farther away, so she picked up her pace to get to it while keeping her eye on the white car. She was just starting up her rental when the woman passed her, talking on her phone. Isabel pulled out and followed right behind. Minutes later they were getting on the freeway and driving through downtown Milwaukee.

Keeping up with the white car was no easy task, but Isabel managed to stay with it for the next several miles until the car's right blinker began signaling as they approached the next exit. At the bottom of the off-ramp, the white car made another right turn, and Isabel followed for a few more minutes into a leafy, upscale neighborhood with stately old homes. Two minutes later, the white car turned into the driveway of a large, elegant redbrick mansion with white columns. It looked like Dr. Colleen Doyle had done very well for herself.

But as Isabel pulled off to the side of the quiet, tree-lined street, she noticed an unobtrusive sign at the head of the drive: HILL HAVEN. ASSISTED LIVING AND REHABILITATION RESIDENCE. So this *wasn't* Dr. Doyle's home. It also wasn't a very encouraging development. Was Jacob a resident here? And if so, why? But it then occurred to Isabel that Colleen was probably just stopping to visit a patient. That made more sense. She pulled into the drive and parked as close as she could to the white car, then reached into her file and pulled out the photo of Colleen and Jacob that Ramush had given to her. As she waited for the woman to get out of her car, she quickly studied Colleen's face in the photograph. When she passed by, six feet in front of her windshield, Isabel was now 100 percent convinced that Dr. Colleen Doyle was the former Colleen Gallagher. Granted, the photo was taken thirty years before, give or take, but she really hadn't changed all that much.

Then Dr. Doyle stopped abruptly and returned to her car, reaching into the back seat and pulling out a large gift bag and a small bouquet of happy birthday balloons. Isabel's stomach sank and she was suddenly overcome with sadness. She *was* here to see Jacob, after all. This really was an unhappy turn of events. She didn't know what to do next. She couldn't confront Dr. Doyle here because that would just be creepy. Maybe she should wait until the doctor left then go inside and see what she could find out about Jacob's condition. That sounded like the better plan, although she'd have to be very surreptitious about it. It wasn't like she could just sashay up to the nurses' station and ask to see his chart.

Then Isabel had an idea. She remembered passing a supermarket after getting off the freeway, so she started up her rental car and drove the mile or so back to the market. She parked near the entrance, then went straight to the bakery section and picked up a little birthday cupcake, then to the floral department, where she grabbed a small bouquet of sunflowers and a happy birthday balloon.

When she got back to Hill Haven, fifteen minutes later, she pulled into the same parking spot and sat in the car, stress-eating a Hershey's almond bar that somehow found its way onto the belt while she was checking out. Just as she popped the last chunk of chocolate into her mouth, she spotted Dr. Doyle walking toward her. *That was a short visit*, she thought. As she got closer, Isabel could see that she had been crying. The sadness Isabel was already feeling was growing by the minute. Next to finding out Jacob was dead, which was of course the worst-case scenario, finding out that he was so badly injured or disabled that he required round-the-clock nursing care was the second-worst scenario she could possibly have imagined.

She waited until Dr. Doyle pulled out of the parking lot, then gathered up her courage—along with the cupcake, the flowers, and the balloon—and with her arms full, headed for the front entrance of the building, then through the automatic front doors and into an elegantly appointed lobby. Now it was show time. Looking very excited, she approached the front desk to speak to the stern-looking nurse sitting behind it who was already scowling at her. Isabel was duly intimidated by this woman, whose overall demeanor made Nurse Ratched look like a candy striper. But she was not going to abandon her plan now.

"Hi there," Isabel said in the nicest way possible. The nurse looked up but said nothing. "I'm afraid I just missed my sister, Colleen . . . Dr. Doyle? She was here a few minutes ago to see her son, my nephew—it's his birthday. I was supposed to meet her but I was running late . . . I'm his Aunt Sharon." Isabel couldn't believe that at that very moment she had remembered that Colleen's sister's name was Sharon.

The nurse turned her head and busied herself at the computer for thirty seconds, then turned back to Isabel. "Sorry. You're not on the visitors list. Can't let you in."

"Well, I don't live here, so I wouldn't be on the regular visitors list."

"If you're not on the visitors list, then you can't visit.

That's why we have a list." The condescension was practically dripping from the corners of the nurse's mouth.

"I understand that, but could I see him just long enough to give him a birthday kiss and drop off these flowers and this cupcake?"

"Still counts as a visit, so no. Sorry. It's against Hill Haven security regulations, and I would be breaking—"

"Oh, for the love of Pete!" came a disembodied voice from around the corner.

A handsome African American woman wearing a white lab coat and carrying a clipboard suddenly appeared. "Would it kill you to be a little friendlier to our guests, Nurse Lacy?"

Nurse Lacy was unmoved. "I was just explaining our regulations about visitation to this lady, Dr. Finnie, and I told her—"

"Yes, I heard you. But couldn't you find it in your heart to be a little more flexible? Here this nice lady is standing in front of you holding flowers, a cupcake, and a balloon for one of our patients, and you're going to just send her away?" The doctor shook her head and dropped her clipboard onto the desk. "I can hold down the fort here for a little bit, Nurse. I have some paperwork to do anyway. Why don't you go take a little break. You seem a little stressed out."

Nurse Lacy didn't argue. She was up and away from the desk in a matter of seconds. Dr. Finnie shook her head again and rolled her eyeballs as she watched her walk away, then smiled at Isabel. "I'm sorry. Nurse Lacy can be a little ill-tempered. If she were a dog, we'd probably have to put her down. I was just talking to your sister, Colleen. You *just* missed her."

"I'll catch up with her a little later. We're having dinner together. But I was so hoping I could see my nephew first." Isabel was slightly alarmed at how easily these lies were rolling off her tongue now.

"I've heard Colleen talk about you. I think it would be fine if you wanted to go down and see him. He's in Suite Two-twenty-two-West. Just go down that hallway and he's about halfway down on your right."

Isabel was touched—touched and now feeling guilty. She hadn't anticipated that lying was going to be one of her *go-to* investigative tools. That was not a topic they covered in her correspondence course. This nice young doctor was making a lovely gesture of trust, and it was all based on a big, fat lie. Well, Isabel told herself, she'd just have to feel bad about that later. She was on the verge of solving her first official case as a private investigator, and in record time, so she was going to forge ahead. "That's so nice of you, Doctor. I can't thank you enough."

The doctor was already getting busy with her work, but looked up and smiled. "You're very welcome. Oh, and visiting hours are over at six."

"Understood. And thank you again." Isabel headed down the hall, hoping she wouldn't have to pass Nurse Lacy on the way. She always felt bad for people like her whose default disposition was to be unfriendly and rude. In her mind, it was just so much easier to go through life being friendly and polite. It must be exhausting, she imagined, to wake up every morning and have to find something new to be mad about.

Isabel remembered a lesson she had learned from her mother, and one that she never forgot. "Being friendly, and polite, and smiling at others doesn't mean your life is perfect and trouble free," Helen Peabody told her impressionable young daughter. "It just means you're doing your best." Isabel was glad to have adopted her mother's philosophy as opposed to her father's, which was, "Show me the man who goes around smiling all the time and I'll show you the village idiot."

When Isabel got to 222-West, she slowly pushed on the partially open door until she saw the shadowy figure of a man sitting in a chair in front of a large picture window, looking out across a bright green lawn, and beyond that, a pond surrounded by colorful summer perennials. She took a few cautious steps in. "Jacob?" The man didn't budge. "Hello, Jacob? I brought you a birthday cupcake. I hope you like chocolate. You don't know me, but my name is Isabel . . . I'm a private investigator, and I was hired to find you." Nothing. He didn't even glance her way. Isabel moved a little closer. "Do you remember your grandfather, Jacob? Here I have a picture I can show you." Isabel reached into her purse and pulled out the photograph of Colleen and Randolph Bachmeier at little Jacob's birthday party. As she moved closer to show him the photo, she heard a voice at the door, "Aunt Sharon? Is that you?"

Isabel froze as the lights came on. The jig was up. She had been undercover for less than five minutes and her cover was already blown. Now all that remained to be seen was whether she was going to be able to talk her way out of this or be arrested for trespassing and possibly stalking.

"I didn't even know you were coming," the man's voice continued.

Isabel slowly turned around, using the cupcake, the flowers, and the balloon almost as a shield from whatever might be coming next. She couldn't believe she had put herself in such a ridiculous situation. But all those concerns fell away when she locked eyes with the young man standing in the doorway.

"You aren't Aunt Sharon. I'm sorry . . . I thought the nurse said my aunt was visiting. So who *are* you, if I might ask? I don't believe we've met. I'm—"

"You're Jacob," Isabel said softly. She knew instantly it was him. He was quite a handsome young man, with a beard;

long, dark hair; and jet-blue eyes. And even with all the hair and whiskers, he was the spitting image of his grandfather.

"I am . . . and I'm here to wish *this* guy a happy birthday!" Jacob walked over and pulled a chair up next to the young man sitting by the window and tousled his hair with his hand. "How are you, buddy?" The young man slowly turned his head and looked at him, but without expression. "I brought your favorite." Jacob reached into the backpack he was carrying and pulled out several bags of what looked like gummy bears. He opened a bag with his teeth, then reached in and took two bears out. "Here . . . I know you like the red ones." The young man slowly reached up and took the piece of candy, then just as slowly put it into his mouth. "Happy birthday, little brother." Jacob patted his shoulder and popped the other gummy into his own mouth, then turned back to Isabel and pointed the bag of candy at her. "Care for a gummy?"

Isabel shook her head. "Oh, no, thank you."

"I'm sorry, but *who* are you again?" he asked as he chewed his gummy.

It was time to fess up and tell him as much as she could about who she was and why she was looking for him. Ramush made very clear that Miss Bachmeier wanted to be the first to discuss the pending family matters with him, which was just as well because she wasn't quite sure she understood it all, anyway. There seemed to be a lot of moving parts.

"My name is Isabel Puddles. I'm a private investigator. I was hired by a member of your father's side of the family to find you."

He looked at her with an expression that was difficult to read. "Then what are you doing here with my little brother?"

"Well, I thought he was you. What's your brother's name?" she asked as she set the cupcake down on the desk and tied the balloon to the chair, then dropped the sunflower bouquet into her tote bag.

"Paul . . . Paul Doyle." Jacob smiled and handed his brother another red gummy. "What made you think he was me? This is all very confusing."

Isabel needed to move things along before Jacob started asking too many more questions. Discovering that she had just stalked his mother and then lied about being his aunt probably wouldn't go over well. "May I show you a photograph, Jacob?" She didn't wait for an answer, instead pulling out the photograph again. "Do you recognize anybody?"

He took it from her and looked it over. "I recognize my mother and myself."

"And the older gentleman?" Isabel asked.

"No idea." He looked a little closer. "Are we related? We do kind of look alike."

Isabel smiled and took a moment to think about the information she was about to impart to him, and how it would eventually, and inevitably, change his life forever. "He's your grandfather." Jacob looked at the photo again as she continued. "I'm sorry to say he has long since passed away, but his daughter, your aunt, has hired me to find you, and she would very much like to meet you."

Jacob stared at the photograph a little longer, then handed it back. "Why?"

"I'm afraid I'm not at liberty to fill you in on the exact details, but what I can tell you is that it's very important that you *do* meet her."

Jacob was processing. "Is my mother involved in this somehow?"

"No. . . I attempted to speak with her but, to be honest, she wanted nothing to do with me. That's why I had to find a way to get to you directly. I then learned that she was coming to see her son on his birthday, so I just assumed she was coming to see you."

Thankfully Jacob didn't ask how any of that came about,

instead he pondered for a moment as he reached back inside the bag of gummies. "You know it's only a fluke you caught me here. I live in Michigan now. I only come back to Milwaukee twice a year to see this guy." He reached over and tousled Paul's hair again, then handed him another red gummy. "I come at Christmas and on his birthday. I wish I could come more often now that they've stuck him in here, but it's hard to get away."

"Who's 'they,' if I might ask?"

"My mother and father, well, step-father. Paul apparently had become too much of a burden for them."

"So Paul is your half brother from that marriage, I gather."

"Yes. My step-father, David, is a doctor too, so it wasn't like they couldn't afford to keep him at home. I think they just decided they didn't want to be tied down anymore." It was clear that Jacob was still angry about this. "Paul was living in their guest house with round-the-clock care and had two caregivers who were completely devoted to him. Now he's just sitting here by himself staring out the window and surrounded by strangers." He looked back over at Paul and rubbed his shoulder. "People don't think he knows the difference, but I know he *does*. If I could take him home with me I would."

Isabel was nearly moved to tears. She wanted to ask why Paul was in this condition but she didn't feel it was appropriate, at least not now. She did want to keep the conversation going, though. "So I take it you and your parents are not on very good terms right now."

"No . . . Not since they did this to Paul. I won't even stay with them anymore. I sleep in my van when I come over. Security lets me park in the employee parking lot out back. I came over on the *Badger*, but I have to head back to Michigan tomorrow."

Isabel smiled. "I'm from Michigan, too . . . Gull Harbor. I came over on the *Badger* myself just this morning. And now that I've found you, I'll be going back tomorrow."

"What time? I'm on the one-thirty crossing," Jacob said as he dug around in his backpack.

Isabel hadn't yet decided when she was going back until now. "So am I," she said, recognizing an opportunity to learn more about Jacob Gallagher on the trip back.

"Great! Then we can talk more about how this introduction to my aunt is going to happen. I'll meet you at the dock."

"Wonderful! So I can tell her you're willing to meet?"

"If she went to all the trouble to hire a private investigator to find me, I guess the least I can do is meet her, so sure."

"Is there a way for me to reach you in case something comes up?" Isabel asked.

"I'd give you my cell phone number but I don't have it with me and I don't have the number memorized." Jacob laughed. "I hate cell phones, but I did finally have to get one after they put Paul in here. I've been living off the grid for so long, I don't remember the last time I had a phone number."

"Off the grid . . . meaning you have no electricity?" Isabel was fascinated with this "off the grid" living she had read about. And although she was unabashedly tech-averse, there were some things she couldn't live without. Electricity was pretty high on that list.

"Nope. No electricity . . . I use solar and wind for what little energy I need, some hydro energy, and I have a wood-stove for heat in the winter. But I do need to maintain *some* contact with the outside world, so I go to a coffee shop in town once every couple of weeks so I can go online and check messages. The owner is a friend of mine. My mother has the number there in case of an emergency. But I'll be at the boat tomorrow, don't worry. Now, I don't mean to be rude, but

Paul and I have a birthday ritual where we watch *Ace Ventura: Pet Detective* on my laptop together. And I get the nurses to micro popcorn for us." Jacob pulled a laptop and two packs of microwave popcorn out of his backpack.

"All right, I will leave you two alone. Thank you for making this so easy, Jacob. I'm going to give you my card, so if anything comes up, please give me a call." Isabel pulled a card out and set it down on the desk next to the cupcake. "I'll look forward to spending some more time with you on the boat tomorrow. Then I can get you up to speed with what details I *can* provide. Would you be amenable to meeting with your aunt as early as tomorrow evening after we dock, assuming I can arrange it? She lives very near Port Wellington."

"I don't see why not. But I won't have much time. I live up near Petoskey, and I have a lot going on at home right now, so I really need to get back."

"I know how anxious she is to meet you, so I'm sure that will be fine. You can follow me back to her house after we dock. Thank you again, Jacob. I'll be at the ferry terminal by noon tomorrow at the latest. I'll keep an eye out for you."

"Okay, I'll keep an eye out for you too. I have a blue VW camper van with a banged-in passenger-side door."

"See you then. Good night . . . And enjoy your movie." She looked over at Paul, who was still staring out the window, expressionless, and chewing on a gummy bear. "Happy birthday, Paul," Isabel said as she walked toward the door. Jacob waved goodbye and turned his attention back to Paul. Isabel got another lump in her throat watching Jacob showing such care and compassion for his little brother. She couldn't imagine any better evidence his aunt Abigail would need that her nephew was exactly the kind of young man she hoped he would be.

As she passed the front desk to leave, Isabel looked over at Nurse Lacy, who was back at the desk and still scowling.

When she realized she was still carrying the sunflowers in her tote, she walked over and laid the bouquet down on the desk in front of her. "Here . . . You look like you could use some cheering up." Isabel turned and walked through the doors without looking back. If she had, she might have witnessed just a hint of a smile.

Chapter 16

At first Isabel was feeling pretty good about what she had accomplished after just one day in Milwaukee. She was so looking forward to telling Abigail that she had found Jacob *and* that he had made such a good impression on her. Given how many possibilities there were for less positive outcomes, this was sure to come as welcome news. While she was certainly happy to have found him, another part of her was thinking that this had all been just a little too easy. She hadn't really accomplished anything that Jim Rockford or Joe Mannix couldn't have accomplished in the first five minutes of the show. Then they'd still have fifty-five minutes left to squeeze in an attempt on their life and a car chase before the crime was solved and the criminal was brought to justice. Isabel was starting to think maybe there was more to be revealed, and that this particular show might not be over, either. She would just have to take things one step at a time, she told herself, and today was definitely a step in the right direction.

Pulling up to the luxurious-looking hotel Charlie had booked for her along the waterfront was a happy surprise. She had called him to book a room for her because she knew he used some sort of website to get good deals on hotel rooms that she could never afford to pay full price for and wouldn't, even if she could. She couldn't remember the last time she stayed in a hotel where she didn't pull in and park right next to the front door of her room. To have a valet park her car and then to take an elevator to a room ten floors up was getting pretty highbrow for Isabel Puddles. After entering her spacious and beautifully appointed hotel room, she walked over to the window and pulled open the drapes to reveal a sweeping view of the Big Lake and a good chunk of downtown Milwaukee. She was amply impressed. Milwaukee was a much nicer city than people gave it credit for being.

Sitting down on the edge of the bed, she called Ramush to give him the good news, but he was not nearly as responsive as she expected him to be. When she asked to speak to Miss Bachmeier, hoping she might be a little more enthusiastic, he asked her to hold off telling her about Jacob for now. "I'm not second-guessing you, Isabel, I just need to be certain it's really him before we get Miss Bachmeier's hopes up."

"I am one hundred percent certain it's him, Ramush," she responded emphatically. "He recognized himself and his mother in that photograph you gave me, but not Mr. Bachmeier. All he said was that he thought they looked kind of alike. Maybe he'll remember more after you meet him and reminisce a little about the time you spent together in Madison."

"Well, I must say I'm impressed with how quickly you were able to track him down, that is assuming he is the Jacob we're looking for."

"I really don't see how he couldn't be, but I understand your needing to make sure. By the way, he lives in Michigan now, up near Petoskey, and we're coming back across on the *Badger* at the same time tomorrow. We're scheduled to dock in

Wellington at five-forty p.m., and Jacob agreed to come back to the house and meet with Miss Bachmeier before he drives north the next morning."

"You didn't mention her or the Bachmeier name to him, did you?" Ramush asked with a degree of alarm.

"No, of course not. I told him the man in the photograph was his grandfather, on his father's side, and that his aunt was the one who hired me to find him. That's it."

"Good. I do think it's best I meet you there at the port to-morrow. Once I see him and talk to him in person I'll know if we have the right young man. So I'll look forward to your arrival tomorrow evening. Thank you for calling, Isabel, and have a safe voyage back."

Isabel was a little disheartened that Ramush seemed so unenthusiastic, and his doubting that she had found the right Jacob was also a bit annoying. For a moment she thought about calling back to insist on talking with Miss Bachmeier. After all, *she* was her client *and* the one who was signing the checks, not Ramush. But she decided this was not a good time to be rocking the boat, and she didn't want to get on Ramush's bad side by going over his head. He must have his reasons for keeping it from her for the time being. She just hoped they were not nefarious ones.

Try as she had, Isabel still couldn't completely shake this whispering suspicion in her head that Ramush might have somehow played a role in the death of one Bachmeier, and the disappearance and probable death of another, but again, she had to remind herself again that she wasn't hired to in-vestigate a cold-case murder or a current disappearance. She was hired to find the long-lost Bachmeier heir, and she had accomplished her mission. Case closed!

It was a muggy evening, so Isabel put on a cool linen shift dress Carly had given her for her birthday and went out for a stroll along the waterfront, looking for someplace to have dinner, although the idea of dining alone in an unfamiliar city was not all that appealing. She hadn't gotten more than a block from the hotel when she was reminded of why she was in downtown Milwaukee in the first place. Several hundred yards ahead of her stood a massive brick building lording over a collection of smaller brick buildings that must have taken up three or four city blocks. Stretched across the highest point, on the tallest building, sat an enormous vintage neon sign that read BACHMEIER BREWERY. Next to it, a neon beer bottle tipped itself into a neon beer mug, and poured itself into a full mug of neon beer, complete with an overflowing foam head. Isabel watched the display repeat a few times before turning in to a quaint-looking seafood restaurant on the waterfront where she ordered a Bachmeier beer and an order of fish and chips. She wasn't really a beer drinker, but tonight it felt like the right thing to do.

Isabel arrived at the *Badger* terminal a little earlier than expected, so she bought her ticket and sat down near the entrance of the waiting area, where she would be able to spot Jacob when he drove his van in. But before she knew it they were announcing that boarding would soon begin, and still no sign of Jacob. She pulled her phone out to see if she had missed any calls, but there was only one call from Frances, who she had forgotten to tell she was coming to Milwaukee. She would no doubt be admonished for such a breach, but she would rather wait and tell her at breakfast in the morning and take the inevitable scolding in person.

Isabel got up and walked around the crowded waiting area, but still no sign of Jacob. She was starting to grow more and more anxious that he might not show up. Not having his phone number was making her even more anxious. How would she be able to reach him if he didn't make it on time? She should have at least asked for his e-mail address. That lapse would have to be filed under *rookie mistake*.

When they announced last call she reluctantly got on board, still struggling with whether or not she should leave without him. If Jacob had been held up for whatever reason, why hadn't he called? Just as she found her seat, her phone rang. It was a Milwaukee area code. Hopefully this was him now, she thought. "Hello, Jacob?"

"Is this Isabel Puddles?" a woman with a familiar-sounding voice asked.

"Yes, it is."

"What may I ask were you doing in my son Paul's hospital room yesterday?" Isabel now recognized the voice of Colleen Doyle. "I know you were there because I found your business card sitting on the desk in his room this morning, just in case you're thinking about denying it."

There was no point in denying it, but answering the question was going to be tricky, too, since she was pretty sure nothing she could come up with was going to fly. It was probably best to just tell her the truth, minus the part about stalking her from her office to the hospital. "I'm sorry, Dr. Doyle, but I was hired to find your son, Jacob, and when I wasn't able to convince you to help me do that, I had to find another way. When I found out your son was a patient at Hill Haven, I assumed it was Jacob. I had no idea you had another son."

"It's none of your business how many sons I have or do not have. How dare you lie your way into a private hospital. And claiming to be my *sister*? You know you could have been arrested for trespassing? And if I had been there, I would have seen to it that you were. Now, I have already asked you respectfully to leave my family alone, which was a request you clearly chose to ignore. If you make any *further* attempts to contact me, or *anybody* in my family, I will seek a restraining order against you, *and* Abigail Bachmeier. And then I will instruct my attorney to file a harassment suit against both of you. Do I make myself clear?"

Isabel was a very patient and understanding person, but she was not a person accustomed to being threatened or spoken to in such a threatening tone. "Dr. Doyle, I certainly understand why you would be upset that I circumvented you to get to your son, but threatening me simply for doing the job I was hired to do is not going to deter me. I'm sorry your son Paul is unwell, but Jacob, who seems to be a wonderful young man, and a devoted brother, is an adult who is entitled to know why Abigail Bachmeier wants to find him. Your decision to keep his father's identity a secret was yours to make, and not anybody's business, but every lie has an expiration date, and I'm afraid the shelf life on this one is up. Miss Bachmeier has every right to want to meet her nephew, and you have no right to prevent her from doing so, nor do you have any right to threaten me, or stand in the way of me helping her achieve that end. Now, do *I* make myself clear?"

There was a deafening silence on the other end of the line while Colleen Doyle processed Isabel's surprisingly terse response. "We'll just see about that. You should expect a call from my lawyers very soon." And with that, she hung up.

Isabel always did her best to avoid confrontations whenever possible, but when push came to shove, she was not afraid to shove back, so she was proud of herself for standing her ground. It also struck her as selfish on Colleen's part to feel she had any right to deny Abigail from meeting Jacob, or him from meeting her, not to mention incredibly ungrateful, given the generosity her father had shown to her and her son years before. Yes, Skip Bachmeier was a louse, and the jury seemed to have delivered that verdict very clearly. But even at nineteen years old, Colleen Gallagher shared equal responsibility for the situation she found herself in. Nobody gets pregnant alone. And she had fared much better, and had more help, than the vast majority of young women who found themselves in similar situations.

The *Badger*'s horn bellowed twice to announce its departure from the dock, and it shook Isabel to attention. There was no turning back now. Her best hope was that perhaps Jacob was already on board and that she had just somehow missed him. But why wouldn't he call? It then occurred to her that if his mother had found her card, he had simply forgotten it on the desk where she had left it. In that case, he would have no way to reach her.

Isabel sat down and looked out at the lake and back at the shoreline as it began to fade into the distance, but she was feeling way too antsy to sit still for very long, so she got up and began to walk around the boat, thinking how foolish she had been to think that this case was going to be wrapped up so quickly and neatly. She was also feeling more than a little unsettled about Colleen Doyle's threat to take legal action against her. She was going to talk to Beverly when she got home and see if there was anything she needed to be concerned about. Getting sued would not exactly be an auspicious beginning to her investigative career.

Isabel had been wandering the decks of the *Badger* for a while, lost in thought. Although it was another calm, beautiful day on the Big Lake, she had forgotten to take her Dramamine, so she was beginning to feel the onset of seasickness. She went down a flight of stairs to a lower deck, where she saw her old friend Sandy again behind the snack bar. After the berating she had just gotten from Colleen Doyle, she was happy to see a friendly face. "Hello again, Sandy. How are you?"

"Oh, hi! It's nice to see you again . . . Isabel, right?"

"Isabel, yes. It's nice to see you again too. May I have a

bottle of water please? I just remembered I forgot to take my Dramamine."

Sandy grabbed a bottle of water out of the cooler and set it down on the counter, waving Isabel away when she reached into her purse for her wallet. "I was hoping I'd see you again, Isabel. I have a question for you: Did you run into anybody you knew when we were crossing yesterday?"

That was an odd question to ask, Isabel thought. "No . . . Not a soul. Why do you ask?"

Sandy looked around, then leaned over the counter and lowered her voice. "Well, after you and I chatted, this gentleman—and I use the term loosely—came over and asked me if I knew you. He was a real sketchy-looking character . . . kind of a biker type, you know, tattoos all over his arms, even on his knuckles. I asked him what business it was of his, which got me kind of a scary look, but then he tried to play nice. He said you looked familiar to him but he couldn't place you. But he didn't look like the type of person *you* would be familiar with, unless maybe you worked the carnival circuit. Then he asked me if your name was Isabel." Isabel was growing increasingly concerned. "I told him I didn't have any idea what your name was. Anyway, I was hoping I'd see you again before we docked so I could tell you about him. I tried to take a picture with my phone but he kept his eye on me until he disappeared up the stairs, almost like he was making sure I *didn't*."

Isabel felt a chill. Who in the world did she know matching *that* description? Nobody, thankfully, but it sounded like he was following her.

"Thank you for bringing this to my attention, Sandy. I'm going to give you my business card. If you see this man again, will you please call me?" She slipped Sandy her card.

"Isabel Puddles . . . Private Investigator. Wait! *Puddles*? Aren't you the lady who solved the murder of that poor old farmer last year! I read all about you. You're famous! Now I remember seeing your picture in the paper. So maybe that's how this guy knew you."

"I suppose that's possible, but I'm afraid it might have more to do with the case I'm currently working on," Isabel replied before popping her Dramamine and taking a sip of water.

Sandy became instantly annoyed when a man approached the counter to order, then cleared his throat impatiently. Sandy shook her head. "These people . . . I guess I better go."

Isabel forced a smile. "Thank you again, Sandy. And please do call me if you see this person again."

"I promise I will. You be careful now, Isabel." Sandy looked concerned as she watched her new friend walk away, a look quickly replaced with one of annoyance when her new customer cleared his throat again. "You need something for a sore throat or are you just trying to make a point?" Sandy yelled down the counter as she took her time getting to her customer.

Isabel climbed the stairs to the top deck and sat down on a bench at the stern of the ship. Mesmerized by the *Badger*'s churning wake, she tried to make sense of why some biker type with knuckle tattoos would be following her. She thought about who knew she was going to be traveling to Wisconsin on the *Badger* yesterday. Freddie and Andy knew, and so did Justin, her dog sitter. She had also mentioned it to Kayla and Jazz when she stopped by the Land's End to drop off a dress for Kayla, who had to attend the wedding of a cousin she didn't like, so she didn't want to buy a new one. And then something hit her like a rogue wave. What if that nagging fear she had, that she might somehow be sealing Jacob's fate by finding him, was real? Had she just led somebody intending to do him harm straight to him? And was that why he wasn't on the boat?

Now the idea that Ramush might be involved in a murder

conspiracy came roaring back. What if he was making sure Abigail's plans for the family fortune were not in jeopardy by eliminating yet another Bachmeier heir? It was a possibility that was beginning to make more and more sense, no matter how hard Isabel tried to tamp it down, while an obvious fact pattern was developing in her head: Skip Bachmeier died not long after he tried to wrest control of the estate from his sister, and under circumstances many considered beyond co-incidental. Then, twenty-odd years later, his son mysteriously disappears after *he* is suspected of trying to do the same thing. Now that threat seems to have been neutralized too. Could eliminating Jacob be next?

Where things got even more diabolical, if a scenario this bizarre was actually true, was the possibility she had already considered, no matter how briefly. Perhaps this was not simply a family servant whose loyalty went to homicidal extremes, but that Abigail Bachmeier *herself* was calling the shots. And maybe this character Sandy had warned her about on the *Badger* was some goon who had been hired to make sure the newest heir to the Bachmeier fortune would not be a threat to Abigail's plans. Her concern over whether Jacob was deemed worthy or not might have been merely a ploy. Was it possible she was being played for a fool, and that Ramush and Abigail were simply gifted actors who were counting on Isabel to blaze a trail that would lead them to their third and final victim?

She took out her phone to call Colleen Doyle to see if she had any idea where Jacob was. She didn't expect anything close to a friendly response, but if her son was potentially in any kind of danger, it was only right his mother should know. Unfortunately that idea went nowhere fast when she looked at the screen on her phone: NO SERVICE.

Typical, Isabel thought. She had once read a story about a man who had been buried in a building collapse after an earthquake who was able to call for help on his cell phone and was eventually rescued. She recalled another about a woman who had been abducted and was able to use her cell phone to call 911 from the trunk of her kidnapper's car. She, too, was rescued. But if Isabel couldn't get a signal standing on the open deck of a boat an hour off the coast of Wisconsin, she wasn't going to lay any bets on cellular technology saving *her* life if she ever ended up in the trunk of a Buick on her way to a landfill.

Isabel got up and began pacing the perimeter of the deck again, wrestling with the idea of whether or not such an elaborate murder plot was grounded in reality and that she was being used as a pawn, or was this, as she dearly hoped, just her overactive imagination at work? Whatever the case, a sense of dread was building, especially now that Jacob was missing in action. If she had unwittingly put him in harm's way, she would never forgive herself.

The *Badger* made good time getting across, but with Isabel's mind racing the way it was, imagining all manner of terrible outcomes, the four-hour trip seemed interminable. As she got ready to disembark, she rehearsed how she was going to handle Ramush, who she assumed was waiting for her to arrive with Jacob as he said he would. Once again she had to remind herself that she had absolutely no proof that Ramush or Miss Bachmeier meant for any harm to come to Jacob, and that this whole plot she had devised in her head sounded completely outlandish, even to her. And why would Ramush insist on meeting them at the boat if he really *had* sent a goon to follow her and lead him to Jacob? Then two words popped to mind: *plausible deniability*.

Isabel decided to just play it cool and calmly tell Ramush that Jacob had not made it to the boat in time and that he had probably just gotten stuck in traffic or had car trouble. He'd call or show up anytime. But she did plan to watch Ramush's reaction to the news very carefully.

Well, if he's acting, Isabel said to herself, *he's putting in an Oscar-worthy performance.* Ramush appeared completely crest-fallen when Isabel broke the news that Jacob had not shown up to catch the boat. So she had to make a decision right then and proceed accordingly. *Was* she working for one or more murderers or *wasn't* she? Coincidence and vague sus-picion were nothing close to evidence, so unless or until she had something concrete to go on, she had no right to accuse them of such heinous acts, especially if this entire conspiracy plot was all just happening in her head. And it's very possible whoever it was who asked Sandy about her on board the *Badger* could well have been somebody who recognized her from all the unwelcome press she received following the Jonasson case, just as Sandy had suggested. Though he may not be the fan base she would necessarily find desirable, that didn't make him a hired hit man.

Isabel suggested to Ramush that they walk over to a port-side coffee shop so she could debrief him about everything that had happened in the past twenty-four hours. Then, as they sat down, she remembered she had gone back and asked Jacob if she could take his picture to show her client, and he had graciously agreed. She took out her phone and pulled up the photo, then handed it to Ramush.

He stared at it expressionless for a few moments until a warm smile crossed his face, and his eyes welled up with tears. He finally handed the phone back.

"That's Jacob. Even with the beard and the long hair, I can see he has his grandfather's eyes."

And to think even for a second that she considered Ramush a possible killer. Isabel was ashamed of herself. She went on to tell Ramush about going to Colleen Doyle's office, and everything that unfolded from there. She was relieved that she could put the fear that Jacob was in any danger out of her mind, but now her concern was that he would have no way of reaching her if he no longer had her card, and that he would soon be home, off the grid, and much more difficult to track down.

They both agreed they should give it a day or two to see if Jacob got in touch, and not mention anything to Abigail, although Isabel didn't feel great about withholding the information. After they said their goodbyes, Isabel promised to let Ramush know the minute she had any news.

Chapter 17

Isabel obviously hadn't been to the Land's End for breakfast yesterday morning, and she hadn't called Frances to let her know she wasn't coming, which was their policy if one of them wasn't going to make it, so she knew she was about to get an earful as soon as she walked in the door.

"Well, good morning, Mrs. Puddles," Frances said, giving her newspaper a slightly aggressive shake.

Isabel could always tell from her tone of voice when Frances was in a mood . . . and she was definitely in a mood. "Nice of you to make time for us. Let's hope Chef remembers how you like your eggs."

But Isabel was in a bit of a mood herself this morning. "Well, Mrs. Spitler, I have a lot on my plate right now, so breakfast hasn't been my number one priority. But I've missed you, if that counts for anything."

Isabel sat down and waved at Kayla and Jazz, who were both taking orders across the room. The diner was busy, but she didn't recognize a soul. By this time in the summer, most of the locals had given up and turned the Land's End over to the tourists. Folks in Gull Harbor were not used to crowds anyway, but eating breakfast surrounded by affluent strangers chatting about their trips to Europe or their tennis games was a lot to handle for folks trying to figure out how they were going to come up with the money to buy their kids new clothes for school in the fall or pay to have their transmission fixed. But Isabel and Frances always had their little table in the corner waiting for them at eight a.m. sharp. Isabel turned over her coffee cup with a sigh and looked across the table at a scowling Frances. "So what's got *your* goat this morning?"

"What does that even *mean*?" Frances asked. "My goat is just fine. But imagine my surprise when I was told you wouldn't be joining me for breakfast yesterday because you had gone off to Milwaukee *by yourself,* without even *telling* me."

Jazz was suddenly there with a smile and a pot of coffee. "Did you have a nice trip to Milwaukee, Mrs. Puddles?"

"I did, thank you, Jazz. It was a quick but very productive trip. I hadn't been to Milwaukee in years, but you know it's actually a very nice city."

"I really do miss it, especially in the summers. I'll put your orders in now. Welcome back."

"Thank you, Jazz," Isabel said, being extra-nice to compensate for her breakfast partner's less than pleasant demeanor.

Frances waited until Jazz was out of earshot. "And to have to learn from Olive Oyl there that my closest and dearest friend in the world had sailed across Lake Michigan without telling me was just a little bit embarrassing. I'd like to know how *she* knows your business and I don't?"

"Frances, please . . . If you're going to get indignant about something, at least wait for something that's worth getting indignant *about*. I stopped by to drop off a dress for Kayla the day before I left and I casually mentioned to them I was going."

"And you didn't think to invite me to come along?" Frances asked, still stewing.

"No, I didn't, Frances. This wasn't a pleasure trip. It was work having to do with the Bachmeier case. Perhaps you've forgotten, I've been—" Isabel suddenly noticed Jazz standing next to their table and looking apologetic.

"Kayla said Chef didn't peel enough potatoes this morning, so we only have one order of hash browns left." She was careful to give the bad news to Isabel and not Frances, whom she tiptoed around like a sleeping guard dog she was afraid to wake up.

"Frances, I want you to have that last order of hash browns," Isabel said in an effort to cajole her friend out of her funk. "It's my way of apologizing for leaving the state without asking for your blessing."

"Sarcastic has never been a pretty color on you, Isabel," Frances said. "Not much of an apology, but I'll accept it." She looked up at Jazz, who once again avoided eye contact. "And tell Chef to make sure they're nice and crispy. Nothing worse than soggy hash browns."

"Sure thing, Mrs. Spitler," Jazz answered as nicely as possible. Poor Jazz just kept trying to win Frances over, but Isabel knew that by now it was a lost cause. Once Frances passed judgment, it was all over. It was a personality trait that had earned her the nickname "Judge Judy" with her kids.

" 'Sure thing, Mrs. Spitler,' " Frances mimicked once Jazz was out of earshot.

"Frances, what *is* it with you and Jazz? I mean, you're not exactly Miss Congeniality *anyway*, but why you have taken such a dislike to this poor girl is just beyond me."

"Poor girl . . . Nothing poor about that one. You go ahead and feel sorry for her, Iz, but I can spot a phony when I see one, and that girl's a phony."

"A phony *what*, Frances? She's a good waitress! We ask her to bring us things and she brings them! What more do we need to know about her?"

Frances opened her newspaper again, clearly unwilling to share whatever reasons were behind her open disdain for their waitress. "Cold cuts are on sale at Kroger. I'm going to go stock up. Hank's on a steady diet of sandwiches now because I'm on strike! My kitchen is closed until we resolve our current situation. Want me to pick anything up for you?"

"No, thank you. You know, they're saying now that processed meats aren't good for you."

"Good. I hope he eats a lot of it," Frances said just as Jazz set their plates down in front of them.

"Extra-crispy hash browns for you, Mrs. Spitler, and extra bacon for you, Mrs. Puddles. Chef feels bad about running out of hash browns."

"You can tell Chef that I'm going to forgive him, but just this once," Isabel said as she reached for the salt and pepper. "And please thank him for the extra bacon."

Extra-crispy hash browns didn't do much to shake Frances out of her mood, so the overall tone didn't get much better over the course of their breakfast. But Isabel was too preoccupied with Jacob's whereabouts and how she might track him down if she didn't hear from him soon, so she wasn't paying much attention to Frances's litany of grievances du jour. The gist seemed to be that she was still determined not to move to Grand Haven and she was still mad at Hank for even suggesting it. And now she was mad at Hank's company for giving him the promotion in the first place and creating so much chaos in her life.

Isabel had to get to work, so after finishing her coffee, she dug some bills out of her purse to pay her bill and stood up to leave. "I need to get down to the hardware, Frances. I'll see you for breakfast tomorrow . . . and please try to have a sunnier outlook on the world."

Oblivious to Isabel's remarks as she paid her own bill, Frances had one more thing on her mind. "So I heard the

Indian drum again this morning. Very early," she said casually. "Care to make a bet that by tomorrow morning we will have heard about somebody else drowning in the Big Lake?"

"No, I do not care to wager that somebody is going to *die* or not. It's ghoulish." Isabel shook her head as she started for the door. "You and your drum . . . Honestly, Frances."

After the sour reception she got from Frances at breakfast, Isabel was happy to see the smiling faces of Freddie and Andy again when she walked into the store. After a chat about whatever details she *could* share about her trip to Milwaukee, they all dispersed and got to work. Freddie went to the office to do his bookkeeping, and Andy went back to lawn and garden, which he had looking more lush and inviting than it ever had before. It wasn't lost on Freddie or Isabel that sales in that department were up, too, thanks to Andy's hard work and a very green thumb.

Isabel was finding it hard to concentrate on hardware store work. She was still trying to figure out how she might track Jacob down in case she didn't hear from him, so she brought her laptop along, hoping she could get some work done in between customers. She remembered he said he frequented a friend's coffee shop to check e-mails, so running down coffee shop leads was going to be her first line of attack. How many coffee shops could there be in Petoskey, Michigan?

She was just taking her laptop out of its case when Andy walked up to the counter carrying an enormous lavender hydrangea that blocked the entire upper half of his body. Following behind him was an attractive, thirtysomething woman, whose pair of sunglasses, perched on her head, held her blond hair away from her face. Definitely a summer person. The woman put her purse down on the counter and smiled warmly at Isabel. "Are you Isabel Puddles by any chance?" she asked in a lilting English accent.

"Yes, I am," Isabel replied with a cautious smile. The woman looked familiar, but Isabel was certain they had never met.

"Hello, Isabel, I'm Elizabeth, Teddy Mansfield's daughter," she said, putting her hand out. "I've heard so much about you."

Isabel excitedly took her hand. "*That's* why you look so familiar! You have your father's eyes! How nice to meet you, Elizabeth. I remember your father telling me you and your husband bought a summer place in Gull Harbor. How are you and your family liking it here?"

"We love it! Living and working in the city, and with three teenagers at home, can be—let's see, what's a nice way of putting it?—a nightmare you can't wake up from?" They both laughed. "But as soon as we pull up to the cottage, not only do I start to feel my blood pressure come down, I begin to reconsider my desire to sell my kids to the circus."

Isabel laughed again. She could see Elizabeth had her father's flair for drama and his mischievous sense of humor, along with his sparkling eyes. "I'm happy to hear you like it here. I've never lived anywhere else." She leaned over the counter and said quietly, "But please don't tell your city friends about us. As you can see from the traffic this summer, we're already at capacity."

"I haven't breathed a word. When people ask where our new summer place is, I just say, 'Up in Michigan.' The last thing I need is to start seeing people from my office up here!"

"Good! Let's keep it on the—what do the kids say?—the low-down? I hope your dad still plans to come for a visit this summer."

"He very much wants to, but he's still trying to find somebody to watch Fred and Ginger for him—the two most pampered corgis in Great Britain outside of Buckingham Palace. My aunt Matilde usually does that for him, and she minds his rose garden too, but she took a little spill a few weeks ago and broke her wrist, so I'm afraid she is indisposed for the time being."

"Poor lady. What happened?"

"Well, dear old Aunt Matilde enjoys the occasional gin and tonic, and when I say *occasional*, I mean three, four, sometimes five a day, every day, which tends to make her a little wobbly. She would like us to believe she has an inner-ear problem, which makes her dizzy and sometimes lose her balance, and *not* the gin, so we all play along. But she's pretty sure gin was what kept the Queen Mother alive past a hundred, so there's no convincing her to moderate. At any rate, until Daddy finds somebody he can trust with those dogs, I'm afraid he'll be staying put. I suggested he check them into a kennel for two weeks, which went over about as well as suggesting to Aunt Matilde that she lay off the gin. Daddy is *completely* devoted to those dogs."

Isabel smiled. "That I can understand. I just had to leave my dogs in my neighbor's care for twenty-four hours and I felt guilty. I think once your kids leave home, if you're a dog person, they kind of fill the void."

"I look forward to testing out your theory. Did I mention I have three teenagers?" Elizabeth had a hearty laugh like her father.

"I remember the teenage years well—*too* well. But mine made it with flying colors, and my ulcer went away eventually. You'll get through it."

Elizabeth laughed again as she reached into her purse for her wallet. "I should let you get back to work, Isabel. I was just driving by and saw these beautiful hydrangeas, and then I remembered Daddy telling me you worked at the hardware store here in Hartley, so I just had to stop and see if you were in. And you're just as lovely as he said." Elizabeth put her credit card down on the counter. "I do hope he makes it over so we can all spend some time together before the summer is over."

"That would be wonderful. And thank you for stopping by, Elizabeth. What a pleasure to meet you." Isabel noticed Andy was straightening some shelves nearby. "Andy, will you please help this nice lady out to her car?"

"Yes, ma'am."

"Goodbye, Isabel. See you again soon, I hope," Elizabeth said as she held the door for Andy and her new hydrangea.

"Goodbye now. I'm going to write to your dad and tell him we met!"

Freddie popped out of his office as the door closed behind Elizabeth. "Did I just hear Mary Poppins out here?"

"Yes, Freddie. She came to borrow a spoonful of sugar. No, *that* was my friend Teddy's daughter, Elizabeth."

"You mean your mystery writer friend and future husband? How nice you could get acquainted with your future step-daughter," Freddie said, with a big grin.

"Don't be ridiculous, Freddie. Why does everybody think I'm in the market for a husband?"

Andy came back in the door and caught the tail end of the conversation. "My uncle Pete's single, Mrs. Puddles. My mom's always trying to set him up on dates. Nice old guy. Do you like cats? I'm thinking maybe—"

"I'm thinking maybe you can stop right there, Andy, my dear. I'm sure your uncle Pete is a very nice *old guy*, but I have no desire to date *anybody* of *any* age, with or without cats."

"She's going to marry a famous English mystery writer anyway, Andy. Hey, Iz, what if he were given a knighthood? You'd become Lady Puddles! But I think that would be a step down from being Kentwater County's Asparagus Queen of nineteen . . . what year was it again?" Freddie got nothing but a deadpan stare from Isabel in reply. "You should have seen her, Andy! Pretty as a picture. In fact, we do have a picture around here somewhere of her crowning. I'll try to dig it up and show you. She had a bright green Cinderella gown and a crown made of freshly picked asparagus. And remember at your coronation when they sang 'Age of Asparagus'?"

Isabel shook her head and flipped open her laptop. "I think that's enough reminiscing, Freddie, don't you? I'm going to do a little work here until we get our afternoon rush if you don't mind."

"You go right ahead. I'm going back to my office." Freddie walked away, humming.

Andy was about to head back to lawn and garden when he noticed Isabel's laptop. "That's a nice laptop, Mrs. Puddles. My mom has the same one. It's a good mom computer."

Andy was as sweet as he could be, and yes he was the best stock boy they had ever had. And although she knew he meant no harm, some of the things that came out of his mouth made her want to smack him. "*Mom* computer? Well, it's my first computer of any kind, so I don't have anything to compare it to, but it seems to be working out just fine. Although it keeps reminding me to make my bed in the morning, which is a little annoying."

Andy laughed. "You're a funny lady, Mrs. Puddles."

The front door jingled and a customer came in looking for a new garden hose, so that got Andy out of her hair so she could turn her attention to her mom laptop. After compiling a list of every coffee shop she could find in Petoskey and the surrounding area, almost thirty in all, she planned to take her lunch break in her office and start calling to see if one of them might be owned by Jacob's friend. But then she found herself researching something that didn't really have anything to do with finding Jacob, but it was a question she felt needed answering: What exactly happened to Paul Doyle that put him into a rehabilitation facility? It didn't take long, given Isabel's increasingly adept Google skill set, to discover the sad news.

According to a five-year-old article in the *Milwaukee Journal Sentinel*, Paul David Doyle, age twenty-two and the son of two prominent area physicians, Dr. David Doyle and Dr. Colleen Doyle, had been involved in a near-fatal motorcycle accident. A picture of the smiling young man at his University of Wisconsin graduation, wearing his cap and gown and posing with his parents and older brother, brought tears to her eyes. The article said Paul had several broken bones, a ruptured spleen, and suffered a severe head injury, which left him in a coma.

Isabel was surprised to see that the accident had occurred in Michigan, near Petoskey, when a drunk driver ran a red light and hit him broadside. There were no updates on the story or his condition. Paul was obviously no longer in a coma, but he *was* obviously still suffering from his brain injury.

Business picked up a little in the afternoon, and Isabel had just sold a set of socket wrenches to one of her regulars when her cell phone rang. It was another Milwaukee number. She crossed her fingers that it was Jacob. It wasn't. It was his mother, again. After Dr. Doyle identified herself, Isabel's heart skipped a beat. *Please don't let this be bad news about Jacob*, she said to herself.

"I'm calling to apologize for the tone of my phone call yesterday, Mrs. Puddles." Isabel breathed a sigh of relief. "I didn't mean to come across as threatening, but I'm afraid that's exactly how I *did* come across." Isabel said nothing. "I don't know whether or not you have children, Mrs. Puddles, but—"

"I do. I have two of them. And if I felt either of them was in any kind of danger, or that they were about to have their lives disrupted by a total stranger, I know I would not be very happy about it, either. So I accept your apology. And I'm truly sorry to be the one to cause this disruption in your family. I know you're concerned about Jacob, and I am as well. I did meet him at the hospital, just by happenstance. We had a very brief conversation, but I was most impressed with him, especially by the love and devotion he showed toward his brother."

There was what felt like an emotional pause on the line before Dr. Doyle continued. "When I found your card I assumed that the two of you had met. I knew Jacob was there to see his brother, and because he has refused to speak to me for some time now, I let him have his time alone with Paul."

"Coincidentally, Jacob and I both planned to be on the *Badger* for the one-thirty crossing yesterday. I was hoping to get better acquainted with him. But he never showed up, which has had me quite concerned."

"I wouldn't worry," Dr. Doyle assured her. "Jacob is an artist and he marches to his own drummer. He also has a different concept of time than the rest of us, so the fact that he missed the boat is not unusual. He was born three weeks after his due date and he has been tardy ever since."

Isabel was happy to see Dr. Doyle had a sense of humor.

"Mrs. Puddles, would I be correct in assuming Mr. Bajrami is still working for Miss Bachmeier?"

"Yes, he is," Isabel answered.

"I think I'd like to come over and talk to you both, maybe even meet with Miss Bachmeier, so I can better understand what all this is about. Are you free tomorrow afternoon by any chance?"

"Tomorrow afternoon would be fine, and I will call Ramush right now and ask him to join us. I'm sure he'll be delighted." Isabel gave Dr. Doyle her office address.

"I'll catch a flight over tomorrow morning. Shall we say two o'clock?"

"I will see you here at two. My office is upstairs above the hardware store."

"Thank you, Isabel. I look forward to meeting you. And, again, please forgive my abruptness with you."

"It's already forgotten. I will see you tomorrow."

As soon as she hung up, Isabel called Ramush on his cell phone. She was excited to tell him about the meeting she had just set up with Colleen, but her call went straight to voice mail. That had never happened before. She was determined to track him down as soon as possible, so she dialed Bachmeier Hall, hoping to reach him there. Sinclair answered and told her that Ramush and Miss Bachmeier had left for Ann Arbor early that morning for a doctor's appointment at the University of Michigan Medical Center. They wouldn't be back until tomorrow. That was odd, too, because Ramush had made no mention of going out of town or of Miss Bachmeier's having an upcoming doctor's appointment. What was troubling Isabel now, though, was knowing that the only reason anybody from the west side of the state would ever go all the way to Ann Arbor to see a doctor, which was more than a three-hour drive each way, would be to see a specialist, as it was one of the country's premier hospitals.

"I hope it's nothing serious," Isabel said to Sinclair. "Miss Bachmeier seems to me to be the picture of good health."

A short pause followed before Sinclair replied. "It's Ramush who is seeing the doctor, Mrs. Puddles. They're running some tests, so he'll be staying in the hospital overnight. I don't expect them back until tomorrow evening. I thought he might have mentioned it to you."

"No not a word . . . Is he all right?"

Another pause. "I suppose that remains to be seen. We'll know more once the tests are completed. I'm afraid I have no other details to share with you, Mrs. Puddles, so if you'll pardon me, I'll say goodbye to you now. I *will* however mention that you called should I hear from either Ramush or Miss Bachmeier today."

"Please ask Ramush to call me as soon as possible, will you please, Sinclair? It's rather urgent."

"Yes, Mrs. Puddles. I'll convey the message."

Isabel was so distracted by this latest wrinkle that she forgot to say goodbye before hanging up. Why had Ramush not mentioned anything this important? Then again, maybe she was overthinking things, per usual. If Ramush were seriously ill, he would certainly have told her. Whatever the case, there was nothing she could do but wait until he called back, so there was no point in worrying. Instead, she would start thinking about how best to handle her meeting with Jacob's mother. She had already had a taste of Dr. Doyle's Irish temper, so she knew she better tread lightly.

Chapter 18

When Colleen Doyle walked into her office, Isabel was immediately taken with her beauty. This was the first time she had seen her up close, after all. She was dressed professionally in a dark brown suit and an emerald-green blouse, which accentuated her thick, flowing strawberry-blond hair. But despite how smart and pulled together she looked, Isabel could read the tension in her face, and see it in her eyes. "Dr. Doyle, it's such a pleasure to meet you." Isabel reached out and they shook hands.

"The pleasure is mine, Isabel. Thank you for agreeing to see me. And please call me Colleen."

"Thank you for coming, Colleen. We have a lot to discuss, so I'm happy we can do it in person. Unfortunately, Ramush is unable to join us. He and Miss Bachmeier are out of town until tomorrow."

Dr. Doyle was clearly disappointed. "That's a shame. I was so looking forward to seeing him again after all these years."

"He was very much looking forward to seeing you as well. He speaks very highly of you. But I'm sure we can arrange for you to meet very soon. Please sit down, won't you?"

Having exchanged the few requisite niceties, Colleen was

ready to get down to business. "I can only assume that in light of Trey Bachmeier's disappearance, Ramush finally broke his silence and told Miss Bachmeier that she has another nephew."

Isabel nodded affirmatively. "He said he made a pledge to Mr. Bachmeier Senior that he would not divulge Jacob's identity, or yours, to Miss Bachmeier unless it became necessary. Ramush felt that time had come."

Colleen looked into Isabel's eyes and nodded slowly. "I guess what concerns me is not having a clear understanding of what Miss Bachmeier's agenda is in wanting to meet Jacob. I don't want his life disrupted. It's been difficult enough these past few years, for all of us. Another layer of drama is the last thing my family needs."

"I'm not sure I fully understand Miss Bachmeier's agenda myself. But I do think I can share with you an observation based on my conversations with her . . . I believe what she is looking for with Jacob, at least in part, is having a touchstone to her father. Once she found out your son existed, and learned how important he had been to her father, she understandably wanted to meet him herself."

Colleen nodded slowly again as if searching for what to say next. "That may be true, but having dealt with the Bachmeier family in the past, I learned that things were often not as they seemed. Now, from what I understand, Abigail Bachmeier is a very fine woman, and a dedicated philanthropist. I know her father thought the world of her. I also know she has had her share of heartbreak in life." Collen took a deep breath and straightened up in her chair. "I owe a great debt of gratitude to Randolph Bachmeier. I don't know what I would have done without his emotional and financial support after making such a terrible mistake in judgment as believing Jacob's father loved me and intended to marry me."

"I can only imagine what a difficult time that must have been for you, Colleen," Isabel offered sympathetically.

"It was the worst time of my life, up until Paul's accident, that is. I brought shame onto my family, and to myself. But Mr. Bachmeier never judged me. Thankfully that shame was immediately washed away the day Jacob came into the world." A slight reminiscent smile crossed her face. "And I know Mr. Bachmeier loved Jacob with all his heart. I wouldn't change a thing about anything that happened. So, as I said, I owe Mr. Bachmeier everything for seeing me through some very dark days, and for giving my son and me the opportunity to start a new life. However—and I know this will sound harsh— I owe his daughter *nothing*. And neither does Jacob."

Isabel respected Colleen Doyle's directness. Now she was going to be direct as well. "Why did you never tell Jacob who his father is? Or was?"

Colleen shrugged slightly. "I never saw any reason to tell him. As far as Jacob knew, his father was someone I had a brief relationship with when I was very young, but someone I didn't see as the kind of father I wanted him to be raised with. All of that of course is true. His name wasn't impor- tant, and Jacob never pried. I met my husband, David, when we were both in medical school. He's a wonderful man who came into our lives when Jacob was just six. I did confide in *him* about who Jacob's father was, and the circumstances that surrounded his birth, and he agreed that there was no reason to tell him. David always treated Jacob as his own, so he was never wanting for a father. He had one. Paul came along five years later. And Jacob was about the best *big* brother any *little* brother could ask for. Jacob's never been the same since Paul's accident."

Colleen was getting emotional. She took a moment to compose herself before continuing. "Anyway . . . once I heard from you, and made the safe assumption that it was Abigail Bachmeier who was looking for my son, I knew it was time to tell him the truth. I'd rather that he hear it from me than from you, nothing personal, or from his aunt, or have him hear about it in the press if it were to become public. Although I don't think he follows the news anymore. My fear now is that this revelation regarding the identity of his biological father will not only widen the gap in our relationship but may end up ultimately ruining his life. Money can do terrible things to a person, and there is no better example of that than the Bachmeier family."

Isabel was imagining herself in Colleen's situation and relating to her now as a mother, not as a private investigator. "Colleen, may I ask how long this estrangement with Jacob has been going on?"

"Since the day we admitted Paul into Hill Haven. I've tried reaching out to him countless times, but he wants nothing to do with me or my husband. He did respond to one e-mail I sent about a year ago. The gist of his message was that the day we bring Paul back home will be the day we can resume communicating."

"Do you mind if I ask about Paul's prognosis? I do know it was a motorcycle accident that happened here in Michigan. It sounds like he's lucky to be alive."

Colleen took a deep breath and paused for a moment before speaking. "Is he? I know that's a terrible thing for a mother to say, but sometimes I question whether the state Paul is in counts as being *alive*. Before the accident he was the most alive person I knew. Selfishly, I'm grateful I can visit him, and sit with him, and hold his hand, rather than having to visit a gravesite, but Paul is still a young man, so to think of him living out his life in a hospital room staring out a window is devastating beyond words."

"Is there any hope he might recover?" Isabel asked carefully.

"They say the last thing to go is hope, right? So yes, we still hang on to the hope that one day, with enough time and enough rehabilitation, he might come out of this, at least partially. I know Jacob is desperately clinging to that hope. But that's how my husband and I feel as parents. As doctors, we know there is very little chance of that happening."

A knock on the door broke the sadness that was hanging in the air. Isabel excused herself and went to open it. It was Andy. "I'm sorry to bother you, Mrs. Puddles, but there's somebody downstairs to see you. I'm sorry I forgot to ask his name."

"Please tell whoever it is that I'm in a meeting, will you, hon?"

"I told him that, but he says it's very important and that he can't wait."

Isabel turned to Colleen. "I'm so sorry, but I need to leave you alone for two minutes. I'll be right back."

Isabel hurriedly followed Andy back down the stairs. As she entered the store, she could not have been more surprised, but very pleasantly so. There stood Jacob, chatting with Freddie. He turned to her with a bright smile. "Hello, Mrs. Puddles!"

"Jacob! There you are!" She wanted to hug him but she barely knew him so she was afraid he might find it awkward.

"I'm really sorry I missed the boat yesterday. My van broke down, and I forgot your card in Paul's room so I had no way of getting in touch. Anyway, I took the *Badger* over this morning, and here I am."

"No apology necessary. I'm just happy to see you! But if you didn't have my card, how did you find me here?"

"Well, your name is a hard one to forget for one thing, and I remembered you said you lived in Gull Harbor. I figured, how many Isabel Puddles could there be in one little town? So I drove down after I got off the boat and stopped by a little diner in town to grab some lunch. I asked the nice lady who waited on me if she happened to know you, and she

told me you were one of her regulars, and that I could probably find you here." He laughed before continuing. "After she
gave me directions, the lady at the table next to me got mad
at her and asked her why she would give out that information
to someone who looked like Charles Manson! I personally
think I'm much better-looking than Charles Manson, so that
kind of hurt."

Isabel laughed. "That was Frances. She's my oldest friend,
and she is not shy about sharing her opinion. And she would
have reacted the same way if Mr. Rogers had come in looking for me, so don't take it personally." In her excitement to
see Jacob, Isabel almost forgot who was waiting upstairs. Just
as she was about to tell him, the front door bell jingled. Isabel
cringed as she watched Jacob's face and demeanor completely
change.

"Hello, Jacob," his mother said softly.

Jacob looked at Isabel. "Is this some kind of setup? Are
you working for my mother?"

As Isabel attempted to explain, Colleen spoke up. "No,
Jacob. Mrs. Puddles contacted me on behalf of her client, your
aunt, hoping I could help locate you. I came over this morning because I felt I needed to meet with her to get a better
sense of *why* she was looking for you, and to explain our current family situation."

"You mean, explain why you had my brother committed?
That situation?" Jacob had gone from all smiles with Isabel
to a look of contempt directed at his mother. He then turned
back to Isabel. "I'm sorry, Mrs. Puddles, but whatever's going
on here, I don't think I want any part of it after all. I need
to get back up north." Jacob made a move for the door, but
his mother firmly grabbed his arm. "Jacob, we need to talk.
Now. There's something you need to know." She looked at
Isabel. "May we please use your office, Isabel?"

"Absolutely. Take all the time you need." Jacob was resisting so Isabel decided to chime in. "Jacob, your mother has something very important to talk to you about. You really should hear her out."

Jacob finally relented with a deep sigh. "All right, fine."

After Colleen and Jacob went upstairs, Isabel paced nervously around the counter, waiting to find out how their conversation had gone. Freddie and Andy, who had been standing away from the conversation but listening intently, were on pins and needles as well. It was obvious there was some high drama afoot, but they knew they were not going to get anything out of Isabel, so they were waiting anxiously for the next shoe to drop. It finally did drop about fifteen minutes later, when Colleen walked back into the store . . . alone. Isabel could immediately tell things had not gone well. "Let's go back up to my office," Isabel said as she turned Colleen back toward the front door. Freddie and Andy watched them leave, looking as if the cable had just gone out five minutes before the end of the movie.

Once they were back in Isabel's office, Colleen sat down and began to explain what happened . . . "I never even had a chance to tell him about his father," she said sadly. "We got right back into it over Paul. He simply will not accept that his brother's needs surpass what we are able to provide for him at home. I'm afraid I lost my temper with him today, though, which is why he left."

"How so?" Isabel asked her.

"I reminded him of the last Easter we were all together at home, and Paul told us he was looking at motorcycles. He had a friend who worked at Harley-Davidson who could get him a great deal. I was furious with him for even considering it." Isabel could hear the anger in her voice, despite doing her best to control it. "My husband is an emergency room physician. He remained calm and tried to reason with Paul, sharing a few horror stories from the ER, which seemed to be having some effect. And then Jacob showed up. I reminded him today that when we asked him to help us persuade his little brother *not* to buy a motorcycle, he told us we should stop being so controlling and that Paul was a grown man who could make his own decisions in life. That was all Paul needed to hear from his big brother. Two months later he bought his Harley, and six months after that he was in a coma. Paul was on his way to visit his brother to show it off when the accident happened." Colleen could no longer contain her tears. "I told Jacob today it wasn't *us* he was angry at, it was *himself.* That's when he got up and left." Isabel reached for a tissue and handed it to her. "I never should have said that. But you know what? My husband and I were angry, too! We're *still* angry! At the world, at the drunk driver who hit him—who is now in prison, where he belongs—and we were mad at Jacob. We were even mad at Paul. Jacob spent every night at the hospital for the next eight or ten weeks, either sleeping in a chair in Paul's room or out in his van, waiting for him to come out of his coma. When he finally did, but just barely, and we began to see some hope he might come out of this, Jacob went back to Michigan to attend to his own life, but he came back as often as possible after we brought Paul home. When we made the decision to admit him to Hill Haven, Jacob cut us off completely."

After hearing this tragic story, Isabel was beginning to think her career as a private investigator might be short-lived. The sadness and the stress were just too much for her. Making pickles and pies and knitting scarves might not be as lucrative as being a P.I., but her emotional well-being was never at stake if she dropped a stich or overbaked a blueberry pie.

Isabel's phone rang. It was Ramush. He was hoping to arrange a meeting the next day with Colleen and Jacob after they got back. He was disappointed to hear Jacob had left, but rather than try to explain what had happened, she handed the phone over to Colleen and went back downstairs. She didn't need to be in the middle of this conversation.

When she laid her eyes on Jacob less than an hour before, Isabel thought she had this case wrapped up, just as she had when she saw him at the hospital in Milwaukee. Now he was gone again, and she *still* had no way to contact him. So it was back to the drawing board. But at least Colleen could arrange to meet with Abigail and Ramush and gain a better understanding of why Abigail wanted to find him, and learn what was at stake.

When Colleen came back downstairs, she handed Isabel her phone back and told her they had made a plan for the three of them to meet the next day in Grand Rapids, where she would be catching her flight back to Milwaukee, and where Ramush and Miss Bachmeier would be driving through on their way back from Ann Arbor. Colleen was still in a bit of a state, so Isabel offered her guest room if she wasn't feeling up to making the drive back to her hotel in Grand Rapids. Colleen thanked her, but politely declined. "The drive will do me good, but thank you for offering, Isabel. You're very kind."

The front door had barely closed behind Colleen when Isabel's phone rang. It was Kayla. "Did cute Jesus find you? I hope I did the right thing sending him to the hardware."

"You did, and yes, he did."

"Whew!" Kayla said with great relief. "Frances was sure you would be in his crawlspace by now. Why is that woman so obsessed with serial killers? And crawlspaces?"

"I think we have both learned by now that Frances Spitler, although we love her dearly, is not rowing with both oars in the water. Thanks for checking in, Kayla. Everything is fine. I'll see you tomorrow."

Chapter 19

Happy to be home after a long and emotionally draining day, Isabel's nerves were instantly soothed by Jackpot and Corky, who came barreling out of their doggie door when they heard her pull into the driveway. They were barely able to contain their excitement, showering her with kisses when she opened the front gate and leaned down to say hello. She knew she had not been a very attentive dog mom these past few days, so to make up for her lapse she quickly changed her clothes and loaded them into the van.

They drove down a road—really more like a path—that wound through some private land owned by old family friends. The dogs knew where they were headed and began to jump excitedly from window to window. After she parked, the threesome hiked down to a pristine stretch of Lake Michigan beach known only to locals. Isabel then took them off leash so they could run around and splash in the water. Corky, being a spaniel, liked the water a lot more than Jackpot did, and she raced straight for the lake. But Jackpot was a brave little guy who was not going to be shown up by his sister, so he was right behind her. Watching them frolic and chase each other in and out of the water and up and down the beach was always a joy. After the day she had just had, a little joy was exactly what Isabel needed. Tomorrow she would get back on Jacob's trail and start calling coffee shops, but she knew that could very well turn into a dead end. Even if she found the right shop, Jacob's friend might not be comfortable talking to her. Her best hope was that Jacob would contact her again after he cooled down. In the meantime, she was going to do her best to put the Bachmeier case out of her head. The Fourth of July was approaching and her kids were coming home soon, so it was time to attend to her own family now.

When she arrived home with two tired, wet, and sandy dogs, she hosed them down in the driveway and left them in the yard to dry off, then went inside to call her kids. After the sad story she had heard today from Colleen, she was feeling more grateful than ever to have two happy, healthy kids, even if they did live on opposite sides of the country. She couldn't imagine what it must be like to have one child who wouldn't speak to her and another who couldn't.

She first called Carly, who, through some kind of telephone magic, was able to patch in her brother, Charlie, too, so all three of them could chat at once. The Fourth of July fell on Sunday this year, so if all went as planned, they would be arriving at the lake in time for dinner this coming Saturday night. That still gave her a couple of days to prepare for their arrival. For the past few years, the kids had been arranging their travel plans, with Carly flying in from Boston, and Charlie from San Francisco, so that they arrived at the Gerald R. Ford International Airport in Grand Rapids at around the same time. That way they could rent a car and drive up to the lake together.

Picking up and dropping off the kids at the airport used to be a biannual ritual for Isabel, and one she always looked forward to . . . the picking-up part, anyway. So when the kids adopted their new protocol and put the kibosh on their old routine, Isabel's feelings were a little bit hurt. But she soon realized it was for the best. For one, it gave brother and sister a chance to catch up with each other without the prying ears of their mother. And it also spared Isabel that terrible sinking feeling she got in her stomach when driving them *back* to the airport, knowing a tearful goodbye was imminent. The drive home alone was even worse. Now after they said their goodbyes, she could immerse herself in some random activity or chore around the house to occupy her mind, or take out her knitting needles to keep from getting too blue.

After a nice long chat with the kids, Isabel was feeling better about the world in general. Conversations with her kids always lifted her spirits. After dinner, which consisted of a Lean Cuisine and half a glass of wine, Isabel was ready for bed, but it was only eight o'clock, which was a little early for bedtime. She remembered telling Teddy's daughter she would write to her father to tell him they had met, so she decided tonight would be a good time to make good on that. She grabbed a pen and her stationery from her antique secretary's desk, which sat in her foyer, then sat down at the kitchen table to write. She had to chuckle to herself when she recalled telling Andy the other day that she was going to buy some new stationery on her lunch break, to which he replied, "What's that?"

Isabel had no answer other than, "Google it." But in her mind, this was exactly why they were writing and not e-mailing, which along with texting, were now the order of the day. When Charlie recently tried to explain to her what Twitter and *tweeting* was all about, she stopped him just as he was introducing the concept of hashtags. "You needn't waste another breath on this, sweetheart," Isabel said to her son. "I know you're only trying to modernize your old mother, but you may as well be speaking Swahili, which I would actually prefer."

When she and Teddy began their correspondence last year, Isabel was a little nervous about writing to such an accomplished writer, but he assured her he relished receiving her letters and found them funny and entertaining. He complimented her on her beautiful handwriting and assured her that her writing was "just fine." Isabel knew that anytime somebody referred to something as "just fine," it probably meant "just okay" at best. But these letters were not meant to impress, they were just a way to share snapshots of their lives with each other and continue cultivating their friendship.

Isabel had never really been a big letter writer, mostly because practically everybody she knew lived in a twenty-mile radius of her, but she did write to her kids frequently while they were away at college, and to her parents during their brief retirement in Florida. She had also been known to write the occasional letter to the editor of the *Gull Harbor Gazette* if she had some community matter on her mind. Today Carly and Charlie insisted she begin e-mailing with them now that she was somewhat computer literate, finally *owned* a computer, and had ventured successfully into the mysterious and daunting world of the Internet. She resisted at first, but the more she resisted, the more they insisted. "Mother, I couldn't tell you the price of a stamp today if you put a gun to my head," Charlie told her to support his position.

Carly shared a similar sentiment. "And if you put the same gun to *my* head, I couldn't tell you where the nearest post office was. I didn't even know you could still buy envelopes."

"Well, it's a shame," Isabel told her kids. And she meant it. "I can't fight the future forever though, so I surrender. You've won this battle. But if you start pressuring me to get involved in any of this other nonsense—the tweeting or that Face-thing—you're going to start getting my letters by way of carrier pigeon."

Isabel stared out at the darkening lake and thought about

how to begin. She remembered her creative writing class in high school and learning about the importance of capturing one's reader from the very start. And being mindful that Teddy was a mystery writer, she knew just how to grab his attention . . .

> *Dear Teddy,*
>   *Well, somewhere in Lake Michigan right now, and for more than a month now, the body of the young heir to a vast Milwaukee beer fortune is either still floating, or more likely, has sunk to the bottom of the lake, and I have been hired to find his long lost half brother, who currently lives "off the grid" in northern Michigan, regularly sleeps in his Volkswagen van, and has no idea he is next in line to one day inherit a fortune . . .*

Nobody could say that wasn't an attention grabber. After Isabel finished her letter to Teddy, which also included telling him how impressed she had been with his daughter, Elizabeth, asking about Fred and Ginger, his rose garden, his sister Matilde, and to let him know she was hoping he would still be coming to visit, she fixed herself a cup of chamomile tea and climbed into bed, where she read for a little while before drifting off to sleep.

Isabel found herself wide awake at six in the morning. It hadn't been her best night's sleep. A thunderstorm had awakened her in the middle of the night, prompting Corky to jump up into bed and hide under the covers, which she never did. Unable to get back to sleep, Isabel couldn't stop thinking about how the meeting between Colleen, Ramush, and Abigail would go tomorrow, along with how she would go about finding Jacob again. She was pretty sure that if she didn't hear from him in the next few days, a trip to Petoskey, a few hours' drive north, would be in her future after the holiday. She had finally stopped allowing her mind to wander back to her previous suspicions that Ramush, and possibly even Abigail, might be involved in a decades-long murder conspiracy, and that Jacob might be next on their hit list. That just didn't make sense anymore, and she was a little embarrassed that she ever thought it did. It also made her question her investigative instincts. But at least now she needn't be concerned that once she found Jacob, he wasn't going to wind up being murdered or sitting in a dungeon at Bachmeier Hall with a couple of Jehovah's Witnesses.

As was often the case with unexpected summer storms that struck in the night, a beautiful morning followed, and today was one of those mornings. So after fixing a pot of coffee, Isabel poured herself a cup and went out to sit on the dock and watch the sun come up over the lake. The trees were as still as they could be, and the lake itself looked almost as if it had been glazed. The only sound was the low, rhythmic squeak of the oars on her neighbor Arnie Edwards's old wooden rowboat as he rowed out to his favorite fishing hole. After she enjoyed some quiet contemplation, and the coffee began to work its magic, the dogs finally came out and joined her. After morning minnow patrol was over, they let her know it was time for their breakfast, so the three of them went inside. As the eight o'clock hour approached, it was time for Isabel to have breakfast, too, and although she wasn't feeling particularly hungry, or in the mood to deal with the Land's End summer crowd, she had assured Frances she would be there this morning, so she got dressed and headed into town.

Isabel arrived before Frances again, and as soon as she sat down, Kayla came over and put an envelope down on the table in front of her, then poured her coffee. "Before I forget."

"What's this?"

"I found it taped to the front door when I unlocked this

morning. Cute Jesus must have left it for you. I know better than to ask what this is all about, but is that boy ever *cute*! Give him a shave and a haircut, and I could go full-on Mrs. Robinson with him!"

Isabel chose not to acknowledge that statement. She opened the envelope and, sure enough, inside was a note from Jacob. He apologized for taking off and had written down his cell phone number, e-mail address, and his address on Logger's Ridge Road. Isabel was awash with relief but didn't want to show it and pique Kayla's curiosity even more. "I wonder where Frances is," Isabel asked her as she dropped the envelope into her purse. "It's already eight fifteen. Maybe I should call her."

"Or maybe we should just enjoy the quiet. She's been in rare form these days, and poor Jazz has been bearing a lot of the brunt." Kayla leaned in so Jazz, who was taking an order nearby, couldn't hear. "Why does Frances have such a problem with her? I just don't get it."

"Who knows? Just Frances being Frances, I guess. Once she's decided she doesn't like you, then that's all she wrote. And she *never* forgets. To this very day she refuses to speak to Edie Rudman because in the fifth grade she cut in front of her in the lunch line and got the last carton of chocolate milk that rightfully belonged to Frances. Granted, Edie *was* kind of a bratty kid, but it was the *fifth grade*, for crying out loud!" Kayla laughed. "That's not all. I was with her at the Rexall over in Hartley not too long ago, and there was Edie working behind the counter. I guess she had to move back home for some reason and obviously wasn't thrilled about working at the Rexall, so she was not, well, let's just say she was not overly friendly to us as we were checking out. Frances bristled when she finally recognized her, and on our way out the door she turned back to her and yelled, with a store full of customers, 'You know what, Edie Rudman? You were a snot back in the fifth grade, and you're *still* a snot!' That woman knows how to hold a grudge."

Kayla laughed out loud and shook her head. "She's one of a kind, thank God. I think she's really on edge about the whole moving to Grand Haven thing. But do you really think they're going to do it? You know I love Frances to death, despite her orneriness lately, so I sure would hate to see her go."

"You know I would too, of course, but I'm not worried. If Frances says she's not moving, the smart money says she's *not* moving. I just hope she doesn't feel like divorce is the only answer. I think she and Hank will eventually come up with a reasonable compromise, but until they do, I think we're just going to have to put up with her being a little testier than usual."

"Who's that?" Jazz asked as she appeared at the table. "Oh, Mrs. Spitler? Boy, I don't know what I did to get under her skin, but she really has a problem with me."

Isabel reached into her tote bag and pulled out her laptop. "Like I've told you before, Jazz, don't take it personally. You're in good company. Frances has a problem with half the people in this county, and the other half have a problem with her. Hey, Kayla, when you get a minute can you help me out here, please, before you get too busy?"

"What can I do for you, Iz?"

"I know you're a lot more computer literate than I am, which is a low bar, but still . . . Isn't there a way you can plug an address in here somehow and it will give you directions on how to get there and how long it takes?"

"Sure, I can help you do that. Where are you headed, Iz?"

"I can't give you any specifics, but you know that case I've been working on?"

"The one you can't talk about?" She turned to Jazz. "I don't know if you've heard this already, but Isabel Puddles is a pretty famous sleuth around here. Michigan's own Miss Marple. With a little bit of Wonder Woman thrown in there."

Isabel scoffed, while Jazz nodded excitedly. "I heard some customers talking about you recently solving some murder around here. Pretty impressive, I must say."

"And now she's a real bona fide private detective," Kayla added proudly.

"Private *investigator,* Kayla. I'm not a detective. Columbo's a detective."

"Columbo? Who's that?" Jazz asked.

"Never mind. Before your time. You can Google him." She turned to Kayla and lowered her voice. "Yes, it's the case I can't talk about, but I *can* tell you that the person who came in here yesterday is the person I was hired to find." Isabel held up the piece of paper with Jacob's contact information and gave it a little shake. "And *this* is what I need to find him once and for all. Then I can finally put this case to bed."

"He did seem a little bit mysterious," Kayla said. Then, turning back to Jazz, she added, "Too bad you weren't here, Jazz. I didn't see a wedding ring, and he was about your age . . . So cute. At least he looked to be underneath all that hair and whiskers. He never told me his name, though. Just signed J.G. on that note for Isabel."

"Good. You don't need to know his name. Not yet. But you and *everybody* will know it soon enough, I'm sure, which, if I'm being honest, is not something I'm looking forward to. Things have finally gotten back to normal since the Jonasson case. Can you imagine what kind of attention the Bachmeier name is—" Isabel stopped herself and winced slightly, remembering she had signed an agreement to either keep quiet or get sued.

Kayla sat down and flipped up Isabel's laptop. "Everybody knows you were working for Abigail Bachmeier, Iz. We just didn't know why. Still don't, so you're fine. Not our business, anyway, right, Jazz? Okay, let me get into Google maps for you."

"How did we ever survive without Google?" Isabel said with a sigh.

"I'm pretty sure the world would stop spinning at this point if we lost the ability to Google. And we wouldn't know *why* it stopped spinning because we couldn't Google it! Okay, what's your password, Izzy?"

Isabel looked contrite for a moment before answering, "My kids' names, in order."

"Not exactly foolproof, is it?" Kayla said as she began typing in the password.

"I know, but it's the only password I can ever remember."

A large party of summer people came in just as Kayla got to work on the laptop. "Jazz, will you go make a fresh pot of coffee, please? Looks like we're about to get our rush a little bit early. I'll be done here in five minutes. And tell Chef to make sure he has plenty of Hollandaise sauce. That crew has eggs Benedict written all over them."

"Fresh pot of joe coming up!" Jazz answered as she headed for the kitchen.

Not a minute passed before Kayla turned Isabel's laptop toward her. "Boy, cute Jesus really lives out in the boonies!"

Isabel looked at Kayla and frowned. "Would you please stop calling him that?"

Kayla laughed. "Why? He looks like a cute Jesus! Not that real Jesus wasn't cute, but who knows? Why? Is it sacrilegious?"

"It's just weird. Let's just go with JG." Isabel took out her glasses to take a closer look. "He did say *off the grid*. Guess he wasn't kidding. Not a grid in sight! Thank you, Kayla. Now can I save this?"

Kayla took the laptop back, hit a few keys and pushed it back. "There . . . saved."

Isabel was impressed. "How did you get so good with computers?"

"I took a few classes. And I've got three kids who *live* on their laptops. I think I got most of whatever knowledge I do have through sheer osmosis."

"How are those adorable kids of yours doing, anyway? I haven't seen them in ages." Kayla was the single mother of twin boys about to enter junior high, and a daughter who was a freshman in high school. How she managed to work full-time with three kids and keep body and soul together always amazed Isabel.

"You haven't seen them since they moved on from adorable." Kayla laughed. "They're fine. The twins are obsessed with zombies. Last night we spent a good hour at the dinner table arguing over whether zombies could swim or not . . . and with no resolution. Still don't know. And my daughter is obsessed with some British sci-fi show—and I mean *obsessed*. Only speaks with an English accent now. So it's a little bit *Night of the Living Dead*, and a little bit *Mary Poppins* around my house these days." Kayla stood up to get back to work and looked over at the front door as it opened. "Well, speak of the devil! Mrs. Spitler is here to lift our spirits again. Good morning, Frances."

"Good morning, Kayla . . . good morning, Izzy." Frances's tone was clipped, which was never a good sign. Isabel had by now learned to read Frances like a weatherman reads a Doppler radar screen. But, like the weather, she was never entirely predictable. Frances dropped a folded newspaper down on the table in front of Isabel. "Now, put that in your peace pipe and smoke it." Kayla raised her eyebrows at Isabel and made a break for it.

"What are you talking about now, Frances?" Isabel asked, as she slid the newspaper away from her.

"Shall I read it to you? This is from the *Wellington Chronicle*." Frances unfolded the paper and cleared her throat. " 'Two Coast Guard cutters were joined today by a helicopter north of Wellington to continue their second day of searching for a Detroit man who was reported missing by his family, after he went fishing alone on his boat, a thirty-eight-foot Chris Craft named *Anchor Management*.'" Frances lowered the paper and looked across at Isabel. "Very clever . . . Lotta good it did him." She took a breath. "'According to the Wellington harbor master, the man, whose name is still being withheld, was last seen leaving the harbor at approximately seven o'clock Monday morning. Cell phone and radio calls have since gone unanswered, and the Coast Guard has so far reported no sign of the man or his boat. This is a developing story.'"

Frances put the paper down and looked across the table with a smug expression. "What do you have to say about that?"

"What do I have to say about a poor man who's gone missing in the Big Lake? I'm not sure what you're getting at Frances, but I'd say it's terrible, and sad. Can you imagine what his family must be going through?"

"And do you not remember me telling you I heard the Indian drum again the other morning?"

"Oh, no. Here we go again. Frances, if I tell you that I believe the Indian drum story is real, will you stop bringing it up every fifteen minutes?"

"You can believe it or not, Ripley. But I know it's true." Frances flipped over her coffee cup. "What do I have to do for a cup of coffee around here? Where's Olive Oyl?"

A timid-looking Jazz approached cautiously with a pot of coffee. "Good morning, Mrs. Spitler," she said politely.

Frances grunted a greeting. "Is that fresh?"

"Yes, ma'am . . . Just made it."

Shockingly, Frances managed a thank-you, then looked over at Isabel, who had taken a section of the paper and started to read. "So, Iz, when are the kids coming? I haven't seen Charlie or my goddaughter since Christmas."

"I haven't, either, Frances. They haven't been here since Christmas. They arrive tomorrow evening."

"So what do you need me to bring for the barbecue, other than the wine?"

"How about a more festive attitude than you've been displaying lately, for one? And your three-bean salad."

"I'll work on *festive*, but I can't make any promises. I *will* bring the salad, though. Maybe I'll get crazy and make it four-beans. And I'll come early to help you set up."

"That would be splendid. Then you can spend some time with the kids. I'm thinking about hiring a little extra help this year, too, so I can spend less time working and more time socializing."

Jazz arrived with more coffee. "Did I just overhear you say you were thinking about hiring some extra help?"

"Yes . . . for my Fourth of July barbecue. Are you interested?" She didn't wait for an answer. "I was going to invite you to come along with Kayla, but if you'd rather work . . ."

Jazz jumped at the chance. "I'll be happy to do it! Just tell me where and what time to be there."

"Terrific! I'll let you know." Isabel took a sip of coffee and teased Frances with a smile after Jazz walked away. "At least one of us can be fair-minded with the poor girl."

"Phooey," Frances said as she rolled her eyes and picked up her newspaper, giving it a shake as she opened it. It was one of their quieter breakfasts.

After she climbed into her van, Isabel pulled out the envelope Jacob had left for her and placed a call to him, but unfortunately got his voice mail. His outgoing greeting said he would be on Mackinac Island until after the Fourth of July, but to go ahead and leave a message and he would return calls on Monday after he returned. She decided to skip leaving a message. Maybe what she should do instead of calling was to drive up to Petoskey and talk to him in person. That way she would know where to find him *and* he wouldn't be such a moving target. And if she could talk to him face-to-face, she might be able to put his mind more at ease than she could over the phone. The poor guy must be wondering who this mysterious aunt of his was, and why this middle-aged woman who worked in a hardware store was chasing him around. So that was what Isabel resolved to do. On Monday, after the kids left, she would drive up to Petoskey to see Jacob in person, and at the same time she could learn just what "off the grid" living even meant.

Ramush was waiting for Isabel outside her office when she arrived. He was looking pensive. "What's wrong?" she asked him as she got out of her van. "Did things not go well with Colleen?"

"Hello, Isabel. I was just running some errands and thought I would stop by and see you."

"Would you like to come up?" Isabel asked as she unlocked the door leading upstairs.

Ramush shook his head. "No, I really have to get back."

"All right, but can you tell me what happened first?"

Ramush hedged for a moment before he began. "Yes . . . Well . . . it was cordial enough at first. I was most happy to see Colleen after so long, and I think she felt the same way. She and Miss Bachmeier were getting along fine, *slightly* awkward, but it was fine. But then things got a little, shall we say, tense? Miss Bachmeier was frustrated that Colleen didn't know how to reach her 'own son,' as she put it, which put Colleen on the defensive. And Colleen wanted to know the details regarding why Miss Bachmeier was so eager to meet Jacob, before she would make any effort to find him herself. Miss Bachmeier then may have insinuated Colleen *did* know how to reach him but was deliberately withholding the information. She also made clear any details would be shared only with Jacob. That ruffled Colleen's feathers even more, so that brought them to an impasse in fairly short order. I was happy we met for coffee and not dinner, because I don't think we would have made it through the salad course. Then Colleen took offense to something else Miss Bachmeier said, and that was the end of the meeting."

"What did she say?"

"Well, I've heard her say this before, and she does speak from some experience, but when Colleen said her concerns were as a mother, and not about whatever money might be involved, Miss Bachmeier responded by telling her that in her experience, 'the minute somebody says it's not about the money . . . you can be sure it's about the money.' Colleen was insulted, and I suppose understandably, so she got up from the table and left. I followed her to her car and tried my best to get her to stay and talk things out, but she refused. So that's where we are this morning."

"Well, that's not good. I'm sorry things took such an unhappy turn. I do have some good news, though, if you're interested."

Ramush raised his eyebrows. "I'm not sure I know how to handle good news anymore, but try me."

"Jacob left his contact information for me after *he* took off yesterday, so I was thinking after the holiday on Monday I would drive up to pay him a visit in person. And it just occurred to me that it might be a good idea if you came along with me."

Ramush thought it over for a moment. "Yes . . . I think that's a very good idea. But why must we wait until Monday?"

"I already called him, but his outgoing message said he was away until Monday and would return calls then. Besides, my annual Fourth of July barbecue is on Sunday and my kids are coming home, so I have lots to do. But I can leave first thing Monday morning after they head for the airport."

"Okay, that's fine. I'll let Miss Bachmeier know I'll be gone for the day."

"And if you are so inclined, and don't have other plans, I would love it if you would come by my barbecue. It starts at four p.m. And please extend the invitation to Miss Bachmeier too."

"Thank you, Isabel . . . I will."

"I probably don't need to tell you that this is not a fancy soiree. Nothing like the big to-do they have down at the yacht club, if that's what you're used to, but we always have fun. Good food and good people. It would give you both a chance to mingle with the natives. But if you *don't* make it, let's meet right here Monday morning at, say, ten? That will put us in Petoskey early afternoon. I'll drive."

"I will see you here at ten a.m. sharp, if not at your barbecue. Thank you again for the invitation."

"You're very welcome. Now I'm going to get a little work done upstairs before I report for hardware store duty. We tend to get busy just before the holiday. Goodbye now, Ramush. Hope to see you Sunday!" Isabel waved and went upstairs to her office. She knew they wouldn't come, but it would have been rude not to invite them.

Business at Freddie's Hardware had not been as busy as it usually was in the week leading up to Fourth of July, which concerned her, despite her trying to stay positive for Freddie's sake. She hoped there would be an uptick in the few days remaining. Freddie hadn't really been himself lately, and she was worried he was becoming increasingly stressed out about business. And with his heart condition, that was not a good thing. But Freddie's stress level was difficult to manage because the store was where he spent the majority of his time if he wasn't at home or on the golf course, and it was the business that was causing all his stress. Freddie was convinced the chain hardware megastore that had opened two years before in Wellington was slowly suffocating his business, as well as every other independently owned hardware store in the county, and that eventually it would drive him out of business.

Despite the hardware doomsday scenario he was forecasting, he hadn't been squeezed out yet, and Freddie was a fighter, so he was determined to figure out a way to stave off what he had resigned himself to be inevitable for as long as he could. So between the stress of fearing he would lose his business and the stress of trying to figure out ways to save it, he was not doing his cardiovascular system any favors. He recently admitted to Isabel that he had, more than once, driven the thirty miles to Wellington to nose around the massive store, incognito, and see what he could learn about how it operated, to check the prices, and to pester the workers on the floor by asking a lot of questions that clearly had nothing to do with the garden shed he claimed to be building.

He also told her about the day his hardware espionage missions came to an end, after he was spotted by one of his loyal regulars, Biff Atkins, who was there only because Freddie didn't stock the copper piping he needed. Biff recognized him despite his John Deere cap and sunglasses and called him out in the plumbing department. "I sure hope this doesn't get back to Isabel, Fred!" Biff yelled down the aisle, laughing. "If she finds out *you're* shopping here now, you're going to have a lot of explaining to do!" Freddie took it in stride and did his best to explain to Biff why he was there, and then swore him to secrecy. If it ever got around he was shopping there, he was convinced it would be the final death knell for Freddie's Hardware.

Freddie's father was her father's older brother, and Freddie was a few years older, so Isabel had known him her entire life. She couldn't imagine her life without him in it, so she had been pretty vocal about his needing to start taking better care of himself. And she wasn't alone. Freddie's wife, Carol, his kids, and his doctors were all emphatic that he had to slow down and find ways to reduce his stress levels, adopt a better diet, and get more exercise. Freddie wasn't big on being told what to do, but a chorus of loved ones and health care professionals telling him he needed to get his act together wasn't something he could easily ignore.

So in an effort to at least flirt with, if not embrace, a healthier lifestyle, Freddie *had* become more careful with his diet, and he and Carol had started walking daily. But when Carol suggested he join a local gym, that was a bridge too far. "Next thing you know, she's gonna want to move that Richard Simmons fella into the basement and have me *Sweatin' to the Oldies!*" he grumbled. Isabel suggested he try meditation, which he finally agreed to do at a local yoga studio, but that was not a great success either. "I think meditation is just a fancy name for a nap," he told her after his first session. "I laid down on that mat and I was out like a light. The yoga lady had to come and poke me with her foot. She said my snoring was disturbing everybody's chakras, whatever *that* means."

Isabel had tried meditation once herself, after Charlie, a practicing Buddhist, had given her an instructional DVD for Christmas out of his growing concern that *she* needed to reduce her stress levels too. It didn't work. For Isabel, knitting was her go-to form of meditation, and although there hadn't been a lot of time for it lately, whenever she felt her brain was in danger of reaching overload, or she was worried or ruminating about one thing or another, she made the time. After a few hours staring out at the lake with her knitting, and a cap or a tea cozy later, all was right with the world again.

Chapter 20

On the day of the kids' arrival, Isabel was almost giddy with excitement. Now that the Bachmeier case looked on the verge of being successfully closed, or would be as soon as she could talk to Jacob again, she could concentrate on her kids and her barbecue for the next few days. Fortunately, business had picked up at the store and it had been quite busy, which certainly was good news. Freddie's idea to provide free hot dogs and hold a raffle to give away a gas grill on Saturday had paid off. Anybody who spent ten dollars or more was automatically entered to win, and between the dynamic sales team of Freddie and Andy, Isabel had a line at the counter all day long. By the time they closed, her fingers were numb from punching the cash register. As nice as it was to see so many of their regulars having fun, visiting with one another, and, more importantly, actually shopping, it was nicer still to see Freddie being himself again. His gregarious nature, combined with his thorough knowledge of hardware and old-school devotion to customer service, which, it seemed to Isabel, had gone the way of letter writing, served to remind any customers who were thinking about straying that they would never find the kind of personal touch Freddie Peabody provided anywhere else. When the crew of Freddie's Hardware finally said good-bye to their last customer and locked the door, they breathed a collective sigh of relief, then Isabel immediately whipped off her apron and hung it behind the door.

"Hate to run off so quickly boys, but I have loads to do before Carly and Charlie get here, and loads more to get ready for my barbecue. Freddie, I will see you around three?"

"With bells on, Cousin."

"Super! Andy, I hope you can make it too. And please bring your mom and dad along."

"Thank you, Mrs. Puddles. Not sure if they've made plans or not, but I'll ask them."

"All right. I'm off! Looks like Freddie's Hardware is back!"

"From your lips, Izzy!" Freddie yelled to her as she flew out the door.

By the time Isabel got home, she had only a couple hours to get ready for the kids' arrival. They had already requested the evening's menu, a favorite family summer classic: fried perch with Isabel's special homemade tartar sauce, Gran Mac-Gregor's pineapple-and-poppy-seed coleslaw, and a simple side of boiled potatoes with butter and parsley.

Isabel had gotten most of the prep work out of the way last night, so all that was left to do was thaw the perch she had caught herself earlier in the summer, then batter it up and fry it when they got there. Carly and Charlie were disappointed when their mother told them that because she had to work all day, she probably wouldn't have time to bake the strawberry-rhubarb pie that usually accompanied their traditional summer fish dinner. But, thanks to picking up a store-bought pie crust on the way home, she was able to rally and get one in the oven.

This was one of the few meals Carly ever requested and actually enjoyed eating. She called it a "cheat day." Fourth of July was a cheat day for her too. For the past few years, Carly had been a marathon runner, which in a roundabout way was how she ended up living in Boston. Most of the time she ate like a bird, unless it was the day before a race, when she could put away enough pasta to feed a small Italian village. Isabel had witnessed what Carly called "carb loading" when she went to Boston to support her daughter on her first marathon. She had a whole group of marathon friends over doing the same, and it was something to see.

Breakfast for Carly was a fresh fruit-and-yogurt smoothie with some kind of mystery powder she brought with her, along with a handful of baby carrots or celery sticks. And "snacking" for her meant walking around with an open bag of frozen peas, picking out one at a time and popping them into her mouth. It drove her brother crazy, and Isabel too, a little bit.

The kids pulled into Poplar Bluff right on time and honked their arrival. Isabel and the dogs hurried out to meet them in the driveway, and as she always did when they came home, she felt an immediate sense of calm. They were home, and they were safe. For the next four days, she could see them, touch them, cook for them, and hear about all the exciting things happening in their lives.

After they got settled into their old bedrooms, which were technically an office/den and a guest room now, they all walked out onto the dock to watch the sunset. Carly rarely if ever drank, so she brought a bottle of some fancy French water she was partial to, Isabel had a glass of wine, and Charlie brought a bottle of beer, which he had stopped to buy on the way up. When he raised it to his lips, Isabel noticed it was a Bachmeier beer. She was not planning to talk about anything having to do with her newest case with the kids. This holiday was about them, not work, but she had to ask. "Is it any good?"

Charlie shrugged. "It's okay, I guess. It was on sale."

Charlie also inherited his mother's frugality. After another outstanding perch dinner, some lively conversation, and strawberry-rhubarb pie à la mode for dessert, the kids did the dishes while their mother got out the Scrabble board. They sat down to play, just as they had done hundreds of times before. She looked up at her kids as they carefully arranged their tiles in their racks. Carly, by far the most competitive member of the family, already had a look of fierce determination on her face, while Charlie, who brought his Buddhism to his Scrabble game, just smiled and hummed quietly to himself. For Isabel Puddles, life couldn't get any better than this.

On the morning of the barbecue, Isabel was up with the birds making Belgian waffles for Charlie, a tradition on Fourth of July morning. He insisted she still serve them with a happy face made with strawberries, blueberries, and whipped cream, in keeping with the holiday, just as she had been doing since he was three years old. Charlie was very much a traditionalist. Carly, naturally, wanted no part of her mother and brother's waffle tradition. She had already been for her run and taken a swim, so she sipped on her fruit smoothie and crunched on her baby carrots with a look of slight consternation while watching her brother and mother pass the butter and syrup across the table to each other. "Stop judging us," Charlie said to his sister as he got up to get the can of whipped cream out of the fridge, squirting more onto his mother's waffle and then his. He then handed the can to his sister, who looked at it as if he had just pointed a gun at her.

"I'm not judging *anybody*," Carly said defensively but un-convincingly.

"Want a bite?" Charlie asked his sister, pointing a gooey forkful at her.

"Are you kidding? If anybody in my running club even

saw me sitting this close to that sugary mess on your plate, they would probably drum me out."

Isabel was suddenly reminded of something and had to ask, "Oh! Speaking of *drums*, do you kids ever remember hearing about the Indian drum when you were growing up?"

Charlie got a look on his face, but waited to swallow before speaking. "We don't say Indian anymore Mom. It's Indigenous, or First Peoples, or—"

"Yes, I know, honey, and I do try to be mindful of that, but they still call it the Indian drum. People around here only recently stopped saying Oriental, so. . ."

Carly bit into another carrot. "Isn't that where the drum beats whenever somebody drowns in the Big Lake?"

"Yes, and as ridiculous as that sounds, there are lots of people here who believe it. Aunt Frances is one of them. She's a little obsessed with it lately."

"Aunt Frances has always had an interesting relationship with fact versus fiction," Charlie offered. "She thought *ET* was a documentary."

Carly took another bite of carrot, then nonchalantly added in between crunches, "Granddad and I heard it once out at the lighthouse." Isabel and Charlie looked up at each other and then at Carly, staring at her until she offered more details.

She took the hint. "Well, we heard this pounding sound, and there was no bad weather approaching so it wasn't thunder, and there was nothing else to account for it . . . and then the next morning in the newspaper there was an article about a man who had gone missing off his sailboat. Coincidental? Maybe . . . maybe not."

Charlie shook his head. "So you think the Great Spirits of Michigan's First Peoples have nothing better to do with their time in the spirit realm than sit around with their drums and keep track of who's drowning in Lake Michigan?"

"*Now* who's being judgy? There are plenty of mysterious phenomenons in this world that have yet to be explained. For instance, why, after eating the breakfast you just did, haven't you lapsed into a diabetic coma?"

Isabel laughed. She always got a kick out of her kids' back-and-forth banter. They were as devoted to each other as any brother and sister could be, but they loved to tease each other, oftentimes creating arguments just for the fun of it and to entertain their mother.

It was shaping up to be a beautiful day, which was good news. Although guests wouldn't begin to arrive until around four, there was still a lot to do before then, so after breakfast she sent Carly and Charlie outside to decorate the yard with red, white, and blue balloons and crepe-paper streamers, along with a handful of flags, and to set up the tables and chairs. It was hard to predict how many people would show up, but Isabel always made sure she had enough to feed at least a few dozen people, and kept a side stash in case of overflow.

She remembered her mother, who was known as one of Gull Harbor's consummate hostesses, telling her daughter that the worst thing that could happen at any gathering was running out of food. Her father argued that running out of booze was much worse. This was not an argument worth having or one she would have any hope of winning. Helen eventually revised *her* position after one fateful dinner party where Clancy Winger, an agent with Buddy's insurance agency, had a gallbladder attack just before dessert was served and had to be taken away in an ambulance. Clancy was fine in the end, but it was still not a good look for any hostess, and a terrible way to end a meal, especially when Helen had made such a beautiful cheesecake. And, as was to be expected, Clancy teased her for the rest of his life about the night she tried to poison him.

"If he doesn't shut up about it," Helen once said to her

husband and daughter after bumping into Clancy in town one day, "I'm going to start wishing I had."

So for Helen Peabody, moving into the number one slot of the worst things that could happen to a host or hostess was having a guest leave your home on a stretcher. Running out of food dropped to number two. Buddy of course still insisted running out of booze remained the cardinal sin of entertaining, but it was one he had never committed.

Isabel's barbecue guest list fluctuated from year to year, but her closest family and friends were almost always in attendance; Carly and Charlie were usually there, of course, as were Freddie and Carol, and Frances and Hank; Gil Cook and his family usually attended, as did Brent Buchanan and his girlfriend, whichever one it happened to be that year. Meg and Larry Blackburn came most years unless they were with Larry's family on Mackinac Island, which was where they were this year. And Ginny and Grady, still traveling somewhere in America in their RV, would be missing Isabel's barbecue, Ginny, for the first time ever. She was going to miss them. Ginny was always fun at parties, and Grady would be missed because having the sheriff there had a way of keeping guests on their best behavior. Kayla had made it to only one of Isabel's barbecues a few years back, but with three young kids who wouldn't stay away from the lake, she was a nervous wreck the entire time, so she was always a "maybe" but usually a no-show.

There were going to be some first-timers this year too. Beverly Atwater would be coming, which would be her first Fourth of July as a summer resident of Gull Harbor, and Isabel's new friends, Zander and Josh, were going to be there too. She hadn't seen them since attending their wedding last summer in Saugatuck, so she was excited to see them again.

Isabel was glad she had decided to take some of the pressure off of herself and the kids this year by hiring on some help. Now they didn't have to be tasked with patrolling the party and could just have fun. This year Jazz would be in charge of making sure the buffet table was supplied, and staying on top of cleanup. Isabel also hired Roger, who had until very recently been—well, there was really no nice way to put it—the town drunk. But Roger had turned his life around, and Isabel had grown quite fond of him over this past year, and admired how he had pulled himself together. Once he seemed to be committed to staying on the straight and narrow, Isabel had helped get him a job cleaning kennels and walking dogs at the animal shelter where she volunteered. Today, after a full year of sobriety, and steady employment, Roger had rehabilitated both his reputation, and his appearance, quite nicely. It was hard to tell how old he was during his drinking days, but now she guessed he was probably in his early forties, with eyes that were now bright blue instead of bright red. After putting on some much-needed weight, cutting his hair, and shaving his scraggly beard, Roger was virtually unrecognizable as the man he had been just one year before. In fact he was now catching the eyes of some of the single women in town, and a few married ones too.

When Roger's backstory began to get out, nobody was surprised to learn that he had once owned a little dive bar in downtown Detroit. But after the factory where most of his customers worked closed down, he lost it. What *did* surprise people was that Roger had recently been hired as a bartender at the Black Bear Tavern for the summer. It wasn't a spot Isabel ever frequented, but she did know that lots of tourists and other summer people enjoyed going into the Black Bear to mix it up with the locals, so it was busy almost every night. It was also the only bar in Gull Harbor. The locals were, for the most part, friendly with the tourists and vice versa. But inevitably, most every summer, you would hear about some kind of a dustup, which usually led to some drunk man in Bermuda shorts and boat shoes being dragged out of the bar by his friends with a black eye or a fat lip. The regulars at the Black Bear could put up with only so much from rich city people.

To those who had gotten to know Roger over the course of his newfound sobriety and reentry into Kentwater County polite society, working in a bar and serving drinks seemed like it might be tempting fate. Isabel had run into Roger out at the shelter recently and asked him, point-blank, purely out of concern for his well-being, if he was worried about being in that environment. Roger laughed and thanked her for her concern, but told her that being around all that booze, and watching people get falling-down drunk nearly every night, reminded him of why he quit. Isabel decided nobody could argue with that.

The plan was for Roger to mind the bar at Isabel's barbecue until he had to report to the Black Bear for Gull Harbor's post-fireworks rush. All he had to do at Isabel's party was fill beer mugs from a keg and pour wine. She didn't serve liquor at her barbecues . . . anymore. Not since she decided to do margaritas one year and ended up having to plead with Frances to come down off the roof, *and* keep her top on at the same time.

Freddie always supplied the bratwurst, which he special-ordered from a German butcher he knew in Wellington, and he always manned the grill. That way he could talk to everybody, and Freddie loved to talk. Isabel knew she could count on him to set up the bar for Roger too, so he could make sure he would have easy access to it from the grill, because Freddie loved his beer too.

Her biggest challenge every year was making enough of her potato salad, baked beans, and cherry buckle to go around. Although it was becoming more and more tempting every year to cut corners with store-bought potato salad, baked beans, and dessert, Isabel didn't really see that as a viable option. She knew she wouldn't be able to deal with the look of disappointment on her guests' faces.

One year she didn't get around to making her spiced mixed nuts, always served in a big silver bowl, for her annual Christmas Eve open house. Isabel could still remember her plumber, Mort, practically tearing up when she broke the news to him. She was afraid she had ruined the poor man's Christmas, so she got up extra early on Christmas morning, made a batch of spiced mixed nuts, and sent Charlie to deliver a big jar of them to Mort's house, just so the guilt wouldn't ruin her holiday too.

Isabel had finally wrapped things up in the kitchen, so she went out to survey the venue. Carly and Charlie had done a wonderful job decorating, and the yard looked very festive. They had even found the old American flag out in the garage and raised it at the end of the dock. Charlie had put himself in charge of music years ago, so he always had a new playlist, although some years his musical selections were more popular than others. Freddie and Carol were the first to arrive with two kegs of beer and two big boxes of bratwurst. While Carol caught up with the kids, Freddie got busy setting up his grilling station and the bar, making sure the keg was within arm's reach in case Roger got too busy. Frances arrived next with the wine, her yearly contribution, and her three-bean salad, and Kayla arrived shortly after that with a beautiful flower arrangement picked from her own garden.

"Where are the kids?" Isabel asked Kayla.

"They're spending the holiday weekend with their father in Traverse City this year," she answered with a sigh of relief.

"Oh, that's a shame," Isabel said, admiring the bouquet Kayla had just handed her.

"Shame? It's the best gift I could ask for! Talk about Independence Day! I can have as many beers as I like, *and* I don't have to spend the whole time worrying about them falling into the lake!"

Jazz arrived next and got right to work setting up the buffet. Isabel had to scold Frances for giving her the side eye. "Please, Frances, just for today, can you try to be nice to her?" Frances answered by lifting her eyebrows, shrugging her shoulders, and walking away.

Next to arrive was Roger, wearing a crisp white shirt, blue pants, and a red bowtie. After Isabel introduced him to Freddie, she headed back inside, where Frances stopped her on the front stoop. "Is *that* Roger? That can't be him . . . there's no way."

"That's Roger, all right. Doesn't he look great? And he came in red, white, and blue—so cute! It's amazing what a difference a year can make, isn't it?"

"It's amazing what a difference not having breakfast, lunch, and dinner on the rocks every day can make! Who knew he was handsome?"

"Frances, you're a married woman."

"For now!"

Isabel had almost forgotten about *that* ongoing drama. "I'm sure you'll work it out. But if you do end up single again, please stay away from Roger. I don't know anybody who could knock the poor man off the wagon any faster than you could. Where *is* Hank, by the way?"

"He can't come. It was his turn to babysit Mother Spitler, so he's picking her up and taking the old gal up to his sister's in Wellington for a little family barbecue. Hate to miss that! Who doesn't love off-brand turkey franks, beans out of a can, and macaroni salad from the Kroger deli?"

"You could have had Hank bring his mother over here, Frances."

Frances looked at her as if she had just gotten a whiff of burned broccoli. "I'm going to pretend you didn't just say that, Isabel. I would rather light a sparkler and put it—"

"Okay, got it! Don't be crass, Frances. It's America's birthday, for God's sake. I want you to be on your best behavior today, can you manage that?" Another lift of the eyebrows and a shrug was her only response, which was not a real confidence builder.

Isabel did one last walk around to make sure everything was ready, and when she determined it was all systems go, she told Charlie to turn on the music. He opened, as he always did, with a crackling recording of Kate Smith singing "God Bless America." If he had already gotten into the beer, Freddie usually marched around the lawn with sparklers and sang along to mark the official beginning of Fourth of July at Poplar Bluff. The weather was gorgeous. Sunny, but not too hot, with a nice, gentle breeze blowing from the west, so all the elements were in place for another memorable Puddles barbecue.

Isabel went into the kitchen to do a final check on operations, and could see that Carly and Charlie were on top of everything. They had already put the beans, with the brown sugar and bacon crust, into the oven, and had three large pans of cherry buckle ready to go in after that. She panicked for a moment when she couldn't remember if she had bought vanilla ice cream from the Amish dairy, but after a quick check in the back freezer, she remembered she had done it last week. Cherry buckle without vanilla ice cream from the Amish on the Fourth of July would be catastrophic.

Freddie came in to collect the bratwurst rolls and the condiments, including the homemade sauerkraut he also got from his German butcher, and a bowl of what was now referred to as "Charlie's Chutney," a mouthwatering concoction made with caramelized onion, sweet peppers, and golden raisins, along with a smattering of secret ingredients he would not divulge. Charlie had started making it a few summers ago, and because everybody raved about it, he had to keep making larger and larger batches of it every year. Charlie had inherited his mother's passion and talent for cooking. He loved the classic Midwest comfort foods he had learned from his mother and both grandmothers, but after living for the past ten years first in San Francisco, and later across the bay in Sausalito, he had taken his culinary prowess to the next level, using ingredients Isabel had often never even heard of and making dishes that were more ambitious than anything she would ever attempt. Isabel knew her culinary lane and she stayed in it. Her days of experimentation ended the day she ruined a fifty-dollar cut of tenderloin attempting to make beef Wellington. But, funny enough, it was his mother's special pot roast that Charlie's city friends, with their worldly, sophisticated palates, requested he make most often.

Now that all the prep work was done, and Freddie had turned on the grill, it was time for Isabel to change into whatever red, white, and blue ensemble she had decided on this year, one of three or four holiday specific outfits she rotated from one year to the next. This year it was red Capri pants and a sleeveless navy-blue blouse with white polka dots. Once she was dressed, as a final festive touch, Isabel put little American flag collars around Jackpot and Corky, who were getting increasingly excited with all the activity, probably sensing that at some point there was going to be some food hitting the grass.

By five o'clock, the barbecue was going full swing and people seemed to be having great fun. Along with the usual suspects, a dozen or so neighbors from around the lake and a handful of friends from town had showed up too. Freddie was in his element—talking, grilling, and drinking beer. Roger seemed to be enjoying himself too, and he and Freddie had become fast friends. In fact, Freddie didn't even realize he was the same Roger he had known until after the party. Jazz was working away diligently, always wearing a smile, assisted by Kayla, who couldn't help herself when there was food to bring out and plates to clear. With Diego tucked under her arm and dressed in an Uncle Sam outfit, trying to maintain some dignity, Beverly made the rounds as if she were running for office, shaking hands and introducing herself to everybody, unaware that everybody already knew who she was, and still in the process of deciding whether they liked her or not. For Frances, though, the jury was in, and Beverly Atwater was another one on her list of people whom she was committed to holding a grudge against. But she had finally accepted the fact that she and Isabel had become good friends, so she would just have to get used to her being around, like it or not. Likewise, Beverly wasn't a big Frances fan, but she did a much better job of hiding her opinion. Killing Frances with kindness was Beverly's way of secretly annoying her.

Zander and Josh appeared to be enjoying themselves, and had charmed everybody they met. On her way out, Mildred Campbell, who had always been a little slow on the uptake, commented on what nice young men they were to Isabel. "Shame their wives couldn't make it, though." The comment stumped Isabel for a moment until she realized Mildred must have noticed them both wearing wedding bands, but apparently not noticing that they were *matching* wedding bands. Two married men, married to each *other*, was just not a blip that would ever appear on Mildred's radar screen.

As the party began to wind down, Frances walked up to Isabel with an odd-looking grin on her face. "So what do you think about *that*?"

"What do I think about *what*?" Isabel asked with a puzzled expression.

"That." Frances pointed with her chin to the table where Zander, Josh, and Charlie were sitting together and laughing.

Isabel shook her head. "I'm not following, Frances."

The odd-looking grin returned. "Those three seem to be getting along awfully well, don't you think?"

"So?"

"So . . . have you ever thought maybe Charlie belonged to the same club?"

"Oh for the love of Benji, Frances! I am *not* going to have this conversation with you. Stop being such a busybody!" Isabel walked away, genuinely annoyed. Yes, of course she had considered that Charlie might belong to the "same club" as Zander and Josh. He was in his early thirties, good-looking, smart, funny, successful, belonged to a gym, and living in San Francisco. To her knowledge, he hadn't had a girlfriend since high school, when during his junior year he dated Becky Culver, the captain of the girls' softball team. But she couldn't imagine if her son *were* gay, that he wouldn't tell her. That alone was reason to think he wasn't, because she and Charlie had always been able to talk about anything, so it was impossible for her to conceive that he would hide such an important part of himself from her. Granted, there had been a time when discovering her son was gay would not have had her doing cartwheels on the front lawn, but that would be true for a lot of parents, even the most loving and understanding. Isabel grew up in a generation where Charles Nelson Reilly and Paul Lynde were considered merely *peculiar*. For her parents' generation, Liberace was only single because he hadn't met the right girl. And, despite all the rumors, Helen Peabody never believed for a second that Rock Hudson, her favorite movie star of all time, was gay, and she never would. She had also never stopped lamenting the fact that he and Doris Day had never married because "they make such a beautiful couple. And their chemistry!"

For Isabel, the only thing she would find troubling about either of her children being gay would be not wanting them to be judged, or bullied, or discriminated against, or worse, feel *less than*, just for being different. No loving parent would want that for their child, knowing they were powerless to protect them from it. But thanks in part to having gotten to know Zander and Josh, and seeing what exceptional young men they were, how much they cared for each other, and how open and proud they were of who they were, she would support Charlie one hundred percent today if he were to tell her he was gay. All she wanted for Carly and Charlie was for them to have fulfilling and productive lives, with as much happiness, and as little heartache and strife, as possible, which was what any good mother would want for her kids. Isabel was both happy and proud that both her kids *were* living fulfilling, productive lives, they seemed to be very happy, and so far, had avoided the proverbial slings and arrows life would inevitably shoot their way. Naturally she would like for them each to find a soulmate with whom to travel through life. Grandchildren would be nice one day too, but she never pressured them on that front.

What Charlie's dating life in California looked like was a mystery to his mother. And now that he was a Buddhist, who knew what that meant? Did he have to date other Buddhists? Were Buddhists even allowed to date? Was there such a thing as gay Buddhists? Whatever the case, she hoped he was on the right path to meet someone someday, of whatever persuasion.

When it came to dating and romance, his sister was a completely different story . . . Carly was a pretty girl and had always been outgoing and popular. In high school she had three boyfriends, and in college, three more, but she always seemed to find a reason to break things off. Today she had a busy life and a successful banking career, but she assured her mother that she still found time to date, at least occasionally.

But the method by which she was meeting men was one Isabel found perplexing. Carly didn't believe in dating anybody she worked with, which her mother agreed was a good rule to follow, and she found her fellow bankers dull anyway.

After recently educating her mother about what an "app" was, Carly proceeded to demonstrate one of the *dating* apps she and millions of others of her generation were apparently using to meet prospective partners. As Isabel understood it, it all had to do with sweeping (or was it swiping?) to the left or the right, yea or nay, and it all seemed based entirely on a single photograph. If the person in the photograph was someone you liked, you swept, or swiped, in one direction or the other. If they liked you back, they swept, or swiped, in the same direction, which meant there was then the potential for a date. To Isabel, it all seemed rather rushed and impersonal, not to mention a little bit shallow, but she kept that opinion to herself.

Carly claimed she wanted to marry and have kids, and she knew her mother wanted grandkids, whether she said so or not. But Carly was a few years older than Charlie, so if she really did want to get married and have a family, it seemed to her mother that she might want to start sweeping or swiping a little bit faster and more often. But she was not the kind of mother who was going to badger her kids about finding a partner. She trusted that whatever path they chose for themselves, or whatever path was chosen *for* them—and for whom, if anybody, they traveled that path with—would be the right one.

As dusk began to fall, only a handful of guests remained. Gil Cook and his family had another party to go to, so they left fairly early. The twice married, and twice divorced, Brent Buchanan and his girlfriend—Debbie was this one's name—also had another party to attend. When Brent was on his way out, Isabel told him she thought his new girlfriend seemed very nice, but that she had stopped retaining the names until she had met them more than twice. He laughed and told her he was sure Debbie was the one, and that she was going to be his next wife . . . which was the same thing he had said about his last half dozen girlfriends. In fact she seemed to remember there might already have been a Debbie somewhere in the mix.

Isabel was thrilled that Zander and Josh had been able to make it, but they had to get back down to Saugatuck for a boat party some friends were having. Both Beverly and Kayla had been a little overserved, so Isabel tipped Roger a little extra and asked him to drive them home on his way to work. Freddie had turned off the grill, filled a pitcher with beer, and plopped down in a lawn chair on the water's edge, while Jazz was still busy cleaning up. The remaining guests took chairs down to join Freddie and get ready to watch the annual Gull Harbor fireworks display, which was less than a mile away, so it always made for an impressive show. Isabel was pleased with how the party had gone, and rated it one of the best barbecues she had thrown in a while.

She had just gotten settled in between Frances and Carol with a cup of coffee when Charlie leaned down and asked if he could talk to her. Was this it? she thought. Was her son planning to have his big coming-out-of-the-closet reveal accompanied by fireworks? They walked out onto the dock before he felt it was safe to speak. "Who's the girl cleaning up right now? I forgot her name."

"That's Jazz. She's working with Kayla for the summer down at Land's End. Why?"

Charlie looked around again before speaking. "Well, I just saw her coming out of your office, and she got this strange look on her face when she saw me, then told me she was looking for the bathroom."

Isabel wasn't quite sure where he was going with this. "Okay . . . and?"

"And . . . She already knew the bathroom was on the other side of the house, because I showed it to her shortly after she arrived. So either she was poking her nose where it didn't belong or she's got some serious short-term-memory issues."

Isabel smiled. "I don't think there's anything to worry about, honey. I'm sure she just got turned around. She's been waiting on us for weeks now and seems like a very nice girl."

Charlie shrugged his shoulders. "All right, Mom. I just got a weird feeling from the look on her face, but if you trust her, fine. Just thought you should know."

As they turned to walk off the dock, Jazz was walking toward them with a big smile. "I've put all the food away, Mrs. Puddles, cleaned the kitchen, loaded the dishwasher, and broken down all the tables and chairs. So I think that's everything."

"Perfect! Thank you so much, Jazz. You did a great job! Let me go get my purse so I can pay you."

Isabel walked up to the house and went into her bedroom where she had left her purse in its usual spot, an antique chair that belonged to her mother. But it wasn't there. She looked around her bedroom but saw no sign of it. She walked back out to the kitchen, checked her office, but her purse was nowhere to be found. *How strange*, she thought as she went back to her bedroom to look again. But she *knew* that's where she had left it. Naturally the conversation she had just had with Charlie immediately came to mind. She didn't want to believe Jazz would steal from her, but if she did, would she—or anybody, for that matter—be so brazen as to steal the whole purse instead of just the wallet? And how would she have hidden it? Carly, who had just woken up from a nap, came down the hall and popped her head in. "Great party, Mom. You did it again."

"I'm glad you had fun dear. Couldn't have done it without you and your brother, though. Hey, have you seen my purse around? I was sure I put it right here in this chair."

"I put it in your closet. There were a few unfamiliar faces around here coming in and out so I thought it best to stash it away. Can't be too careful these days, Mom. You know you're *way* too trusting."

Isabel instantly felt ashamed she had even entertained the idea that Jazz had stolen her purse. "I happen to think it's better to be *too* trusting than not trusting enough."

"Really? Have you watched the news lately, Mom?" Carly walked over to the closet and retrieved her mother's purse.

Isabel laughed as she took her purse and looked inside. "I hope my coupons are still in here! Thank you, honey. I do appreciate you looking after your mother." She opened her wallet and took out two fifty-dollar bills for Jazz . . . and an extra twenty-dollar tip to make up for thinking she was a criminal.

"Well," Carly added, "after what happened last year, I think you might *need* a little more looking after."

Isabel gave her a hug. "Don't you think if your old mom could get through an ordeal like that unscathed, she can probably get through just about anything?"

Carly smiled. "I don't think we should tempt Fate. The next time, you might end up getting scathed. Come on. Let's go out and watch the fireworks."

"Wait, I need to put the dogs in the office. Fireworks make poor Jackpot crazy, and Corky is a lot more high strung than he is, and this is her first Fourth of July at the lake. I'll meet you out there."

Isabel grabbed the dogs' daybeds in the kitchen and lured them into the office with treats. She tossed the beds down and threw doggie biscuits into each, then assured them in doggie-speak that she'd be back in a little while. But as she started to close the door, she happened to glance over at her desk. Her laptop was sitting right where she had left it, but something caught her attention . . . A folder sitting next to her laptop was definitely not how she had left it.

Isabel was a stickler for organization, and the papers inside this particular folder were sticking out in disarray. She would never have left them that way. So once again, her conversation with Charlie about Jazz came back to her. But why would she be poking around her desk? She stopped herself and quickly dismissed the idea. Somebody had probably just come in looking for something, maybe a pen and paper. Now she felt a little silly for letting her kids plant suspicions like this in her head. Isabel loved that Carly and Charlie were so protective of her, but they were both city people now, so they saw the world a lot differently than their small-town mother did. They may have become skeptical of people's intentions, and maybe that was necessary if you lived in a big city. But here in tiny little Gull Harbor, she was going to keep on trusting people, at least until they gave her good reason not to.

Isabel came back outside and handed Jazz her cash and invited her to stay to watch the fireworks. Jazz thanked her but said she needed to go meet some friends at the beach. "All right, well, thanks again for doing such a great job today."

"Thank *you*, Isabel, I enjoyed it. You have a very nice family, *and* friends. Guess I'll see you at breakfast again soon!" And with that, Jazz waved goodnight just as the first fireworks exploded in the sky.

Chapter 21

The holiday weekend went by far too quickly, and now Isabel found herself standing in the driveway waving goodbye and blowing kisses to her kids as they pulled out of the driveway on their way to the airport. She was managing to keep a smile on her face, while simultaneously trying to fight back tears, when her cell phone rang. It was Ramush. She needed a minute to compose herself, so she decided to wait five minutes and call him back. By the time she had pulled herself together, he had left a voice mail apologizing for not being able to attend the barbecue and to let her know he would not be driving to Petoskey with her this morning, after all. "When I told Miss Bachmeier you had located Jacob in Petoskey, she insisted on going up to meet him before he disappeared again. We'll be leaving very shortly and will be staying at the Bayshore Inn. Please call me once you get to Jacob's and tell him his aunt would like him to join her for dinner at the hotel this evening. I've made an eight o'clock dinner reservation for the four of us. Miss Bachmeier is counting on you to make sure he is there. Oh, and I've reserved a room for you at the hotel for this evening, as well. We'll look forward to seeing you later."

Isabel was disappointed Ramush wouldn't be coming along to keep her company on the drive up. She was already missing the kids and they hadn't even been gone fifteen minutes. Driving a few hours alone would now feel that much lonelier.

After packing an overnight bag and picking out something nice to wear for dinner at the Bayshore Inn, an elegant old hotel that had once been the summer home of a wealthy Ohio rubber magnate, Isabel had an idea . . .

"Good morning, Frances . . . How would you feel about driving up to Petoskey with me today and spending the night?" She looked out the kitchen window and waved at her neighbor, Justin, who was coming over to dog-sit again. "There's no catch . . . I just thought it would be fun for us to spend a little quality time together, you know, before you move . . . I'm just kidding, Frances!" She chuckled as she watched the dogs excitedly greet Justin as he came in the gate. "But if you'd rather do laundry than spend time with your best friend, I understand . . . You're right! He *should* get used to doing his own laundry." She took her last sip of coffee. "Can you be ready in thirty minutes? Great. I'll see you then."

After a couple hours on the road, with about ten minutes of their conversation devoted to Isabel's visit with her children, and another five minutes on the barbecue, the next one hundred minutes were unsurprisingly devoted to Frances's current issues with Hank. What Isabel had somehow missed was that Hank was now in his new position, and living in an extended-stay hotel in Grand Haven. Fortunately, he had been outbid on the waterfront condo he had put an offer on, so they didn't have that to deal with. But now he was pressuring her to come down and look at other places. Because Hank's promotion had put Mr. and Mrs. Spitler into a new tax bracket, they could keep looking for something on the water, he told her, but Frances was still as defiant as ever.

"What's this man's obsession with living on the water, anyway? Next thing you know, he's going to be looking at houseboats! If I want to be on the water, I can drive to the beach, or just come over to your house," Frances declared.

Isabel reiterated her suggestion that as long as they could afford it, why not buy something there, keep their house in Gull Harbor, and then split their time? But she was officially done offering advice. Frances and Hank were just going to have to work this out on their own.

Isabel and Frances were beginning to feel peckish. With another ninety minutes to go before they got to Petoskey, and then however long it was going to take to find Jacob's place, they decided they should start looking for a place to stop for lunch. A sign for a Cracker Barrel caught their eye, so they agreed to stop there. The experience didn't get off to a great start.

Because it was lunchtime, the place was packed. Although it was just off the highway, the place seemed to be most popular with locals from the surrounding farming communities as opposed to tourists. Frances grumbled something about the place looking like the studio audience for *Hee Haw*, a comment Isabel ignored as she held up two fingers for the blue-haired hostess who approached them with an armload of menus and a warm smile. "Hello, ladies, welcome to Cracker Barrel. I have a nice booth over by the window if you'll just follow me."

Frances's assessment of the crowd was pretty spot-on. When two middle-aged women from Gull Harbor passed for city folk, you knew you were really in the country. After they reached their booth, the hostess assured them their waitress would be right with them. Isabel looked at her name tag. "Thank you, Laverne," she said as she slid into the booth.

"Look," Frances said as she slid in and gestured out the window into the crowded parking lot, "I haven't seen this many pickup trucks in one place since Conway Twitty played the county fair."

Isabel opened the menu, "Please try to be on your best behavior, Frances. I'm hungry, and I'd rather not face the humiliation of being thrown out of a Cracker Barrel."

Frances was poking around in her purse for her reading glasses. "I don't know *what* you're talking about, Isabel."

After having been seated for about a minute, two glasses of water suddenly landed on the table, startling them both. They looked up from their menus at a woman with an imposing figure, a wrist brace on her right hand, and the look and manner of someone who had obviously been doing this for a while. Her name tag read: Edna. "You ready to order?" Edna asked with a heavy sigh and all the enthusiasm of someone about to have an impacted wisdom tooth removed.

Frances was digging through her purse. "Hold your horses there, Edna. I don't even have my glasses on yet."

Edna glared down at Frances with an expression that instantly made Isabel nervous. Their waitress clicked her ballpoint pen a few times, then turned her attention to Isabel, who quickly moved into damage control. "How are *you* doing today, Edna?"

"Well, I'm sixty-four years old, I've got bursitis in my left shoulder, carpal tunnel in my right hand, fallen arches on both feet, and I'm workin' at the Cracker Barrel . . . so that's how I'm doin'."

Frances put her glasses on and gave the menu a look. "How about we see what we can do to brighten up your day a little, Edna."

Isabel was immediately suspicious. What kind of game was she playing now? Frances was many things, but a brightener of days was not on that list. "Good luck with that," Edna replied. "If the vodka didn't do the trick this morning, I don't see much chance you can pull it off. You need a little more time?"

"Yes, please. Thank you, Edna," Frances replied with a smile.

"You got it," Edna replied, tucking her pen behind her ear and moving on to her next table.

Isabel looked over the top of her menu at Frances. "What's going on here, Frances?"

"I know when not to poke a bear with a stick. Edna obviously woke up on the wrong side of the cave this morning, and since she's going to be in charge of our lunch when we can't see it, I'm playing it cool."

"So if Jazz were more intimidating and unfriendly, you'd be nicer to her?"

"Doubt it. Listen, I know you like her, Iz, but I'm telling you, something isn't right about that girl."

"Okay, well, we're just going to have to agree to disagree. Are you ready to order? Edna's coming our way again, and if we aren't ready, I'm afraid what—oh, hi, yes, I think we're ready Edna."

Edna stood next the table with her eyebrows arched and her pen clicking. "Super . . . So what'll it be?"

Isabel folded her menu up. "I'm going to have a BLT on whole-wheat, mayo on the side," she said as she handed her menu to Edna.

"And I'll have the chef salad, with Thousand Island dressing *not* on the side, please. I don't like having to dress my own salad." Frances handed her menu back to Edna with a forced smile.

"Yes, that's real drudgery, dressing your own salad," Edna replied. "Anything to drink?"

Isabel jumped in. She knew Frances had her limits. "We'll each have an iced tea, unsweetened, with lemon. Thank you." Edna nodded and left without saying a word.

When their orders arrived, Isabel's mayo was on the side as requested, but so was Frances's salad dressing, which she had gone out of her way *not* to request. She looked up at Edna. "I believe I specifically asked you *not* to bring my dressing on the side."

"That's right, I believe you did. Well, let's fix that." Edna reached down, picked up the ramekin filled with Thousand Island dressing, and poured it over Frances's salad. "There we go. Anything else?"

"Some crackers, please," Frances asked through teeth that were already beginning to clench.

"We ran out of crackers, sorry. The barrel's empty."

Frances took a deep breath and looked up at their waitress. "You know, Edna, waitressing is a little like a game of fetch. Most dogs manage it quite nicely, and with a lot less attitude."

Edna paused for a moment, then calmly asked, "Are you calling me a dog?" Isabel was bracing for the worst.

"No. . . I *like* dogs," Frances answered, then looked over at Isabel. "How about we take our lunch to go, Iz? I'd rather eat in the car. If you would be so kind as to bring us our check and a couple to-go containers, we'll be on our way. Then you can go back to pulling the wings off flies, or whatever it is you do for fun."

So that was their Cracker Barrel experience. But at least they left of their own accord, as opposed to being kicked out. Isabel made sure she picked up the check so she could leave Edna a nice tip, despite her nasty demeanor. Everybody can have a bad day, she reminded herself, and it looked as if poor Edna had strung quite a few of those together. After eating their lunch in the van with the engine running and the air conditioning on, the next few miles on the road were pretty quiet . . . until Isabel suddenly started to giggle. Frances looked over and joined in. For the rest of the trip, it was one bout of the giggles after another as they relived their experience with Edna. Isabel had to admit that, given a choice between the subdued and polite Frances, who did her best to disarm their charm-challenged waitress or the Frances who finally snapped and put her in her place, the latter was much more entertaining.

After she had decided to come along with Isabel on this road trip, Frances called her cousin Louise who lived in Petoskey and arranged to stay the night with her. She and Isabel agreed they would meet in the morning at the hotel, then do some shopping and have lunch before driving home.

Petoskey was a charming little town that sat on Little Traverse Bay. The historic hamlet was famous for its many quaint shops, including a chocolate shop that both Isabel and Frances agreed made the best fudge in the world, and where they both intended to load up. After arriving at Louise's cute little Cape Cod home near the bay, they were having a chat in the driveway until a look of panic crossed Isabel's face. "What's wrong?" Frances asked her.

"I didn't bring my laptop! It has the map of how to get to Jacob's in it!"

"Do you still have it written down?" Frances asked.

"I think it's still in my bag . . . Oh, please let it be there." She walked over and reached into her van, pulling out her tote bag. After digging around for a minute she found it. "Whew! Here it is."

"Give it to me and hand me your phone," Frances said, putting her hand out. After she plugged the information into

Isabel's phone, she handed it back in thirty seconds. "Voilà! You're back in business."

Isabel thought it might be a good idea to call Jacob first so he didn't feel like she was sneaking up on him. "Excuse me, ladies." Isabel got back in her van and placed the call, while Louise showed Frances around her immaculately kept front garden. Jacob picked up on the second ring. "Hello, Jacob, it's Isabel Puddles calling . . . I'm just fine, how are you? Great . . . and you're home now? Well, it just so happens I'm in Petoskey, and I was wondering if it would be all right if I came by . . . According to my phone map, you are thirty-three miles away, and it will take me forty-one minutes to get there . . . What will they think of next? I feel like Jane Jetson . . . Oh, never mind . . . before your time . . . All right, then, I'll see you within the hour."

Isabel put her window down and said her goodbyes. Louise said she wanted to come shopping with them, so they all agreed to meet in the lobby of the Bayshore Inn the next morning at eleven. Isabel backed out, tooted her horn, and was on her way, directed by a woman's voice coming from her phone. *Who doesn't know who Jane Jetson is?* she asked herself. *Am I really that old?*

For a very long time Isabel had avoided anything she deemed too high tech, which included laptop computers, cell phones, and the Internet. Even after her family and friends, many of whom were older than her, joined the twenty-first-century technological revolution, and despite constant encouragement bordering on nagging from her kids, she stubbornly refused to cave to the pressure. In truth, Isabel felt more like Wilma Flintstone trapped in Jane Jetson's world for quite some time. But in the past year she had slowly entered the modern era. First with a cell phone—a birthday gift from Beverly Atwater—and next, with a laptop—a gift to herself. Although she still found the Internet intimidating, she was also finding it quite handy, and she had learned to use the Google, and use it quite proficiently. The final frontier would be trying to figure out the remote control for her new flat-screen television, which had come close to sailing into the lake more than once. *Baby steps,* she told herself.

After driving a few miles, Isabel began to find the map lady's voice rather comforting, making for a much less sassy copilot than the one she had just dropped off.

Chapter 22

After driving down a deserted dirt road lined with northern pines for a good ten minutes, and with virtually no sign of civilization other than the road itself, Isabel thought the map lady must be lying to her. She pulled over and called Jacob again to make sure she was on the right course, and not on her way to the Canadian border.

"Do you remember seeing an old abandoned farmhouse with a rusty pickup truck out front?" Jacob asked.

"Yes, but that was a good five miles back."

"Good, then you're on the right road. Do you remember crossing over a rickety old wooden bridge?"

"No."

"Well, once you cross that bridge, you'll have three-point-seven more miles to go. You'll see me out in front. I'm unloading my van next to the barn."

"Boy, you weren't kidding when you said you were living off the grid," Isabel said as she put her van back into gear and started off down the road again.

"And if I could get farther away from civilization, I would!" Jacob added before hanging up.

Isabel soon crossed the rickety wooden bridge, then drove

several more minutes until she spotted a clearing in the distance. She slowed down and was relieved to see a VW camper van and a weathered old barn set well away from the road. Jacob came out of the barn and waved as she pulled in and parked. At first glance, the place looked like a roadside attraction of some kind. A modestly sized log cabin was still partially under construction, with large blue tarps covering portions of the uncompleted roof, and next to it, an old Airstream trailer in need of a good polish. The old barn was more like a very large wooden lean-to shed, unlike the style of old barns typically found in Michigan. Scattered all around the property were large, rusty iron sculptures in abstract designs, stacks and stacks of wooden cherry crates, and piles of lumber stacked here and there. To one side of the barn there were a series of fenced-in livestock pens, and in front of it, a vintage Sunoco gas pump. There was no mistaking that this was the home of an artist, and an eccentric one at that.

As soon as Isabel got out of her van she was greeted enthusiastically by two large, very friendly dogs who ran out ahead of Jacob. The two shepherd mixes were smiling and wagging their tails furiously as Isabel reached down to pet them. "The black-and-white one is Bucky and the other one is Scout," Jacob yelled to her. She then greeted them by name and scratched their heads some more. Suddenly a bloodhound came barreling out of the barn, ears flapping in the wind, then body-checked Bucky and Scout to get in on the petting action. Jacob reached out to shake Isabel's hand. "And this is Molly. She's kind of an attention hog. I just got her last month. She flunked out of the police academy because she has doggie ADD. Poor girl can't decide what scent she wants to follow, so she tries to follow them all. Apparently that's not what they're looking for in a tracking dog, so she ended up at our local animal shelter . . . and now here."

"She's beautiful," Isabel said as she scratched her head.

"Looks to me like she lucked out coming here. Better than chasing fugitives through the woods, I would think."

"She seems pretty happy. Bucky and Scout aren't sold on her yet." Isabel looked over at the two sidelined shepherds sitting nearby and looking dejected. "We don't get many visitors out here, so this is a very big deal." Jacob then smiled contritely. "I'm sorry I took off on you like that last week. Must have been a little awkward for you, but I could see where things were headed with my mother and it was no place good. I just couldn't stay for it. Plus I really needed to get back here."

"No apology necessary. I'm just sorry you and your mom are so at odds. That must be hard on both of you." Jacob had no reaction, so she continued scratching behind Molly's ears a little more, then looked up and around the place. "This is quite a spread you have here, Jacob."

"It's a work in progress. But the progress ebbs and flows. As you can see, there's been a work stoppage on the cabin. I kinda ran out of money, so I sleep in the Airstream for now. But the cabin's kitchen and bathroom are finished, so I'm not roughing it that much."

"But what do you do in the winter? How do you keep warm?" Isabel asked with motherly concern.

"I pull the trailer into the barn as soon as the first snow flies. I have an old potbellied stove in there that keeps the whole place pretty warm. My studio is in there, too, so I can work all winter. And, speaking of pot bellies. . ." Isabel followed Jacob's eyes and saw a large potbellied pig coming out of the barn. "That's Gary. He just woke up from his nap, so he's a little cranky." Gary came over and sniffed Isabel's pant leg, looked up at her, then moved on with a snort. "That's about as personable as he gets. There are a couple more guys for you to meet but I have to keep them penned up if I'm not able to keep an eye on them. They are *serious* troublemakers."

Isabel followed Jacob over to the large fenced-in pen

where two brown-and-white speckled goats were standing at the fence, waiting to be introduced. "That's Flora and that's Fauna. You can probably tell Flora's pregnant. I have a friend who watches the place and takes care of the animals when I'm away, and he brought his male goat over a while back and, well, apparently he had chemistry with Flora, and nature took its course. So pretty soon we're going to have a couple baby goats around."

Isabel swooned. "Which are just about the cutest creatures on the planet!"

Jacob nodded in agreement as he pointed to another part of the property. "And over there is the chicken coop. I've got nine Rhode Island Reds. They keep me well stocked with eggs. The goats and the chickens come into the barn in the winter too. And there's an old owl who lives in the rafters I named Doctor Hoo." Jacob then pointed to the other side of the property. "And over there is my vegetable garden, which is the reason Flora and Fauna are on lockdown. I've taught the dogs to scare the deer and raccoons away, but these goats aren't afraid of them in the least. If anything, it's vice versa."

"I am so impressed, Jacob. You're like a cross between Henry David Thoreau and Dr. Doolittle . . . with maybe a little Noah thrown in there too."

Jacob seemed fine with the analogy. "I read Thoreau in college. He was a big influence on me. I even made a trip to Walden Pond a few years ago. I knew I wanted to live off the grid before I even knew it was really a thing. I plan to have more animals too. I may even turn the place into an official animal rescue at some point. I have twenty acres, so why not?"

"Looks to me like you're already pretty official."

"Getting there. It all kind of started with a donkey named Festus. There was this local farmer I got to know who had to sell his farm—it was either that or the bank was going to take it—but the new owner didn't want Festus, so I took him. He threw the goats in too. Festus and I had an instant bond. The goats played hard to get for a while, but Festus followed me everywhere and talked to me constantly from day one. I talked to him too. And we understood each other. I know that sounds crazy."

"Not crazy at all. I talk to my dogs all the time, and I think we do understand each other to a degree," Isabel said as she reached over the fence to pet the goats. "Where's Festus now?"

"I lost him last year. I still get choked up if I let myself think about him for too long. Anyway, since I already had Festus and the goats, why not take in a few more, right? So next it was Bucky and Scout, who I got at the local shelter, and then one day Gary arrived. Somebody just dropped him off in the night. When I woke up, he was lying up on the cabin porch, waiting for breakfast. I guess word had gotten out that I was a soft touch." Gary walked by at that moment with a cat riding on his back. "Oh, yeah, and some cats found me somehow too. Gary hates them."

Isabel was fascinated with Jacob's life off the grid and wanted to know more. "This whole concept of living off the grid is kind of new to me. My son told me about it. He just bought some land in northern California and plans to build something *off the grid*, but not to live full-time. So you don't have electricity here?"

"Sometimes. I have solar panels on the roof of the barn, on the other side, but you can't always count on the sun in this part of the state. And you see that old windmill over there? I've got that hooked up to a battery, and I get some power out of that too, depending on the weather. Come with me and I'll show you something else."

They walked through a stand of trees behind the cabin, and as they got closer, Isabel could hear running water. They came upon a stream falling over a beautiful waterfall about ten feet high and into a large crystal clear pool of water surrounded by moss-covered boulders.

"I get all my water from the stream. This pond, which I'll admit is man-made, is my swimming hole all summer long, but I've got a little homemade hydroelectric system set up, which you can't really see from here. I'm still perfecting it, but it gives me a decent amount of electricity. I don't really need much, though. So I'm *mostly* off the grid. My only concession, and the purists would criticize me mercilessly for it, was putting in a septic tank. I built an outhouse when I first bought the land and started building the cabin. Then I came out one morning and saw a big black bear coming out of it. He looked like he had spent the night in there and I was pretty sure he would be back, so I called the septic tank people that day and added a bathroom to the cabin. I grew up in the suburbs. I'm not trying to live prehistorically here. I just believe in living as self-sufficiently as possible. I also have a gas-powered generator, just in case, which is another big no-no for the purists. Come on, I'll take you inside the barn."

Isabel was beyond impressed. She already knew Jacob was a good man after watching him interact with his brother in the hospital, but anybody who could run an operation like this alone was also very smart. And he had an animal lover's soul to boot. If Abigail Bachmeier was hoping her long-lost nephew would turn out to be a man of strong character, somebody she could trust to oversee her beloved foundation after she was gone, she couldn't do any better than Jacob.

When they walked into the barn, Isabel was what her friend Teddy called "gobsmacked." One entire wall had shelves made from old fruit crates, displaying thirty or forty different ceramic pieces. The opposite wall was completely covered with vintage signs, with dozens more leaning against it.

"I don't know if my mother told you, but I'm a ceramicist.

I have my potter's wheel in that corner, and my kiln is out in back of the barn. I used to go to a bunch of art shows every summer to sell my stuff, but that got much harder once the ark started filling up. I have that friend I mentioned who will come out and watch the place when he's available, so I can still hit the big summer art shows. In fact I have one in Saugatuck coming up. There are some folks who collect my stuff who'll show up every year at those big shows. Some who are more adventurous will actually drive out here."

Isabel walked over to take a closer look at some of Jacob's work—beautifully glazed vases, bowls, and jugs of all sizes and shapes, some in earth tones, others in an array of bright colors. There was also a collection of sculpted candelabras, and a smattering of sculptures that seemed to have no purpose other than to be interesting and unique. Isabel was taken with one sculpted candelabra in particular, lifting it gently to admire it. "Your work is beautiful, Jacob," she said as she carefully set the piece back down. "Just beautiful."

"Thank you, Isabel. I love it . . . the whole process. It's very tactile and messy, and also quite therapeutic. When I sit at my wheel and get my hands on that clay, it's like meditation for me. I tried iron sculpture for a while, as you may have noticed out in the yard. That was a fail. Welding is not at all therapeutic, and I wasn't very good at it anyway." Jacob turned around. "And over here is my collection of vintage signs. I've been collecting them for years."

They walked to the other side of the barn, where he began to sort through some of the old signs leaning against the wall. "I'll show you one of my favorites." Jacob reached back and pulled out a large, slightly rusty tin sign with a smiling, winking man wearing a fedora and holding a pint of beer. It read: REFRESHING OLD WORLD GOODNESS . . . BACHMEIER BEER. He leaned it against the others and stood back to admire it. "From the late 1940s, maybe early '50s. It's a Milwaukee beer . . . I think the first beer I ever drank was a Bachmeier. You know it's strange, I don't know what it is, but I feel this weird connection to this sign, and to this beer. I'm saving this one to put up in the cabin if I ever finish it."

Gobsmacked didn't begin to cover what Isabel was feeling right now. She looked at Jacob and tried to come up with something to say but was completely tongue-tied. Jacob put the sign back where he had found it, then looked back at Isabel and smiled, taking a moment before speaking. "I've known for years, Isabel. *And* I know who hired you to find me. What I don't yet understand after all these years is why?"

Isabel was still in a partial state of shock as she tried to process what Jacob had just told her. After he made them some tea, they sat down in some Adirondack chairs positioned around a fire pit that also served as a grill.

"I make this tea with fresh mint that grows wild all over here. Do you like it?"

"Delicious. You really do live off the land, don't you?"

"As much as humanly possible. I eat out of my garden from spring to fall, and I learned to can and jar from the wife of that old farmer I got Festus from. That gets me through the winter. I usually buy a stag in the fall—I don't hunt, but lots of folks around here do—so I eat a lot of venison in the winter. I don't ever go hungry. The only food I really buy is for the animals. Learning to bake bread is my next culinary endeavor."

Isabel was completely captivated by this young Renaissance man living deep in the north woods, but what she was dying to know was how he discovered he was a Bachmeier. And then it was almost as if he had read her mind. Was he clairvoyant, too?

"So you're probably wondering how I found out Skip Bachmeier was more likely than not my father."

"I'd be lying if I said I wasn't," she answered before taking another sip of tea.

"Well, one day I overheard a conversation between my mother and my aunt Sharon. They thought I had gone outside to play, but I was really in the basement playing with my trains. I always heard everything that was going on in the kitchen above me. Anyway, that day they were talking about somebody named Skip dying in a plane crash. I remember hearing my mother say, 'Are you sure Jacob's outside?' I was only, I don't know, maybe twelve years old at the time, but it still didn't make any sense to me why they would be talking about this guy and a plane crash. And why were they being so secretive about their conversation? Then I heard my aunt say, 'I think you need to tell him. He deserves to know who his father is.' And I remember my mother saying, emphatically, 'Absolutely not. Jacob has a father now. What's the point? Maybe someday, but right now it will just confuse him.' That ship had already sailed because then I was *really* confused. I still am, by the way. And then I saw Skip Bachmeier's picture on the front page of the newspaper the next day and read the article about the crash, and about him being the only son of Randolph Bachmeier. I knew my mother had worked at the Bachmeier Brewery, along with my grandparents, but I still didn't really get the connection."

"And do you ever remember Mr. Bachmeier visiting you?"

"Just vaguely. I remember a nice old guy bringing me toys, and a few other memories, like little snapshots of him. One of him pushing me on a swing . . . another of riding a Ferris wheel with him and eating cotton candy. Later on I figured out who he was. I know I said I didn't recognize him when you showed me that photograph, but my mind was racing at the time, and I'm just so used to keeping it all a secret, I kind of froze. I also remember he always had this mysterious-looking man with him who always had on a black suit. Then around Christmastime one year I remember my mom telling me the man died, and I remember her being so sad about it. I was maybe five years old at the time. But that's really about it. Since I met you that day, though, I've had some other flashes of memories, like his smile, and his mustache."

"And you never asked your mother about your real, or rather, your biological father?"

"I love my mother, even though I'm angry with her now, but she is not the easiest person to talk to. She has a short Irish temper, and she used to get depressed from time to time, another Irish trait, so I never wanted to say anything that might upset her. I've always instinctively known that whatever the story was behind her relationship with Skip Bachmeier, it wasn't a happy one."

"That's quite a secret to keep all these years, Jacob. And your mother obviously still has no idea you know?"

"Nope. But it looks like that cat's about to jump out of the bag, right?" Jacob added as he finished his tea.

"Your aunt Abigail, and that mysterious man in the black suit you remember, whose name is Ramush, are at the Bayshore Inn right now waiting to meet you. Ramush was your grandfather's chauffeur, but he's worked for your aunt ever since he died. They'd like you to come for dinner tonight."

Jacob nodded and stared off into the distance before speaking. "Bayshore Inn. Very fancy. I've never been inside, but I think I heard they require a sport coat for men, and I don't have one," Jacob said as he reached down to pet Molly, who had just shoved her head into his lap, demanding to be petted.

"I wouldn't worry about that. I'm pretty sure your aunt has some pull. Anyway, all that's important is that you finally meet. So you'll come tonight?"

"Sure . . . why not? I've certainly been curious about all

this since you found me. I'll try to come up with something presentable to wear so I don't embarrass anybody."

"Ramush made an eight o'clock dinner reservation." Isabel looked at her watch. "So if I leave now, that gives me just enough time to get checked in and get ready myself." She got out of the chair, but it took some effort. "Whoever designed Adirondack chairs was either a sadist or a contortionist. I've always loved the way they looked, but I've never once been comfortable sitting in one." Jacob laughed as they walked over to her van and he opened the door for her. Isabel looked at him before getting in. "I'm a little afraid to leave you here. I don't want to lose you again."

Jacob smiled. "I'll be there . . . Promise. I just need to feed this menagerie and then lock them down, which is no small undertaking. When they get the sense I'm leaving they all get a little weird and start hiding. But I should be able to make it there by eight." With that, Jacob gave Isabel a hug. "Thanks for going to all this trouble to find me, Isabel."

"Thank *you* for letting me. I didn't know for sure who or what to expect if I was *able* to, but you have been a very happy surprise. I know you will be for your aunt too. And Ramush is very anxious to see you again after all these years."

Jacob looked like he might be on the verge of getting a little emotional. "Drive safely Isabel. I'll see you at eight."

As she drove back into Petoskey, Isabel's mind was reeling. She called Ramush to let him know Jacob would be there at eight, but she didn't get into any details regarding their surprising conversation. It wasn't her place, just as it wasn't her place to tell Jacob why it was his aunt Abigail wanted to meet him. As she thought more about the time she had just spent with Jacob, she was not only taken with what a happy, self-contained person he seemed to be, and how devoted to his art and to his animals he was, but also fascinated by the fact that for all these years he had known he was related by blood to a beer dynasty, yet he never chose to divulge that to his mother or to the Bachmeier family and try to cash in. Here was a young man who looked like he was about to become the sole heir to a vast fortune—unless Trey Bachmeier miraculously turned up alive somehow—who lived in an Airstream trailer next to a cabin with a half-finished roof. Her only hope now was that, whatever came of Jacob's new relationship with his aunt Abigail, it wouldn't change his life too drastically or alter his admirable character. Because as it had been proven, time and again, money can do terrible things to a person.

Chapter 23

After checking in to the classically elegant Bayshore Inn and then racing to get ready in time, Isabel met Miss Bachmeier and Ramush in the stylishly appointed hotel lobby. She hadn't seen Abigail in a while, but what she picked up on right away was how pensive she seemed to be. Isabel attempted to make small talk, but neither she nor Ramush were very interested. They both seemed miles away. A slight feeling of dread began to creep in. What if this reunion turned out to be unpleasant or even combative, like Abigail's meeting with Colleen? But it was too late to worry about that. There was no slowing this train down now.

Abigail, sitting contemplatively in an exquisite antique chair, suddenly got up and said she wanted to go outside and wait for Jacob. Moments later, there they were, standing in the grand portico of the old inn and waiting . . . and waiting. Isabel looked at her watch. It was now almost ten minutes after eight and she was starting to get nervous. What if Jacob got cold feet? Then, in the distance, she heard the faint but familiar sound of a Volkswagen engine. *Please let that be him*, she said to herself. When she saw Jacob's van turning into the long driveway, lined with summer flowers, slowly putt-putting its way up to the portico, she felt a rush of relief.

"Here he is!" Isabel said cheerfully. Her eyes were suddenly diverted when she noticed Abigail reach over and grab Ramush's hand.

The young valet in the red jacket looked ready to go out to tell the driver of the camper van he had made a wrong turn. After parking the most expensive cars on the market all summer long, this was likely the only explanation for why this less-than-mint-condition Volkswagen van was suddenly idling under the grand portico of the Bayshore Inn. When Jacob walked around the front of the van, after thanking the still confused valet and waving at his welcoming committee, Isabel was stunned to see that Jacob had shaved his beard, pulled his hair back into a ponytail, and was dressed in a pair of khakis and a yellow polo shirt. Isabel knew he was handsome, but not *this* handsome. He smiled brightly at them all as he made his way up the steps. What happened next was a moment Isabel did not see coming, and one she would never forget . . . the sight of Abigail and Ramush, both with tears running down their cheeks.

Jacob stopped halfway up the steps. "I thought this was supposed to be a *happy* occasion! What's with all the tears?" Abigail tried to say something but couldn't speak. Her nephew went right up to her and took both her hands as she reached out to him. He looked her in the eyes for a moment, then lightly kissed her cheek before embracing her gently. Isabel was so touched she had to turn away and wipe her tears away. When she looked back, she saw Ramush with his hand on Jacob's shoulder. At that moment, any concerns she had had about this reunion going poorly dissipated completely.

After Abigail finally let go of Jacob's hands, she looked at his face again, patted his cheek, and finally found words. "I'm your Aunt Abigail, Jacob."

Jacob grabbed both her hands again. "Well, it's nice to meet you, Aunt Abigail. I guess that makes me your nephew, Jacob."

She took one of his hands and raised it to her cheek. "You're the spitting image of your grandfather. It's just remarkable. Isn't it remarkable, Ramush?"

Ramush finally composed himself, and now reached out to shake Jacob's hand. "Remarkable," he said softly.

Jacob shook his hand, then pulled him in for a hug. "Come on Ramush . . . bring it in."

Abigail took a deep breath. "Well, shall we go in and sit down? I requested a table with a view of the bay. And what a beautiful evening it is."

"Let's do it." Jacob took his aunt by the elbow and turned her toward the door. As he did, she looked back at Isabel and stretched her hand out to take hers.

"Thank you, Isabel. This means the world to me."

This time Isabel was speechless.

Dinner began with some friendly chitchat about Petoskey and Abigail reminiscing about what it was like before the tourists found it, just as they had Gull Harbor. She had not yet mentioned her last name, so in her mind she was still just Aunt Abigail, Jacob's father's sister, but Isabel was sure she had probably already thought about how she would begin a more formal introduction to her, and the world he was about to enter. Nobody had opened their menus yet, and Abigail and Ramush could barely take their eyes off Jacob. The waiter politely interrupted and asked for a drink order. Abigail ordered a kir royale, and just water for Ramush and Isabel who were, after all, both technically working. When it came around to Jacob he ordered a beer. "A Bachmeier if you have it." He was happy to hear they did, then smiled, avoiding eye contact with Isabel, who of course was wise to what he was doing.

"I love an ice-cold Bachmeier. Nothing like it . . . but it's so hard to find in northern Michigan. I'm still a Milwaukee boy at heart, I guess." Abigail and Ramush looked at each other in wide-eyed amazement until Jacob smiled and reached over and grabbed his aunt's hand. "I'm just teasing. I know who you are, Aunt Abigail . . . And I've known about who my father was for years."

Abigail's expression registered both shock and happiness. She took his hand and started getting emotional again. Jacob then went on to share the same story with them that he had shared with Isabel earlier, about the day he overheard that conversation between his mother and his aunt in the kitchen. At one point, while talking about Mr. Bachmeier's visits, he looked over at Ramush. "I do remember you now too, Ramush. I could only remember a man in a black suit before, but now that I see your face again, I remember you very clearly."

Ramush was touched. "I remember you too, Jacob . . . very clearly."

Then Jacob smiled as if he had just conjured up a fond memory. "You always had a pack of Juicy Fruit gum with you, I remember. You'd slip me a piece when my mother wasn't looking because she wouldn't allow me to have gum."

Ramush reached into his jacket pocket and pulled out a pack of Juicy Fruit. "I'm still never without. When I first came to America from Albania, the stewardess gave me a piece of Wrigley's Juicy Fruit just before our plane landed in Chicago. I was crying because my ears were hurting and popping and she said chewing gum would help. I thought that piece of gum was manna from heaven. I've been chewing it now for more years than I care to admit. But never in front of your aunt Abigail. She will not abide gum chewing. Consider yourself forewarned."

Abigail smiled at Jacob. "Nor could I abide the Wrigleys. My mother and father, your grandparents, used to invite them over to Bachmeier Hall every summer. They had a boy about my age, he was the grandson of William Wrigley, the patriarch who I suppose we have to thank for the charming invention of chewing gum. I've forgotten the boy's first name but I remember he went by Packy. And, lucky for me, Packy had a terrible crush on me. The boy was always chasing me around the grounds, trying to kiss me. What I also remember quite vividly, unfortunately, is that Packy had the most *atrocious* breath! I remember asking my father why anybody belonging to a family that made their fortune with peppermint gum would have such a bad breath problem." Abigail led the table in a big laugh.

During dinner Jacob talked about his fondest memories of Mr. Bachmeier. More and more details were coming back to him the longer he talked, and Ramush's memories were triggering others for him. Abigail was completely enthralled, with a softness Isabel had never seen before, or even imagined existed. There was no longer any trace of the sadness and the loneliness she *had* seen, or the resentment, when she spoke of Skip and Trey. She and Ramush were both completely captivated as Jacob shared some of the details of his life: his art, his animals, his home, and his commitment to living off the land as much as possible. The more he talked, the more pleased with her nephew Abigail became, periodically looking over at Isabel with sparkling eyes and a smile.

After the waiters cleared their plates, Abigail asked Isabel and Ramush if she could have a few minutes alone with Jacob. It was evidently time for her to talk to him about family business matters. Isabel and Ramush were happy to excuse themselves. They walked out onto the dock in front of the inn to take in the rest of a glorious western Michigan sunset over the bay. Ramush had a few questions for Isabel about Jacob, which she answered politely by telling him that they were questions he should be asking of him rather than her. But then he asked a question that stumped her. "Do you think he knows anything about Trey?"

Isabel thought it over for a moment. "I certainly didn't tell him, and he never brought it up. But I would think so, given that it was in all the papers on both sides of the lake. Then again, maybe life off the grid for Jacob includes staying away from the news too."

"Well, if he didn't already know about Trey's mishap, I'm sure Miss Bachmeier has now told him."

"Mishap? Is that what we're calling it now, Ramush?" Isabel asked.

"What would you prefer we call it, Isabel?"

"It's not my business . . . I'm sorry. You're entitled to call it whatever you like. It's just that *mishap* seems a little cavalier."

"Okay, let's call it an accident." Ramush smiled at her.

Isabel nodded her head slowly as she watched the sun sink into the lake and disappear from view. "As I said, Ramush, this is not my business. Call it what you like, but unless or until his body is found, other possibilities can't be entirely ruled out."

"Like murder, for instance?" Ramush offered.

"I'm sorry for bringing it up. No need to get back into all that," Isabel insisted. "Let's just concentrate on the positive! Looks like things have turned out better than expected. Miss Bachmeier is like a new woman, and even *you* got emotional seeing Jacob again after all these years. I recall you telling me you hoped he would give Miss Bachmeier a sense of family again." Ramush nodded as Isabel continued, "It looks to me like that's the path they're on. But it's also pretty obvious to me that Miss Bachmeier considers you family too, Ramush."

"I've spent far more of my life with the Bachmeier family than I ever did my own. Sadly I barely remember my own parents. I don't know what would have become of me if Mr. and Mrs. Bachmeier hadn't brought me to America."

Isabel remembered something she wanted to ask Ramush about now that she had seen where Jacob lived. "It's probably none of my business, but since when has that stopped me, so I'm going to ask anyway. Miss Bachmeier told me that her father had taken a sizable portion of Skip's stock in the company and used it to set up a trust for Jacob. So whatever happened to that? I mean, if he doesn't have the money to finish putting a roof on his cabin, and sleeps in a trailer instead, it doesn't sound to me like he's ever come into that kind of money."

"I had suspected it for years, but Colleen confirmed that Skip, with the help of his lawyers and a couple of corrupt trustees, found a way to raid Jacob's trust after Mr. Bachmeier died. It was the sort of unconscionable thing he would do and think nothing of. By the time Colleen had discovered what happened, it was too late. To try to recoup what he stole would have required a lawsuit and the publicity that would come with it. And, before you knew it, Skip was dead. There was some money left, but not much. When Jacob came of age, she told him he had inherited some money from a relative in Ireland. Apparently he set it aside and used it to buy his land and at least *start* building his cabin. When she learned of this from Colleen, Miss Bachmeier immediately replenished what her brother had stolen, which was an amount I was privy to. He hasn't learned of that yet, and I probably shouldn't be telling you, but I know you'll keep that under wraps."

"That's very generous of her," Isabel said.

"Miss Bachmeier is incredibly generous. And in this case she is simply ensuring that her father's intentions are being honored, even if it is a few decades later. He'll learn about it in due time. But when he does find out, I do hope he'll dip into that trust to at least put a roof over his head."

The more Isabel learned about Skip Bachmeier, the more she thought maybe he *did* get what he deserved, however it came to be. Who steals money from his own child?

Ramush stared out at the horizon for a few moments, then turned to Isabel again. "I want to thank you for all you've done, Isabel. You have gone above and beyond."

"I only did what you hired me to do, Ramush. But I couldn't be more pleased that things have turned out as they have."

Just then one of the waiters walked out onto the dock and approached them. "Miss Bachmeier has asked that you please come back inside."

When they got back to the table, Isabel looked at Jacob and smiled. He smiled back, but his look told her there was a lot more on his mind now than there had been when she left. Jacob had clearly just been given a lot to digest. Abigail looked across the table at Isabel. "I want to thank you for all you've done in bringing this moment to fruition, Isabel." She then turned to Jacob and took his hand. "And this young man has exceeded, well, I can't say he has *exceeded* my expectations, because I've learned to manage those in my life. But he has certainly exceeded what my hopes were for the sort of young man he would be." She looked back at Jacob. "I know your grandfather is smiling down on us right now. Jacob will be coming to visit us at Bachmeier Hall very soon, but I'm afraid he has to leave us now."

Jacob was still looking a bit discombobulated, as if maybe he needed some time to himself to process whatever he had just learned from his aunt about the Bachmeier family and his place in it now. "Yes, I need to get back to the home front, but I will be seeing you all again very soon." Jacob stood up to leave. "Thank you for finding me, Isabel. And Ramush, Aunt Abigail, thank you for looking for me."

After Jacob said his goodbyes, the waiter brought coffee for the table. Just then, Ramush's cell phone rang. He pulled it out of his jacket pocket and looked to see who was calling. He turned to Abigail. "It's Sinclair."

"You talk to him, Ramush. I don't want to hear about any staff drama right now."

Ramush excused himself from the table to take the call. Abigail reached over and took Isabel's hand. "He's just a lovely young man, isn't he, Isabel? He reminds me so much of my father at that age, minus the ponytail. Not only in appearance, which is indeed striking, but in the tone of his voice, his demeanor, even his mannerisms. It's quite remarkable what one inherits. I'm pleased to know that all my father's wonderful traits live on after skipping a generation."

There was that dark, biting humor again, but Isabel was still happily surprised to see such warmth coming from a woman she had previously written off as cold and somewhat heartless.

"He is indeed a wonderful young man. I'm very happy for you, Abigail. And relieved too. Things could have gone in a very different direction." She had barely gotten the words out when Ramush reappeared at the table looking slightly shell-shocked.

"The sheriff just called and spoke to Sinclair. Trey's body has been recovered."

Chapter 24

After receiving the stunning news about the discovery of Trey Bachmeier's body, Abigail and Ramush left immediately to go back to Gull Harbor to meet with Sheriff Chase, but Isabel decided to stay the night as planned. There was no need for her to go with them. As she kept reminding herself, Trey Bachmeier's fate was not her business. And she didn't like to drive at night. That didn't mean she could put this sad development out of her head though. It wasn't exactly shocking news, given that, for weeks now, everybody, including Abigail and Ramush, had made the assumption that Trey Bachmeier was dead. But it didn't make the news less jarring or tragic. Whatever his less-than-admirable personality traits might have been, people do change. But the opportunity for this young man to one day change his colors and perhaps become a better person had been preempted by tragedy.

Anticipating that the story would be covered by local news, Isabel waited for the eleven o'clock report. Not surprisingly, it was the lead story. Sheriff Chase was the first person interviewed. According to the sheriff, a badly decomposed body, believed to be that of Trey Bachmeier, was discovered by local fishermen tangled up in their nets early this morning. The cause of death was assumed to be drowning, but the county coroner would be doing an autopsy to confirm. The sheriff did, however, say there was no indication of foul play. Trey had been tentatively identified by the monogram on his shirt, and personal identification found in his wallet which was still in the zipped pocket of his windbreaker.

Isabel immediately thought about what this would mean for Jacob. Now that Trey's death was confirmed, the weight that was about to be put on his shoulders was going to be a terrifically heavy burden for anybody to carry, especially someone who seemed to have very little interest in the material world.

After a restless sleep, Isabel got up in the morning, had her coffee, checked out, and then got into her van to drive home, forgetting all about Frances until she started to back out. It was only nine, and they were not due to meet until eleven, so she pulled back into her spot and went inside. The tempting breakfast buffet she had opted to pass up an hour before was now summoning her back. After breakfast she still had time to kill, so she walked out to the lawn, sat down in a wicker chaise, and looked out at the spectacular view of the bay, the water glistening in the morning sun.

Shopping with Frances and Louise was about the last thing she felt like doing today, but she knew there was no getting out of that. The best she could do was try to expedite the excursion. At eleven, Isabel sat down on a bench under the portico and waited for them to show up, and when they did, Isabel was in for a lucky break. She walked over to the car and looked inside to see that Frances and Louise did not seem to be in very good condition. Before she could even ask what was wrong, Louise cleared things up.

"Three bottles of wine . . . I knew opening the second bottle was a bad idea, but after bottle number two, number three practically opened itself. I'm sorry, Isabel, but I need to just go home and climb back into bed."

Frances then chimed in. "And all I'm interested in shopping for right now is some aspirin, Iz. Would you mind if we just headed home?"

Isabel thought it was only polite to pretend she was disappointed, when in reality she was thrilled. She began with a heavy sigh. "All right, well, I'm sorry you gals are under the weather, but I understand. Maybe we can plan to come back in December and do some Christmas shopping. This town always looks so cute at Christmas."

"Great idea!" Louise said as she put her car back into gear. "Thanks for being such a good sport, Isabel. It was nice to see you again. I'm coming down for Thanksgiving so I'll probably see you then." Frances was already out of the car and had reached in to grab her overnight bag from the back seat. She leaned back in to say goodbye, and Cousin Louise was off with a parting farewell honk.

Isabel looked at Frances and shook her head. "Three bottles of wine. What were you thinking?"

"It was actually four. I hid the last bottle after we emptied it."

Once the aspirin kicked in, Frances slept most of the way home, making it a very contemplative drive for Isabel. By the time she dropped Frances off and got back to Poplar Bluff, it was late afternoon. Justin was sitting out on the dock fishing, with Jackpot and Corky sitting next to him, patiently anticipating what he might pull out of the water. When they saw that their mom was home, they tore down the dock and up the lawn to greet her. Justin waved and began to reel in his line.

After she paid Justin and sent him on his way, she unpacked her overnight bag and walked into the kitchen. The house seemed empty with the memory of having the kids at home so fresh. She loved her home, and she loved *being* home, but it always felt so much homier when Carly and Charlie were in it, so whenever they left, there was an inevitable period of readjustment.

Isabel decided to write a quick e-mail to Jacob. She wasn't going to bring up anything having to do with Trey, but she wanted him to know how much she had enjoyed meeting him and that she was there for him if he ever needed to talk. But when she walked into her office and over to her desk to get her laptop, it wasn't there. Had she left it at the office? At the store? No, she was certain she had brought it home, because she and the kids had used it to set up a personal e-mail account for her, which was in the morning just before they left, and she knew her laptop was on her desk then.

She looked around the house just in case, but finally picked up the phone to call Justin and ask him if he had seen it. Maybe he moved it for some reason. "No, Mrs. Puddles . . . I never went in your office, and I only remember seeing your laptop once on your kitchen table. And I only remember *that* because my mom has the same computer."

Isabel thanked him and hung up. There was now only one conclusion. She had been robbed. She ran straight to the drawer in her bedroom dresser where she kept her jewelry and found it had been untouched, which came as a great relief because she had her mother's, grandmother's, and great-grandmother's wedding rings there in her collection. The television was still there, and the cookie jar in the kitchen where she kept emergency cash was also untouched. She went around and checked all the doors and windows, but there was no sign of a break-in. Then a knock at the door startled her. She looked through the peephole. It was Justin. She invited him in and noticed he was wearing a funny expression. "What is it?" she asked.

"Okay . . . well, yesterday I took the dogs on a walk over to the Big Lake. It was late afternoon, and we got about a quarter of the way there and I remembered I hadn't locked the glass slider when we came in off the deck earlier. I always make sure your doors are locked when I leave, but I figured it would be fine. Nothing bad ever happens on Gull Lake, so I just kept going. When we got home, the slider was open. Just a little bit, but it was open. Then I got mad at myself for being so careless. It's bad enough to forget to lock it, but to not even close it all the way? Now I'm afraid that's how whoever took your laptop probably got in." Isabel was taking it all in but saying nothing. "I'm so sorry, Mrs. Puddles. I feel terrible. I'm going to buy you a new laptop."

"Don't be silly. You'll do no such thing. And do not beat yourself up about this. I forget to lock the doors all the time. But why would anybody want my laptop? It wasn't an expensive one. It's just a mom computer, right? And why wouldn't they take anything else?"

"Maybe when they heard the dogs and me coming back, it scared them off?"

"Yes, I suppose that's possible." Isabel looked at her watch. The hardware was still open. Isabel always went to Freddie when she found herself in situations she wasn't quite sure how to handle, and this landed squarely into that category. Isabel Puddles was not someone who frightened easily, but the idea that somebody had come into her home and robbed her left her feeling anxious and vulnerable. For the first time in her life, Isabel felt unsafe in her own home. After assuring Justin again that she did not hold him accountable, she locked up, put the dogs in the van—because now she was afraid to leave them home alone—and drove to the hardware store.

Although she tried to be calm when she told Freddie what had happened, he could tell she was rattled. Freddie told her she needed to go to the sheriff's office immediately and file a report and offered to go with her. He turned to Andy, who was listening and looking concerned. "Do you think you could mind the store alone for an hour, Andy?"

"Sure, Mr. Peabody. No problem." Then, turning to Isabel, "I'm sorry this happened, Mrs. Puddles. It's not the kind of thing you think about ever going on around here."

Isabel thanked them both for their concern, but told Freddie she was fine with going to file the report alone. "Andy, if you could watch the dogs while I'm gone, that would be helpful. They're out in the van."

"Sure, let's go get them. I'll take them back to lawn and garden and they can sniff around."

Isabel put Jackpot and Corky on their leashes and introduced them to Andy, who she could tell was a dog lover. After crouching down to say hello, he stood up and took their leashes from her. "Do you think it was somebody you know who stole your laptop, Mrs. Puddles?"

"I sure hate to think so, Andy, so I'm going to assume that is *not* the case."

"Well, it's a shame either way. I had my brand-new Schwinn ten-speed stolen a week after my mom and dad gave it to me for my birthday. I locked it up to a street sign, but they somehow lifted it up and over. I know this will sound very melodramatic, but it changed the way I saw the world. It really did . . . and I was only twelve."

Isabel was touched. "That's terrible, honey, but I understand what you mean. I wonder if it's better to learn firsthand at *that* age that there are people out there who steal, or be reminded of it when you're my age. Well, that's a conversation for another day. Thanks for watching these guys. I'll be back shortly."

Isabel walked the few blocks to the sheriff's department and for a moment forgot about her stolen laptop. Instead she began hoping Sheriff Chase would be there, and would be willing to provide some more details about Trey Bachmeier. But when she got to the office, he unfortunately was out. She had no choice then but to sit down with Melanie Hodges, who took the job as the department's office manager after her cousin Ginny retired. Melanie was not a big Isabel fan. She had never forgiven her for winning the title of Asparagus Queen when *she* only made second runner-up, so Melanie had always been a little snarky whenever their paths crossed. The feeling was mutual, but Isabel had always countered her snarkiness by being overly nice and polite, something that really got under Melanie's skin. Once she took the job with the Sheriff's Department, it was as if she had gone to work for the FBI tracking down America's most wanted fugitives. How well her previous job as the office manager of a carpet store had prepared her to become a crime fighter, however, was questionable.

Isabel took a breath and sat down across from Melanie at her desk. She patiently sat through a ten-minute interrogation, which included being asked about possible persons of interest, and if anything of a sensitive nature was on the laptop. But after Melanie asked if any blood was found at the scene, Isabel's patience ran out. "I'm sorry, Melanie, but blood at the scene? Really? Do you think maybe they stopped to chop an onion on their way out and cut themselves?" Melanie looked at her unamused and said nothing, then reached into a drawer and presented her with a four-page form to fill out. Isabel forced a smile. "You know, I think I'll take this home and fill it out. I'll bring it back in tomorrow."

"We won't be able to assign a detective to the case until we have that form filled out, just so you know. And please only use black ink," Melanie said slamming the drawer shut for punctuation.

"I wasn't aware we had detectives in Kentwater County. And if I have a black pen, I'll use it. Otherwise you'll have to live with blue." Isabel folded the form in half and stood up to leave.

"Well, you're the famous super-sleuth, Isabel Puddles. I

would think you would be able to solve this crime all by yourself anyway."

"Thank you for your help, Melanie . . . always a pleasure. Would you please ask the sheriff to call me when you speak to him next?" She didn't wait for an answer, but as she opened the door to leave, she felt an urge to be a little snarky herself. She turned back to Melanie. "Wasn't the asparagus outstanding this season? Fit for a king! Or a queen."

On her way back to the store lost in thought, several blasts of a car horn brought her to attention. It was Frances, who pulled up next to her. Isabel climbed in, and after telling her about the theft, asked her if she would come over and spend the night. "I just don't want to be there alone tonight," Isabel said with some sadness in her voice.

"Yes, of course I will! Do you want me to bring Hank's gun?" Frances asked in earnest. "I shot it out at the range with him a few times, so I'm pretty sure—"

"Please don't, Frances. I don't want a gun in my house. You're as bad as Beverly. I doubt they would come back, anyway, but even if they did, I wouldn't shoot somebody over a four-hundred-dollar laptop."

"I would! If anybody came into my house uninvited, I would shoot 'em dead, call the sheriff, and then make myself a cup of coffee."

"You're all talk, Frances. Remember when you ran over that gaggle of wild turkeys? You were absolutely bereft. And those were turkeys. You wouldn't even roast a turkey that Thanksgiving because you felt so guilty."

Frances closed her eyes as if reliving the tragic incident. "I thought they were going to get out of my way. How was I supposed to know turkeys couldn't fly? I think I still have feathers stuck in the grille of this car."

"Too bad for those poor turkeys you didn't pay more attention in our seventh-grade science class. Miss Drolan did a whole thing about indigenous Michigan wildlife, including wild turkeys, *which do not fly*."

Frances was suddenly indignant. "Well, maybe they should learn! What's the point of having wings if you don't use them?"

Isabel was not digging any deeper into this rabbit hole. "What time can you come over? I'll make dinner."

"I'll follow you home now. I was just picking up my dry cleaning. Hank's not home anyway, like it matters."

"Perfect. Let's go. I'm parked in front of the store."

Isabel went straight for comfort food when it was time to make dinner. Her Grandmother Peabody's bacon and tomato mac and cheese always made her feel cozier and comforted. With a nod to good health, she made them each a nice green salad and, just to annoy Frances, put her dressing on the side. After dinner they each took a bowl of black cherry ice cream from the Amish and went out and sat on the dock until the mosquitoes started biting. Frances was still paying the price for the previous night's excesses, so she went to bed early, and Isabel sat up for a while and skimmed through her latest edition of *Better Homes & Gardens*, but without much enthusiasm.

She was still feeling very unsettled, but it helped knowing Gull Harbor's own Dirty Harry was in the front guest room. She tossed her magazine onto the coffee table and got her knitting out. She had been working on a scarf to give to Andy when he headed back to school in the fall as a thank-you for all his hard work. Just when she was getting into her rhythm, her cell phone rang. Coincidentally enough, it was Andy. He had never called her before, so when she heard his voice, her heart skipped a beat, dreading that he might be delivering bad news. He wasted no time getting to the purpose for his call. "I think I might know who stole your laptop, Mrs. Puddles.

I can't be positive, and I probably shouldn't say it unless I was . . . but I think Jazz, our tenant downstairs, might have stolen it."

Isabel was beyond shocked. "But why in the world would you suspect Jazz, Andy?"

"When she first moved in, I asked her if she wanted the Wi-Fi code, and she said she didn't have a computer. But last night she suddenly asked me if she could have the code. I also know she worked for you at your barbecue, so she knew your house. Just now I had to go down to her unit to get to the circuit box because we blew a fuse. It took her a minute to let me in, and although I didn't see a laptop, I did see a charger, and it's the same charger my mom has for her laptop. Remember I told you yours was the same as my mom's?" Isabel was starting to feel a slight flush, which got stronger when she remembered Charlie being suspicious when he saw her coming out of her office. "My mom says there's something about Jazz she doesn't trust, and she has this boyfriend who's been coming around on a loud motorcycle that my parents are not happy about. It's just a summer rental, so they're giving her the boot after Labor Day weekend. Anyway, I felt like I needed to tell you that."

"Well, thank you for your concern, Andy. I'm going to have to think this over. I just can't imagine what she would want with my laptop. But thank you."

Andy had offered some good circumstantial evidence with Jazz suddenly requesting the Wi-Fi code right after Isabel's laptop had gone missing. And if the charger he saw *did* belong to her laptop, that was some hard evidence to go along with it, but it felt too scant to take to Sheriff Chase. What also occurred to her was how Jazz could even get into her computer without knowing the password. Having this idea planted in her head added yet another layer of confusion and angst, but now she was starting to feel angry. If Jazz was the person who stole her laptop, she was determined to get it back and see to it that she was held accountable. But first she would need more evidence. Isabel intended to pay very close attention to how Jazz reacted when she told her and Kayla about the theft at breakfast in the morning. If she had anything to hide, Isabel was sure she would be able to tell.

"What do you mean she quit?" Isabel said to Kayla after she delivered the news.

"Well, Iz, I think that's what you call it when you just don't show up for work or even bother to call in."

Isabel shook her head and let out a heavy sigh. "Frances is going to *love* this."

"Where is she?" Kayla asked.

"Parking the car. We drove in together. I'll tell you what happened when you get a break."

Isabel's cell phone rang. It was Andy again. "Good morning, Mrs. Puddles. I thought you should know that Jazz moved out of the apartment at some point last night . . . probably when my parents and my sister and me went out for ice cream after dinner. We only noticed this morning because she left the door open. She owed a month's rent too. And that computer charger was gone."

"Thank you for calling, Andy. I'll see you at the store later."

Isabel expected Frances to run with the *told you so* ball and spike it in the end zone, but she was surprisingly quiet as she listened to Isabel share the news Andy had delivered about Jazz possibly stealing her laptop, culminating in her moving out in the night, owing a month's rent, and then not showing up for work. Frances seemed to be feeling bad for Isabel instead. "I'm so sorry, Izzy. You are the most trusting person I know, and the most honest. It takes a special kind of evil to steal from someone who was as nice as you were to that girl . . . Of course I told you from the beginning she was no good. Knew it the minute I met her."

And there it was. But Frances was right. She *had* seen it, and so had Andy's mother, so why hadn't she? "I guess I just had a blind spot with her for some reason. But Kayla liked her too! So it wasn't just me," Isabel said, defending herself.

Frances scoffed at that line of defense just as Kayla approached the table. "Kayla was just desperate for help. She would have hired Squeaky Fromme if the woman could carry a tray full of waffles."

"Who's Squeaky Fromme?" Kayla asked.

"Google her!" Frances replied, laughing.

Isabel shook her head. She looked defeated. "What I can't figure out is how she planned to get into my computer without my password." Kayla heard that last bit when she came over with coffee and suddenly got a funny look in her eyes. "What is it?" Isabel asked her.

Kayla hesitated. "You remember the other day when you were in here with your laptop and I asked you for your password so I could do the Google map thing for you?" Isabel nodded. "And remember you told me your password was your kids' names?" Isabel nodded again. "Well, Jazz was standing right there when you said it. And then a little later, while we were closing up and making some small talk, she asked me about your family and your kids. I told her you had two, and I'm pretty sure I mentioned their names."

Now it all made sense. It definitely *was* Jazz. The question now was, what if anything could be done about it?

Chapter 25

Isabel was so shocked at discovering that it was Jazz who stole her laptop that she had lost her appetite, so she barely touched her breakfast. She simply could not wrap her head around the fact that this young woman, whom she had defended from Frances's wrath all summer, and whom she had gone out of her way to be nice to, even hiring her to work in her home, had stolen from her. She was left with a tossed salad of emotions: She felt violated, confused, angry, embarrassed, but mostly she just felt sad. The laptop could be replaced, but her trusting nature had taken a blow. As it turned out, being fair-minded and trusting people you didn't know very well had its risks, even in Gull Harbor. Carly and Charlie were right. Maybe, she had to ask herself, seeing the good in people only made sense if you had already ruled out what might *not* be good in them.

As they pulled into the driveway at Poplar Bluff, Frances asked Isabel if she wanted her to stay over again that night. She thanked her for staying over the night before but didn't see the need tonight. Now that she knew it was Jazz, and that she had apparently skipped town, she was not feeling nearly as anxious. "If I see her, I'm going to make a citizen's arrest," Frances told her.

Isabel laughed. "I'm not really sure that's a thing, Frances, but thank you for the sentiment. Just don't shoot her."

"Can't make any promises. All right, Izzy, I'll call and check in on you later."

Business was slow at the hardware, but it always dropped off a little in August, so Isabel spent a good part of the day dusting and reorganizing shelves, going aisle by aisle. She was busy in the lightbulb department when Ramush came into the store carrying bags of baked goods from Hobson's. "Good afternoon, Isabel."

"Hello there, Ramush. I've been thinking about you and Miss Bachmeier ever since Petoskey. How are you doing?"

"Everything is fine. Status quo, as they say. But I wanted to let you know that Miss Bachmeier is having a memorial service for Trey this Friday at noon, at Bachmeier Hall. She would very much like it if you would come. Jacob will be there as well. He's stopping on his way to an art show in Saugatuck, I believe."

Isabel couldn't think of anything she would rather do less. "Of course I'll come, but I have to say that it surprises me a little that she would host a memorial for Trey, given how she felt about him. It wasn't exactly a sentiment she tried to hide." Isabel wasn't going to go as far as calling it hypocritical because she was not in any position to judge Abigail's true motives, but if she had to choose a word . . .

"I think perhaps she's remembering now what he was like as a boy, when she was genuinely fond of him. I always thought he was a little brat, but I had very little to do with him, thankfully. Plus it wouldn't look good not to do *something* for him, would it."

That made sense to her. It was sad but it made sense. "It's a shame Jacob has to become acquainted with the half-brother he never knew at his memorial service. Not a very happy situation, is it?"

"I would agree it's less than ideal, but what is it they say now? It is what it is? Anyway, we are focusing on the positive. Jacob being brought back into the fold after all these years has made all the difference in Miss Bachmeier's outlook for the future. I think knowing the grandson her father knew and loved will someday carry on the family legacy is a great comfort to her. It almost restores your faith in the justice of the universe . . . almost."

Isabel remembered she had something she had been meaning to ask Ramush about. "I hope you don't think I'm prying, Ramush, even though I am, but I know you were in Ann Arbor recently having some tests done. Is everything all right?"

"You mean did I pass?" Ramush replied with a smile before continuing. "I appreciate your concern, Isabel, but everything checked out as I expected it would. When you get to be my age, your cylinders just don't fire the way they used to, and your chassis starts to rattle a bit. It's like that old station wagon. If I'm not driving it, I'm fixing it. But it keeps on running."

"Well, good. I'm happy to hear it's nothing serious."

Ramush nodded. "Everything is just fine. So we'll see you Friday at noon, then?"

"I'll be there," Isabel replied as she got back to work.

Isabel was up on a stepladder with a broom, swatting at a cobweb in the corner, when the front doorbell jingled. She turned around to see Sheriff Chase standing at the counter. "Hello there, Isabel."

"Hello, Sheriff," she said as she climbed down from the ladder. "How are you?"

"Been busy, as you may have heard, but things are getting back to normal now. I understand you came in to file a report yesterday. You had your laptop stolen, Melanie tells me."

"Yes, I'm sorry to say I did . . . and even sorrier to say I know who stole it."

"Do I need to make an arrest?" the sheriff asked as he slowly turned a rack of key chains sitting on the counter.

"Looks like she skipped town," Isabel said, putting the broom away in the office. "So I'm afraid there's not much you can do about it now, Sheriff."

"She? Do I know her?" he asked.

"You know the girl who was helping Kayla out at Land's End this summer?"

"Jazz?"

"Yes . . . But you've got bigger fish to fry than worrying about my laptop. I have all the important stuff saved on a flash drive, which is something I only recently learned about, so that's a blessing. If she needed a laptop that bad, let her have it."

"You know there was something I just didn't trust about that one. I couldn't quite put my finger on it."

"Yes, that seems to be the consensus." Isabel didn't need to be reminded of what a sucker she'd been, so she quickly changed the subject. "I saw you on the news the other night, Sheriff."

"I wish you hadn't! I hate being on TV! Grady was good at it, but I *hate* it. Anyway, I'm glad we've finally been able to put that case to bed. I understand you've been working for Abigail Bachmeier."

"I have, but in a matter unrelated to her nephew. I'm curious, though. Have you heard back from the coroner?"

"Not yet, but I do have something I'd like to ask you about. I met with Miss Bachmeier again, and her, whatever he is, chauffeur? Bodyguard? He's a bit . . . I don't know . . . intimidating isn't the right word, but he's . . ."

"Ramush is unusual, and he can be a little off-putting at first, but he really is a lovely man. He's very loyal to his boss, and *very* protective. Abigail's actually very nice too, once she gets to know and trust you. Then she lets her guard down a little."

"She wasn't what I would call *devastated* when I first spoke to her the day her nephew went missing. And the news that we'd found his body didn't get much of a rise out of her, either. If anything, she seemed relieved."

"I can't really say very much about any of that, Sheriff, but there was a lot of Bachmeier family strife that I think accounts for her *detachment*, I guess you could say."

"Yes, she hinted at that. She got very annoyed with me when I asked her if her nephew had any enemies that she knew of, and before I even got the question out, she answered, 'Yes, me! So am I now a murder suspect? Shall I call my lawyer?' I assured her I was just crossing t's and dotting i's so I could close the case, at which point she told me I could, quote, 'practice my alphabet someplace other than her living room,' then got up and left me sitting there alone with what's his name."

Isabel had to keep from smiling. "This probably isn't any of my business—in fact, I know it's not—but I'm going to ask anyway. Do you suspect there may have been foul play involved in Trey Bachmeier's death?"

"Well, because you have such a sterling and well-deserved reputation, Isabel, I'm going to tell you something in confidence. Do I have your word you'll keep this to yourself?"

"Scout's honor, Sheriff. Actually I wasn't a scout, but Brownie's honor."

"A man from Wisconsin called me yesterday after he heard the news about Trey Bachmeier's body being found. He's been up in the Canadian wilderness fishing for several weeks and wasn't following the news, so he hadn't heard about Trey's disappearance in the first place. He told me that he had crossed on the *Badger* the same day as Trey and had talked to him about the car he was bringing over. This man is also a car collector and had seen him arrive at the boat with a vintage red Mercedes convertible, I guess it was. When he introduced himself as Trey Bachmeier, the man immediately knew who he was. They chatted for a little while and then it was, you know, nice to meet you and that was it. He didn't think anything of it.

"A little while later, the man was walking around the boat and saw Trey again on the top aft deck talking with a young woman. He said it appeared they knew each other, and that it was not a very friendly-looking conversation. All he could tell me in the way of a description was that she looked to be in her thirties and was wearing a loose-fitting summer dress with a floral print. She also had on a floppy sun hat and was wearing big sunglasses. He said in retrospect it was an outfit that looked almost like a disguise, but he didn't think anything of it at the time. Probably just having a fight with his girlfriend, he figured.

"After the man's truck was delivered to him, and he was leaving the parking lot, he saw the same woman in the passenger seat of a black, late-model SUV badly in need of a wash, driven by a bald, heavyset man who most definitely was not Trey Bachmeier. He had no reason to get the tag number, but he did remember seeing Texas plates. That was it. He said he just thought the responsible thing to do was to let me know just in case it proved to be useful information."

"And is it useful information, Sheriff?" Isabel's asked.

"I don't know. If the coroner comes back with a report that says his cause of death was something other than drowning, it would be. Otherwise, with no cameras and no witnesses, how he ended up in the water is anybody's guess. What's your gut tell you, Isabel? I trust your instincts."

"You do? Because I was evidently the only sucker in town who thought Jazz was a great gal, so I may have lost my touch."

Sheriff Chase laughed. "I doubt very much that's true."

"I guess I wouldn't rule out foul play just yet. These days you just never know. I mean, one day you own a laptop, and the next day your waitress steals it. I guess it's wait and see at this point, right?"

Sheriff Chase laughed. "I guess that's all we *can* do. I'll keep you posted, Isabel." The sheriff turned to leave, then turned back. "Oh, did you ever fill out that report Melanie gave you?"

"Nobody's got that kind of time, Sheriff. Besides I didn't have a black pen at home, and she seemed pretty adamant about that."

"Yeah, she's a stickler for a black pen. I'm not sure what that's all about. We sure miss Ginny around the office. You think there's any chance she'd reconsider her retirement?"

"I wouldn't bet on it, Sheriff. I'd just get used to black pens if I were you."

Chapter 26

Trey Bachmeier's memorial service was not exactly standing room only. There were a handful of college friends who came to pay their respects, but paid them mostly at the bar and at the buffet. There was the young woman who was alleged to have been his girlfriend at the time he went missing, who, in a show of real class, brought her new boyfriend as a date. "She seems to be taking it well," Ramush muttered to Isabel under his breath. There were a few Milwaukee Pipps, of Pipp's Pretzels, who attended—cousins from his mother's side apparently—but they were not throwing themselves on the casket, either. His late mother's husband, Trey's step-father, was invited, but chose not to attend.

Ramush informed Isabel that the coroner had released Trey's body that morning after officially ruling his death an accidental drowning, so they were able to have him cremated. "His ashes were still warm when I picked him up. I wish I'd thought to bring oven mitts." Ramush chuckled while Isabel slowly turned her head to him and grimaced. But Ramush wasn't done regaling her with morbid small talk. "Miss Bachmeier felt the service needed a focal point, so she had Cook's deliver a casket for the occasion. I asked Mr. Cook what their return policy was, but he thought I was joking. I wasn't. Miss Bachmeier said maybe we'd use it as a planter until somebody needs it, or she'd give it to Sinclair for Christmas."

Isabel cringed again. If it wasn't obvious to her already, it was now. Abigail and Ramush were not people who showed a lot of deference when it came to the topic of death. Isabel excused herself at that point and went to the bar and ordered a glass of Chardonnay. Her nerves were already shot and the service had yet to begin.

There were maybe thirty-five people in attendance, but strangely enough, the person who looked the most forlorn was Jacob. He turned to Isabel after they sat down together and shook his head. "It's just so sad that I only find out I have another half-brother after he's dead. I know, based on what Aunt Abigail and Ramush have told me, that he wasn't the greatest guy in the world, but I still would have liked to meet him." Isabel had no words. She just smiled warmly and patted him on the leg.

After a short service held on the west terrace, conducted by the very elderly minister from the Lutheran church in Milwaukee where the Bachmeier's had once worshipped—and who had to keep being reminded of the deceased's name— the attendees mingled back at the bar and the buffet for exactly one hour, after which Ramush had been instructed to send them all on their merry way.

Jacob walked Isabel out to her van. When she arrived at Bachmeier Hall she hadn't noticed his camper van parked near the garage with a cargo trailer attached. "Looks like you're off to that art show in Saugatuck from here?" she said.

"Yes. It's a big one. I know most of the other artists so it's always nice to catch up and see everybody's work. Wait here just a minute, Isabel, I need to run to my van." He returned moments later with a cardboard box and handed it to her. "A token of appreciation for all you've done. I can't tell you how freeing it is to finally be honest about my true lineage. I hadn't even realized how much psychic energy was required to keep all this a secret for so many years."

"And I can't tell *you* how happy I am things have turned out the way they have for you, and for your aunt." She set the box down on the low wall that hugged the driveway and reached inside. Wrapped in tissue paper was the ceramic candelabra she had admired in Jacob's barn. "Well, aren't you just the sweetest thing ever. Thank you, Jacob. It's beautiful." She put the gift back in the box and gave him a hug.

"I was happy to see you liked that piece. It's one of my favorites too."

She lifted it out and looked at it again. "I know just where I'm going to put it."

"Isabel, I have something I'd like to talk to you about. Is it okay if I stop by your office on my way out of town a little later? I should probably get back inside now."

"I'm heading home from here, but you're welcome to come by my house if you'd like. I'm just over on Gull Lake."

"Okay, great. I'm going to be here for a little while. Aunt Abigail says she has a few more things she needs to talk to me about. I'm already on overload, but I'm doing my best to take it all in. Who would have thought, right?"

Isabel could see that a lot was weighing on his mind. She wrote down her address and told him he could come by anytime. He thanked her and went back inside. Isabel spent her drive home wondering what Jacob wanted to talk to her about, but at this point, she was ready for anything.

Dusk was blanketing the lake by the time Jacob arrived. After greeting Jackpot and Corky, and after Isabel showed him the place of prominence his artwork now occupied in the middle of her dining room table, she made them some tea and they went out to the screened-in porch to talk.

"Tell me what's on your mind, Jacob?" She paused. "That was a dumb question. I know you've got way too much on your mind to unload over a cup of tea."

Jacob nodded in agreement. "It's a lot. But what I wanted to talk to you about is kind of unrelated to the rest of this. Let's see, where do I start? Well, a few years ago, actually it was about twelve years ago now, I fell head over heels in love with a girl from Milwaukee who worked in a coffee shop I used to hang out in. Chloe was her name. I had just taken a job teaching art at a private school up in Bayfield, which is a little town at the very western edge of Lake Superior. Mom and David had a summer home there, so I was going to live in the house and teach school. My brother Paul was still in high school, and the plan was that he would come up and work in the summers. But I had that whole summer off, so Chloe and I spent a lot of time together. When it was time for me to head north, I couldn't bring myself to leave her, so I asked her to come with me. And to my surprise, she said yes.

"The first couple years were great. I was teaching and she was working in another coffee shop up there. And for those first couple of summers she and Paul got along really well, and although my mom didn't really like her, David seemed to. I knew this was the woman I wanted to marry and start a family with, so I finally decided it was time to propose, so I did, very romantically, on my knee at the beach at sunset . . . and she turned me down flat. She said she loved me, but she had no interest in being married. Her parents had both been married and divorced a few times, so they had not set very good examples, and she was afraid getting married would ruin everything. I was disappointed, of course, more like devastated, but I had to respect her feelings. I thought eventually she'd cave, though. So it was a few months after my ill-fated proposal, and we were in a pub in town with some friends and somebody started buying tequila shots. On top of the tequila, I'd had a few too many beers—Bachmeier beers—so by the time we left, I was completely sloshed. And on our walk home, I ended up telling her my big secret, which I had never shared with anybody, that my *real* father was the late Randolph Bachmeier Junior. The next morning I didn't even remember telling her, but she did, and she wanted more details. So I told her everything I knew about how it all came to be, which wasn't much, and explained to her that it was a family secret, and that's where I wanted to leave it."

Isabel could see where this was going. "So after she discovered you were a Bachmeier, I'm guessing marriage didn't sound like such a bad idea anymore?"

"Exactly. And then the browbeating began. She wouldn't stop talking about it. Kept telling me I needed to go to the Bachmeier family and demand to somehow be compensated or I should threaten to go public about it. She just turned into this money-hungry, I don't know what, but she wasn't the woman I fell in love with. It was pretty demoralizing. And heartbreaking. It was obvious she didn't really love me, but she kept pressuring me to marry her. Finally I couldn't take it anymore, so I broke up with her. Or I tried to. But she wouldn't leave. She would *not* move out. So the day after the school year ended, I packed up my car while she was at work, put all her things out on the front porch, had the locks changed, and I left town.

"I spent that whole summer living in Petoskey, which by the way was where I started taking ceramics classes. Chloe kept calling and leaving me messages, telling me how much she loved me and wanted to be with me, which I knew was a complete crock of you know what. Finally I just stopped taking her calls. Then she started calling my friends, even calling my family, trying to find out where I was, but they were not about to tell her. When I came back in the fall to start the new school year, I was afraid she would still be there, but thankfully she was gone. My buddy, who was a bartender down at the pub, told me she took off with some guy. I was so relieved."

"What a terrible experience that must have been. But it sounds like you really dodged a bullet with that one."

"She was the first woman I ever really fell in love with . . . and the last."

"I'm sorry you had to learn such a hard life lesson, but better to learn her true character before you married her." Isabel paused for a moment and looked at Jacob, who was staring into the trees outside as darkness fell. "I'm honored you would trust me enough to tell me all this, Jacob, but I'm wondering why."

"Actually, this is where it gets complicated. I ran into Chloe's brother, Craig, at the art show in Saugatuck last summer. I'd met him years before and we'd even gone fishing together a couple times . . . nice guy. He and his family live in Grand Rapids now and they have a place in Saugatuck. He and Chloe had been estranged for a long time, but he saw her at a family reunion earlier that summer and she introduced him to her husband, who he said he didn't like very much. And then she introduced him to their son, Austin, who he figured was ten or eleven. He told me he was, in his words, 'completely blown away,' because it was obvious to him that Austin was *not* her husband's son. He was mine. 'Spitting image of you,' he said. And, well, the math makes sense."

That was a shoe Isabel did not see dropping. She was almost left speechless. "That is . . . wow . . . that really is something. Boy, nobody can say you haven't had your share of surprises in life, Jacob."

"And I'd be happy to never have another, but I need to know if this kid really is my son. I have a picture her brother sent me. Can I show you?" Jacob reached into his wallet and pulled out a photograph of a smiling young boy that, had she not known better, she would have assumed was a picture of Jacob at that age.

"Awww . . . what a little cutie." She held the photo out in front of her and next to Jacob's face. "I'd be shocked to find out he *wasn't* your son. You can skip the DNA test."

Jacob hesitated but finally asked. "Her brother said he had no contact information for her. Do you think maybe you could help me find him, Isabel? I'll pay you, of course."

"I will be happy to help, and, no, you will not pay me. If you'll write down all the details you can think of for me, I'll start looking first thing tomorrow. I can't make any promises, but I'll do my best."

Jacob smiled. Isabel could read the relief on his face. "It would mean the world to at least be able to meet him."

"You are entitled to meet him, and you should. And he's entitled to meet you . . . and I will do my very best to make that happen."

"I can't thank you enough. One more thing. Please don't mention this to anybody. I haven't told my mother or Aunt Abigail. I don't want to tell either of them they may have a grandson or a great-nephew until I know for sure we can even locate him."

"Mum's the word," Isabel answered with an assuring smile.

"I better get going. I'll shoot you an e-mail with all that information ASAP."

"Great! Have a safe trip, Jacob, and enjoy your show. Next year I'll make sure to come down for it."

Isabel got to her office early. Her shift at the hardware store didn't begin until ten, and thanks to Freddie lending her his laptop, she could start her search for Jacob's son. She was hoping she would find an e-mail from Jacob waiting with the information she needed to start, but nothing had arrived. She had gotten lucky finding Colleen, thanks mostly to Andy's mother, who got the ball rolling for her, and she had gotten even luckier meeting Jacob, almost accidentally. This might take a little more gumshoeing. But until she had something to go on, she was in limbo.

She still had some time to kill before work, so she decided it might be a good time to take a look at the fall class schedule and figure out what classes she still needed to take, and how many she thought she could handle next semester. For some reason she had been putting this off. While looking at the classes that were still required for her to earn her criminal justice degree, she began to feel herself losing steam. It wasn't because she was getting tired of school. She was thrilled to be back in college, even at her age, and she enjoyed being back in a classroom after all these years. But what suddenly was not thrilling her was the idea of studying criminal justice any longer. She had been so caught up in the Jonasson case that after it ended, she felt a career bringing criminals to justice sounded very exciting, and she did seem to have a knack for it. But, more and more, it was starting not to feel right.

When she had first gone away to college, Isabel planned to study education, get her teaching credential, and then teach English and American literature, just like her favorite teacher, Gladys DeLong, and ideally teach in Gull Harbor. But instead she got married and had a family. Her love for literature had never gone away, though. In fact the older she got, the more she appreciated how important it was for the world, and for her. Now, for whatever reason, her thoughts were drifting back to that time in her life. Maybe she needed to make an honest assessment of where she wanted to go from here. If her career in criminal justice was just going to be a series of trying to solve murders, and bear witness to other peoples' tragedies, she wasn't sure she was cut out for that anymore. There was just no getting around the fact that it was sad and depressing!

She was still determined to get her degree, but what would she rather do, she had to ask herself; sit down and read a great book or sit down and look at crime scene photos, or autopsy photos, or learn more about how blood spatters when someone is shot or bludgeoned to death? The answer was beginning to come into pretty clear focus, so she clicked on the English department's class catalog and began to scroll through. She didn't have to decide today, but there was no harm in looking, and thinking about what path would be most rewarding.

It was a slow Saturday at the hardware, and although Saturdays were usually their busiest day of the week, it was ninety-four degrees today with very high humidity, so whatever projects the good people of Kentwater County had planned to tackle this weekend had been put on hold. Suddenly the door jingled and in came Gil Cook. "Hiya, Izzy! How's tricks?"

"Boy, you're in a good mood," she said, "but then you usually are in a good mood. Unless somebody's backed into your car."

"I've gotten over that! And yes I do try to stay on the sunny side of the street. Who says funeral directors have to be dark and gloomy all the time? I'm shattering the stereotype, Iz!"

"That you are, and as one of your oldest and dearest friends, I support you wholeheartedly. But if I came in to discuss funeral arrangements for a loved one, I'm not sure I'd want Jerry Lewis as the Nutty Mortician making those arrangements for me."

Gil howled with laughter. "I know how to tone it down when I need to, Izzy. I express myself very discreetly when I'm at work. Nobody, for instance, would ever know that under my black suit I might be wearing Bugs Bunny boxer shorts."

"I didn't need to know that either, Gil."

Gil laughed again. "Anyhoo, I just bought a new patio boat, and we're putting it in the water tomorrow. Want us to come by and pick you up?"

"That's exciting. I didn't know you were boat shopping."

"I've had my eye on this boat down at the marina all summer. I was waiting for the owner to bring the price down a little, but he would not budge. So because I sold two caskets in two days, I decided, what the hell! Life is short! Thank God, or I'd be out of business!"

Isabel rolled her eyes. "Yes I saw the one you sold Abigail Bachmeier."

"Oh, that's right! You were at the memorial. And it wasn't cheap! The other one I sold to the family of a man from Detroit who went missing last week. He washed up a couple days ago. They sprang for a nice one too."

Isabel already knew this would be the lead story on the Frances Spitler news hour tonight. The Indian drum legend would live on.

"Well, Gil, I could talk caskets with you all day, but I need to get back to work. Let me know when you get out on the lake tomorrow and maybe I'll jump on."

"All righty, then. Bye, Iz! A couple more beats of the Indian drum before the end of summer, and I may be back in to buy that new riding mower Freddie just got in! Boy, that's a beauty!"

"Not you, too, Gil!"

"Not me, too, what?"

"You don't really believe that silly Indian drum folktale, do you?"

Gil shrugged. "Can't be proven, can't be disproven."

"That's because you can't disprove something that doesn't exist in the first place," Isabel replied in a sensible tone of voice.

"Whoa! This is getting *way* too deep for me, Iz. I gotta go!"

Just as the door closed behind him, it opened again, and there stood Ramush. "Good afternoon, Isabel. Boy, it is a hot one out there."

"Hello, Ramush. People are going to start talking if we keep up these rendezvous."

"I'm sorry, I don't mean to be a pest."

"I'm just kidding. Yes, it's pretty miserable, isn't it? I'm looking forward to getting home and taking a dip in the lake. That was quite a memorial service yesterday. Not like any I've been to before."

"I'm glad to have it over with." This was not the usual sentiment attached to a memorial service, but there was no reason to be surprised at this point. From the very beginning, both Ramush and Abigail had reacted to Trey's disappearance as if they had misplaced a set of keys. Ramush then reached into his vest pocket and pulled out an envelope. "I intended to give this to you at the service yesterday but I lost track of you before you left. Payment in full for your services, per our agreement."

Isabel took the check and dropped it into her tote bag, tucked under the counter as usual. "Thank you, Ramush."

"Aren't you going to look at it?"

"I remember our agreement. I trust you."

"Miss Bachmeier added a little bonus. She was very happy with your work, *and* with you. You know she doesn't like many people, but she likes you."

"Well, that's nice to hear. I like her too. And I like you, Ramush. It's been a pleasure working with you. Please send her my thanks. I hope our paths will cross again soon, but in a more sociable way. You'll have to come to one of my Sunday suppers one of these days."

"That sounds delightful. Well, I have to get to Hobson's before he closes. Saturday is cheesecake night. Miss Bachmeier is quite enamored of Mr. Hobson's cherry cheesecake. It makes Chef very jealous, which is always fun. So I will bid you a good afternoon, Isabel."

And that was it. Ramush nodded his nod and he was gone. Her work for Abigail Bachmeier was officially finished, and she could finally afford that new garage roof, and maybe even a new mom computer. All she was left with now was a craving for Bobby Hobson's cherry cheesecake. She picked up the phone and called Bobby to ask him to hold one for her. Just like Gil, she felt she deserved to splurge a little too.

Chapter 27

Isabel enjoyed what may have been the first Sunday all summer when she could truly relax, with nothing work related hanging over her head. She began her day by going to church. Because her usual church partner, Ginny, had been away all summer, and because she didn't like going alone, she'd been playing hooky for weeks now. But today she felt like going for some reason. Fortunately Congregationalists were forgiving people, or at least they were supposed to be, so she was welcomed back into the fold with open arms . . . by everybody but Melanie Hodges from the sheriff's department who was also a member of her church. Melanie, true to form, had been throwing her dirty looks at the kaffeeklatsch, which was held in the basement after the service every Sunday. Still annoyed by her attitude the other day, Isabel made it a point to comment on how dry the blueberry muffins were, within earshot of Melanie, after being told she had baked them.

"If I drank the amount of coffee I'd need to wash these down, I'd be awake until Tuesday!" she said to the group she was standing with, as she wrapped her napkin around the remainder of the muffin and tossed it in the garbage. She knew it was petty, and she knew it wasn't what a good Congregationalist should do, but the expression on Melanie's face was worth whatever demerits from above she might receive. There were not many people in Kentwater County who Isabel Puddles didn't like, and even fewer who didn't like her, but Melanie Hodges had been on both lists for a very long time.

Isabel hadn't been home for more than five minutes when, coincidentally, Ginny called, and the two had a nice, long-overdue chat. She and Grady were in Maine now, and although they had thoroughly enjoyed their U.S. tour, they were both getting a little homesick, so they were going to start making their way back soon. After she hung up with Ginny, she called the kids. After a brief chat with them, she took the book she had been trying to finish all month outside, climbed into her rarely used hammock, and swung gently back and forth while the dogs napped beneath her. Ten minutes later, the book was lying on her chest, and Isabel was sound asleep too.

How long she had been napping she couldn't say, but it felt like the first deep sleep she had experienced in a long while. Unfortunately that deep sleep was interrupted by the sound of a boat horn. She groggily lifted her head to see Gil pulling up to her dock with his new patio boat. Although she would have preferred to go back to dozing, she wanted to be a good sport, so after she put the dogs inside, she climbed aboard and took a loop around the lake with Gil and his family. The lake was getting quieter now and things in Gull Harbor were already starting to wind down. After the usual Labor Day surge, which was fast approaching, the summer people would decamp entirely. The locals could then have their town back and return to the quiet rhythm of life in Gull Harbor.

After Gil—whose captaining skills would never be described as top-notch—nearly took out her dock trying to drop her off, and after she narrowly escaped a fall into the drink trying to jump onto her dock on his second pass, Isabel waved goodbye and counted her blessings. As she headed inside to satisfy a sudden craving for a piece of cherry cheesecake, she saw a man coming around the corner waving at her. She took off her sunglasses so she could see a little better. He looked familiar, and as he got closer, she realized it was the real estate agent again. She'd had better luck getting rid of ants. "Hello again, Mrs. Puddles. How are you?" he yelled. "Have you been having a nice summer?"

Isabel was now officially annoyed. The skunk had arrived at the picnic, and now an otherwise perfect Sunday afternoon had been interrupted. Once again she had to take time out of her life to convey to this person that she had no interest in selling her property—not now, and not ever. "I'm sorry I don't remember your name, but I know why you're here, and although I hate to be rude, I also hate being put in a position where I have to be. I have not changed my mind, I never will, and I don't think it's very good form to show up unannounced, on a beautiful Sunday afternoon, and try to make me change my mind."

The agent was looking contrite. "I'm very sorry, Mrs. Puddles, but I'm obligated to make a new offer if my client wants to make one."

"Whatever obligation you have to your client has nothing to do with me."

"I understand that, Mrs. Puddles, but my client has come up with a number, for all three parcels, which I think you'll find quite tantalizing."

"Tantalizing? Numbers are not tantalizing to me. The cherry cheesecake sitting in my fridge right now, *that's* tantalizing. Nothing *you* have to say to me could possibly fall into that category. You really needn't waste your time making another visit." Isabel started for the stairs to the deck, then turned back. "You know, maybe it would help if you were to pass along a message to your clients from me. Although it may be a difficult concept for them to grasp, and perhaps for you as well, there are people in this world—and I'm happy to say many of them live right here in Gull Harbor, Michigan—who find value in things *other* than money; things like family and friends, privacy, trees, nature, and maybe, most importantly, memories. And this place is full of wonderful memories for me, and a place where my family and friends and I intend to create many more. And *that* you cannot put a price on, no matter how *tantalizing* others may find it." She walked up onto her deck, then turned and peered down at the forlorn looking agent, for whom she was starting to feel slightly sorry. "Can I bring you out a slice of cheesecake?"

"No, thank you, ma'am. I guess I'll just be on my way. I won't bother you again."

"Thank you. I know you're just doing your job, but when somebody tells you they aren't interested, three times, it would behoove you to believe them and not waste any more of your time. Or theirs. Take care and go out and enjoy this beautiful day!"

He nodded and tried to smile before he turned and made his way back to his car.

As Isabel was slicing off what she had intended to be a sliver of cheesecake, but turned into more like three slivers, she heard the agent start his car and drive away slowly. Isabel was a patient and tolerant person, and it was not in her nature to be rude—Melanie Hodges encounters aside—but there were times when there really was no other option. Sometimes, when traveling the high road, the altitude could get to you. But, as Frances liked to say, "If your car breaks down on the low road, your walk back into town is a whole lot shorter."

Isabel got to the office again early Monday morning, hoping to get a little work done before she had to report for hardware duty downstairs. She immediately checked her e-mails to see if Jacob had written with the information she would need to start searching for his ex-girlfriend, Chloe, and his son, Austin. She was pleased to see he had written, and according to the time stamp, he must have sent it before leaving Saugatuck last night:

Hi, Isabel . . . Hope you had a nice weekend. I had a successful show and sold out, which is always a good thing, but that's not the big news. I ran into Chloe's brother, Craig, again here in Saugatuck. I think I mentioned he has a place here. He told me that Chloe and her husband showed up out of the blue just a couple days ago, with Austin. Apparently they were headed up north and were just stopping to say hello. Craig asked where they were living now, but she said they were in transition, which he thought sounded a bit vague. He tried to get some alone time with her to talk about Austin, and tell her he had seen me, but her husband wouldn't let her out of his sight. And she wouldn't give him any way to contact her. But Craig showed me a photo he took of them with his phone just before they left, which I'm forwarding on to you. The other photo I've attached is an old one I found of Chloe and me back in Wisconsin in happier times. Not sure if they are of any use to you as far as tracking them down, but thought I'd send them along anyway. I've also included whatever other information I could remember about her; birthdate, hometown, and the high school she went to.

Getting ready to drive back home tonight. Please let me know if I can do anything else to help you in your search. Thank you again for your help with this. After seeing this photo of him, I'm pretty convinced, and Craig is, too, that Austin is my son, so I really want to find him. Especially now, with all these new developments in my life, which will affect him too. Frustrating to know he's somewhere in Michigan right now but still so far out of reach.

Best, Jacob

Isabel downloaded the first photo he sent, which was taking a while, so she went downstairs to make a pot of coffee.
Freddie and Andy would be in shortly, so she filled up her big
thermos cup and left the rest for them. Back at her desk, she
put her coffee down while her eyes slowly fixed on the screen.
She grabbed her reading glasses and moved in for a closer look
at the photo that was now fully in view. There was Austin,
bookended by his mother, and her husband, who had been
accurately described by Andy as sketchy-looking. They were
leaning against the rear of a black SUV, one badly in need of
a wash, and with Texas plates.

But what made Isabel's heart skip a beat was that Chloe
was wearing a floral-print summer dress, a floppy hat, and
sunglasses. Her gears were quickly clicking into place. It was
the same getup worn by the woman Trey was arguing with
on the deck of the *Badger*, according to the description by
the man who had spoken with Sheriff Chase. Even with the
shadow the hat was casting across her face, she looked oddly
familiar.

Isabel clicked on the other photo. When that one finished
downloading, her heart went from skipping a beat to racing,
and she suddenly felt faint. It was a smiling Jacob, ten years
younger, sitting on a boat with his girlfriend, Chloe. Only it
wasn't Chloe . . . it was Jazz! She looked back at the woman
in the sunglasses and the floppy hat and realized she was a
well-disguised Jazz. Isabel's immediate instinct was to e-mail
Jacob back, but when she looked at his message again, she
noticed a postscript she had missed:

PS: Forgot to mention that for whatever reason Chloe
apparently goes by Jasmine now.

Isabel grabbed her cell phone and called Jacob, pacing
around her office while it rang, until it went to voice mail.

"Jacob, it's Isabel! Please call me the minute you get this message. It's very important." She continued to pace her office as she tried to make sense of all this, then stopped to look at the first photo again. This time she noticed Chloe's husband had what appeared to be tattoos on his knuckles. Isabel quickly realized he may very well have been the same man at the snack bar Sandy had warned her about. If those two were both aboard the *Badger* the same day Trey Bachmeier was crossing, and Chloe, aka Jasmine, aka Jazz was seen having an argument with him, it certainly stood to reason that Trey might very well have had a little help going over the railing. But, Isabel asked herself, what would their motive be to get rid of Trey Bachmeier?

After giving that question a little more thought, Isabel quickly developed a theory. If Jazz had done her research, she knew that with Trey out of the picture, Jacob, the father of her child, would then become the sole heir to the Bachmeier fortune. The next question she had was why would she have to work undercover as a waitress at the Land's End? The only reason that made any sense was that she had somehow found out that Isabel had been hired to find Jacob, and she hoped maybe she would eventually lead her to him. And that left her with only one terrifying conclusion, perhaps she had just that.

Now, with Trey dead, Jacob was the only person standing between her son, Austin, and all that Bachmeier money, because he would automatically become the heir if Jacob were out of the picture too. And now that Jazz had his contact information, which was stored in the laptop she had stolen, probably for that very reason, she and her husband might be on their way to take care of their Jacob problem at this very moment!

Desperate to warn him that his life may be in danger, she tried to call Jacob again, but still no answer. She had to find a way to warn him, hoping it wasn't too late. Isabel could only think of one course of action now, so she grabbed her phone and called Sheriff Chase. Luckily he had given her his cell phone number so that she could circumvent Melanie if she needed to reach him.

Thankfully the sheriff answered right away, and Isabel explained as best she could, and as quickly as she could, what she feared was happening in real time, and that she believed Jacob was in grave and imminent danger. Sheriff Chase, knowing Isabel's track record, and how his former boss, Grady Pemberton, rued the day *he* didn't listen to her, immediately agreed to help. He asked her to e-mail Jacob's address, and to read off the license plate number on the SUV, then asked her to e-mail the photos. He told her as soon as they hung up that he was going to notify the Michigan State Police and the county sheriff in Petoskey who was an old friend of his. He would ask them all to get to Jacob's place as quickly as possible. Isabel thanked him profusely and hung up. Now feeling completely helpless, and in a cold sweat, Isabel began pacing again.

She tried Jacob's number one more time. Nothing. And then something else struck her. What if Jazz and her husband were planning to go one diabolical step further? Once they had both Trey *and* Jacob out of the way, what if they didn't feel like waiting for Miss Bachmeier to pass away to have access to her money? At least not of natural causes. Maybe they wanted Austin to inherit what they believed to be his rightful fortune *now*! And because Austin was a minor, Jazz and her husband would control it all.

Isabel called Ramush, but he didn't answer. Not a good sign. She ran downstairs and ducked her head in the door and saw Freddie and Andy chatting at the counter. "I gotta go fellas! I'll fill you in later!" She ran out the front door, jumped in her van, and squealed out of her parking space, with Freddie and Andy peering out the window, both looking quite confused. Freddie turned to Andy. "Well, Andy, I believe that splashing sound you just heard was my dear cousin Isabel finally going off the deep end."

As Isabel raced toward Bachmeier Hall, she thought she had better let Sheriff Chase know this murderous duo might have plans to murder Abigail Bachmeier, too, and perhaps intended to start with her. Or maybe they had split up. She looked around for her cell phone, then remembered she left it charging on her desk. Naturally.

Isabel made it to the guard's gate at Bachmeier Hall in record time, but as she skidded to a halt, Bernard, the guard who was usually on duty, was nowhere to be found. She jumped out of her van and ran around to open the gate herself, and found him lying on the ground inside the gate house . . . and then she saw blood. He had obviously been struck in the head, but he was still breathing. He then started coming to, rubbing his head and groaning, which indicated to Isabel that he probably hadn't been out for very long. "Sorry, Bernard! I'll be back as soon as I can!" she yelled.

Isabel, now in full panic mode, jumped back into her van, and just as she was ready to hit the gas, something caught her eye. Off to the side of the road, leaning against a tree, was a motorcycle. She remembered Andy telling her that Jazz's boyfriend—who she now knew to be her husband—rode one. It looked as if they *had* split up. The husband was here to do in Abigail, while Jazz was in the black SUV, on her way to Petoskey to take care of Jacob.

Isabel jumped out of her van again and ran back to the gate house, picked up the landline, and called 911. When the dispatcher answered, she yelled "It's Isabel Puddles! Please call Sheriff Chase and tell him to come to Bachmeier Hall immediately! I think Abigail Bachmeier is about to be murdered!"

She hung up, jumped back in her van, and tore up the drive before suddenly skidding to a stop. If there was any way she could prevent whatever was about to happen inside, she didn't want to lose the element of surprise, so she pulled over and parked. As she snuck up the driveway, nothing looked any different than usual, but it did seem eerily silent. Chills shot through her body as she thought about what might be unfolding inside, or what was about to. She climbed over some shrubs, crawled up to one of the living room windows, and cautiously raised her head to peek inside.

There, in the cavernous living room was Abigail, sitting in a chair, clutching one of her Pomeranians. She looked frightened, and Isabel instantly could see why. Standing a few paces away from Abigail was a creepy-looking man wearing a sinister smile, pointing a gun at her. And he had tattoos on his knuckles. Isabel froze, not knowing what to do . . . and then she heard a click.

Chapter 28

Isabel knew that sound. She'd heard it enough from watching a thousand different detective shows on TV. She turned around slowly to find Jazz standing about ten feet away and pointing a gun at her. She was no longer the poor, put-upon waitress Isabel had befriended and defended all summer long. Instead, she was wearing a menacing smile, and had a look of pure evil in her eyes.

"Hello, Isabel. It's me. I'm very sorry you got dragged into this. But, well, you did, so here we are." Isabel was too frightened to say anything. "I'm not going to hurt you, Isabel. Not yet, anyway. You've been so nice to me. And you could come in very handy, because after we take care of the old lady in there, we're heading up to visit Jacob, whose address you were kind enough to provide. Now that you're such good buddies, after he sees *you* with us, he'll be a cinch to take care of."

Isabel was terrified, but she was determined to keep her cool. She just needed to find her voice and start talking. The longer she could keep her engaged, the more time the sheriff would have to get there before anybody got shot. "So, Jazz, or do you prefer Chloe?"

"I couldn't care less. My real name is Brenda, anyway."

"Well, you'll always be Jazz to me. And that's your husband in there right now, I presume? What's his name?"

"Stewie."

"I'm curious. Were you planning to introduce your son to
his real father before you killed him?" Jazz glared back at her
while Isabel continued, "Where is Austin, anyway?"

"I left him with a friend. And he's *just* fine," she answered
indignantly, as if her mothering skills were suddenly being
questioned. "Jacob knows nothing about Austin. And how do
you know anything about my son anyway?"

"You hear things from people, you know, like your
brother, Craig." Jazz's eyes narrowed. "But it's nice you have
a friend to keep an eye on your golden goose while you and
that charming husband of yours are out on your little murder
rampage. He looks like a real catch by the way."

"Stewie is a great husband, I'll have you know. A better
one than that idiot Jacob would ever have been. Just not as
rich. But *that* little problem is about to be solved."

"You don't really think a couple of flunkies like you and
Mr. Hell's Angels in there are going to end up inheriting the
Bachmeier fortune, do you?" Isabel forced a slight laugh.

"You don't have any idea what you're talking about." Jazz
was getting increasingly agitated. "You know you're starting
to get on my nerves, Isabel."

"Oh, dear . . . Can't have that. But I do have to hand it to
you, Jazz. You really had me fooled. Nobody else liked you,
and I mean *nobody*. But I did. Just goes to show you my instincts are not always that great."

"Well, that's very nice of you to say, Isabel. I liked you
too. But not a morning went by when I didn't think about
slipping some rat poison into your friend's eggs. I only wish
we had time to shoot her too, just for kicks."

"You know, it's funny, Frances was the one who first
called it, right from day one. There was something in your

eyes she said that she just didn't trust. I really had to eat some crow when I told her you turned out to be a thief. Of course, *now* I can see what she was talking about."

"If it'll make you feel any better, you can have your stupid laptop back. It's in the back of our car, which is parked up in Wellington. All I needed out of it was Jacob's address. He's been so hard to track down!"

"Why would I need my laptop *now*? I'm not dumb enough to think you and your accomplice in there plan to let me go."

"I guess you're right. Bummer. Well, maybe we'll give you a chance to send some farewell e-mails," Jazz said, followed by an unnerving laugh.

"That would be nice. But just so you know, if you're under the impression you're going to get away with any of this, the authorities are already on to you. Seems a man who was crossing on the *Badger* with Trey that day just came forward and identified you as the woman he saw arguing with him on the upper deck."

"Please. Do I look stupid? You're making that up."

"Floral-print summer dress, floppy hat, sunglasses. And when he was leaving he saw you and Prince Charming get into a black SUV with Texas plates. Ring a bell?" Isabel could see this had really unnerved her, although she was trying to disguise it. "So what happened, Jazz? You just threw poor Trey overboard? Do you think that was the smartest plan?"

Jazz thought it over for a second. "Well, I guess the cat's out of the bag now, isn't it. We actually had another plan altogether at first, and if Trey had been a little more cooperative he might still be around. All we were trying to do was make a deal with him."

"Oh? And what was that?" Isabel asked, trying to buy more time.

"I found out where he lived, and then Stewie and me waited for him one day outside his fancy condo in downtown

Milwaukee. When he came out we asked if we could talk, and he just laughed in our faces and looked at us just like we were garbage. What a snob."

Isabel smiled. "I guess Trey had some pretty good instincts."

"That wasn't a very nice thing to say, Isabel. Maybe I should just shoot you now."

"Wait until after you tell me the whole story, please. I've been so curious. So what was the deal you were trying to make with him?"

"That I wouldn't tell his aunt about his half-brother, Jacob, or his nephew, Austin, as long as he paid us a hundred thousand dollars, which would have been nothing to him, but he called us some not very nice names and got into his sporty little red Mercedes convertible and took off. Then I remembered Memorial Day weekend was coming up, and he would more than likely be heading over here to Gull Harbor, so we staked out his building for a couple more days, and sure enough, he pulled out one morning with some luggage in the back seat and we followed him up to Manitowoc, and right on board the *Badger*. We thought maybe then, with a more captive audience, we could convince him we meant business."

"Sounds like that didn't really work out," Isabel said.

"Not really. So, yeah, we had a heated exchange I guess you could call it on the top deck. He didn't believe what I was telling him until I showed him a picture of Jacob, and then another one of Austin. Then he knew right away what I had just told him was the truth. Those Bachmeier men all have a very particular look, don't you think? But he told me to go to you know where, and that he wasn't going to pay us a penny. And he said he was going to call the police and have us arrested for trying to blackmail him. Then all of a sudden the weather started to turn real bad, real fast, and you could see the rain approaching, so everyone on deck headed downstairs in a hurry. Stewie had been off to the side watching us, and he was losing patience. So after everybody had cleared the deck he walked over just as Trey snatched the pictures out of my hand and threw them overboard. Then he looked at my husband and called him biker trash, and some more not very nice things, and, well, then it was out of my hands. If you're dumb enough to insult a biker with muscles the size of my Stewie's while you're standing against the railing of a ship? Well, you shouldn't be *too* surprised when he lifts you up and tosses you overboard like a rag doll."

Isabel shook her head slowly. *What a horrible fate to meet at the hands of two such horrible people*, she said to herself. "So did you take the job at Land's End just to try to get information about Jacob out of me? How did you know I was even looking for him?"

"Oh, no! I took the job because I was just about broke! We thought we should stick around the area to see if Trey's body washed up, and while we were waiting, and waiting, we came up with this other plan. Bigger risk, but a much bigger reward if we could pull it off. Since we'd already killed one Bachmeier, why not go for two? But then Stewie found out he had a court date back in Texas—that's where we live now—so he had to go back to appear. And then they locked him up for thirty days! You know, it's just always something, isn't it? So I sent Austin over to visit an old friend of the family who has a little farm down in Paw Paw. That kid loves animals, so he was happy as could be, and I stuck around here. Got that crappy job, found that crappy basement apartment, and then I waited for Stewie to get back. It was pure luck I ran into you. Once I found out you were this famous private investigator, and learned who you were working for, well, then I was all ears. It really could not have worked out any better. At least for us. So I have you to thank for leading us straight to Jacob. Once we take care of him—and you know I think I might do that myself after the way he treated me—then my little Austin is going to be one very rich kid. I already have the DNA I need to prove he's a Bachmeier because I grabbed a little bit of Trey's hair as he was headed over the railing. Pretty clever of me, don't you think? And then we'll all live happily ever after. The end."

Suddenly a gunshot rang out, followed by another, and then another. Jazz smiled and shook her head, "Doesn't sound like old lady Bachmeier wanted to tell Stewie where to find her jewelry. These rich people are just *so stingy*. Come on, let's go inside."

Jazz directed Isabel toward the door with her gun and instructed her to open it. When they walked into the foyer, with Jazz holding her gun to Isabel's head, they both looked down and saw her husband lying in a heap in the middle of the living room. Jazz screamed, "*Stewie!*" just as Isabel, with as much force as she could muster, drove her heel right into Jazz's flip-flopped foot so hard she was sure she heard toes breaking. Jazz's gun flew into the air, and when it landed, Isabel kicked it across the floor of the foyer, where Ramush suddenly appeared with a smile and holding a gun of his own. He leaned over, picked up the other gun, and dropped it into a porcelain umbrella stand. Jazz limped over and began sobbing uncontrollably over the body of her dear, looked-to-be-departed, Stewie.

"Boy, he did *not* go down easy," Ramush said with a chuckle. "Three shots! I once took down a water buffalo on safari in Botswana with Mr. Bachmeier with just two." He put his arm around Isabel, who was watching the scene before her in shock. "Are you all right, Isabel?"

Isabel slowly composed herself. "I'm fine, but they clobbered your security guard Bernard over the head pretty bad. I better run down and check on him." She turned toward the door just as Bernard stumbled into the foyer, holding his head.

"Did I hear gunshots?" he asked before collapsing in the first chair he could find.

"Nice of you to stay on top of things, Bernard," Ramush said to him with a smile.

"Where's Abigail?" Isabel asked.

"Here I am, Isabel! Just went to put the dogs away. They aren't used to such commotion. And I don't want them tracking through all that blood." She looked down at Jazz hovering over her dead husband, still sobbing. Abigail looked down at her as she passed by. "Don't make a scene, dear. It's not very becoming. Looks to me as if he's a goner, so you'll not bring him back with such histrionics."

"I'm sorry about the rug, Miss Bachmeier. I know it's one of your favorites," Ramush said as he walked over and gave it a closer look.

"I do love it. Expensive too. Persian Tabriz. I think I paid a little over thirty thousand dollars for it at Sotheby's, and that was some years ago. But rugs come and go. And I do think the right cleaning agent should take care of the blood. Do you happen to know, Isabel? Don't such matters fall under your purview?"

Isabel shook her head. "I really couldn't tell you, Abigail. I'm just trying to process somebody paying thirty thousand dollars for a rug."

Abigail threw her head back in laughter. "I just *adore* your sense of humor Isabel."

Isabel suddenly felt a wave of relief when she heard sirens approaching.

After the dead biker's massive body was removed, and Jazz was led away in handcuffs, Sheriff Chase had a few questions for Ramush and Miss Bachmeier, who both answered so nonchalantly, it was as if they were taking a survey about what they looked for in a bath soap. Ramush then left with the sheriff to go into town and make a statement, so Isabel sat down with Abigail in the living room. "Are you okay?" she asked.

"I'm *just* fine. About time we had a little excitement around here! The servants are still nervous wrecks. I found them all hiding in the pantry after the shots were fired. Do you know I had no idea Ramush kept a gun in the house? Or that he was so clever with one. Three shots square in the chest. Most impressive. Worthy of a stuffed bear at your county fair, I would think. Of course he was rather a large target, wasn't he."

Two housekeepers, both still looking like the nervous wrecks Abigail had just described, slowly appeared out of nowhere and began rolling up the rug. "Just put that out in the carriage house, girls. We can try to clean it later. Maybe baking soda and a little distilled vinegar will do the trick. Didn't you use that when I spilled tomato juice on it once? Worth a try. And then why don't you and Chef and Sinclair take the rest of the day off. Go into town and have yourselves some fun. Go out to dinner. My treat. Take your minds off all this hullabaloo!"

"Thank you, ma'am," one of them said quietly. The other just nodded as they lifted the rolled-up rug together and began to carry it away. "Oh, and tell Chef you'll have to take his car. Ramush is still working on the station wagon. He's got it out there in a million pieces!" She turned to Isabel. "Always fixing something, but then in a household this size, and with six automobiles, there always seems to be something that needs fixing."

This little morsel caught Isabel off guard. "I didn't know Ramush was a mechanic."

"Oh, yes. Father sent him to school for it so he could maintain our cars. I just don't know what I would do without him. And now he's gone and saved my life! It's not the first time, either, mind you. I nearly drowned out in that lake one day many years ago, but Ramush pulled me to shore and gave me CPR. I think he's deserving of a much bigger Christmas bonus this year, don't you?"

When Isabel got home that evening, she was still in a state of shock. She couldn't quite believe what had just happened. As it turned out, there actually was a murder conspiracy in the works, but not the one she had conjured up in her head involving Ramush and possibly even Abigail. No, instead it involved the woman who had been pouring her coffee all summer. She really did need to take a long, hard look at whether or not she wanted to stay in this line of work, if it meant constantly putting herself in situations where she could get herself killed. At some point her luck was sure to run out. The Jonasson case was a different animal, because ultimately that was about helping an old friend and her family. The Bachmeier case, on the other hand, was her first professional case of any real substance, and she wasn't sure how she felt about risking her life for money, no matter how generous the sum. If Jazz *had* ended up killing her, her funeral expenses would be covered, but that was cold comfort.

After a couple of hours contemplating everything, sitting in her favorite overstuffed chair with Jackpot snuggled up on one side and Corky on the other, and her knitting in her lap, the phone call she had been waiting for finally came. It was Jacob. He had been fully debriefed by Ramush, and he too was in a state of shock. They spent a good hour on the phone going over the events of the day, but on a positive note, as they were talking, Jacob was on his way to the farm near Kalamazoo where Austin was staying. Austin's uncle Craig would meet him there too, and they would both break the news to the boy, as delicately as possible, that his mother had been arrested, his step-father was dead, and that Jacob was in fact his real father. Before they hung up, Jacob promised to stay in touch. He was "looking forward to being able to introduce Austin to the woman who had made it possible," he said.

After talking to Jacob, Isabel began to see the flip side of things. Yes, this case had been stressful, and unsettling, and in the end, potentially deadly, and not only for her, but for people she had grown very fond of. But she also had to look at what were some very positive results. Jacob would soon be united with the son he never knew he had, and Abigail had already been united with a nephew she never knew *she* had, *and* a grand-nephew, so she felt good about having had a hand in making all that happen. She still felt a strange sadness about Trey Bachmeier's death though, despite having never met him, or never hearing anybody say anything nice about him. But dying such a terrible death, as a result of other peoples' greed and cruelty, was still a horrible tragedy.

Isabel finally decided she had done enough ruminating for one night, so she put away her knitting and got ready for bed. But first, she could hear the last piece of cherry cheesecake faintly calling her name from the fridge. Cheesecake always had a calming effect on her, so tonight, she told herself, it was purely medicinal.

Chapter 29

Isabel was at the store marking down prices for their upcoming end-of-summer sale when she got a call from Abigail Bachmeier *herself*, inviting her to Bachmeier Hall that evening for a special dinner. No details were provided as far as what exactly the specialness of the dinner was, but Isabel had no other plans, so she was happy to accept the invitation. A couple of weeks had passed since her last trip to Bachmeier Hall, one that resulted in both her and Abigail's nearly being shot to death. But her nerves had settled down enough by now so that she felt it was probably safe to accept a dinner invitation. She still might ask to be seated facing the door though.

It had been an emotional day at the store today because she and Freddie finally had to say goodbye to Andy that morning when he stopped by with his mom on his way back to school to say thank you and goodbye. Freddie, being an old softie under his macho hardware man exterior, could barely speak. He had grown very fond of Andy, and was so impressed with his positive attitude and impressive work ethic. "Maybe there's hope for this next generation after all with the likes of Andy leading the charge," he said to Isabel one day, then lamented the fact that science wasn't further along with cloning technology. Freddie shook his hand, but Andy went in for a hug, which pushed Freddie closer to the brink of tears. He then handed him an envelope with five hundred-dollar bills inside. "It's your summer bonus, son . . . a token of my appreciation for a job well done. Just a little extra spending money for school this year," he told him. Freddie also told him his job would be waiting for him next summer if he wanted it. Andy thanked him, hugged him again, and assured him he would love to come back next year.

Next it was Isabel's turn to thank him, not only for all his hard work, but especially for his help in solving the stolen laptop mystery. "Maybe I'll follow in your footsteps, Mrs. Puddles, and become a private investigator," Andy said, at which point his mother jumped in.

"But we're still keeping our sights set on medical school, right, honey?"

"Yes, Mom. Maybe I'll be a doctor who fights crime on the side."

Everyone laughed, and Isabel handed him a gift bag with the scarf she had knitted for him inside. "A token of *my* appreciation, and a little something to help keep you warm this winter."

Andy hugged her too. Then *he* got a little emotional. "You're about the nicest people a guy could ever hope to work for. And to think I almost took a job at the Home—" Freddie and Isabel both raised their fingers to their lips to stop him. His eyes widened for a second, and then they all started laughing again. "Thank you for everything. I'll come and see you at Thanksgiving and Christmas too!" And with that, Andy, stock boy extraordinaire, was gone, and already the store seemed empty.

"What are we going to do about Frank when Andy comes back next summer, Freddie?" Isabel asked as she began her counter-straightening ritual.

"I'm going to tell him he can go home and take a nap from Memorial Day to Labor Day," Freddie answered as he disappeared down the plumbing aisle, then yelling back. "Either that or break his other leg."

Isabel hadn't had time to go out and buy a hostess gift for Abigail that would be appropriate for a *special* dinner, so after changing into something casual, yet elegant, she went into her pantry and grabbed two of her last jars of pickles. She wasn't sure bringing pickles to a hostess as sophisticated as Abigail Bachmeier was entirely copacetic, but it was either that or regifting a box of praline pecans Ginny and Grady had sent her from their turn through Georgia.

After she rang the doorbell, Sinclair answered the door with his usual formality, and the usual nod, but this time with an actual smile. Ramush then appeared in the foyer to greet her. "Isabel! How lovely to see you again! And without a bloody, bullet ridden corpse lying in the middle of the living room this time!" He then leaned in and kissed her on the cheek, something he had never done before. "Dinner will be served on the west terrace this evening," he told her as he put his arm around her and guided her down the hall. She had never seen Ramush so animated, and the energy in Bachmeier Hall had gone from dark and dreary to cheerful and upbeat, certainly a welcome change. As she passed the portraits of Mr. and Mrs. Bachmeier on their way to the west terrace, even they looked more content, this time with eyes that seemed to sparkle instead of pierce.

But an even bigger surprise was still to come . . . When they stepped out onto the west terrace, Isabel was dumbfounded by what she saw. Where a massive wall of trees and vines and overgrown shrubs had once been, there was now the most expansive and magnificent view of Lake Michigan Isabel had ever seen in her life. She stood in awe for a moment and took it all in. Abigail stepped quietly onto the terrace and watched her with a smile before speaking. "I've had a little yard work done since you were here last." Abigail then gave her a warm hug. "Hello again, my dear."

"Hello, Abigail. It's just spectacular. I've lived here all my life, and I have never seen a view of the Big Lake so breathtaking."

"Yes, I'd forgotten what a pretty view we had from here. It's the reason Father bought the land in the first place, so I thought it was about time we cast our eyes upon it again."

Isabel handed her the gift bag. "I brought you some of my bread-and-butter pickles."

Abigail took the bag and immediately reached in and pulled out a jar. "Are these the legendary Puddles Pickles I've heard so much about?"

"I don't know about legendary, but yes. I hope you'll like them."

"I'll warn you, Isabel, I'm a dill girl, but that's just the German in me. I am most anxious to give these a try. I'll have Chef put a dish of them out with dinner." She handed them off to Sinclair, who always seemed to be exactly where he was supposed to be at all times. Isabel looked over at a large, beautifully set table, sparkling with silver and crystal. She wondered how a dish of Puddles Pickles could possibly fit in. Then she noticed the table was set for eight. "We have some special guests joining us for dinner tonight whom I think you'll be happy to see. I know they're anxious to see you."

"Hello, Isabel." She turned around to see Jacob stepping out onto the terrace, smiling from ear to ear as he walked over and wrapped her in a bear hug.

"I believe you remember my nephew, Jacob," Abigail said as she patted him on the back. Isabel was too moved to speak, so Abigail continued, "And I'd like you to meet my *grand*-nephew. Where did he go? Austin dear, where are you?" A very shy-looking Austin peeked his head out the door, then cautiously stepped onto the terrace. Dancing at his feet were four Pomeranians, with a fifth tucked under his arm. "Austin, please say hello to Mrs. Puddles," Abigail said gently.

Austin walked over and stood next to his father, who put his hand on his head. "It's okay. Go say hello to Mrs. Puddles, son."

Austin stepped over and put his hand out. "Hello, Mrs. Puddles. It's very nice to meet you. I'm Austin." He looked up at his father. "But I'm not sure what my last name is anymore."

Jacob laughed. "We'll figure that out later."

Abigail jumped right in. "Well, whatever you decide on, first and foremost, you're a Bachmeier!"

Isabel was barely holding it together at this point. She leaned down to make eye contact with Austin. "It is such a pleasure to meet *you*, Austin. I've heard a lot about you. I see you've made some new friends." Austin smiled and looked down at the little fur ball he was holding who then licked his face.

"They just adore him," Abigail said. "The whole lot of them barely know I exist anymore." Abigail was glowing as she looked down at Austin and patted him on the head. "They all slept in bed with you last night, didn't they?"

Austin nodded. "They snore too."

Isabel's attention was suddenly drawn back to the terrace doors again, where she saw Colleen Doyle step out looking very chic, followed by her handsome husband, David. After she was introduced to David, Isabel looked over at Jacob, whose smile indicated that he and his parents had resolved their issues, at least for now. Sinclair appeared on the terrace again and walked over to Abigail. "Chef would like me to serve the canapés now if it's all right with you, madam."

"Yes, that will be fine, Sinclair, but in the meantime, let's have a toast, shall we?"

Ramush, who had been standing quietly and observing this whirlwind of happy introductions, lifted a dripping-wet bottle of champagne out of a silver ice bucket with a flourish and popped the cork, followed by a round of applause. After carefully filling everyone's crystal flutes, he reached into his pocket and pulled out a small bottle of ginger ale, and filled the last flute for Austin. They all then raised their glasses, and Abigail made a toast.

"To family, to friends, and to Randolph Bachmeier, who I know is finally at peace and smiling down on this gathering tonight as we all embark on these new chapters in our lives." They all clinked glasses. "And special thanks to the extraordinary Isabel Puddles, whose shrewdness and tenacity, and her very big heart, have made all this possible."

Isabel was humbled and smiled shyly. "Thank you, Abigail. I am honored to be a part of such a wonderful reunion, and to have played some small role in helping to bring it about has been a great privilege. The pieces were all there, all I did was help you put the puzzle together."

"Chin-chin," Abigail offered, and they clinked again. After some friendly chitchat and milling about over champagne and canapés, Isabel was anxious to hear from Jacob about how he was holding up, so she asked him to walk out onto the lawn and take in the view with her.

"I'm doing fine," Jacob said with a faint smile. "I mean, I guess. It's a lot to digest as you might imagine, but Austin is obviously my first concern. All the stuff about the foundation and the money, we'll just figure out as we go along. I can't think about it right now. But I made it clear to my aunt that none of that is going to change the course of my life, or the life of my son, any more than it has to. It's not going to be an easy road ahead for either one of us, but especially for Austin. He's still confused about what happened, the poor kid. I mean, imagine this stranger shows up out of the blue and tells you he's your father. But you know what's funny is that it was as if the moment he saw me, he knew, and we began to bond almost immediately. He's just such a sweet, trusting kid. I'm so glad he's away from his mother and that step-father, and safe with us now."

"What have you told him about his mother?" Isabel asked with some hesitancy.

"He understands that his mother is in jail, and that's upsetting to him of course, and he knows his stepfather is dead. But I got the impression that was much less upsetting. He understands they did some very bad things. There's no textbook for dealing with something like this, so we'll just have to muddle through it. I've already enrolled him in school, and I rented a house in town so my life off the grid is going to be revised a little. I'll still go out every day to work and hang out with my four-legged crew, but I'll be back every day by the time he gets home from school. And we can spend weekends out there. He was the happiest I've seen him yet when I took him out there and showed him the place. The kid didn't want to leave! He couldn't care less about this massive estate, he just wants to go back and see Gary and the goats and sleep in the trailer."

"I can't tell you how happy I am to hear this. I think you two will be just fine. I'm also happy to see you have mended fences with your parents."

"That brings me to some other pretty incredible news . . . I hope it's incredible, anyway. Austin and I flew home to Milwaukee a few days after I picked him up so I could introduce him to his grandparents and to his uncle Paul. All the stuff between my parents and me just kind of lifted when they met Austin, and he understood he now had grandparents who immediately showered him with love. I've never seen them so doting. His mother had been estranged from her family for years so Austin never met her parents, which is just as well, because I *did*, and they were not the grandparent types. So after they all got acquainted, we went to see Paul. We walked into his room together, and Paul was sitting at the window as usual. I said hello and hugged him as I always do. Austin was a little shy, but I pulled him over by the arm and I said, 'Paul, this is your nephew, Austin.' And the kid just instinctively knew something, I don't know what, but he connected with Paul on some other level. He didn't say anything, just leaned over and hugged him. And do you know that for the first time since the accident, Paul actually smiled. I was crying, my parents were crying, the nurses were crying, and Austin just sat there with him. I don't know what it means, and maybe it doesn't mean anything at all, but it's the first glimmer of hope we've seen, and I intend to hang onto it for as long as I can."

That was it. Isabel couldn't wipe the tears away fast enough. Then she looked up and saw Colleen standing beside her. "I just told her about Austin meeting Paul," Jacob told her as he put his arm around Isabel and the other around his mother.

Colleen grabbed Isabel's hand and looked her in the eyes. "I know that as a mother you understand what this means to me, and to my family. I will never be able to repay you for what you've done for us. You really have put us back together, Isabel."

Isabel took a breath and tried to collect herself. "No . . . You put yourselves back together. All the love was there."

Sinclair stepped out onto the lawn to announce that dinner was being served. When the three of them came back onto the terrace, Austin was sitting on David's lap, deep in conversation, while Abigail and Ramush were laughing together and acting more like a couple than employer and employee, which made Isabel wonder if their relationship might be a little more complex than she had previously thought, or even imagined. Could there be a romantic connection she had failed to pick up on? Or one they concealed for some reason? Or was she just letting her imagination get the better of her *again*? She would likely never know the answer, but she hoped maybe it was true.

After one of the most memorable dinners of her life, not merely because of the food, which was stupendous—even Puddles Pickles had received rave reviews—but because of all the love she felt at the table, and the promise of a happy future for this newly formed family, it was time for Isabel to say good night. So after many more hugs and thank-yous, and promises to stay in touch, Ramush walked her out, while Abigail remained on the terrace with her family, all of them overnight guests of Bachmeier Hall. Isabel knew it had likely been a very long time since Abigail's lavish guest rooms had received actual overnight guests. When they reached the driveway, Ramush turned to her and smiled. "Is there anything you feel we've left unresolved, Isabel? Anything unanswered?"

"What do you mean, Ramush?"

"I mean, is there anything that's still weighing on your mind?"

Isabel looked at him with a puzzled expression. "Like?"

"Well, Miss Bachmeier tells me you had asked about Skip Bachmeier's unfortunate accident, and asked her if she thought there was any possibility it was not an accident, but rather something a bit more deliberate."

Isabel didn't see this coming at all, but since he asked. "It did occur to me that, given the circumstances, there would certainly have been motive for somebody to arrange for her brother's plane to crash."

Ramush held her stare for a beat, then smiled, looking almost wistful. "While we're on the subject of motive, what I can tell you is this. Skip Bachmeier murdered his own father out of fear his inheritance was in jeopardy. This is something I knew then, and know to this day, to be a fact, and so does

Miss Bachmeier. He then set about trying to destroy *her* life, which another man had already done quite a good job of doing before him." He continued. "Randolph Bachmeier was not only the kindest man I ever knew, but the man I owed my life to. And he was the man his daughter worshipped. He was all she had, and her brother took him away from her."

Isabel was flummoxed. Was Ramush covertly confessing to being involved in Skip Bachmeier's murder? That's sure what it felt like. But before she could fully compute this, he had even more to say. "Which brings us to Patrick Pendleton, who shattered the heart and the life of a beautiful young woman, who had been nothing but loyal and loving and completely devoted to him. And how did he thank her for her devotion? By heartlessly abandoning her for another woman, and then publicly humiliating her."

Now she had really been thrown for a loop. Why was he bringing this up now? Although Isabel had briefly flirted with the idea that Ramush, or somebody in Miss Bachmeier's inner circle, might have played a role in Skip Bachmeier's death, she had never even considered the possibility that they might have had a hand in her former fiancé's death. All she had ever heard was that he had died in a car crash in the south of France. Not even Isabel's vivid imagination had taken her that far. But if her imagination hadn't run away with her before, it was now running away so fast it was about to take flight.

Ramush looked very intently into Isabel's eyes. "These were two very bad men, Isabel, who both hurt a very fine woman and robbed her of the life she deserved. And sometimes in this world, but not often enough, bad people get what they deserve." His eyes stayed fixed until tears began welling up. He looked away for a moment, then back at Isabel with a smile. "Thank you for giving Abigail a family again, Isabel. I know Jacob and Austin, and the Doyle's, will provide her with great comfort in the years to come. Now I no longer have to worry that she'll be alone." Isabel had been studying his face, and he knew it. He extended his hand and took hers. "I'm very happy we came to you for help. Your investigative skills, as well as your instincts, are indeed *exceptionally* good. Almost as good as your pickles!" He then kissed her on the cheek. "Please do stay in touch."

With that, Ramush turned around and walked back toward the grand front entrance of Bachmeier Hall. Just before going back inside, he turned and looked at her with a smile and a wink.

Chapter 30

Labor Day weekend had come and gone, and life in Gull Harbor had more or less gotten back to normal. And so had life for Isabel Puddles. Breakfasts at Land's End were back to normal, too, and Frances was back in rare form—inappropriate and as sassy as ever, but without all the brooding and the mood swings they had all been forced to endure over the summer. Her improved attitude had to do with what most would call a catastrophe, but for her, was a four-alarm blessing.

Over Labor Day weekend a fire had destroyed the corporate headquarters of Hank's company in Grand Haven, so they were forced to relocate their entire operation to their Kentwater County facility. Nobody was hurt, or Frances would have tried to do a better job of hiding her glee, but it did put an immediate end to the turmoil over moving to Grand Haven. If Frances had not been with her at the lake on the day the fire broke out, she would never have stopped wondering who set the blaze. But because this did nothing to affect Hank's new role as a vice-president, or his new salary, Frances was now actively looking at properties in Gull Harbor . . . on the water. "Who wants to live in that old dump we've been in all these years now that we can afford to live on the water?" she snorted one morning while leafing through a real estate catalog.

In other local real estate news, Beverly put her lake house on the market. It was too big for just her and Diego, and she decided it wasn't her responsibility to provide a vacation home for her family. She was looking at a condo on the water too, until she found out Frances was looking in the same development. "I think I'm going to wait until I see where she lands before I make any decisions," she told Isabel.

Jazz had been charged with second-degree murder in the death of Trey Bachmeier, and two counts of conspiracy to commit murder in the plot to kill Jacob and Abigail. She was being held without bond, and her trial date had not yet been set, but interest in the Trey Bachmeier murder case had gradually begun to fade. Most people were either not interested or too confused about the conspiracy plot to give it that much attention. After the press finally lost interest, the whole sad story just kind of fizzled, which was just fine by Isabel. Fortunately, because the handful of people who knew about her involvement in the case were still staying mum, she hadn't been dragged into the spotlight as she had been in the Jonasson case, so that came as a great relief for her.

Frances of course was unrelenting in her ability to find a new Jazz jab to launch at Isabel nearly every single day. In fact, that was what Isabel had taken to calling them. She had no defense for her lapse in good judgment and she didn't bother trying to come up with one. She admitted, and more than once, that she was wrong. "It happens! A lot! And to a lot of people. This time it happened to me. And you know what? It might just happen again!" she finally proclaimed at breakfast one morning. "Now can we *please* just move on?"

But because spotting somebody who was guilty of murder, and who was in the middle of plotting a brazen double murder, was supposedly now Isabel's department, it did still sting a little. And when that same homicidal conspirator had been bringing you your eggs almost every morning all summer, it stung even more.

Teddy had written back to say how much he regretted not being able to visit over the summer, but he had not been able to find anybody he could trust to watch Fred and Ginger. It had to be somebody they knew and whom he trusted, but his sister was still *indisposed*, as he put it. In order to make sure he could still make his regular trip to Chicago at Christmas to see his daughter and her family, he planned to move them down to a country house he had in Cornwall where he had a housekeeper who had agreed to look after them. Isabel stopped to Google where in the UK Cornwall was, exactly, as she was only familiar with their hens. Daughter Elizabeth, he wrote, had suggested the family spend Christmas in Gull Harbor this year, so he hoped they could see each other again then. Teddy then asked her something she didn't see coming. He invited her to come and stay at that same country house he mentioned in Cornwall. Teddy said that springtime in southwest England was "magical." He had a little guesthouse where she could stay with all the privacy she could want or need. It was obvious this was his way of making clear he was extending the invitation as *a gentleman*. Very Mr. Darcy, Isabel thought. Teddy asked her to think it over and they could talk about it at Christmas. She had never been abroad, and as a devoted fan of English literature, Agatha Christie, *My Fair Lady*, and someone who had watched the entire *Downton Abbey* series twice, Great Britain was the place in Europe she most wanted to visit.

Isabel hadn't seen Abigail or Ramush since their dinner together at Bachmeier Hall with Jacob, Austin, and the Doyle's, but she had received several e-mails from Jacob, one that included a picture of a very happy-looking Austin on his first day at his new school. She wrote back to tell Jacob she thought of them often and wished them all the best in building their new lives together as father and son. The poor boy's mother was likely going to spend the rest of her life in prison, where she belonged, so that wouldn't be easy for him. But with Jacob as his father, she knew Austin's life promised to be much happier than it otherwise would have been.

Although she was pleased there had been happy endings all around—Jazz, her husband, and Trey Bachmeier being the obvious exceptions—there was one nagging question she couldn't shake, and one she decided to bring up with Beverly over dinner at the Old Cottage Inn the night before she was heading back to Detroit to take on a new case.

"Just curious, Bev . . . Am I still constrained by the nondisclosure agreement I signed regarding the Bachmeier case?" Isabel asked casually as she reached for a piece of bread.

Beverly seemed slightly surprised by the question, but she was quick with an answer. "Until the day they close the lid, yes, unless you want to be in litigation with the Bachmeier estate until the day that happens."

Isabel thought Beverly's rather grim response over for a minute. "What if you were my attorney? Wouldn't whatever I told you fall under attorney-client privilege?"

"Yes, it would. Now give me a dollar and you can put me on retainer."

"Really?"

"Yes. Give me a dollar and I will officially become your lawyer. Anything you tell me is then privileged and confidential."

Isabel reached into her purse and took out her wallet. "All I have are two twenties."

"Fine. Give me a twenty and I'll apply nineteen dollars to your half of the check." Isabel handed the bill across the table.

Beverly already knew about the suspicions swirling around Skip Bachmeier's death because she was the one who had told

Isabel all about it, along with Skip's failed plan to have Abigail committed. But Beverly knew nothing about the accident in the south of France more than fifty years before that had taken the life of the man who abandoned Abigail Bachmeier at the altar.

Isabel shared all she knew about the story, and Beverly was enthralled. "It's starting to sound like a Hitchcock movie! So what you're saying is that you think these two *accidents* are related?"

"I think they very well could be. Related in that there may have been one perpetrator for both," Isabel replied after a sip of wine. "Obviously I have no proof, but I *can* tie them together with a little piece of circumstantial evidence I've discovered."

"Do tell," a rapt Beverly urged.

"Well, both accidents could likely have been the result of some kind of mechanical failure."

"And?"

"*And* Ramush, Abigail Bachmeier's most loyal and devoted servant, I recently learned, is apparently quite a knowledgeable mechanic."

Beverly was not impressed. "That's the very definition of circumstantial, Isabel. Mechanical failure doesn't mean tampering was involved, it just means the mechanics failed. What else have you got?"

Isabel then went on to describe the oddly touching conversation she'd had with Ramush in the driveway of Bachmeier Hall a few weeks before. "It just felt to me like he was confessing. He obviously sees himself almost as her protector," she said, trying to bolster her case. "But then here's the next question that begs to be asked: Let's say Ramush *did* somehow arrange for these accidents to happen. What, if anything, did Abigail know? And if she did know anything, when did she know it?"

"Oh, *that* old chestnut? Isabel, let's get real. She may have been the one who put him up to it, for all we know. But at this point nobody will ever know what or when the old lady did or didn't know anything. And nobody cares. Except maybe you. My advice is to let it go. The wondering and the ruminating over all of it are going to drive you nuts. I hate to sound condescending by saying you've read too many murder mysteries and watched too many detective shows, Isabel, but I think you've read too many murder mysteries and watched too many detective shows. There was never any evidence that Skip Bachmeier's plane crash was anything other than an unfortunate accident for him, but happened to be a fortunate one for his sister. All I did was share the suspicions some people had at the time. And even if it *were* murder, that case is so cold it could preserve a woolly mammoth. As far as the car crash on the French Riviera goes? That sounds more like Karma than murder to me." Beverly reached for the bottle and refilled their glasses. "But let me ask you this, why do you think this gentleman, Ramush, would confess to you, even in the round-about way you described?"

"Maybe to clear his conscience?"

"Could be. But there's a line in *Rear Window*, my favorite Hitchcock movie of all time, where Grace Kelly says to Jimmy Stewart, something like, 'A murderer would never parade his crime in front of an open window.' " Beverly took a long, thoughtful sip of wine, before continuing. "But then again . . ." she raised her glass in a toast.

Isabel picked up her glass. "What are we toasting to?"

"To the *possibility* that Ramush is a homicidal exhibitionist who *did* confess to you, and who has gotten away with murder not once but twice."

Isabel put her glass down. "I'm not toasting to cold-blooded murder, Beverly."

"Okay, well, suit yourself." Beverly clinked her water

glass. "I'm not endorsing revenge murders, but I think we should all be so lucky to have somebody in our lives so devoted to us that they would go to such lengths to protect us."

Isabel scowled. "I don't want anybody killing anybody on *my* behalf, thank you very much."

Beverly shrugged. "Well, I will tell you this. You can't always count on the law to punish horrible people for the horrible things they do to others. People get away with doing awful, horrendous things to others every day and are never even caught, let alone punished. Sometimes, when the law fails to do its job, Karma takes care of it. But you can't depend on Karma either. So, having been in the murder business for a while, what I've found is that for some people, people just like you and me, the only way they see to prevent, or to punish cold-blooded murder, is by committing cold-blooded murder themselves. In the case of your friend Ramush, well, you know what they say."

"No. What do they say?"

"Murder is like a bag of M&M's. It's hard to stop at just one."

Isabel shook her head. "I'm sorry I ever brought it up. Let's look at the dessert menu."

Chapter 31

Isabel woke up the next morning and felt the autumn chill in the air when she stepped out on the deck with her coffee. It would soon be time to break out the sweaters and the warm socks again. Her conversation with Beverly about Ramush was still on her mind, but she knew Beverly was right. There was no point obsessing over something that may or may not have happened decades in the past. Accidents happen, coincidences happen, and often the twain *do* meet. Her feelings about what Ramush may have been insinuating when talking about the deaths of Skip Bachmeier and Patrick Pendleton were just that, feelings. And feelings, she reminded herself, are not facts. *From this day forward*, Isabel told herself, she would choose to believe that her new friend Ramush was not a murderer, and that her other new friend, Abigail, was not an accessory to murder. End of story.

Looking for ways to take her mind off it once and for all, Isabel decided it was a good morning to ride her bike into town for breakfast. Traffic was no longer an excuse, and the weather being too hot wasn't, either. She dug her faded old Michigan State sweatshirt out of a drawer and slipped it on, then got on her bike and pedaled into town. Halfway there, feeling invigorated by the wind in her face, she wondered why she didn't do this every morning, weather permitting, of course.

When she walked into Land's End, her cheeks were flushed from the chill in the air and her first real exercise in quite some time. When she walked in Isabel was ready to proudly announce to the room that she had finally ridden her bike to breakfast. But Frances beat her to the headline. "Well, Isabel, I heard them again."

"I did, too . . . twice," Kayla chimed in as she flipped Isabel's cup over and poured her coffee.

"Are we talking about what I think we're talking about?" Isabel asked as she sat down and unzipped her jacket. Kayla answered with her eyes. "Not you too, Kayla," Isabel said with a groan.

"I'm just saying that I heard something that sounded like drumbeats last night, and it was at the same time Frances did."

"Then why didn't I hear it?"

Kayla had an easy explanation. "Maybe you can't hear it unless you *believe* you can hear it."

Isabel sighed and shook her head. "That makes absolutely no sense." Just as she took her first sip of coffee, Gil burst through the door and plopped himself down at their table. "And here's another believer. Good morning, Gil."

"Good morning, one and all," Gil replied as he flipped his coffee cup over. "What are you talking about? What do I believe?" he asked as Kayla handed him a menu. "Just coffee for me, thanks, Kayla."

"What's your hurry?" Isabel asked.

"Gotta get up to Wellington and pick up a couple'a floaters." Isabel winced. She had heard Gil use the expression many times before and it never ceased to creep her out. Gil poured sugar into his coffee and stirred as nonchalantly as if the topic at hand was the weather before continuing. "Seems a couple guys stole a boat last night, and when the harbor police caught up with them, they jumped in the lake and tried to escape. It didn't turn out very well for them."

Frances and Kayla both grinned knowingly at Isabel.

"What am I missing here?" Gil asked before being distracted by the smell of freshly baked cinnamon rolls. "Hey, Kayla, maybe I do have time for a cinnamon roll. Why not? Where are they going anyway?"

"Coming right up," Kayla said as she headed to the kitchen window.

Frances looked over at Isabel, who was trying to will this conversation away, then turned to Gil. "Kayla and I both heard the Indian drum last night." She took a dramatic pause and raised two fingers, "Twice."

"Yeah, I heard the drum last night too. Those spirits have had a busy summer, haven't they?"

Kayla was back with Gil's cinnamon roll. Now all three of them were looking at Isabel as if waiting for her to jump aboard the Indian drum train. She stood it for as long as she could, then suddenly realized the path of least resistance was right in front of her. She took a long, contemplative sip of coffee before offering a little pearl of wisdom that had just come to mind. "All the world is made of faith, and trust, and pixie dust."

A brief moment of silence followed until Frances finally barked. "What's *that* supposed to mean?"

"It's from *Peter Pan*, Frances. My favorite Disney movie. It just means I believe. There. I said it. That was easy enough. Everybody happy?" Isabel reached over and tore a piece off of Gil's cinnamon roll and popped it in her mouth. One thing Isabel Puddles had learned in life, and as she had very recently been reminded, was that sometimes changing your mind was just that easy. Who was she to decide what was real and what wasn't, or what others should or shouldn't believe. After all, she was well into junior high before finally accepting the truth about Santa Claus . . . and it was a disappointment she never completely got over.

The newspaper delivery man startled the whole table when he came in and dropped a stack of papers into the rack. Isabel got up to grab one and returned to the table. "I think he gets a kick out of doing that," she said as she unfolded the paper. On the front page was the story about the men who drowned after stealing a boat, which by now was already old news. But also on the front page was the story that really captured her attention. The headline read: ABIGAIL BACHMEIER TO DONATE FAMILY ESTATE TO TOWN OF GULL HARBOR. Isabel was flabbergasted. She hadn't spoken to Ramush in a while, or Miss Bachmeier, but how had she not heard about this development until now? She took the section of newspaper and excused herself from the table and stepped outside to call Ramush, but got no answer. Next she called Jacob to see what she could find out, but his phone was turned off. Finally she called Bachmeier Hall, hoping Sinclair would answer, but no answer there, either.

Forgetting to say goodbye to her friends back inside, Isabel got on her bike and pedaled home as fast as she could, and with her head spinning. What could possibly have prompted Abigail Bachmeier to give up the family estate where she had lived for fifty years? She pulled off the main road, and as she got closer to Poplar Bluff, she could see the old station wagon Ramush always drove around town starting to back out of her driveway. Oh, good, she said to herself, now she would get some answers. But as she got closer, she could see it wasn't Ramush driving, it was Jacob. And sitting next to him was Abigail. Isabel rang the bell on her handlebars to alert them she was coming. Jacob waved and pulled back into the drive. He and Abigail were both getting out of the car when she pulled up and got off her bike.

"Where's Ramush?" Isabel asked with a smile. "Have you hired a new chauffeur, Abigail?"

Abigail smiled, but only slightly. Isabel immediately recognized it as a sad, reflective smile and her heart began to sink. Something was terribly wrong.

"We've just come back from Ann Arbor. I'm afraid we have some very sad news, Isabel," Abigail said calmly. "My dear, sweet Ramush passed away late last night."

Isabel was stunned silent. Abigail took both her hands. "He had been ill for quite some time before he ever told me. By the time we went to see the doctors in Ann Arbor, his illness was too far along for anything to be done, except to make him as comfortable as possible when his time grew near. He died with both of us at his bedside. He had been sleeping comfortably all day while we sat with him. Then he suddenly opened his eyes, smiled at us both, squeezed our hands, and took his last breath. He didn't suffer, which is something I will be eternally grateful for."

Isabel was still speechless. He must have known he didn't have much time left when she last saw him at their dinner at Bachmeier Hall, despite looking perfectly healthy. And not just healthy, he also seemed unusually calm and content and in very good spirits. Isabel struggled to find words as her eyes filled with tears. "I'm so sorry, Abigail . . . I had grown so fond of Ramush."

"And he was very fond of you too, Isabel. He admired you very much," Abigail said with a kind smile. "And he absolutely loved your pickles!"

Isabel smiled. She could see Abigail was putting on a brave front, but she knew how devastated she must be. "I don't think I've ever seen anyone more devoted or loving than Ramush was to you."

Abigail's eyes said it all. "Nor will there ever be again . . . Ramush Bajrami was a true blessing, not only to me but to my father, who I know has welcomed him with open arms and thanked him for the love and devotion he showed us all, and for bringing Jacob and me together. *And* his great-grandson, Austin." She put her arms around Isabel and hugged her. "Thanks to you and Jacob, Ramush was able to leave this earth knowing I would not be left alone." She reached over and grabbed Jacob's hand who was now fighting back tears himself. Abigail then found a burst of happy energy. "And since I saw no point in my rattling around in that old house any longer, especially without Ramush there with me, I decided to give up Bachmeier Hall, which you may have heard about. I'm moving closer to my nephew and grand-nephew. I've purchased a quaint little cottage overlooking the bay, and it's just a couple of miles from the boys."

Jacob chuckled and wiped his eyes. "A *quaint* cottage on ten acres, with six bedrooms, a guesthouse, a pool, and a tennis court."

"Well, I can't very well turn that geriatric staff of mine out onto the street, can I? I have to keep them employed and with a roof over their heads. And they need something to do, don't they? But what I really needed was to get away from all those memories—some happy, many not—and build some happy new memories with my new family with whatever time I have left. Ramush and I discussed it when we knew the end was near for him, and he wholeheartedly approved. We agreed that the village of Gull Harbor would put Bachmeier Hall to good use. It has more than served its purpose for the Bachmeier family, so now it's time to pass it along. Pay it forward as they say."

Isabel smiled. "I'm so sorry about Ramush, but it's nice that such sad news can be followed by such happy news. I think maybe he stayed around just long enough to make sure you would be okay."

"I'm certain of it," Abigail said, patting Isabel's cheek.

"I'm going to miss having you as my neighbor though, Abigail."

"Well, you will always be welcome to visit us, and I insist that you do. We're just a hundred some miles up the coast, so I will expect to see you very soon. Now we must be off so we can get back in time to pick up Austin from school."

After saying their tearful goodbyes, Jacob and Abigail backed out of the drive and were on their way with a honk. But fifty feet or so away they stopped and slowly backed up. Isabel walked her bike over to the passenger side as Abigail rolled down her window.

"I forgot to say how enchanting your Poplar Bluff is, Isabel. It's just as I pictured it. It suits you very well, indeed."

Isabel was touched. "Thank you, Abigail. And if you ever find yourself missing Gull Harbor, you are more than welcome to visit me too. I just have the one guest room, but it's cozy."

"Thank you. Perhaps I'll take you up on that one day." And with that, Abigail and Jacob waved goodbye again, and they were off.

Isabel watched them turn onto the main road, knowing this case, and this chapter in her life, had officially ended. She hoped she would see them again, but wondered if she ever really would. She put her bike in the garage and was soon greeted at the front gate by Jackpot and Corky. After a slathering of kisses, Isabel reached inside the front door and grabbed their leashes. It was shaping up to be a beautiful autumn day, and the perfect morning for a reflective walk over to the Big Lake. The dogs were, as usual, ecstatic once they saw the leashes. Isabel harnessed them up and off they went, their stumpy little tails wagging wildly as they guided her toward the trail they knew so well.

As they entered the woods, her thoughts were with Ramush. Given the state of his health when they last spoke, it now seemed far more likely than not that he *was* confessing to her, in his own way, that he was somehow involved in the deaths of Skip Bachmeier and Patrick Pendleton. And although she obviously found the act of murder abhorrent, no matter how dastardly the actions that may have provoked it may have been, she knew in her heart that Ramush was not an evil man. Maybe, as Beverly pointed out at dinner, you couldn't always count on the law or on Karma to settle a score or right a wrong, but what kind of a world would it be if everybody decided to murder the people in their lives who had done them wrong or wronged somebody they cared about? A less populated one, that's for sure. And how could you ever be sure *you* weren't on somebody's list?

As Isabel and the dogs cleared the woods and took in the spectacular view of a glistening, bright blue Lake Michigan, she stopped to soak it all in and try to shake off the unhappy thoughts running through her head. She took a deep breath and thought about how lucky she had been in her life. She had wonderful, adoring, and devoted parents; a happy childhood; a marriage that was, well . . . meh, but one that gave her two beautiful children; she was surrounded by loving family and friends; and she had always enjoyed good health. Isabel lived a graced life and she was grateful for it every day. She felt sorry, bordering on guilty, for the countless others who were just as deserving as she, but who had been denied those gifts and instead led lives fraught with sadness and tragedy. The randomness of the universe, and the injustice in the world had always perplexed and saddened Isabel Puddles, and it always would.

She looked down at the empty beach, the sand smooth and strewn with driftwood, and remembered the story of the Armistice Day Storm. She could almost see all those people from town who went down to the shore in the freezing cold that night and stood on the beach holding lanterns for the poor souls they thought might be out there, struggling to survive after their ships sunk, just so they would know they were not alone. Maybe the best we can do in this life, Isabel had come to believe, is to hold a lantern for those people who are less fortunate. People we may not know, and may never meet, but who are in need of someone to shine a light for them. And maybe that's what she had unwittingly done for Ramush. Whatever he did or didn't do was between him and the universe. But if she was able to help him see his way to unburdening himself before he left this world, she was glad she could be the one to hold the lantern for him.

Connect with Us

Visit us online at
KensingtonBooks.com
to read more from your favorite authors, see books
by series, view reading group guides, and more.

for sneak peeks, chances to win books and prize packs,
and to share your thoughts with other readers.

facebook.com/kensingtonpublishing
twitter.com/kensingtonbooks

Tell us what you think!

To share your thoughts, submit a review,
or sign up for our eNewsletters, please visit:
KensingtonBooks.com/TellUs.